CALAMITY

Also by Brandon Sanderson from Gollancz:

Mistborn
The Final Empire
The Well of Ascension
The Hero of Ages
The Alloy of Law
Shadows of Self
The Bands of Mourning

The Stormlight Archive
The Way of Kings Part One
The Way of Kings Part Two
Words of Radiance Part One
Words of Radiance Part Two

The Reckoners
Steelheart
Mitosis
Firefight

Elantris
Warbreaker
Alcatraz
The Emperor's Soul
Legion
Legion: Skin Deep

CALAMITY

BRANDON SANDERSON

GOLLANCZ

LONDON

The right of Brandon Sanderson to be identified as the author
of this work has been asserted by him in accordance with the
Copyright, Designs and Patents Act 1988.

First published in Great Britain in 2016 by Gollancz
An imprint of the Orion Publishing Group
Carmelite House, 50 Victoria Embankment, London EC4Y 0DZ
An Hachette UK Company

A CIP catalogue record for this book is available
from the British Library

ISBN 978 0 575 10466 2 (Cased)
ISBN 978 0 575 10483 9 (Export Trade Paperback)

1 3 5 7 9 10 8 6 4 2

Printed in Great Britain by Clays Ltd, St Ives plc

The Orion Publishing Group's policy is to use papers that
are natural, renewable and recyclable products and made
from wood grown in sustainable forests. The logging and
manufacturing processes are expected to conform to the
environmental regulations of the country of origin.

For Kaylynn ZoBell
> A writer, reader, critiquer, and friend,
> who has spent ten years in a writing group
>> with a bunch of loudmouths
> and still raises her hand politely to make comments,
>> instead of murdering us.
> (Thanks for all your help over the years, Kaylynn!)

Prologue

I'VE witnessed the fearsome depths.

I was in Babilar, Babylon Restored. Formerly New York City. I stared into the burning red star known as Calamity, and knew—with no uncertainty—that something inside me had changed.

The depths had claimed me as one of their own. And though I've pushed them back, I still bear their hidden scar.

They insist that they will have me again.

PART ONE

1

THE sun peeked over the horizon like the head of a giant radioactive manatee. I crouched, hidden in a tree of all places. I'd forgotten how weird the things smell.

"We good?" I whispered over the line. Instead of using mobiles, we were relying on old radios we'd rigged to work with headsets. The audio snapped and popped as I spoke. Primitive technology, but essential for this job.

"Wait a sec," Megan said. "Cody, you in position?"

"Sure am," crackled the reply, laced with a calm Southern drawl. "If anyone tries to sneak up on you, lass, I'll put a bullet up his nose."

"Ew," Mizzy said over the line.

"We'll move in five," I said from my perch. Cody had called the contraption I was using a "tree stand," which was really a glorified camp chair strapped some thirty feet up the trunk of an elm. Hunters had used them back in the day for hiding from game.

I put my Gottschalk—a sleek, military-style assault rifle—to my shoulder and sighted through the trees. Normally, in this sort of situation I'd be sighting on an Epic: one of the super-powered individuals who terrorized the world. I was a Reckoner, same as my team, dedicated to bringing down dangerous Epics.

Unfortunately, life for the Reckoners had stopped making sense about two months ago. Our leader, Prof, was an Epic himself—and had been caught in a rival's intricate plot to find a successor. Consumed by his powers, he had left Regalia's empire in Babilar, but had taken with him her hard drives, complete with notes and secrets. We intended to stop him. And that led me here.

To a large castle.

Seriously. A castle. I'd figured those were just in old movies and foreign countries, yet here one was hidden in the woods of West Virginia. And despite the modern metal gates and high-tech security system, this place looked like it had been around since long before Calamity appeared in the sky—lichen covered the stonework, and vines twisted up one of the weathered walls.

Pre-Calamity people had been weird. Awesome too—evidence: castle—but still pretty weird.

I looked away from my scope and glanced at Abraham, who was hiding in a nearby tree. I could pick him out only because I knew exactly what to look for. His dark outfit blended well into the dappled shades of morning, which was—our informant said—the best time to assault this particular location: Shewbrent Castle, also known as the Knighthawk Foundry.

The world's primary source of Epic-derived technology. We'd used their weapons and tech to fight Steelheart, then Regalia.

Now we were going to rob them.

"Everyone have their mobiles off?" I asked over the line. "Batteries out?"

"You've asked that three times already, David," Megan replied.

"Check anyway."

They all gave the affirmative, and I took a deep breath. So far as we knew, we were the last cell of Reckoners. Two months in and we still had no sign of Tia, which meant she was probably dead. That left *me* in charge—though I'd gotten the job by default. Abraham and Cody had laughed when I'd asked if they wanted it, while Mizzy had gone stiff as a board and almost started hyperventilating.

Now we were putting my plan in motion. My crazy, foolhardy, incredible plan. Honestly, I was terrified.

My watch buzzed. Go time.

"Megan," I said into my radio, "you're up."

"On it."

I shouldered my rifle again, peering through the trees toward where Megan would launch her assault. I felt blind. With my mobile, I could have tapped into Megan's view to follow her attack, or I could have at least brought up a local map and watched my team represented as blips. Our mobiles, however, had been built and distributed by Knighthawk—who also maintained the secure network they ran on. Using those to coordinate an attack on Knighthawk's own installation seemed about as smart as using toothpaste for salad dressing.

"Engaging," Megan said, and soon a pair of explosions shook the air. I scanned through my scope and picked out the smoke trails rising in the sky, but couldn't see Megan; she was on the other side of the castle. Her job was to make a frontal assault, and those blasts had been grenades she'd thrown at the front gate.

Attacking the Knighthawk Foundry was, of course, *absolutely* suicidal. We all knew this, but we were also desperate, low on resources, and being hunted by Jonathan Phaedrus himself. Knighthawk refused to deal with us, and had gone completely silent to our requests.

Our choices had been to try to take on Prof unequipped, or to come here and see what we could steal. This seemed the better of two bad options.

"Cody?" I asked.

"She's doing fine, lad," he said over the crackling radio line. "It looks just like that video. The place released drones right after the explosions happened."

"Pick off what you can," I said.

"Roger."

"Mizzy?" I said. "You're up."

"Groovy."

I hesitated. "Groovy? Is that some kind of code word?"

"You don't know . . . Sparks, David, you can be a real square sometimes." Her words were punctuated by another series of explosions, larger this time. My tree shook from the shock waves.

I didn't need my scope to see the smoke rising from my right, along the castle's flank. Soon after the blast, a group of basketball-sized drones—sleek and metallic, with propellers on top—popped from windows and flew toward the smoke. Larger machines rolled out of shadowed alcoves; spindly and about as tall as a person, each had a gun arm on the top and moved on tracks instead of wheels.

I followed these with my scope as they started firing into the woods where Mizzy had planted flares in buckets to give

8

off heat signatures. Remotely firing machine guns enhanced the illusion that a large squad of soldiers was out there hiding. We kept all the shots aimed high. We didn't want Abraham in the crossfire when it was his turn to move.

The Knighthawk defense played out exactly as we'd been shown on the video from our informant. Nobody had ever successfully breached the place, but many had tried. One group, a reckless paramilitary force out of Nashville, had taken videos, and we'd managed to get copies. Best we could guess, most of the time all of those drones were inside patrolling the hallways. Now, however, they were out fighting.

Hopefully that would give us an opening.

"All right, Abraham," I said into the line, "your turn. I'll cover."

"And off I go," Abraham said softly. The careful, dark-skinned man rode a thin cable down from his tree, then slipped silently across the forest floor. Though he was thick of arm and neck, Abraham moved with surprising nimbleness as he reached the wall, which was still shadowed in the early-morning light. His tight infiltration outfit would mask his heat signature, at least as long as the heat sinks on his belt were functional.

His job was to sneak into the Foundry, steal whatever weapons or technology he could find, and get out in under fifteen minutes. We had basic maps from our informant claiming that the labs and factories on the bottom floor of the castle were stuffed with goodies ripe for the plucking.

I watched Abraham nervously through my scope— pulling the aim point to the right so an accidental discharge wouldn't hit him—to make sure no drones spotted him.

They didn't. He used a retractable line to get to the top of the short wall, then another to reach the castle's roof. He hid beside one of the crenellations while he prepared his next step.

"There's an opening to your right, Abraham," I said into the line. "One of the drones popped out of a hole beneath the window on that tower."

"Groovy," Abraham said, though the word sounded particularly odd coming from him, with his smooth French accent.

"Please tell me that's not a real word," I said, then raised my gun to follow him along as he made for the opening.

"Why wouldn't it be?" Mizzy asked.

"It just sounds weird."

"And things we say today don't? 'Sparks'? 'Slontze'?"

"Those are normal," I said. "Not weird at all." A flying drone passed by, but fortunately my suit was masking my heat signature. That was good, since the wetsuitlike clothing was pretty darn uncomfortable. Though mine wasn't as bad as Abraham's; his had a face mask and everything. To a drone I'd have a tiny heat signature, like a squirrel or something. A secretly very, very deadly squirrel.

Abraham reached the alcove I'd pointed out. Sparks, that man was good at sneaking. In the moment since I'd looked away, I'd lost him, and had trouble locating him again. He had to have *some* kind of special forces training.

"There's a door in here, unfortunately," Abraham said from his alcove. "It must close after the machines exit. I will try to hot-wire my way in."

"Great," I said. "Megan, you good?"

"Alive," she said, puffing. "For now."

"How many drones can you see?" I asked. "Have they rolled out the larger ones on you yet? Can—"

"Little busy, Knees," she snapped.

I settled back, anxiously listening to the gunfire and explosions. I wanted to be out there in the mess, firing and fighting, but that wouldn't make sense. I wasn't stealthy like

Abraham or . . . well, *immortal* like Megan. Having an Epic such as her on the team was certainly an advantage. They could handle this. My job as leader was to hang back and make judgment calls.

It sucked.

Was this how Prof had felt during missions he supervised? He had usually waited it out, leading from behind the scenes. I hadn't realized how tough that would be. Well, if there was one thing I'd learned in Babilar, it was that I needed to rein in my hotheadedness. I needed to be like . . . half a hothead instead. A hot chin?

So I waited as Abraham worked. If he couldn't get in soon, I'd have to call off the mission. The longer this took, the greater the chances that the mysterious people who ran the Foundry would discover that our "army" was only five people.

"Status, Abraham?" I said.

"I think I can get this open," he said. "Just a little longer."

"I don't . . ." I trailed off. "Wait a sec, what was that?"

A low rumbling was coming from nearby. I scanned below me and was surprised to see the mulchy forest floor *buckling*. Leaves and moss folded back, revealing a metal doorway. Another group of drones flew out of it, zipping past my tree.

"Mizzy," I hissed into my headset. "Other drones are trying to flank your position."

"Bummer," Mizzy said. She hesitated a moment. "Do you—"

"Yes, I know that word. You might need to institute the next phase." I glanced down at the opening, which was rumbling closed. "Be prepared; it looks like the Foundry has tunnels leading out to the forest. They'll be able to deploy drones from unexpected positions."

The door below stopped, half shut. I frowned, leaning

down to get a better look. It appeared that some dirt and rocks had fallen into one of the door's gears. Guess that was the problem with hiding your entrance in the middle of a forest.

"Abraham," I said into my headset, excited, "the opening out here jammed open. You could get in this way."

"I think that might be difficult," he said, and I looked back up to note that a couple of drones had retreated after a barrage of explosions from Mizzy's side. They hovered near Abraham's position.

"Sparks," I whispered, then raised my rifle and picked the two machines off with a pair of shots. They fell; we'd come prepared with bullets that fried electronics when they hit. I didn't know how they worked, but they'd cost basically everything we could scrounge up in trade, including the copter that Cody and Abraham had escaped Newcago in. It was too conspicuous anyway.

"Thanks for the assist," Abraham said as the drones dropped.

Beneath me, the gears on the opening scraped against one another, trying to force their way closed. The door moved another inch.

"This entrance is going to close any second," I said. "Get here fast."

"Stealthy is not fast, David," Abraham said.

I glanced at that opening. Newcago was lost to us; Prof had already attacked and ransacked all of our safehouses there. We'd barely gotten Edmund—another of our Epic allies—out to a safe hiding spot.

The people of Newcago were terrified. Babilar was little better: few resources to be had, and old minions of Regalia's were keeping an eye on the place, serving Prof now.

If this robbery went bust, we'd be broke. We'd have to

set up somewhere off the map and try to rebuild over the next year, which would leave Prof with free rein to rampage. I wasn't sure what he was up to, why he'd left Babilar so quickly, but it bespoke some kind of plot or plan. Jonathan Phaedrus, now consumed by his powers, wouldn't be content to sit in a city and rule. He had ambitions.

He could be the most dangerous Epic this world had ever known. My stomach twisted at that thought. I couldn't justify any more delays.

"Cody," I said. "Can you see and cover Abraham?"

"Just a sec," he said. "Yeah, I got 'im."

"Good," I said. "Because I'm going in. You have ops."

2

I slid down my rope and hit the forest floor, crunching dried leaves. Ahead of me, the door to the hole finally started moving again. With a yelp, I dashed toward the opening in the ground and jumped in, skidding a short distance down a shallow ramp as the door closed with a final grinding sound behind me.

I was in. Also, likely trapped.

So . . . yay?

Faint emergency lights running along the walls revealed a sloping tunnel that was rounded at the top like a giant's throat. The incline wasn't very steep, so I climbed to my feet and started inching down the slope, gun at my shoulder. I switched my radio, carried at my hip, to a different frequency—protocol for whoever made it into the Foundry, to let me focus. The others would know how to reach me.

The dimness made me want to flip on my mobile, which could double as a flashlight, but I restrained myself. Who knew what kind of backdoors the Knighthawk Foundry might have built into the things? In fact, who knew what the phones were truly capable of? They had to be some kind of Epic-derived technology. Phones that worked under any circumstances with signals that couldn't be intercepted? I'd grown up in a pit underneath Newcago, but even I realized how fantastical that was.

I reached the bottom of the incline and flipped on my scope's night-vision and thermal settings. *Sparks,* this was an awesome gun. The silent corridor stretched out before me, nothing but smooth metal, floor to ceiling. Considering its length, the tunnel had to lead under the Foundry walls and into the compound; it was probably an access corridor.

Contraband photos of the Foundry interior showed all kinds of motivators and technology lying around on workbenches down here. That had enticed us to try this all-in plan. Grab and go, hope we ended up with something useful.

It would be technology built, somehow, from the bodies of Epics. Even before I'd discovered that Prof had powers, I should have realized how much we relied on Epics. I'd always dreamed that the Reckoners were some kind of pure, human freedom force—ordinary people fighting an extraordinary foe.

That wasn't the way it happened though, was it? Perseus had his magic horse, Aladdin had his lamp, and Old Testament David had his blessing from Jehovah. You want to fight a god? You'd better have one on your side too.

In our case, we'd cut off pieces of the gods, trapped them

in boxes, and channeled their power. Much of it had originated here. The Knighthawk Foundry, secretive purveyors of Epic corpses made into weapons.

My headset crackled and I jumped.

"David?" Megan's voice, dialed into the private radio line. "What are you doing?"

I winced. "I found a drone access tunnel in the forest floor and managed to sneak in," I whispered.

Silence on the line, followed by "Slontze."

"What? Because it's reckless?"

"Sparks, no. Because you didn't take me."

An explosion shook somewhere near her.

"Sounds like you're having plenty of fun," I said. I kept moving forward, my rifle up and my focus ahead, watching for drones.

"Yeah, sure," Megan said. "Intercepting mini-missiles with my face. Loads of fun."

I smiled; the mere sound of her voice could do that to me. Hell, I'd rather be yelled at by Megan than be praised by anyone else. Besides, the fact that she was talking to me meant she hadn't *actually* intercepted any mini-missiles with her face. She was immortal in that if she died, she'd be reborn—but she was otherwise as fragile as anyone else. And because of recent concerns, she tried to limit using her powers.

She'd be doing this mostly the old-fashioned way. Ducking between trees, lobbing grenades and taking shots while Cody and Mizzy covered her. I imagined her cursing softly, sweating while she sighted at a passing drone, her aim perfect, her face . . .

. . . Uh, right. I should probably stay focused.

"I'll keep their attention up here," Megan said, "but be

careful, David. You don't have a full infiltration suit. You'll have a heat signature to those drones, if they look closely."

"Groovy," I whispered. Whatever that meant.

Ahead of me the tunnel started getting lighter, so I turned off the night vision on the scope and slowed my pace. I crept forward and stopped. The access tunnel ended at a large white corridor that stretched to the right and left. Brightly lit, with tile floors and metal walls, it was completely empty. Like an office when the shop down the street has free donut day.

I pulled our maps, such as we had, from my pocket and checked them. Didn't say much, though one of the photos looked a lot like this corridor. Well, somehow I had to find useful technology in here, steal it, and get out.

Prof or Tia could have come up with a way better plan, but they weren't here. So I picked a direction at random and continued walking. When the tense silence was broken a few minutes later by a quickly approaching sound echoing through the corridor, it was actually a relief.

I dashed toward the sound; not because I was eager to meet it, but because I spotted a door up the hall. I reached it in time to pull it open—thankfully, it wasn't locked—and slip into a dark room. My back against the door, I heard a group of drones zip past outside. I turned and looked through the little window in the door to watch them buzz down the white corridor, then turn into the access tunnel.

They hadn't spotted my heat signature. I flipped my radio to the open line and whispered, "More drones are going out the way I came in. Cody, status?"

"We've got a few tricks left," Cody said, "but it's getting frantic out here. Abraham did manage to get in through the roof though. The two of you should grab what you can find and get out ASAP."

"Roger," Abraham said over the line.

"Got it," I said, glancing around the room I'd entered. It was completely dark, but judging by the sterile smell, it was some kind of lab chamber. I flipped on my night-vision scope and gave the place a quick once-over.

Turned out I was surrounded by bodies.

3

I choked back a cry of alarm. Rifle to my shoulder, I scanned the room again, my heart thumping. It was filled with long metal tables and sinks, interspersed with several large tubs, and the walls were lined floor to ceiling with shelves packed with jars of all sizes. I leaned in to get a better look at those jars on a shelf near me. Body parts. Fingers. Lungs. Brains. All human, according to the labels. This had to be a laboratory where bodies were dissected.

I shoved down my nausea and focused. Would they keep motivators in a room like this? Anything I found that used Epic technology would need a motivator to work—the mission would be useless unless I found a stash of those.

I started looking for them—they'd be small metal boxes, about the size of a mobile's battery. Sparks. Everything was bathed in the green of the night vision, and through the tunnel view of my rifle's scope, the place took on another level of eerie.

"Yo," Mizzy's voice said on the line, and I jumped again. "David, you there?"

"Yeah," I whispered.

"Fighting on my side has moved over toward Megan, so I've got a breather," Mizzy said. "Cody told me to see if you needed anything."

I wasn't certain what she could do from such a distance, but it was good to hear someone's voice. "I'm in some kind of lab," I answered. "It has shelves full of body parts in jars and . . ." I felt nauseous again, swinging my gun to get a better look through the scope at the tubs nearby. They each had a glass lid, and they were full. I gagged and recoiled. ". . . and some vats filled with floating chunks of something. It's like a bunch of cannibals were getting ready to go bobbing for apples. Adam's apples, at least."

I reached out and opened a cupboard, where I found an entire shelf of pickled hearts. As I moved onward, my foot touched something that squished. I jumped back, gun toward the floor, but it was only a wet rag.

"Mizzy," I whispered, "this place is super creepy. Think I'm safe to turn on a light in here?"

"Oh, that'd be waaaay smart. The people with a hyper-advanced bunker and flying attack drones aren't going to have security cameras in their labs. Nope. Not a chance."

"Point taken."

"Or they've already spotted you and a squad of death-copters is heading your way. But in case you're *not* trapped and about to be executed, I'd err on the side of being careful."

She said it all in an upbeat, almost excited voice; Mizzy could be perkier than a sack of caffeinated puppies. Usually that was encouraging. Usually I wasn't on edge from sneaking through a room full of half corpses.

I knelt, touching the rag on the floor. That it was still wet might imply someone had been working in here overnight, and had been interrupted by our attack.

"Anything you can swipe?" Mizzy asked.

"Not unless you want to stitch yourself up a new boyfriend."

"Ew. Look, just see what you can grab and get out. We're already over time."

"Right," I said, opening another cabinet. Surgical utensils. "I'll hurry. It— Wait a sec."

I froze, listening. Had I heard something?

Yes, a kind of rattling. I tried not to imagine a corpse rising out of one of those tubs. The sound had come from near the door I'd entered through, and a tiny light flicked on suddenly near the floor in the same area.

I frowned, inching toward it. It was a small drone, flat and round, with whirring brushes along its bottom. It had come in through a little flap near the door—kind of like a cat door—and was buffing the floor.

I relaxed. "Only a cleaning bot," I said over the line.

The bot immediately went silent. Mizzy started to reply, but I lost the words as the little cleaning bot reengaged and zipped back toward its door. Throwing myself to the ground, I stretched out a hand and barely managed to grab the little drone before it could scoot out through the small hinged flap.

"David?" Mizzy asked, anxious. "What was that?"

"Me being an idiot," I said with a wince. I'd knocked my elbow on the ground as I dove. "The bot recognized something was wrong and made a break for it. I caught it before it got out though. It might have warned someone."

"Might anyway," Mizzy said. "It could have a link to the place's security."

"I'll be quick," I said, climbing to my feet. I set the cleaning bot upside down on a shelf near a rack of blood pouches hanging in a small cooler with a glass door. Several more were lying out in the open on the counter. Ick.

"Maybe some of these body parts are from Epics," I said. "I could take them, and we'd have DNA samples. Could we use those?"

"How?"

"I dunno," I said. "Make weapons out of them somehow?"

"Yeaaaah," Mizzy said skeptically, "I'll staple a foot to the front of my gun and hope it shoots lasers now or something."

I blushed in the darkness, but I didn't see the need for the ribbing. If I stole some valuable DNA, we could trade it for supplies, right? Though admittedly, these body parts probably wouldn't do. The important parts of Epic DNA degraded quickly, so I'd need to find frozen tissue if I wanted something I could sell.

Freezers. Where would I find freezers? I checked one of the tubs, lifting the glass lid, but the water inside was chilly, not frozen. I let the top back down, scanning the room. There was a door at the rear, opposite the one that led out to the hallway.

"You know," I said to Mizzy as I walked toward the door, "this place is exactly like I'd expect it to be."

"You *expected* a room full of body parts?"

"Yeah, kinda," I said. "I mean, crazy scientists making weapons from dead Epics? Why *wouldn't* they have a room full of body parts?"

"Not sure what you're driving at with this, David. Other than creeping me out."

22

"Just a sec." I reached the door, which was locked.

It took a few kicks, but I got it open. I wasn't too worried about the noise—if someone nearby was listening, they'd already have heard me struggling with the little drone. The door swung back, revealing a dark corridor, smaller than the hallway outside and completely unlit. I listened, heard nothing, and decided to see where it went.

"Anyway," I continued, "it makes me wonder. How *do* they make weapons out of Epics?"

"Dunno," Mizzy said. "I can fix the stuff once we get it, but motivators are out of my league."

"When an Epic dies, their cells immediately start to break down," I said. "Everyone knows that part."

"Everyone who is a nerd."

"I'm not a—"

"It's okay, dude," Mizzy said. "Embrace your nature! Be yourself and stuff. We're all basically nerds, only about different things. Except Cody. I think he's a geek or something . . . can't remember my terminology. Something about eating chicken heads?"

I sighed. "When an Epic dies, if you're fast enough, you can take a sample of their cells. The mitochondria are supposed to be important. You freeze those cells, and you can sell them on the black market. Somehow, *that* becomes technology. Problem is, Obliteration let Regalia perform surgery on him. I saw the scars. They made a bomb using his powers."

"So . . ."

"So why surgery?" I said. "He could have just given a blood sample, right? Why did Regalia call in some fancy surgeon?"

Mizzy went silent. "Huh," she finally said.

"Yeah." Honestly, I'd assumed that an Epic had to be dead

to make technology from their powers. Regalia and Obliteration proved me wrong. But if you could create technology from living Epics, why hadn't Steelheart made a legion of invincible soldiers? Maybe he was too paranoid for that, but surely he would have created hundreds of versions of Edmund, the Epic who powered his city.

I reached a corner in the dark hallway. Using the infrared on my scope, I peeked around it and scanned for danger. The night vision revealed a small room filled with several large freezer chests. I didn't see any distinctive heat sources, though the timer on my scope's overlay warned me I should turn back. Except if I left, and Abraham didn't get anything either, we'd be ruined. I *needed* to find something.

I crouched there, worried I was running out of time—but also bothered by what I'd seen. Beyond the question of making motivators from living Epics, there was another problem with all of this. When people talked about Epic-derived technology, they implied that all the devices came from a similar process. But how could that be? Weapons were so different from the dowser, which let us detect who was an Epic. Both seemed hugely different from the spyril, the piece of Epic-derived technology that had let me fly on streams of water.

I was no nerd, but I knew enough to realize that these technologies were all in very different disciplines. You didn't call a gerbil doctor to work on a horse—yet when it came to Epic technology, it seemed that one expertise was enough to create a variety of items.

I admitted the truth to myself: these questions were the real reason we were here at Knighthawk. Prof had kept secrets, even before succumbing to his powers. It felt like nobody had been straight with me about any of this, ever.

I wanted answers. They were probably here somewhere. Maybe I'd find them behind that group of robotic war drones that were extending their gun arms from behind the freezers in front of me.

Oh.

4

THE drones' floodlights turned on as one, blinding me, and they opened fire. Fortunately I'd spotted them in time, and was able to pull back around the corner before any shots hit me.

I turned and took off at a run, retreating down the corridor. Gunfire drowned out Mizzy's voice in my ear as the robot drones chased me. Each had a square bottom with multidirectional wheels, and a spindly body topped with an assault rifle. They'd be perfect for maneuvering around furniture and through hallways, but sparks, it felt humiliating to be running from them. They looked more like coatracks than machines of war.

I reached the door to the lab with the body parts and ran through it, skidding to a stop, then slammed my back against the wall next to it. The tap of a button patched the view from my scope into a small screen on the side of my Gottschalk rifle, which let me lift the gun around the corner and fire without risking a hit.

The robots scuttled like a group of sparking brooms on wheels. Personally, I'd have been embarrassed to create such stupid-looking robots. I fired in burst mode without much aiming, but the corridor was narrow enough that it didn't matter. I gunned down several of the robots, slowing the others, which had to push past the wreckage. After I dropped a few more, they retreated to take cover around the corner, in the room with the freezers.

"David?" Mizzy's frantic voice finally drew my attention. "What's happening?"

"I'm fine," I said. "But they spotted me."

"Get out."

I hesitated.

"David?"

"There's something in there, Mizzy. A room that was under lock and key, guarded by drones—I'll bet they moved in there as soon as our original attack happened. Either that, or that room is *always* guarded. Which means . . ."

"Oh, Calamity. You're going to be you, aren't you?"

"You *did* just tell me to, and I quote, 'embrace my nature.'" I fired another salvo as I caught motion at the end of the corridor. "Let Abraham and the others know I've been spotted. Pull everyone out and be ready to retreat."

"And you?"

"I'm going to find out what's in that room." I hesitated. "I might have to get shot to do it."

"What?"

"I'll be radio silent for a moment. Sorry."

I dropped my radio and headset, then tapped a button

at the side of my gun that extended a small tripod on the bottom. I set it pointing into the tunnel at an angle, hoping to ricochet bullets off the metal wall toward the robots—but really setting up a distraction. The gun could remote fire, using the slightly melted controller I popped out of its alcove on the side.

I hurried through the room, triggering short bursts of fire to make it seem I was still exchanging shots with the drones. Their floodlights were bright enough that they reflected off glass and metal in this room, giving me enough light to move by. I snatched the little cleaning robot off the shelf, its wheels still whirring frantically, then grabbed a pouch of blood off the counter and a roll of surgical tape I'd spotted in a drawer earlier.

I tore off a piece of tape and affixed the pouch to the top of the robot, then punctured the bag with my knife. I crossed to where I'd originally entered the room, cracked open the door, and set the machine down outside it. It scuttled off down the white hallway at speed—leaving a wide trail of blood drops behind, as blatant as a sudden tuba solo in the middle of a rap single.

Great. Now hopefully I could fake the getting shot part. I grabbed another pouch of blood and stabbed it with my knife. Taking a deep breath, I ran to the door on the opposite side of the room, where the drones were firing on my Gottschalk.

The robots had made progress, shoving the fallen ones out of the way and advancing. I ducked back as the robots started firing at me, then I screamed and sprayed some of the blood on the wall. From there I dashed to one of the tubs, using the pouch to squirt a different trail toward the exit.

I couldn't see much of what was inside the tub, now that I wasn't using my scope, but I pulled it open, gritted my teeth, and climbed in—touching some slippery bits that I was pretty convinced were livers. As I settled into the icy fluid, I was profoundly aware of exactly how gruesome all this was. Fortunately, I was quite accustomed to my plans humiliating me in some way; this time I was merely doing it on purpose. So hey, progress!

I tried to remain still, hoping the tub's refrigeration unit and icy temperature would hide me from any infrared detection the robots might be using. Unfortunately, to not stand out, I had to close the top of the tub and hold my breath. And so I lay there among the bobbing body parts, watching lights flash above as the robots and their floodlights entered the laboratory. I couldn't see much through the water and the glass top, but I couldn't help imagining the robots gathering around the tub, looking in at me, amused at my feeble attempt at a distraction.

I held my breath until I was ready to burst. My face, not covered by my infiltration suit, was *freezing*. Blessedly, the lights finally vanished. I managed to last a little longer before I pushed open the top and, shivering, looked around the lab. Pitch-black.

The robots had apparently taken the bait. I wiped the liquid from my eyes and climbed out. Sparks. As if this place hadn't been creepy *before* I'd decided to crawl into a vat of livers to hide from death robots. I shook my head, crossing over to pick up my radio and gun. I shoved on the headset, but I had gotten blood on it, and it seemed to be on the fritz.

I'd have to use the radio the old way. "I'm back," I said quietly, pressing send and speaking into it.

"David, you're crazy," a voice responded.

I smiled. "Hello, Megan," I said, slipping into the narrow corridor. I jogged past fallen robots. "Everyone pulling out?"

"Everyone who's smart."

"Love you too," I said. I stopped at the corner where I'd first run into the robot guards and peeked around it. The room beyond was dark, like before. I looped my gun's strap around my shoulder, then used the scope to look for lingering robots. "I'm almost ready to go. Give me a few more minutes."

"Roger."

I clicked the radio to send only, so that their chatter wouldn't alert any nearby foes. Unfortunately, I didn't have time to be more careful. My trick with the false trail would soon be discovered. As if in testament to the danger, a distant explosion shook the building.

I felt at the wall and turned on the lights, then crossed the room to one of the large standing freezers. The stainless steel surface reflected my face, which had two weeks' worth of scrub on it. I thought it looked rugged. Megan tended to snicker at it.

Heart thumping, I unlocked the first of the chests and threw it open, releasing a burst of icy air. Inside were rows and rows of frozen glass vials with colorful caps. Not the motivators I'd been looking for, but most likely Epic DNA samples.

"Well," I whispered, "at least it's not a rack of frozen dinners."

"No," a voice responded. "I keep those in the other chest."

5

I stood very still, a chill rising up my spine. I turned, careful not to make any sudden motions, and found that I had—unfortunately—missed a single robot hidden in the shadowed recesses of the room. That beanpole of a body was hardly intimidating, but the souped-up FAMAS G3 assault rifle mounted to its top was something else entirely.

I considered trying to shoot it, but my body was turned the wrong direction. I'd have to swing my gun around and hope to hit the robot before I got shot myself. My chances did not seem good.

"I actually *do* have food in the other one," the voice continued, projected from the robot. A man's voice, tenor, soft. He had to be one of the enigmatic people who ran the Foundry. Most of these drones seemed autonomous, but their masters would be watching—each gun had a camera on it. "Not frozen dinners, mind you. Steaks. A few choice ribeyes left over from the good old days. I miss those more than anything."

"Who are you?" I asked.

"The man you're trying to rob. How did you divert my drones?"

I bit my lip, trying to judge the response time of that gun as I inched to the side and watched it follow me. Sparks. The tracking apparatus was excellent; the gun stayed right on me. The robot's speakers even made a little cocking noise by way of warning, and I froze in place.

But did it have full range of movement? Maybe not . . .

"So this is what has become of the mighty Jonathan Phaedrus," the voice said. "Sending a hit team in to try to steal from me."

Phaedrus? Of course. The Knighthawk Foundry worker thought we were still with Prof. We hadn't exactly trumpeted it out that he'd fallen to his powers; most people didn't even know he was an Epic in the first place.

"We only had to come," I said, "because you refused to trade with us."

"Yes, very honorable of you. 'Trade us what we want, or we'll take it by force.' I expected more of one of Jonathan's special teams. You barely . . ." The voice trailed off, then continued, fainter. "What do you mean there's another one? They stole *what*? How did they even know where those were, dammit?"

Something muffled responded. I tried to step away, but the drone made the cocking sound again, this time louder.

"You," the voice said, turning his attention back to me. "Call your friends. Tell them to return what the other man stole, or I *will* kill you. You have three seconds."

"Uh . . ."

"Two seconds."

"Guys!"

The wall to my right melted in a burst of heat, revealing a shadowy form beyond.

I dove and—against my instincts—rolled *toward* the robot drone. It got off an initial round at me, but—as I'd hoped—when I got too close, its gun couldn't angle down far enough to hit me.

That meant I only got shot once.

It hit me in the leg as I was rolling. Not sure how that managed to happen, but sparks, it *hurt*.

The robot tried to back away, but I seized it, ignoring the searing pain in my leg. Last time I'd been shot, I hadn't felt it at first, but this time I had trouble fighting through the sheer agony. Still, I managed to keep the robot from firing at me again as I reached up and unlocked the device that held the gun to the machine. It dropped free.

Unfortunately, as I'd been struggling, a good *two dozen* drones had unclipped from the ceiling—where they'd been disguised as panels—and hovered down on propellers. I hadn't been nearly as safe in here as I'd assumed, though for now their attention was focused on a figure that stepped through the slag of the wall: a man made entirely of flames, his figure the deep red of molten rock. Firefight had arrived. Too bad he wasn't real.

I grabbed my wounded thigh and scanned the room for Megan. She was hiding near the corner in the corridor leading back to the laboratory. Firefight wasn't real, not completely, but neither was he an illusion. He was a shadow from another place, another version of our world. It wasn't that he had actually come to save me; Megan was just overlaying our world with a ripple from that world, making it seem like he was here.

It fooled the drones—indeed, I could *feel* the heat coming from the melted wall, and could smell smoke in the air. As the drones frantically started firing, I reached into the open freezer and grabbed a handful of vials. Then I limped across the room, joining Megan, who came to me as soon as she was aware that I'd been hit.

"Slontze," she said with a grunt, getting under my arm and hauling me toward cover, then shoved the vials I'd taken into her pocket. "I leave you alone for five minutes, and you go and get shot."

"At least I got you a present," I said, pushing my back against the wall inside the curve as she quickly bound my wound.

"Present? The vials?"

"I got you a new gun," I said, gritting my teeth at the pain as she pulled the bandage tight.

"You mean the FAMAS you left on the floor over there?"

"Yup."

"You realize that every one of the, like, a hundred drones I fought outside had one of those. We could build a fort out of them at this point."

"Well, once you finish using all those for a fort, you'll need one for shooting. So you're welcome! Even comes . . ." I winced at the pain. "Even comes with its own room full of death robots. And maybe some steaks. Don't know if he was lying about those or not."

Behind her, Firefight looked unconcerned, bullets melting before they reached him. It wasn't as hot as it should have been—it was as if the fire were distant, and we felt a breeze that blew out from it.

We barely understood how her powers worked. Those drones that Firefight melted weren't *actually* dead, and that wall hadn't *actually* been opened. The other world's ability to affect this one was fleeting. For a minute, we were all caught in the warping of reality as the two worlds mixed, but in moments it would all fade back to normal.

"I'm fine," I said. "We've got to move."

Megan said nothing, getting under my arm again. The fact that she gave no reply—and that she'd stopped us in the middle of a fight to look at the wound—told me what I needed to know. I was hit bad, and bleeding a lot.

We shuffled away down the corridor toward the laboratory. As we did, I glanced over my shoulder to make sure no drones were following. None were, but I did catch an unnerving sight: Firefight was looking at me, *again*. Through the flames of distortion, two black eyes met my own. Megan swore he couldn't see our world, and yet he raised a hand toward me.

We were soon out of his sight. The loud pops of gunfire chased us as we staggered into the laboratory room with all the organs. We stepped to the side, anxious, as another group of drones scuttled past. They didn't even glance at us. There was an *Epic* to fight.

We crossed the room, then moved into the bright hallway outside. I left a *real* blood trail on the floor.

"What *was* that place?" Megan said. "Were those *hearts* in those jars?"

"Yeah," I said. "Man, my leg hurts. . . ."

"Cody," Megan said, sounding alarmed, "is Abraham out? . . . Okay, good. Prime the jeeps, and have the first-aid kit ready. David's been shot."

Silence.

"I don't know how we're going to do that, Mizzy. Hopefully we can use the distraction like we planned. Be ready."

I focused on keeping myself moving through the pain. We turned up the tunnel leading to the hidden entrance I'd

35

used to sneak into the place. Behind us, the shooting suddenly stopped.

Bad sign. Firefight had vanished.

"You couldn't make him follow us?" I asked.

"I need a breather," she said, eyes forward, jaw set. "This was hard enough in the old days, when I didn't care what it did to me."

"You mean—" I said.

"It's just a headache," she replied. "Like yesterday, but worse. It's as if . . . well, as if something were pounding on my skull, trying to get in. Creating such a large distortion in reality is pushing me to the edge. So let's hope that—"

She stopped. A group of drones was gathered in the access tunnel before us, blocking our path to the exit into the forest. That exit teased me; it was several hundred feet away, but I could see that it had been blown open by an explosion, letting in filtered sunlight. It was likely how Megan had entered, but with those drones between it and us, the exit might as well have been in Australia.

Then, without warning, the ceiling caved in. Huge chunks of metal fell around us, and the tunnel shook as if in a blast. I knew enough by now though to recognize something *off* about the explosion. Perhaps the steel chunks didn't scrape as loudly as they should have, or perhaps it was the way the corridor shook. Or perhaps it was how those steel chunks fell directly in front of us, blocking the drones—which started firing, but missed hitting both Megan and me with any debris.

This was another dimensional illusion, though it was still violent enough to knock me from my feet. I hit with a grunt, trying to roll to my side to protect my wounded leg. The room spun, and for a moment I felt like a grasshopper stapled to a Frisbee.

When my vision wobbled back to a semblance of stability,

I found myself huddled beside one of the fallen hunks of metal. It felt real to me, for the moment. Here, in the blending of two worlds Megan had created, the "illusion" was real.

My blood, which had soaked through the impromptu bandage, stained the floor like someone had wiped it with a dirty cloth. Megan knelt beside me, her head bowed, her breath coming in hisses.

"Megan?" I asked over the sounds of the firing drones. Sparks . . . they'd be on us soon, blockade or no blockade.

Megan's eyes were open wide, and her lips parted, exposing clenched teeth. Sweat trickled down her temples.

Whatever she'd been fighting off when using her powers recently, it was coming for her in force.

6

THIS wasn't supposed to happen.

We'd found the secret, the way to make Epics immune to the corrupting effects of their powers: if you faced your deepest fears, it caused the darkness to retreat.

It was *supposed* to be over; Megan had run into a burning building to save me, facing her fears head-on. She should have been free. And yet there was no denying the frantic cast to her expression—her clenched teeth, her tense brow. She turned toward me, not blinking. "I can feel him, David," she whispered. "He's trying to get in."

"Who?"

She didn't answer, but I knew who she meant. Calamity. Calamity, the red spot in the sky, the new star that had heralded the arrival of the Epics . . . was itself an Epic. I somehow knew Calamity was *supremely* angry that in learning that Epics' fears were connected to their weaknesses, we'd figured out how to overcome its influence on Megan.

The gunfire of the drones stopped.

"That cave-in is an illusion of some sort, isn't it?" the voice from before called, echoing in the corridor. "Which Epic did you kill to gain this technology? Who told you how to build the motivators?"

At least he was talking instead of shooting.

"Megan," I said, taking her arm. "Megan, look at me."

She focused on me, and that seemed to help, though the wildness was still there in her eyes. I was tempted to step back and let her unleash it. Maybe that would save us.

But it would doom her. When Prof had succumbed to the darkness brought by his powers, he'd killed friends without so much as flinching. That man, who had spent his life defending others, was now entirely subject to his powers.

I wouldn't have the same happen to Megan. I reached to my thigh pocket and—wincing as I shifted my wounded leg—pulled out my lighter. I held it up before Megan and flicked on the flame.

She shied back briefly, then hissed and *seized* the flame in her fist, burning her hand. The fallen metal chunks we'd been using as cover wavered, then faded out of existence. The ceiling repaired itself. Fire was still Megan's weakness—and even having faced her fears, the weakness negated her powers. And probably always would.

Fortunately, so long as she remained willing to face that weakness, she could apparently drive the darkness away. The tension left her, and she sank to the ground with a sigh. "Great," she muttered. "Now my head *and* my hand hurt."

I smiled wanly and slid my gun away across the ground, then did the same with Megan's. I raised my hands as the drones surrounded us. Most of them were the tracks-and-assault-rifle type, though there were also a few that flew. I was in luck—they held their fire.

One of the machines rolled closer. It had raised a small screen from its base, which projected a backlit shadowy figure. "That image was of Firefight, from Newcago, right? It fooled my sensors completely," the voice said. "No ordinary illusion could have done that. What technology are you using?"

"I'll tell you," Megan said. "Just don't shoot. Please." She stood up, and as she did so, she kicked something backward with her heel.

Her headset. Still lying on my side, I caught it under my hand and rolled onto it, masking the motion by holding my bleeding leg. I didn't think any drones spotted what we'd done.

"Well?" the voice said. "I'm waiting."

"Dimensional shadows," Megan said. "They aren't illusions, but ripples from another state of reality." She'd stood to face the robot army, putting herself between the robots and me. Most focused their weapons on her—and if they killed her, she'd reincarnate.

I appreciated her protective gesture, but sparks, reincarnating could do unpredictable things to her—particularly with how her powers had been acting lately. She hadn't died since we were in Babilar, and I hoped to keep it that way.

I needed to do something. I curled up, still holding my leg. The pain was real. I could only hope the way I trembled and bled would make the drones dismiss me as I laid my head on the headset and covertly whispered into the microphone.

"Mizzy? You there? Cody? Abraham?"

No reply came.

"Impossible," the man said to Megan. "I've tried numerous

times to capture that type of power in a motivator, and I doubt anyone has the knowledge to do what I could not. Dimensional rifting is too complex, too strong to . . ."

I glanced up at Megan, who stood tall and proud before the arrayed army, even though I knew her head must be splitting with pain. She'd spoken earlier in humility, as if beaten— but her posture told another story. Of a refusal to back down, to bend a knee, or to bow to anyone or anything.

"You're an Epic, aren't you?" the voice said, tone growing hard. "There *is* no technology, no motivator. Jonathan is recruiting, then? Now that he's turned?"

I couldn't stifle my gasp. How did he know about Prof? I wanted to demand answers, but I was in no position to do so. I rested my head against the floor, suddenly drowsy. Sparks. How much blood had I lost?

As my head touched the headset, it crackled and Mizzy's voice cut in. "Megan? Sparks, talk to me! Are you—"

"I'm here, Mizzy," I whispered.

"David? Finally! Look, I've placed charges to collapse the tunnel. Can you get out that way? I can blow it after you pass."

Charges. I glanced at the drones surrounding us.

Megan's illusions . . .

"Do it now, Mizzy," I whispered.

"You sure?"

"Yes."

Then I braced myself.

The explosion blew above, and it somehow seemed *louder* because I'd been expecting it. The chunks of metal fell exactly where they had before, slamming to the ground inches from where I crouched—but I was left unharmed, as was Megan.

The robots, on the other hand, acted like a bunch of youthful dreams and got thoroughly crushed.

Megan was at my side in an instant, handgun pulled from

her thigh holster, firing at the remaining drones. I managed to pull the knife out of my calf sheath and I held it up, drawing a glance from Megan that said, "Seriously?"

"At least it's not a stupid samurai sword," I muttered, putting my back to the debris. As the falling dust cleared, Megan picked off one final drone, sending it spinning to the ground.

I pushed myself to my feet—well, *foot*—and hobbled along the wreckage of the tunnel toward my gun.

"Where did *that* come from?" Megan asked, gesturing toward the broken ceiling. Mizzy's charges hadn't completely collapsed the tunnel—in fact, so far as I could tell, the fallen wreckage was *identical* to the illusory debris that Megan had created.

"Mizzy said she could blow the place after our escape."

"And you had her drop it on *top* of us instead?" Megan said, fetching my gun and handing it to me, then grabbing her rifle.

"I was thinking, your illusions pull from alternate realities, right? And the closer the reality is to ours, the easier it is to pull? You were really tired—"

"Still am."

"—and I figured you used a reality very like our own. Explosion from above. Mizzy had placed charges. So I guessed it would happen the same way."

Megan got under my arm again and helped me limp around the wreckage. She shot a drone that was trying to extricate itself from some fallen stone. "That might not have worked," she said softly. "Things don't always turn out like they do in the other realities. You could have crushed yourself, David."

"Well, I didn't," I said, "so for now we're safe. . . ."

I trailed off as sounds echoed up the corridor, coming from far behind us. Metallic sounds. The whirring of copters. Treads on metal.

Megan looked at me, then at the exit to the forest ahead, still a hundred feet away.

"Let's hurry," I said, hobbling forward.

Instead, Megan took my arm from around her shoulders and placed it against the wall so I could hold myself up. "You're going to need some time to extract," she said.

"So we should hurry."

Megan shouldered her rifle, then faced back down the corridor.

"Megan!"

"That spot beside the rubble is defensible," she said. "I can hold them off for a good long while. Get going."

"But—"

"David, please. Just go."

I took her by the shoulder, then pulled her to me and kissed her. That twisted my leg, causing pain to flare up my side, but whatever. A kiss from Megan was worth it.

I released her. And then I left, as she had said.

I felt cowardly, but part of being in a team was about recognizing when someone else could do a job better than you. And part of being a man was learning to let your immortal girlfriend take a turn being the heroic one.

I'd be back for her though, dead or not. And soon. No way was I going to leave her body to end up like those in the tubs I'd found. I stumbled up the slope, trying not to dwell on what might happen to Megan. She'd have to shoot herself once the drones overwhelmed her, as she couldn't risk getting captured.

Behind me, Megan started firing, the rifle shots echoing in the steel hallway. The drones scuttled and clacked. Automatic weapons fire followed.

I had almost reached the exit, but I saw shadows in the sunlight outside. I was getting sick of drones. I winced as I pulled out my handgun. Fortunately, the shadows resolved into a stout black man in tight, dark clothing, night-vision goggles on his brow and a very, *very* large gun in his hands. Abraham cursed as he saw me, voice softly laced with his French accent.

"How are you?" he said, hurrying down the short slope. "And Megan?"

"She's covering our escape," I said. "She wants us to go without her."

He met my eyes, then nodded, turning to walk with me the last couple of feet. "Drones outside pulled back into the complex once you were spotted," he said. "Everyone else is at the jeeps."

We had a chance then.

"She *is* an Epic."

I jumped, looking around. It was that voice from before. Had a drone found us?

No. A panel on the wall had turned into a display. The same shadowed figure as before was on-screen, facing us.

"David?" Abraham said, standing in the sunlight of the open roof of the exit. "Let's go."

"She is an Epic," I said instead, facing the screen. That figure . . . was it familiar?

A light suddenly switched on, banishing the shadows and revealing a stocky older man with a round head, bald save for some wisps of white hair that stuck up almost like a crown. I *had* seen him before. One time. In a picture of Prof's, taken years ago.

"I have seen something unbelievable today," the man said, "and it leaves me curious. You're the one they call Steel-slayer, aren't you. Yes . . . the kid from Newcago. Don't you *kill* Epics?"

"Just the ones that deserve it," I replied.

"And Jonathan Phaedrus?"

"Jonathan Phaedrus is gone," Abraham said softly. "Only the Epic Limelight remains. We will do what needs to be done."

I didn't say anything. It wasn't that I disagreed with Abraham, but saying the words was hard for me.

The man studied us. Suddenly, the gunfire behind us fell silent. "I have recalled my machines. We need to talk."

In reply, I fainted.

7

"WE wouldn't have had this problem if you'd been willing to deal with us."

Megan's voice. Mmm . . . I lay in darkness, enjoying that sound, and was annoyed when the next speaker wasn't her.

"What was I supposed to do?" It was the voice of that man, the one from Knighthawk. "First I get word that Phaedrus has turned, then you *immediately* contact me and demand weapons? I wanted nothing to do with it."

"You could have guessed that we would resist him," Abraham said. "The Reckoners would not simply join with a tyrant because he was once our leader."

"You're missing my point," the man said. "I didn't turn you away because I thought you were working with him; I turned you away because I'm not a *sparking* idiot. Phaedrus knows too much about me. I'm not going to cross him *or* sell to him. I wanted nothing to do with you people."

"Then why did you invite us in here?" Megan demanded.

I groaned, forcing my eyes open. My leg ached, but it didn't hurt like I expected it to. When I shifted it, I felt only a superficial pain. But sparks. I was *exhausted*.

I blinked, my eyes struggling to focus, and a moment later Megan's head appeared above me, golden hair hanging down around her face. "David?" she asked. "How do you feel?"

"Like a piece of bread at a rock party."

She relaxed visibly and turned around. "He's all right."

"A piece of what?" the Knighthawk man's voice asked.

"Piece of bread," I said, sitting up with difficulty. "At a rock party. You know, because nobody wants *bread* at a *rock party*. They've come to see the cool rocks. So they toss the bread on the floor and it gets stomped on."

"That's the dumbest thing I've ever heard."

"Sorry," I grumbled. "I'm usually more eloquent after getting shot."

I was in a dim room filled with an inordinate number of sofas, one of which I had been lying on. Another one—long, black, overstuffed—near the far wall had a low table in front of it that was covered with an array of monitors and other computer equipment, as well as a small stack of dirty plates. The Knighthawk man sat on a different sofa closer to me, near a little nightstand piled with peanut shells and two large, empty plastic cups. Beside him sat a full-sized mannequin.

Like, really. A mannequin. The type you might find in an old department store, modeling clothing. It had a completely featureless wooden face, and was dressed like the Newcago elite in a wide-brimmed hat and pinstriped suit. It had been positioned to sit in a relaxed pose, legs crossed and hands clasped.

Right . . .

Abraham stood in front of the sofa, arms folded, still in his black infiltration suit. He'd removed his mask—it hung from his belt—but he still wore his imposing P328 gravatonic minigun strapped to his back. Other than Megan, he was the only member of my team in the room.

"Nice place," I said. "I assume you spent your entire decorating budget on the freaky laboratory?"

The man sniffed. "The laboratory needs to remain clean for the work I do there. I have invited you into my home, young man. A rare honor."

"I apologize for not bringing some ceremonial stale pizza crusts as an offering," I said, nodding to the dirty plates on the table across the room. I climbed to my feet, wobbling— although with one hand on the armrest of the couch I managed to remain upright. My leg throbbed, and I looked down to find that my pants had been sliced to get at the wound.

It was scabbed over, and looked like it had been healing for weeks, perhaps months.

"Hmm," the man said. "Sorry that it's not completely healed. My device isn't as powerful as some others."

I nodded to Megan, indicating I was all right. She didn't offer me an arm to lean on, not in front of an enemy, but she did remain close by.

"Where are we?" I asked.

"Underneath my Foundry," the man said.

"And you are?"

"Dean Knighthawk."

I blinked. "Seriously? Like, that's your *name*?"

"No," the man said, "but my name was stupid. So I use this one instead."

Well, points to him for honesty, though my skin crawled at the idea of giving up your name. I wasn't even fond of the nickname people gave me, Steelslayer. David Charleston was good enough. My father gave me that name. These days, it was about the only thing I had left of him.

Knighthawk was indeed the man I'd seen in Prof's photo back in Babilar. The man was older now, more bald and more paunched, with jowls hanging down beside his neck, like melted cheese sloughing off the top of a piece of bread in the microwave.

He and Prof had obviously been friends, and he knew that Prof was an Epic—had known for a long while.

"You were part of Prof's first team," I guessed. "The one with Regalia and Murkwood, when all of them became Epics."

"No," Knighthawk said. "I wasn't. But my wife was."

That's right. There had been four of them, I remembered Prof saying. A woman named . . . Amala? There was something important about her, something I couldn't quite remember.

"I was an interested observer," Knighthawk said. "A scientist, and not the 'Hey kids, watch me freeze this grape with liquid nitrogen' type like Jonathan. A real scientist."

"And a real businessman," Abraham said. "You've built an empire upon the bodies of the dead."

Beside Knighthawk, the mannequin spread its arms apart, hands to the sides, as if to say, "Guilty as charged." I jumped, then glanced at Megan.

"Yeah," she whispered, "it moves. Haven't figured out how."

"Mizzy and Cody?" I whispered.

"Stayed outside in case this was a trap."

"I pioneered motivator technology," Knighthawk said to Abraham. "And yes, I have benefited from it. So have you. So let us not point fingers, Mr. Desjardins."

Abraham maintained a calm expression, but he couldn't

have been happy to hear Knighthawk use his last name. Even I hadn't known what it was; we didn't talk much about our pasts.

"That's great," I said, then walked by Abraham and flopped down onto the couch opposite Knighthawk and his creepy mannequin. "Again, why did you invite us in here?"

"That Epic," Knighthawk said, and his mannequin pointed at Megan, "is Firefight, isn't she? She was a dimensionalist all along?"

It wasn't exactly true. When Megan spoke of Firefight, she spoke of him externally—a being from another dimension who she could bring into ours, fleetingly. She didn't consider herself to be Firefight, though that was a small distinction.

"Yes," Megan said, stepping up and—after considering for a moment—sitting down next to me. She rested her arm along the back of the couch, exposing her underarm holster and making it easily accessible. "There's more to it, but basically . . . yes. I am what you say."

I rested my hand on her shoulder. Megan could be cold—part was her native personality, part was wanting to keep her distance from people because . . . well, Epics tended to be dangerous to get to know. I could see past that, to the tension in the way she watched Knighthawk, the way she wiggled her thumb as if cocking an imaginary revolver. Her hand had a big red blister on it where she'd grabbed the flame.

We knew how to keep the darkness at bay, but this war wasn't won yet. She was worried about what had happened to her earlier. Frankly, so was I.

Knighthawk's mannequin leaned forward in a thoughtful posture and tipped its hat back to better expose its featureless face. "What you did in the lab, young woman," Knighthawk said, "fooled all of my sensors, cameras, and programming. You aren't just any dimensionalist, you're a powerful one. My robots report scarring on the walls of the room, and some of my drones were *destroyed*. Permanently. It's like nothing I've ever seen."

"You're *not* getting my DNA," Megan said.

"Hmm?" Knighthawk said. "Oh, I already have that. I collected a dozen different samples before you two made it to the access corridor. You think you could come in here wearing anything other than a cleanroom suit and escape without me getting some of your skin cells? But you needn't worry; I'm far from creating a motivator based on you. There is more to it than . . . is generally assumed."

The mannequin continued to gesture while Knighthawk talked. *But Knighthawk's not moving at all,* I noticed. *And the overstuffed couches and pillows make it seem like he's wedged into his seat.* Dean Knighthawk was at least partially paralyzed. He could talk—every word he spoke came from his own mouth—but he didn't move anything more than his head.

How could he be disabled? If he had technology to heal me, then why wouldn't he have healed himself?

"No," Knighthawk said, still addressing Megan, "I'm not interested in exploiting your powers right now, but I do want to understand them. What you did earlier was *powerful*. Incredible. The manipulation of reality is no small-scale stuff, young lady."

"I hadn't realized," she said dryly. "What are you getting at?"

"You were going to sacrifice yourself," Knighthawk said. "You stayed behind so the others could escape."

"Yeah?" Megan said. "It's not a big deal. I can survive a lot of things."

"Ah . . . so a High Epic?" Knighthawk said, his mannequin sitting up straighter. "I might have guessed as much."

Megan drew her lips to a line.

"Get to the point, Knighthawk," I said.

"The point is this," he replied, his mannequin waving to us. "This conversation. Such an explosive use of that woman's powers should have driven her to isolation, rage, and a supreme annoyance at anyone near to her. Jonathan is one of the few Epics I know who could control the darkness—and following the use of his powers, he would often stay away from people for days before he was under control again. Yet *this* young lady used her powers but wasn't consumed by darkness at all—as proven by the fact that she subsequently selflessly risked her life for her team."

The mannequin leaned forward.

"So," Knighthawk continued, "what's the secret?"

I looked toward Abraham, who shrugged almost imperceptibly. He didn't know if we should share the information or not. So far, we had been careful about when, and with whom, we talked about how to drive back the darkness in Epics. With this knowledge, we could accidentally tip the power structure in the Fractured States—as the secret of overcoming the darkness *also* gave away the secret to discovering Epic weaknesses.

I had half a mind to broadcast these things far and wide. If the Epics discovered one another's weaknesses, maybe they'd kill each other off. Unfortunately, the truth would probably be more brutal. Power would shift, and some Epics would rise while others fell. We might end up with one group of Epics ruling the entire continent, and be forced to deal with an organized, powerful regime instead of a network of city-states fighting one another and remaining weak because of it.

We'd want to let this knowledge out sooner or later—spread it to the lorists of the world and see if they could start turning Epics from the darkness. But first we needed to test what we'd discovered and find out if we could even make it *work* on other Epics.

I had big plans, plans to change the world, and they all started with one trap. One important hit, perhaps the hardest ever pulled by the Reckoners.

"I'll tell you the secret to turning Epics away from their madness, Knighthawk," I decided, "but I want you to promise to keep it quiet for now. And I want you to equip us. Give us what we need."

"You're going to bring him down, aren't you?" Knighthawk said. "Jonathan Phaedrus. Limelight, as they call him now. You're going to kill Prof."

"No," I said softly, meeting his eyes. "We're going to do something far, far more difficult. We're going to bring him back."

8

KNIGHTHAWK had the mannequin carry him.

I got a better look at the thing, walking beside it. It wasn't your average, everyday store mannequin. It had articulated wooden fingers and a more solid body than I had expected. It was really more of a large marionette, only without the strings.

And it was strong. It carried Knighthawk with ease, sliding its arms through straps in some kind of harness Knighthawk wore. The whole arrangement made the mannequin look like it was hugging him from behind, its arms across his stomach and chest, with Knighthawk remaining upright and strapped in place, his feet dangling a few inches off the ground.

It didn't look comfortable *or* normal. Still, Knighthawk

chatted conversationally while we walked, as if it were perfectly natural for a quadriplegic to be carted around by a tall wooden golem.

"So that's basically it," I said to him as we made our way down the nondescript corridor, heading toward Knighthawk's armory. "The weaknesses are tied to fears. If an Epic confronts the fear, banishes it, then they can drive back the darkness."

"Mostly," Megan said from behind us. Abraham had gone up above to fetch Mizzy and Cody, as we'd decided that—one way or another—we were going to have to trust Knighthawk. We didn't have any other option.

Knighthawk grunted. "Fear. Seems so simple."

"Yes and no," I said. "I don't think a lot of Epics, consumed by their powers, like to think about being weak. They don't confront these things; that's basically the problem."

"I still wonder why no one else has made the connection," Knighthawk said, sounding skeptical.

"We've made it," Megan said softly. "Every Epic thinks about this, I guarantee it. It's just that we think about it all the wrong way— we connect fears and our weakness, but we connect them in *reverse* of the truth.

"It's the nightmares. They're maddening. They drive you from your bed, gasping, sweating, and smelling blood. The nightmares are about your weakness. The loss of power, the return to mortality, the return to being *crassly common,* so a simple accident could end you. It makes sense that we'd be afraid of the thing that could kill us, so the nightmares seem normal in a way. But we never realized that weaknesses grew *out of* our fears—the fears came first, and then the weaknesses. Not the other way around."

Knighthawk and I both stopped in the hallway, looking back at her. Megan met our gaze, defiant as ever, but I could see the cracks. *Sparks* . . . the things this woman had been forced to live with. What we'd discovered was helping her, but in some ways it was also prying those cracks wider. Exposing things inside her that she'd worked hard to cover up.

She'd done terrible things in the past, serving Steelheart. We didn't talk about it. She'd escaped that by being forced to not use her powers while infiltrating the Reckoners.

"We can do this, Knighthawk," I said. "We can discover Prof's weakness, then use it against him. Only instead of killing him, we'll lay a trap that makes him confront his fears. We'll bring him back and *prove* that there's another solution to the Epic problem."

"It won't work," Knighthawk said. "He knows you, and he knows Reckoner protocol. Calamity—he *wrote* Reckoner protocol. He'll be ready for you."

"See, that's the thing," I said. "He knows us, yes. But *we* also know *him*. We'll be able to figure out his weakness far more easily than with other Epics. And beyond that, we know something important."

"Which is?" he demanded.

"Deep down," I said, "Prof wants us to win. He'll be ready to die, so he'll be surprised when what we actually do is save him."

Knighthawk regarded me. "You have a strangely persuasive way about you, young man."

"You have *no idea*," Megan muttered.

"We're going to need technology to beat him though," I said. "So I'm eager to see what you have."

"Well, I've got a few things I could lend you," Knighthawk said, starting down the corridor again. "But contrary to what people assume, this place isn't some kind of massive repository for hidden technology. Pretty much every time I get something working, I immediately sell it. All those drones aren't cheap, you know. I have to order them out of Germany, and they're a *pain* to unpack. Speaking of which, I'm going to bill you for the ones you destroyed."

"We're here begging, Knighthawk," I said, catching up to him. "How do you expect us to pay you?"

"By all accounts you're a resourceful kid. You'll think of something. A frozen blood sample from Jonathan will do, assuming your crazy plan fails and you end up having to kill him."

"It won't fail."

"Yeah? Taking a look at the history of the Reckoners, I'd never bet money on the plan that *doesn't* intend to leave some bodies behind. But we'll see." His mannequin nodded toward Megan.

That mannequin . . . something about it struck me. I thought for a moment, and then it clicked in my mind like the mandibles of a giant poker-playing beetle.

"The Wooden Soul!" I said. "You got some of *her* DNA?"

Knighthawk twisted his head to look at me as we walked. "How in the world . . ."

"Pretty easy connection, once I thought about it. There aren't many puppeteer Epics out there."

"She lived in a remote Punjabi village!" Knighthawk said. "And has been dead for almost ten years."

"David's got a thing about Epics," Megan said from behind. "I'd call him obsessed, but that doesn't do it justice."

"It's not that," I said. "I'm like a—"

"No," Knighthawk said.

"This makes sense. I am like—"

"No, *really*," Knighthawk interrupted. "Nobody wants to hear it, kid."

I deflated. On the floor, a little cleaning drone zipped up. It bumped into my foot in what seemed like a vindictive motion, then scuttled away.

Knighthawk's mannequin pointed at me, though it had to turn sideways to do it, as its arms were strapped into carrying Knighthawk, its hands peeking out the sides. "Obsession with the Epics isn't healthy. You need to watch yourself."

"Ironic words, coming from a man who has built his career by making use of Epic powers—and is using them right now to get around."

"And what makes you think I don't have the same obsession? Let's just say I speak from experience. Epics are strange, wonderful, and terrible all at once. Don't let yourself get drawn in by that. It can lead you to . . . difficult places."

Something in his voice made me think of the laboratory, with the body parts floating so casually in vats. This man wasn't quite sane.

"I'll keep that in mind," I said.

Together we continued down the corridor, passing an open doorway, which I couldn't help peeking into. The small room beyond was strikingly clean, with a large metal box in the center. It looked kind of like a coffin, an impression not helped by the room's dim lighting and sterile, cold smell. Past the coffin stood a large wooden display case shaped like a bookshelf with large cubbies. Each held some small item, many of which seemed to be clothing. Caps, shirts, little boxes.

The cubbies were labeled, and I could barely make out a few: *Demo, The Abstract Man, Blastweave* . . .

The names of Epics. Perhaps those freezer chests were where Knighthawk kept his DNA samples, but this was where he kept his trophies. Curiously, one of the largest cubbies had no plaque, only a vest and what looked like a pair of gloves, set out prominently for display with their own spotlight.

"You won't find motivators in there," Knighthawk noted. "Just . . . mementos."

"And how would I find motivators?" I asked, looking to Knighthawk. "What are they really, Knighthawk?"

Knighthawk smiled. "You have no idea how hard it has been to keep people from figuring out the answer to that, kid. Trick is, I need people out there to collect material for me, but I don't want Joe and Sally knowing how to make their own motivators. That means misinformation. Half truths."

"You aren't the only one who makes these things, Knighthawk," Megan said, stepping up beside us. "Romerocorp does it, as does ITC over in London. It's not some grand secret."

"Oh, but it is," Knighthawk said. "The other companies know how important it is to keep that secret, you see. I don't think even Jonathan knows the whole truth of it." He smiled as he hung limply from his mannequin's arms. I was getting tired of that smirk already.

The mannequin turned and headed down the hall toward another door.

"Wait," I said, hurrying after him. "We're not going in that room with the mementos?"

"Nope," Knighthawk said. "No food in there." His mannequin pushed open this second door, and I could see a stove and refrigerator beyond, though the linoleum floor and slab-like table in the center made it feel more like the cafeteria back at the Factory than a kitchen.

I glanced at Megan as she joined me in the hallway, right outside the door. The mannequin went inside and deposited Knighthawk into an overstuffed easy chair beside a table. Then it crossed to the refrigerator, rummaging for something I couldn't see.

"I *could* do with a bite," she noted.

"Doesn't all this feel a little morbid to you?" I asked softly.

"We're talking about machines made from the corpses of your people, Megan."

"It's not like I'm a different species. I'm still human."

"You have different DNA though."

"And I'm still human. Don't try to understand it. It will drive you crazy."

It was a common sentiment; trying to explain Epics with science was maddening at best. When America had passed the Capitulation Act, which declared Epics exempt from the legal system, one senator had explained that we shouldn't expect human laws to be able to bind them when they didn't even obey the laws of *physics*.

But, call me a fool, I still wanted to understand. I *needed* it to make sense.

I looked at Megan. "I don't care what you are, as long as you're you, Megan. But I don't like the way we use corpses without understanding what we're doing to them, or how it all works."

"Then we'll pry it out of him," she whispered, drawing close. "You're right, motivators might be important. What if the way they work is related to the weaknesses, or the fears?"

I nodded.

More sounds came from the kitchen. Popcorn? I looked in, surprised to see Knighthawk relaxing in his easy chair while his mannequin stood next to the microwave popping popcorn.

"Popcorn?" I called to him. "For *breakfast*?"

"The apocalypse hit us over a decade ago, kid," he called back. "We live in a frontier, a wasteland."

"And that has to do with this how?"

"Means social mores are dead and buried," he said. "Good riddance. I'll eat whatever I sparking want for breakfast."

I went to go in, but Megan caught me by the shoulder,

leaning closer. She smelled like smoke—like detonated ordnance, gunpowder from spent bullet casings, and burning wood from a forest set aflame. It was a wonderful, heady scent, better than any perfume.

"What was it you were going to say earlier?" she asked. "When you were talking about yourself and Knighthawk cut you off, wouldn't let you finish?"

"It was nothing. Just me being stupid."

Megan held on, meeting my eyes, waiting.

I sighed. "You were talking about how obsessed I am. And that's not it. I'm like . . . well, I'm like a room-sized, steam-powered, robotic toenail-clipping machine."

She cocked an eyebrow.

"I can basically do only one thing," I explained, "but damn it, I'm going to do that one thing really, really *well*."

Megan smiled. A beautiful sight. She kissed me then, for some reason. "I love you, David Charleston."

I grinned. "You sure you can love a giant robotic toenail clipper?"

"You're you, whatever you are," she said. "And that's what matters." She paused. "But please don't grow to room-sized. That would be awkward."

She let go, and we entered the kitchen to discuss the fate of the world over popcorn.

9

WE settled down at the large table. It had a fancy glass top that revealed black slate underneath. There was a majestic sense to it, which seemed completely at odds with the peeling linoleum and faded paint of the kitchen. Knighthawk's mannequin sat primly on a stool next to the man's large chair, then began to feed him pieces of popcorn one at a time.

I had no more than fuzzy knowledge of the Wooden Soul, the Epic from whom he'd stolen powers to create such a servant. Supposedly she'd been able to control marionettes with her mind. Which meant this thing in the suit wasn't autonomous; it was more like an extra set of limbs for Knighthawk to use. Likely he wore some kind of device with a motivator that gave him the ability to control the mannequin.

Voices outside the room announced new arrivals. A little

drone scuttled in on the floor—Knighthawk had sent it to lead Abraham, and perhaps to keep him from poking into places he didn't belong. Soon afterward, the tall Canadian man entered and nodded to us.

The other two members of my team followed him. Cody appeared first, a lanky man in his late thirties. He wore a camouflage hunting jacket and cap—though not specifically for this mission. He basically always wore camo. He hadn't shaved in days, which he'd explained was a "true Highlander tradition used to prepare for battle."

"Is that popcorn?" he asked in his strong Southern drawl. He walked over and snatched a handful from the bowl right out of the mannequin's hand. "Brilliant! Boy, Abraham, you weren't kidding 'bout the creepy wooden robot thing."

Mizzy bounced in behind him. Dark-skinned and slight of build, she wore her wild curly hair pulled back so that it exploded in an enormous puff, kind of like an Afro mushroom cloud. She took a place at the table as far from Megan as possible, and shot me an encouraging smile.

I tried not to think of the missing team members. Val and Exel, dead at Prof's hand. Tia, lost somewhere, probably dead as well. Though we were usually silent about such things, Abraham had confided in me that he'd known of two other Reckoner cells. He'd tried to contact them while fleeing New-cago, but he'd had no response. It seemed Prof had gotten to them first.

Cody crunched down his handful of popcorn. "How does a fellow score some more of this? Don't know if y'all realize, but we've had an exhausting day."

"Yes," Knighthawk said, "an exhausting morning spent attacking my home and trying to rob me."

"Now, now," Cody said. "Don't be sore. Why, in parts of the old country, it's considered *polite* to introduce yourself with a fist to the face. Yes indeed, a man won't think you're serious unless you come in swinging."

"Dare I ask . . . ," Knighthawk said. "Of what old country do you speak?"

"He thinks he's Scottish," Abraham said.

"I *am* Scottish, ya big slab of doubt and monotony," Cody said, climbing from his chair—apparently determined to fix his own popcorn, since nobody had offered to do it for him.

"Name one city in Scotland," Abraham said, "other than Edinburgh."

"Ah yes, the Burgh of Edin," Cody said. "Where they buried old Adam and Eve, who were—naturally—Scots."

"Naturally," Abraham said. "A city name, please?"

"That's easy. I can name a ton. London. Paris. Dublin."

"Those—"

"—are *completely* Scottish," Cody said. "We founded them, you see, and then those other folks up and stole them from us. Y'all need to learn your history. Want some popcorn?"

"No. Thank you," Abraham said, giving me a bemused smile.

I leaned toward Knighthawk. "You promised us technology."

"*Promised* is a strong word, kid."

"I want that healing device," Abraham said.

"The harmsway? Not a chance. I don't have a backup."

"You call it that too?" Megan asked, frowning.

"One of Jonathan's old jokes," Knighthawk said, his mannequin shrugging. "It just stuck. Anyway, mine isn't nearly as efficient as Jonathan's own healing powers. It's all I got though, and you aren't taking it. But I have two other bits of fun I can lend you. One—"

"Wait," Mizzy said. "You've got a healing machine, and

you still walk around with Smiles McCreepy there? Why not, you know, fix your *legs*?"

Knighthawk gave her a flat stare, and his mannequin shook its head. As if asking about his disability broke some kind of taboo.

"How much do you know about Epic healing, young lady?" he asked.

"Weeellll," Mizzy said, "the Epics we kill tend to stay pretty dead. So I don't get to see healing often."

"Epic healing," Knighthawk said, "doesn't change your DNA or your immune system. It merely fixes damage to cells. My current state is not the result of an accident; if it were no more than a severed spinal cord, I'd be fine. The problem runs far deeper, and while I've found that healing returns some sensation in my limbs, they soon degrade again. So I use Manny instead."

"You . . . named it?" Abraham asked.

"Sure. Why not? Look, I'm starting to think you don't want me to give you this tech after all."

"We do," I said. "Please, continue."

He rolled his eyes, then accepted another piece of popcorn from his marionette's hand. "So, a few months back, an Epic died in Siberia. A squabble between two despots, kind of dramatic. An enterprising merchant was in the area, and managed to harvest one of the—"

"Rtich?" I said, perking up. "You managed to emulate *Rtich*?"

"Kid, you know far too much about all this for your own good."

I ignored the comment. Rtich—pronounced something like "r'teech"—had been a powerful Epic. I'd been looking for something that would let us go toe-to-toe with Prof. We needed an edge, something he wouldn't expect—

Megan elbowed me in the stomach. "Well? Gonna share?"

"Oh!" I said, noticing that Knighthawk had stopped his explanation. "Well, Rtich was a Russian Epic with a very eclectic set of abilities. She wasn't technically a High Epic, but she was very powerful. Are we talking about her entire portfolio, Knighthawk?"

"Each motivator can only provide one ability," he said.

"Well," I said, standing, "then I assume in this case, you emulated her quicksilver globe. Why are we sitting here? Let's go get it! I want to try it out."

"Hey, Scotsman," Knighthawk said, "will you get me a cola out of the fridge while you're up?"

"Sure," Cody said, pouring a fresh batch of popcorn into a bowl. He reached over and fished a cola from the fridge, the same brand that Tia had liked.

"Oh," Knighthawk added, "and that bin of potato salad."

"Potato salad and popcorn?" Cody asked. "You're a weird dude, if you don't mind me saying." He walked over and slid the translucent bin across the table, cola on top. Then he plopped down beside Mizzy and put his feet—work boots—up on the table, leaning back in his chair and attacking his bowl of food like a man whose house had once been burned down by a particularly violent ear of corn.

I remained standing, hoping everyone else would join me. I didn't want to sit around and *talk* about Epic powers. I wanted to *use* them. And this specific ability should prove to be as exciting as the spyril, but without the water, which I was totally up for. I might have been willing to let the depths consume me in order to save my friends, but that didn't mean water and I *liked* one another. We had more of a truce.

"Well?" I urged.

Knighthawk's mannequin popped open the bin of potato

salad. There, sitting in the middle of the stuff, was a little black box. "It's right here."

"You keep your priceless super power devices," Megan said flatly, "in the potato salad."

"Do you know how many times people have broken in to rob me?" Knighthawk asked.

"Never successfully," I said. "Everyone knows this place is impregnable."

Knighthawk snorted. "Kid, we live in a world where people can *literally* walk through walls. No place is impregnable; I'm just good at telling lies. I mean, even *you* people managed to snitch a few things from me—though you'll find that the ones Abraham grabbed are mostly useless. One creates the sound of a dog barking, and another makes fingernails grow faster—but not any stronger. Not every Epic power is amazing, though I'd like those two back anyway. They make good decoys."

"Decoys?" Abraham asked, surprised.

"Sure, sure," Knighthawk said. "Always got to leave a few things out so people feel like they're grabbing something useful for their efforts. I have this whole routine—furious they've robbed me, swearing to get vengeance. Blah blah. Usually makes them leave me alone, happy to have gotten what they did. Anyway, across dozens of break-ins, you want to guess how many people thought to look in the potato salad bin?"

His mannequin dug the little box out and set it on the table—he'd packed it in a watertight bag, at least—and I sat back down to admire it, imagining the possibilities.

"How do you get the fairies inside something that small?" Cody asked, pointing at the device. "Doesn't it crush their wee wings?"

We all pointedly ignored him.

"You mentioned another piece of technology?" Abraham said.

"Yeah," Knighthawk said, "I've got an old crystal grower lying around here somewhere. Attach it to a pure crystal lattice, and you can grow new formations in seconds. That might be handy."

"Uh," Mizzy said, raising her hand. "Anyone else confused as to why, exactly, we'd want something like that? Sounds cool and all, but . . . crystals?"

"Well, you see," Knighthawk said, "salt is a crystal."

We all looked at him, stupefied.

"You *are* going to chase down Jonathan, right?" Knighthawk said. "And you're aware he's in Atlanta?"

Atlanta. I settled back into my seat. Atlanta would be under the jurisdiction of the Coven, a loose affiliation of Epics who had basically promised not to bother one another. Occasionally one would help another murder a rival who tried to steal their city—which for Epics was practically like being best buddies.

But for all I knew of Epics, my knowledge of the world was spotty. The nature of Babilar, with its glowing fruit and surreal paints, had taken me completely by surprise. I was still at my core a sheltered kid who'd never left his home neighborhood before a few months ago.

"Atlanta," Abraham said softly. "Or what is now Ildithia. Where is it currently?"

"Somewhere in eastern Kansas," Knighthawk said.

Kansas? I thought, the comment jarring my memory. *That's right. Ildithia moves.* But so far? I'd read about it moving, but had assumed it stayed in the same general region.

"Why is he there though?" Abraham asked. "What is there for Jonathan Phaedrus in the city of salt?"

"How should I know?" Knighthawk said. "I'm doing my

best to avoid drawing the man's attention. I watched where he went for self-preservation's sake, but there's no way in Calamity that I'm going to start poking him with a stick."

Knighthawk's mannequin set down the bowl. "I'm out of popcorn, which means it's time to attach some strings to this little gift of mine. You can take the rtich and the crystal grower on the condition that you get out of here now, and you *don't* contact me anymore. Don't mention me to Jonathan; don't even talk about me to one another, in case he overhears. He likes things done right. If he comes here for me, he'll leave a smoldering hole and not much else."

I looked toward Megan, who was staring at Knighthawk, unblinking, lips downturned. "You know we have the secret," she said softly to him. "You know we're close to answers. A real solution."

"Which is why I'm helping you in the first place."

"Halfway," Megan accused him. "You're willing to toss a grenade into the room, but you don't want to look and see if it did the job or not. You know that something needs to change in this world, but *you* don't want to have to change with it. You're lazy."

"I'm a realist," Knighthawk said, his mannequin standing up. "I take the world as it is, and do what I can to survive in it. Even giving you these two devices will be dangerous for me; Jonathan will recognize my handiwork. Hopefully he'll think you got them off an arms dealer."

The mannequin walked to the fridge and removed a few other items, dropping some in a sack. He set one on the table for us; it looked like a tub of mayonnaise, but when he pried off the top, inside was another small device settled into the gooey condiment. The mannequin slung the sack by a strap over its arm, then walked over to lift Knighthawk from behind.

"I have other questions," I said, rising.

"Too bad," Knighthawk said.

"You have other technology you could give us," Abraham said, pointing at the sack. "The ones you've given us are only what you think won't get you in too much trouble with Prof."

"Good guess, and you're right," Knighthawk replied. "Get out. I'll send a bill with a drone. If you survive, I expect it to be paid."

"We're trying to save the world, you know," Mizzy said. "That *includes* you."

Knighthawk snorted. "You realize that half the people who come to me are trying to save the world? Hell, I've worked with the Reckoners before, and you're *always* trying to save the world. Looks pretty unsaved to me so far; in fact, looks a fair bit *worse* now that Jonathan has flipped.

"If I'd given you things for free all along, I'd have gone bankrupt years ago, and you wouldn't even have had the *option* of coming to try to rob me. So don't climb up on a high horse and spit platitudes at me."

And then the mannequin turned and walked out. I stood at my chair, feeling frustrated, and looked back at the others. "Did that exit feel abrupt to any of you?"

"Did you miss the part about him being a really weird dude?" Cody asked, nudging the potato salad bin with his foot.

"At least we got something," Abraham said, turning one of the small boxes over in his hands. "This puts us in a far better position than where we began—and beyond that, we know where Jonathan has set up base."

"Yeah," I said, glancing at Megan, who seemed troubled. So she felt it too. We'd gotten some weapons, sure, but we'd missed an opportunity for answers.

"Grab that stuff," I said. "Cody, search the fridge just in case. Then let's get out of here."

The group moved to do as instructed, and I found myself staring out the door and into the hallway. There were still too many questions.

"So . . . ," Megan said, joining me. "You want me to guide the rest of the team out?"

"Hmm?" I asked.

"Remember how you chased Prof and us into the under-streets of Newcago, after *expressly* being told you'd be shot if you didn't stay put?"

I smiled. "Yeah. Back then, I figured getting shot by the Reckoners would be *so cool*. Think about showing off a bullet scar to your friends, and saying that *Jonathan Phaedrus* himself shot you."

"You're such a nerd. My point is, are you going after Knighthawk?"

"Of course I'm going after him," I said. "Make sure everyone gets out safely, then try to save me from my stupidity if this goes sour." I gave her a swift kiss, caught my rifle as Abraham tossed it to me, then went to chase down Knighthawk.

10

I didn't have to search far.

The hallway was empty, but I stepped up to the room we'd passed earlier—the one with the trophies on the back wall—and peeked in. I was unsurprised to find Knighthawk sitting in an easy chair on the far side of the room. A gas fireplace crackled beside him, and his mannequin lay, its invisible strings cut, on the ground beside it.

At first that worried me. Was Knighthawk all right?

Then I saw his eyes—reflecting the writhing flames—staring at the silvery box in the center of the room, the one that looked like a coffin. As a tear rolled down Knighthawk's cheek, I realized the man had probably wanted to be alone, without even the mannequin's silent gaze upon him.

"Prof killed her, didn't he?" I whispered. "Your wife. She went evil, and Prof had to kill her."

I finally remembered the details of a conversation I'd had with Prof weeks ago, right outside Babilar, in a little bunker where he'd been doing science experiments. He'd told me about his team of friends, Epics every one. Him, Regalia, Murkwood, and Amala. Over time, three of them had eventually gone evil.

Sparks. *Four* of them, when you included Prof.

It doesn't work, David, he'd said. *It's destroying me. . . .*

"You don't listen to instructions very well, do you, boy?" Knighthawk asked.

I slipped into the room and walked to the coffin. Part of the lid was translucent, and I could see a pretty face lying peacefully inside, golden hair fanned out behind.

"She tried so hard to resist it," Knighthawk said. "Then one morning, I got up and . . . and she was gone. She'd been awake all night, judging by the six empty cups of coffee she'd left. She'd been afraid to sleep."

"Nightmares," I whispered, resting my fingers on the glass of the coffin.

"I think the stress of being up all night snapped her. My dear Amala. Jonathan did us both a favor in hunting her down. I *must* see it that way. Like you should discard this foolish notion you have of saving him. End him, kid. For his own good, and for all of us."

I looked up from the coffin toward Knighthawk. He hadn't wiped away that tear. He couldn't.

"You have hope," I said. "Otherwise you wouldn't have invited us in. You saw the way Megan was acting, and your first thought was that we'd found some way to beat the darkness."

"Maybe I invited you in out of pity," Knighthawk said. "Pity for someone who obviously loves an Epic. Like I did. Like Tia did. Maybe I invited you in to give you a warning. Be ready for it, kid. One morning you'll get up, and she'll just be gone."

I crossed the room, rifle over my shoulder, and reached for Knighthawk. I wasn't prepared for how quickly his mannequin could move. It leaped to its feet, catching me by the arm before I rested my hand on Knighthawk's shoulder.

His eyes flickered to my hand, apparently deciding I hadn't intended to harm him, and the mannequin released me. Sparks, its grip was *strong*.

That let my hand fall on his shoulder, and I squatted down before his chair. "I'm going to beat this, Knighthawk, but I need answers only you can give me. About motivators, and how they work."

"Foolishness," he said.

"You kept Amala in stasis. Why?"

"Because I'm foolish too. She had a hole the size of Jonathan's fist in her chest when I found her. Dead. Pretending otherwise is stupid."

"Yet you healed her body," I said. "And preserved her."

"You see those?" he said, nodding to the far side of the room. To the remnants from fallen Epics. "Those powers didn't bring her back. Each is from an Epic with healing powers that I made a motivator out of. None worked. There is no answer. There is no secret. We live with the world as it is."

"Calamity is an Epic," I whispered.

Knighthawk started, then tore his eyes away from the wall, focusing on me again. *"What?"*

"Calamity," I repeated, *"is an Epic*. A . . . person. Regalia discovered the truth, even talked to him or her. This thing that destroyed our lives, it's not a force of nature. Not a star, or a comet . . . it's a *person*." I took a deep breath. "And I'm going to kill Calamity."

"Holy *hell,* kid," Knighthawk said.

"Saving Prof is step one," I said. "We're going to need his abilities to pull this off. But after that, I'm going to get up there, and I'm going to *destroy* that thing. We'll return the world to the way it was before Calamity rose."

"You're absolutely insane."

"Well, I spent some time drifting after killing Steelheart," I said. "I needed a new purpose in life. Figure I might as well aim high."

Knighthawk stared at me, then kicked his head back and laughed loudly. "I never thought I'd meet someone with more ambition than Jonathan, kid. *Kill* Calamity! Why not? Sounds simple!"

I looked toward the mannequin; it had grabbed its belly and was rocking back and forth as if it were laughing.

"So," I said. "You going to help me?"

"What do you know about Epics who were born as identical twins?" Knighthawk asked as the mannequin reached over and wiped the man's cheeks. Tears of laughter had joined the one he'd shed for his wife.

"There's only one set, as far as I know. The Creer boys, Hanjah and the Mad Pen, in the Coven. They've been active lately in . . . Charleston, isn't it?"

"Good, good," Knighthawk replied. "You do know your stuff. You want a seat? You look uncomfortable."

The mannequin pulled over a stool for me and I sat.

"Those two go all the way back," Knighthawk explained, "to about a year after Calamity, around the time that Prof and the others got their powers. First wave, you lorists call it. And they're what started some of us thinking about how the powers worked. They have—"

"—the exact same power set," I said. "Air pressure control, pain manipulation, precognition."

"Yup," Knighthawk said. "And you know what, they *aren't* the only pair of twin Epics. They're merely the only pair where one didn't kill the other."

"That's not possible," I said. "I'd have known about them."

"Yeah, well, my associates and I made sure nobody heard of the others. Because in them was a secret."

"Each set of twins had the same abilities," I guessed. "Twins share a power set."

Knighthawk nodded.

"So it *is* genetic, somehow."

"Yes and no," Knighthawk said. "We can't find anything genetic about Epics that gives clues to their powers. That mumbo-jumbo about mitochondria? We made it up; seemed plausible, since Epic DNA tends to degrade quickly. Everything else you've heard about motivators is technobabble we use to confuse those who might be trying to figure out how to compete with us."

"Then how?"

"You realize that by telling you, I'd be breaking an agreement I have with the other companies."

"Which I appreciate."

He cocked an eyebrow at me, and his mannequin folded its arms.

"If there's even the slightest chance that I'm right," I said, "and I can stop the Epics forever, isn't it worth the risk?"

"Yes," Knighthawk said. "But I still want a promise out of you, kid. You don't share this secret."

"It's wrong of you to keep it," I said. "Perhaps if the governments of the world had possessed this knowledge, they'd have been able to fight back against the Epics."

"Too late," he said. "Your word."

I shook my head. "Fine. I'll tell my team, but I'll swear them to secrecy too. We won't tell anyone else."

He thought about that for a moment, then sighed. "Cell cultures."

"Cell . . . what?"

"Cell cultures," he said. "You know, when you take a sample of cells and keep them growing in a lab? That's the answer. Grab an Epic's cells, stick them in a test tube with some nutrients, and run power through them. Boom. You can emulate that Epic's powers."

"You're kidding," I said.

"Nope."

"It can't be that easy."

"It's not *easy* at all," Knighthawk said. "The voltage of the electricity determines which power you get out. You have to be ready to channel it properly, or you could blow yourself— hell, the entire *state*—to the moon. Most of our experimentation, all of this equipment, is based on harnessing the abilities that come off the cells."

"Huh," I said. "So you're saying that Calamity can't distinguish between an actual person and a pile of cells?" That was a strange mistake for an intelligent being to make.

"Eh," Knighthawk said. "More like they just don't care. If Calamity *is* an Epic, I mean. Besides, maybe there's some kind of interaction with motivators we don't understand. Truth is, those things can be touchy, even in the best of cases. Once in a while, a power simply won't *work* for someone. Everyone else can use it fine, but one person can't operate the device.

"It happens more often to Epics. Jonathan proved that Epics could use motivators, but occasionally we'd run into one that he couldn't operate. Same goes for two different motivators being used by the same person. Sometimes they interfere and one craps out."

I sat back on the stool, thoughtful. "Cell cultures. Huh. Makes sense, I suppose, but it seems . . . so simple."

"The best secrets usually are," he said. "But it's simple only in retrospect. Do you know how long it took scientists in pre-Calamity days to figure out how to make cultures of normal human cells? It was a strikingly difficult process. Well, same with motivators. We slaved to create the first ones. What you call a motivator is really a little incubator. The motivator feeds the cells, regulates temperature, expels waste. A good motivator will last decades, if built right."

"Regalia knew your secret," I said. "She took Obliteration and used his cells to create a bomb."

Knighthawk was silent. When I looked at him, his mannequin had settled against the wall, hands behind its back, head down as if uncertain.

"What?" I asked.

"Making motivators from Epics who are still alive is dangerous."

"For the Epic?"

"Sparks, no, for *you*. They can feel it when their powers are used by someone else. It's terribly painful, and they get a sense for where it's happening. Naturally, they seek out the source of the pain and destroy it."

"That's where the twins come in," I said. "You said . . ."

"One almost always kills the other," he said. "One would be in pain whenever the other used their powers. It's why I don't make motivators out of living Epics. It's a bad, bad idea."

"Yeah, well, from what I know of Obliteration, he probably enjoyed the pain. He's like a cat."

"A . . . cat?"

"Yeah. A freaky, messed-up, scripture-quoting cat who loves to be hurt." I cocked my head. "What? You think he's more like a ferret? I could see that. But Regalia. She performed surgery on Obliteration. Wouldn't she just need a blood sample?"

Knighthawk's mannequin waved dismissively. "Old trick. Used it myself before I decided to stop making motivators from living Epics; helps keep them from realizing how simple it all is. Either way, you have the secret. Maybe it will help; I don't know. But can you leave me to my grief now?"

I climbed to my feet, suddenly very tired. Lingering effects of my healing earlier, perhaps. "Do you know Prof's weakness?"

Knighthawk shook his head. "No idea."

"Are you lying?"

Knighthawk snorted. "No, I'm not. He never let me know what it was, and every guess I had turned out to be wrong. Ask Tia. He might have told her."

"I think Tia's dead."

"Damn." Knighthawk grew quiet, and his gaze seemed distant. I'd hoped that the secret of the motivators would shed light on Prof and what he did by gifting his powers to others. I still didn't have an answer to why some Epics could avoid the darkness that way.

Unless they actually can't, I thought. I needed to talk to Edmund, the one called Conflux.

I walked toward the door, passing the dead Epic in the coffin. I quietly hoped Knighthawk never found a way to bring this woman back; I doubted he'd get what he wanted from the reunion.

"Steelslayer," he called after me.

I turned, and the mannequin approached, carrying a small device on one palm. It looked like a cylindrical battery, of the old bulky style I'd seen in toy commercials during recordings shown after dinner in the Factory. We kids had loved the commercials. They'd somehow seemed more real—more a picture of life in the world before Epics—than the action shows they'd interrupted.

Oh, to live in a world where children ate colorful breakfast cereals and begged their parents for toys.

"What is it?" I asked, taking the device from the mannequin.

"Tissue sample incubator," he said. "It will keep cells fresh long enough for you to send them to me. When you fail, and have to kill Jonathan, get me a sample of his DNA."

"So you can make some kind of device, enslaving his cells to enrich you?"

"Jonathan Phaedrus has the most powerful healing abilities of any Epic I've ever known," Knighthawk said as the mannequin made a rude gesture at me. "He'll create a harmsway far more capable than any I've ever tested. It might . . . it might work on Amala. I haven't tried anything on her for well over a year. But maybe . . . I don't know. Either way, you should let Jonathan keep healing people after he dies. You know it's what he'd want."

I made no promises, but I did take the incubator.

You never knew what might come in handy.

PART TWO

11

I was somewhere cold and dark.

My world was only sounds. Each one horrible, an assault, a scream. I curled up before the barrage, but then the lights attacked. Garish, terrible. *Violent.* I hated them, though that did nothing. I wept, but this too terrified me; my own body betraying me with an assault from within, to pair with all of those from without.

It built to a climax of booms, and flashes, and burning, and crashes, and screeches, and terrible explosions until—

I woke.

I had curled up awkwardly in the back seat of one of the jeeps. We were traveling on a broken highway through the night. The vehicle thumped and jostled as we sped toward Atlanta.

I blinked drowsy eyes, trying to make sense of the dream. A nightmare? My heart was certainly racing. I could remember being absolutely terrified of the noise and confusion, but it hadn't been like any other nightmare I'd experienced.

No water. I vaguely remembered a few nightmares from my time in Babilar, and they'd always involved drowning. I sat back, contemplating. After what we'd discovered about Epics, I couldn't ignore any bad dreams. But where did that leave me? People were still going to have nightmares. How could you tell if one was important, or no more than a random dream?

Well, I *wasn't* an Epic. So it probably didn't matter.

I stretched and yawned. "How are we doing?"

"Good progress tonight," Abraham said from the front passenger seat. "Less rubble on the roads out here."

We traveled at night when possible, spread across two jeeps, with lights off, navigating by night-vision goggles. We changed around who was riding where every few hours at Abraham's suggestion; he said that it helped keep conversation fresh and drivers alert. Everyone took a turn driving except me. Which was completely unfair. Just because of that one time. Well, and that other time. And the one with the mailbox, but seriously, who remembered that anymore?

Right now, Mizzy and Abraham were in my jeep, while Megan and Cody drove in the other. I pulled out my rifle, which I'd stashed at my feet. A touch collapsed the stock, and I could use the night vision and thermal scope to get a look outside.

Abraham was right. This highway, though broken up in places, was in generally better shape than the one we'd taken from Newcago to Babilar, and *way* better than the one we'd taken to Knighthawk's place. We passed derelict cars on the side of the road, and none of the towns in the area were lit—either because they were abandoned, or any inhabitants didn't want to draw the attention of Epics. I figured the former was more likely. People would gravitate toward one of the larger cities, where they would have to be ruled by Epics but also have some access to the necessities of life.

Terrible as Newcago had been, it had still provided a relatively stable life. Packaged foods out of one of the operating factories, clean water, electricity. It wasn't colored fruit cereal, but it beat living in a wasteland. Plus, when it came to Epics, in the city you were like a school of fish—too insignificant to be singled out, you simply hoped not to get killed in a random act of anger.

I eventually caught sight of an old green roadway sign proclaiming that we weren't far from Kansas City. We'd go around that, as Epics reigned there, most notably Hardcore. Atlanta's current position wasn't far beyond it, fortunately. Riding in the backs of these cars was none too comfortable. Sparks, this country had been *big* before everything fell apart.

I got out my mobile. It sure felt good to be using one of these again, though I'd needed to dial the screen brightness way down so it didn't illuminate our car. I typed in a message to Megan.

Kiss.

A second later the mobile blinked, and I checked the response.

Gag.

I frowned until I noticed the text wasn't from Megan, but from a number I didn't know.

Knighthawk? I texted back, guessing.

Well, technically it's Manny, my mannequin, came the reply. *But yes—and also, yes, I'm monitoring your communications. Deal with it.*

You realize everyone claims your mobiles are completely secure, I wrote.

Then everyone is an idiot, he replied. *Of course I can read what you send.*

And if Prof kills me and takes this phone? I asked. *Aren't you worried he'll notice you texted me?*

In response, the texts from him vanished, as did my replies. Sparks. He could hack my phone's memory?

Remember our deal, a new text said. *I want his cells.*

I hadn't made any such deal, but there was no use mentioning that now. I jotted down his number on a piece of paper, then watched as—sure enough—this latest text from him faded. A few moments later, a text came from Megan.

Kiss back, Knees.

Everything all right over there? I asked.

If by "all right" you mean me going insane having to listen to Cody make up story after story, then yes.

I sent her a smile.

You realize he's claiming to have been in the Olympics, she sent. *But a leprechaun stole his medal.*

Wait for the pun, I texted her. *There's usually a terrible one at the end.*

I'm riding with Abraham next leg, she said. *Seriously. I thought I'd gotten over feeling like I need to strangle members of this team. Turns out my desire to murder Cody in a violent, dehumanizing fashion had nothing to do with the darkness. It was completely natural.*

Hmm, I texted back. *We might want to check and see if anything Cody is doing is related specifically to your psyche. There's a chance, though slight, that if facing your fears can dampen the darkness, other environmental stimuli might enrage it.*

A few moments passed.

Nerd, the text finally returned.

I'm just trying to consider all possibilities.

Really, she sent back, *why couldn't I end up dating a guy with a *useful* obsession?*

I smiled. *Like what?*

Romance novels? Make-out techniques? Boyfriend stuff. Maybe then you'd compliment me for something other than my choice in sidearms.

Sorry, I sent. *I don't have a lot of experience in this area.*

You don't need to tell me, she sent back. *Seriously, David, it's a good thing you have such a nice butt.*

You realize Knighthawk is probably monitoring this conversation, I warned her.

Well, his butt is pretty damn ugly, she sent, *so why should I care?*

We hit a rough patch, bumping and jostling. Mizzy slowed, navigating us around it. *Do you miss Newcago?* I found myself asking Megan. *I do sometimes. Strange, eh?*

Nah, she wrote. *It's where you grew up. Where your family was from. I miss Portland sometimes. Last place I lived a normal life. I even had a doll. Esmeralda. Had to leave her.*

I cocked my head. Megan didn't talk about those times much.

If I'm truly cured, she wrote to me, *I can start looking for them. Once I know for certain.*

Your family? I wrote. *Any idea what city they're in?*

If I know them, they're not in a city, Megan wrote. *There are more people than you think, living out there in that darkness. Surviving. I'd bet they outnumber the people in the cities; you just don't see them.*

I doubted that. I mean, would that many people really be so invisible? And what happened when one of them turned into an Epic? New Epics tended to lose control immediately after obtaining their powers. The results were often . . . unsightly.

You know what galls me most about all this? Megan sent. *That my stupid father was right. All his crazy talk about an apocalypse, training his daughters to shoot, preparing for the worst . . . he was right. He thought it would be nuclear, but close enough.*

No more came, and I left her alone with her thoughts. A short time later, Mizzy slowed down. "I need a break," she said. "Wanna switch, Abe?"

"If you are so inclined," he said.

"I'm inclined. Way inclined."

Looks like we're stopping to change drivers, I sent to Megan. *Mile marker . . . 32.*

We're ahead of you a few miles, she sent. *I'll tell Cody to slow down until you catch up. We're almost to the city anyway.*

We pulled over behind an old semi-truck trailer, the cab nowhere to be seen. I inspected it with the scope, noting the remains of a long-cold fire inside.

"I need to stretch my legs," Abraham said. "David, cover please?"

"Sure thing," I said, loading my rifle. He went for a short stroll, and I stood up out the jeep's open roof so I could survey, in case someone or something was hiding in the tall grass beside the roadway. Mizzy slid over to the passenger seat, reclined her chair, and sighed in satisfaction.

"You sure about this plan, David?" Mizzy asked.

"No, but it's the best one we've got."

"Other than straight-up killing Prof," she said softly.

"You too?" I said. "Knighthawk also said we should kill him."

"You know it's what he'd want, David. I mean, he'd be all stern-faced and 'Don't you try to save me, now. Do what needs to be done.'" She fell quiet. "He killed Val, David. He *murdered* her and Exel."

"That wasn't his fault," I said quickly. "We've been over this."

"Yeaaah, I know. It's just . . . you never gave Steelheart a second chance, right? Too dangerous. You needed to save the city. Get your vengeance. Why's it so different here?"

I turned my scope toward a rustling bunch of weeds, until a feral cat popped out and scurried away.

"This conversation isn't really about Prof, is it?" I asked Mizzy.

"Maybe not," she admitted. "I know things are different now. We know the secret to the weaknesses, blah blah. But I keep thinking . . . why do *you* get revenge, but not me? What about *my* feelings, *my* anger?" She bounced her head against the headrest of her seat a few times. "Blaaaahhhhh. That sounds so whiny. 'Gee, David. I'd really like to murder your girlfriend. Why won't you let me?' Sorry."

"I understand the emotion, Mizzy," I said. "I truly do. And don't think a big piece of me doesn't feel guilty for spending so long trying to kill Epics, only to end up with Megan. Who would have thought that love and hate would be so similar, you know?"

"Who?" Mizzy said. "Like, basically every philosopher to ever live."

"What, really?"

"Yeaaah. Bunch of rock songs too."

"Wow."

"You know, the fact that you were educated in a gun factory kinda shows sometimes, David."

Abraham finished his business and walked back toward the jeep. I felt like I should give more of an answer to Mizzy, but what could I say? "We're not doing this merely because we like Prof, or because of my feelings for Megan," I said softly, climbing down into my seat. "We're doing this—going to Ildithia to rescue Prof—because we're *losing,* Mizzy. The Reckoners were the only ones who ever fought back, and now they're basically no more.

"If we don't come up with a way to seriously turn this tide and stop the Epics, then humankind is finished. We can't keep killing them, Mizzy. It's too slow, and we're too fragile. We *have* to be able to start *turning* them.

"We're rescuing Prof not just for the man himself. Sparks, when we succeed, he'll probably hate us for it, since he'll have to live with what he did. He'd probably rather be dead. But we'll do it anyway, because we need his help. And we need to *prove* that it can be done."

Mizzy nodded slowly as Abraham got into the car. I put the gun down.

"Guess I'll have to sit on this thirst for vengeance," Mizzy said. "Smother it real good."

"No," I said.

She turned and looked at me.

"Keep that fire alive, Mizzy," I said, then I pointed out the rooftop. "But aim it at the real target. The one who *actually* killed your friends."

Calamity hung outside, a bright red dot in the sky, like the targeting point on a scope's overlay. Visible every night.

Mizzy nodded.

Abraham started the car, not asking to be caught up on our conversation. As we moved, my phone blinked and I sat back, anticipating another round of banter with Megan.

Instead, her text was brief, yet chilling.

Hurry up. We decided to scout close to the city, to get a glimpse. Something's happened.

What? I messaged back, urgent.

Kansas City. It's gone.

12

I tried to think of a proper metaphor for the way the slag *crunched* under my feet. Like . . . like ice on . . . No.

I stepped across the wide-open landscape of melted rock that had been Kansas City. For once, words failed me. The only proper descriptor I could think of was . . . sorrowful.

The day before, this had been one of the points of civilization on an otherwise dark map. Yes, it had been a place dominated by Epics, but it had also been a place of life, culture, society. *People.* Tens, maybe hundreds of thousands of them.

All gone.

I crouched down, rubbing my fingers on the smooth ground. It was still warm, and probably would be for days. The blast had warped stone and, in an instant, turned buildings into molten mountains of steel. The ground was covered in little ridges of glass, like frozen waves, none taller than an inch. Somehow they conveyed the feeling of an incredible wind blowing from the center point of the destruction.

All those people. Gone. I sent a prayer to God, or whoever might be listening, that some of them had gotten out before the blast. Footsteps announced Megan. She was lit by the morning sun.

"We're dying out, Megan," I said, voice ragged. "We capitulated to the Epics, and we're still getting exterminated. Their wars will end all life on this planet."

She rested a hand on my shoulder as I crouched there, feeling the glass that had once been people.

"This was Obliteration?" she asked.

"This matches what he did in other cities," I said. "And I know of no other with the powers to do this."

"That maniac . . ."

"There's something seriously wrong with that man, Megan. When he destroys a city, he considers it a *mercy*. He seems to think . . . seems to think that the way to truly rid the world of Epics is to destroy every single person who could ever become one."

The darkness had given Obliteration a special kind of madness, a twisted version of the Reckoners' own goal. Rid the world of Epics.

No matter what the cost.

My mobile blinked, and I ripped it off the place where it usually rested, strapped to my jacket's shoulder.

You see this? It was Knighthawk, and he'd included an attachment. I opened it up. It was a shot of a large explosion blasting out from what I presumed to be Kansas City. The photo had been taken from far away.

People are sharing this right and left, Knighthawk sent. *Aren't you guys heading that direction?*

You know exactly where we are, I texted back. *You're tracking my mobile.*

I was just being polite, he sent. *Get me some photos of the center of the city. Obliteration is going to be a problem.*

Going to be? I sent.

Yeah, well, look at this.

The next shot was an image of a lanky man with a goatee walking through a crowded street, long trench coat fluttering behind him, sword strapped to his side. I recognized Obliteration immediately.

Kansas City? I asked. *Before the blast.*

Yeah, Knighthawk wrote back.

The ramifications of that sank in. I scrambled to dial Knighthawk's number, then lifted the phone to my ear. He picked up a second later.

"He isn't glowing," I said, eager. "That means—"

"What are you doing?" Knighthawk demanded. "Idiot!"

He hung up.

I stared at the phone, confused, until another message came. *Did I say you could call me, boy?*

But . . . , I wrote back. *You've been texting me all day.*

Totally different, he wrote. *Didgeridooing invasion of privacy, calling a person without their permission.*

"Didgeridooing?" Megan asked from over my shoulder.

"Profanity filter on my mobile," I said.

"You use a *profanity* filter? What is this, kindergarten?"

"Nah," I said. "It's hilarious. Makes people sound *really* stupid."

Another text came from Knighthawk. *You said that Regalia created a motivator from Obliteration. What do you want to bet she made more than one? Look at these images.*

He sent another sequence that showed Obliteration in Kansas City, working on some kind of glowing object. It was bright, but you could still tell it was doing the glowing, not Obliteration himself.

Timestamp on that last one is right before the place got vaporized, Knighthawk sent. *He destroyed Kansas City with a device. But why use one of those instead of doing it himself?*

Stealthier, I wrote back. *Him sitting in the center of town like he did in Texas, glowing until he blows the place up, is going to give a big warning that people should run.*

That's downright disgusting, Knighthawk wrote.

Can you watch for him on other mobiles?

That's a lot of data to sift, kid, Knighthawk sent.

You have something better to do?

Yeah, maybe. I'm not one of your Reckoners.

Yes, but you *are* a human being. Please. Do what you can. If you spot him in another city, glowing or not, send me word. We can maybe warn the people.

We'll see, he sent.

Megan regarded my phone. "I should be creeped out by how much control he has over the mobiles, shouldn't I?"

She and I took some more pictures of the downtown. After we sent them to Knighthawk, my entire conversation with him faded from my mobile. I showed Megan, though she was distracted, looking across the seemingly endless field of glassy rock-and-steel mounds that had once been a city.

"It would have killed me," she said softly. "Fire. A permanent end."

"It would have killed most Epics," I said. "Even some other High Epics." It was one way to get past their invulnerabilities—nuke them to oblivion. A terrible solution, as some countries had discovered. You could nuke only so many of your own cities before you didn't have anything left to protect.

Megan leaned on me as I put my hand on her shoulder.

She'd climbed into a burning building to save my life, confronting what could have killed her, but that didn't mean her fear was gone. It was merely controlled. Managed.

Together, the two of us joined the other Reckoners, who had settled near the center of the blast—which Abraham had tested for radiation, to be sure it was safe.

"We're going to have to do something about this one, David," Abraham said as I walked up.

"Agreed," I said. "Saving Prof comes first though. Are we agreed on that?"

Around the group, they nodded. Abraham and Cody had been with Megan and me from the start, willing to try bringing back Prof instead of killing him. It seemed I'd persuaded Mizzy with our conversation in the car, as she nodded vigorously.

"Is anyone else here worried about *why* Prof went to Atlanta?" Cody asked. "I mean, he could've stayed in Babilar and had all sorts of Epics obeying him. Instead, he's moved all the way out here."

"He must have a plan," I said.

"He has all of Regalia's information," Abraham said. "She knew things about Epics, their powers, and Calamity—more, I suspect, than anyone else knows. Makes me wonder what he discovered in her data."

I nodded, thoughtful. "Regalia said that she wanted a successor. We know she was involved in things much larger than that one city. She'd been in *communication* with Calamity, had been trying to figure out how his powers worked. Maybe Prof's continuing her work, whatever she was plotting before the cancer grew too bad."

"Possible," Mizzy said. "But what? What was she planning—or alternately, what is *Prof* planning?"

"I don't know," I said. "But I'm worried. Prof is one of the most effective, intelligent people I've ever met. He's obviously not going to sit around as an Epic and merely rule a city. He'll have grander plans; whatever he's up to, it will be *big*."

We left Kansas City a far more solemn group than had entered. We traveled closer together this time, two jeeps driving single file. It took a sickeningly long time to reach a point where we weren't surrounded by melted buildings and scarred ground. We kept going, though the sun had risen. Abraham figured we were close to our target, within a few hours at most.

I decided the best way to distract myself from the horror of Kansas City was to try to get something productive done. So I took out one of the boxes Knighthawk had given us. Mizzy twisted around in her seat, looking back over the headrest curiously. Abraham glanced at me in the rearview mirror but said nothing, and I couldn't read his emotions. I'd known piles of ammunition more expressive than Abraham. The guy could be like some kind of Zen monk sometimes. With a minigun.

I lifted the lid, turning the box so Mizzy could see inside. It contained a pair of gloves and a jar filled with a silver liquid.

"Mercury?" Mizzy asked.

"Yeah," I said, taking out a glove and turning it over.

"Isn't that stuff, like, *reaaaal* bad for you?"

"Not sure," I admitted.

"It causes madness," Abraham said. Then, after a moment, "So no big change for anyone in this particular car."

"Hur hur," Mizzy said.

"Mercury is quite toxic," Abraham said. "Quickly absorbed into the skin, and can even emit vapors that are dangerous. Be careful with it, David."

"I'll leave the lid on until I know what I'm doing. I'll just see if I can get the mercury to move around in the jar."

I pulled on the glove, eager. Immediately, lines of violet light ran down the fingers to a central pool in the palm. The softly glowing purple reminded me of the tensors, which I supposed made sense. Prof had created those to imitate Epic-derived technology. He'd probably used one of Knighthawk's designs.

"This is going to be breathtaking," I said, imagining the things I'd read about Rtich's powers. I held my hand over the jar of mercury, but then paused. How exactly did I engage the abilities? The spyril had been tough to control, though easy to engage in the first place. But with the tensors, it had taken time before I'd managed to make them do anything.

I tried giving mental commands, tried using the tricks I'd used to make the tensors work, yet nothing happened.

"Is it gonna take my breath *now*," Mizzy asked, "or, like, sometime down the road? I'd like to be prepared."

"I have no idea how to make these work," I said, waving my hand and trying again.

"Are there instructions, perhaps?" Abraham asked.

"What kind of super-amazing Epic technology comes with an *instruction* book?" I said. That seemed too mundane. Still, I looked through the box. Nothing.

"It is for the best," Abraham said. "We should wait to try this in a more controlled environment—or at least until we aren't driving on a half-broken road."

With a sigh, I took off the glove, then picked up the large jar of mercury and stared at it. The stuff was *weird*. I'd imagined what a liquid metal would be like, but it defied those expectations. It flowed quickly, lightly, and was incredibly reflective. Like someone had melted a mirror.

I packed the jar away at another prompting from Abraham

and set the box at my feet, though I did send a text to Knight-hawk asking for instructions. Not long after, however, Megan's car slowed ahead of us. Abraham's mobile buzzed.

"Yeah?" he said, tapping it and pressing his earpiece in tighter. "Huh. Curious. We're stopping now." He slowed the jeep, then glanced back at me. "Cody has spotted something ahead."

"The city?" I asked.

"Close. Its trail. Look at two o'clock."

I got out my gun and—unzipping the top of the jeep—stood up. From that vantage, I could see something very interesting off the roadway: a huge plain of flattened, dead weeds. It extended into the distance.

"The city definitely came this way," Abraham said from below. "You can't tell from here, but that's part of a very wide strip—as wide as a city—of dead grass. Ildithia leaves that behind as it travels, like a giant slug's trail."

"Great," I said, yawning. "Let's chase it down."

"Agreed," Abraham said, "but look closer. Cody says he spotted people walking the trail."

I looked again, and indeed several small groups of people trudged along the wide strip of ground. "Huh," I said. "They're headed away from the city. We think it's moving northward, right?"

"Yes," Abraham said. "This confused Cody and Megan as well. Do you want to investigate?"

"Yes," I said, settling back into the jeep. "I'll send the other two."

We turned off the road and moved toward the strip of dead grass as I texted Megan. *See what you two can find out from those stragglers, but don't take any risks.*

They're refugees, she sent. *What kind of risks could be involved? Scurvy?*

. . .

Cody and Megan went on ahead, and we hung back. I tried to catch a nap, but the jeep's seat was too uncomfortable and—even though there really was no reason to worry—I was worried for Megan.

Eventually, her text came. *They *are* refugees. They know about Prof, though they call him Limelight. He's been here for two or three weeks, and some of the other Epics are resisting him, the main one in charge—a guy named Larcener—included.*

The people have fled the city because they think a confrontation between Prof and Larcener is coming, and they figure they'll get away for a week or two—live off the land—before going back and seeing who's ended up in control.

Did they say how far away the city is? I asked.

They've been walking for hours, she sent, *so . . . maybe an hour or two by jeep? They say we'll pass other refugees moving toward Ildithia. People from Kansas City.*

So at least some of the inhabitants escaped. I was relieved to hear that.

I showed the texts to Mizzy and Abraham.

"This note about Ildithian politics is good," Abraham said. "It means that Prof has not stabilized power in the city. He will not have the resources to watch for us."

"Will we be able to get in?" Mizzy asked. "Without looking suspicious?"

"We can hide among the refugees from Kansas City," I said.

"We wouldn't even need that," Abraham said. "Larcener allows people to enter or leave Ildithia without penalty, so there is often a trickle going in and out. We can present ourselves as hopeful workers, and they should take us right in."

I nodded slowly, then delivered the order to continue

off-road, but to give the swath of dead land a wide berth. Working cars—which had to be converted to run off power cells—were a novelty in most parts of the world. Who knew what sort of stupid bravery we could run into if we came too close to people desperate enough?

Megan and Cody rejoined us, and together we traveled across the bumpy ground for about an hour. Watching through my scope, I spotted the first signs of Ildithia: fields. They grew alongside the city, not in the patch of dead ground, but right next to it. I'd expected this; Atlanta was known for its produce.

Shortly after spotting this, I noticed something else peeking over the horizon ahead of us: a skyline incongruously rising from the center of a large, otherwise featureless landscape.

We'd found Atlanta, or Ildithia, its modern name.

The city of salt.

13

I sat on the hood of our jeep, which we'd parked in a little stand of trees a mile or two from Ildithia, and studied the city with my scope. Ildithia was made up of a good chunk of old Atlanta—downtown, midtown, some of the surrounding suburbs. About seven miles across, according to Abraham.

Its skyscrapers reminded me of Newcago—though admittedly, living inside the city hadn't given me a good sense for what its skyline looked like. These buildings seemed more spaced out, and pointier. Also, they were made of salt.

When I'd heard about a city made of salt, I'd imagined a place made of translucent crystal. Boy, had I been wrong. The buildings were mostly opaque, translucent only at the corners where the sun shone through. They resembled stone, not giant growths of the ground-up stuff for eating.

The skyscrapers represented a marvelous variety of colors. Pinks and greys dominated, and my scope's magnification let me pick out veins of white, black, and even green running through the walls. Honestly, it was beautiful.

It was also changing. We had approached from the back—this city definitely had a "back" and a "front." The districts at its rear were slowly *crumbling away,* like a dirt wall in the rain. Melting, sloughing off. As I watched, the entire side of a skyscraper crumbled; then the whole thing came tumbling down with a crash I could hear even at this distance.

The salt piled in lumps as it fell, getting smaller the farther along the trail they were. That made sense; most Epic powers didn't create objects permanently. The fallen salt buildings would eventually melt and vanish, evaporating and leaving the dead, flattened ground we'd traveled along.

As I understood it, on the other side of the city new buildings would be growing—like crystals forming, Abraham had explained. Ildithia moved, but not on legs or wheels. It moved like mold creeping across a piece of discarded toast.

"Wow," I said, lowering my rifle. "It's incredible."

"Yes," Abraham said from beside the jeep. "And a pain to live in. The whole city cycles through every week, you see. The buildings that decay back here regrow on the front side."

"Which is cool."

"It is a pain," Abraham repeated. "Imagine if your home crumbled every seven days, and you had to move across the city into a new one. Still, the local Epics are no more cruel than anywhere else, and the city has some conveniences."

"Water?" I asked. "Electricity?"

"Their water supply is collected from rain, which falls often, because of a local Epic."

"Stormwind," I said, nodding. "And that—"

"Doesn't melt the salt?" Abraham interjected before I could ask. "Yes, but it does not matter much. The buildings on the back side do get weathered by the time they fall, and perhaps they leak, but it is manageable. The bigger problem is finding ways to collect water that isn't too salty to drink."

"No plumbing then," I said. The Reckoner hideout in Babilar had had a septic tank, which was a nice luxury.

"The rich have electricity," Abraham said. "The city trades food for power cells."

Megan strolled up, one hand shading her eyes as she looked at the city. "You sure this plan of yours will get us in, Abraham?"

"Oh, certainly," Abraham said. "Getting into Ildithia is never a problem."

We piled into the jeeps again, then did a careful loop around the city, keeping our distance just in case. We finally ditched our jeeps in an old farmhouse, fully aware that they might not be there when we returned, fancy Reckoner locks or not. We also swapped our clothing for battered jeans, dusty coats, and backpacks with old water bottles at the sides. When we set out, we hopefully looked like a group of loners working to survive on their own.

The following hike left me missing the bumpy ride of the jeep. As we drew close to the leading edge of Ildithia, we walked among more of those fields—things I'd read about, heard about, but never seen before today.

There was more connectivity between city-states in the Fractured States than I'd once assumed. Perhaps the Epics could have survived without any kind of infrastructure, but they tended to want subjects to rule. What good was it to be an all-powerful force of destruction and fury if you didn't have peasants to murder now and then? Unfortunately peasants had to eat, or they'd go and die before you got a chance to murder them.

That meant building up some kind of structure in your city, finding some kind of product you could trade. Cities that could produce a surplus of food could trade for power cells, weapons, or luxuries. I found that satisfying. When they'd first appeared, the Epics had wantonly destroyed anything and everything, ruining the national infrastructure. Now they were forced to bring it all back, becoming administrators.

Life was so unfair. You couldn't *both* destroy everything around you *and* live like a king.

Hence the fields. The ones I'd noticed alongside the city's path had already been harvested, but these cornfields were ripe and ready. People worked them in large numbers, and though it was early spring, they were already harvesting.

"Stormwind again?" I whispered to Abraham, who hiked beside me.

"Yes," he said. "Her rains cause hyperquick growth around the city; they can get a new crop every ten days. Periodically, the people travel with her a few days in advance of the city's path and plant, then she waters. Workers travel ahead and manage the fields, then rejoin the city when it passes them. Oh, and you might want to keep your head down."

I lowered my eyes, adopting the old familiar posture—with flat expression—of one who lived under Epic rule. Abraham had to nudge Megan as she defiantly met the eyes of a guard we passed, a woman with a rifle on her shoulder and a sneer on her lips.

"Move on to the city," the woman said, pointing her gun toward Ildithia. "You touch an ear of corn without permission and we'll shoot you. You want food, talk to the overseers."

As we drew closer to the city, we picked up an escort of

men with cudgels on their belts. I felt uncomfortable beneath their gaze but kept my eyes down, which let me inspect the transition into the city. First there was a little crust on the ground. It got thicker as we drew closer, crunching underfoot and breaking, until finally we stepped onto true saltstone.

Closer in, we passed lumps that indicated where buildings were starting to grow. The white-grey of the salt here was woven with dozens of different strata, ribbons of color, like frozen smoke. The stone had a texture to it I could see, and it made me want to rub my fingers on the rock and feel it.

The place smelled strange. Salty, I guess. And dry. The fields had been humid, so it was noticeable how dry the air was here right inside the city. We joined a short line of people waiting to enter the city proper, where the buildings were the correct size.

There was also a familiarity to the sight: the uniform texture and tone, even with the variations in color, reminded me of the steel of Newcago. This place was probably alien to everyone else, with everything grown out of solid salt, but to me that was normal. It felt like coming home. Another irony. To me, comfort was intrinsically tied to something the Epics had created.

We were given an orientation; the person who spoke to us was surprised that we weren't refugees from Kansas City, but he kept his speech quick and direct. The food belonged to Larcener. If you wanted some, you worked for it. The city wasn't policed, so he said we'd probably want to join one of the established communities, if we could find one that was taking new members. Epics could do what they wanted, so stay out of their way.

It seemed to lack Newcago's structure. There, Steelheart had established a defined upper crust of non-Epics, and had used a powerful police force to keep people in line. In turn though, in Newcago we'd had access to electricity, mobiles, even movies.

That bothered me. I didn't want to discover that Steelheart had been a more effective leader than others, though part of me had known it for a long time. Heck, Megan had told me as much when I'd first joined the team.

Orientation done, we subjected ourselves to being searched—Abraham had warned us of this, so Megan was prepared to use her powers in a very careful illusion on several bags. That disguised some tools, like our power cells and advanced weapons, as more mundane items. She left a nice handgun as a plant, undisguised, for the guards to "confiscate" for themselves, a kind of toll for getting into the city. They let us have our more mundane weapons though, as Abraham had said they would. Weapons weren't illegal in the city.

After the search wrapped up, we were cleared. The guy from before, who'd given us our orientation, pointed. "You can take any building that's not occupied. But if I were you, I'd keep my head down these next few weeks."

"Why?" I asked, slinging my pack over my shoulder.

He eyed me. "Trouble between Epics. Nothing we can bother ourselves with, other than to lie low. Might be less food to be had in coming days." He shook his head, then pointed toward a stack of crates sitting outside the border. "I tell you what," he said to us and a few other newcomers. "I lost my work crew this morning. Sparking morons ran off. You help me cart those crates in, and I'll give you a full day's grain requisition, as if you'd started in the morning."

I looked to the others, who shrugged. If we'd actually been the loners we pretended to be, there was little chance we'd have passed up such an opportunity. Within minutes, we were hauling crates. The wooden containers were stamped with the burned-in mark of UTC, a group of nomadic traders ruled by Terms, an Epic with time manipulation powers. Looked like I'd missed her visit, unfortunately. I'd always wanted to see her in person.

The work was hard, but it did give me a chance to see some of the city. Ildithia was well populated; even with a large number of people manning the fields, the streets were busy. No cars, except the ones on the sides of the road that were made of salt, leftovers from when the city had originally been transformed. Apparently when the city regrew each week, it also reproduced things like these cars. None of them worked of course. Instead, there were a striking number of bicyclists.

Laundry was draped on lines outside windows. Children played with plastic cars alongside one road, their knees covered in salt that had rubbed off the ground. People carried goods purchased from a market that, after a few trips, I managed to pinpoint on a street one over from our path—which ran between the outer edge of the city and a warehouse about a half hour inside.

As I traipsed back and forth with box after box, I was able to get a good feel for how the buildings grew. Right inside the border, bulges formed into the knobs of weathered-looking foundations, like stones that had stood for centuries in the wind. Beyond those, the buildings had begun to fully take shape, walls stretching upward, brickwork emerging. It was like erosion in reverse.

The process wasn't perfect. Occasionally we would pass unformed lumps on the ground or between buildings, like cancerous growths of salt. I asked one of the other people lugging boxes about it, and he shrugged and told me that each week there were some irregularities. They'd be gone the next time the city cycled through, but others would have grown.

I found it all fascinating. I lingered for a long moment

before what seemed like it would become a row of apartments formed out of a black-blue salt with a swirling pattern. I could almost see the buildings rising, ever so slowly, like . . . popsicles getting un-licked.

There were trees too—that was a difference from New-cago, where nothing organic had transformed. These grew up like the buildings, crafted delicately from salt. They were only stumps here, but farther in they were full-blown trees.

"Don't stare too long, newbie," a woman said, hiking past and dusting off her gloved hands. "That's Inkom territory." She was one of the workers from the field, recruited to haul with us.

"Inkom?" I asked, catching up and nodding to Abraham as he passed, carting another box.

"That neighborhood," the tall woman said. "Closed doors—they don't take new members. They're up for degrade on the trailing edge, and usually move into that apartment set until their homes reconstitute. After Inkom moves out, Barchin tends to move in, and you don't want to try to deal with them. Nasty bunch. They'll let anyone join, but they'll take half your rations, and only to let you sleep in a gutter be-tween two buildings until you've been with them for a year."

"Thanks for the tip," I said, looking over my shoulder at the lumpish buildings. "But this place is big—looks like there's lots of empty space. Why would we want to join a family anyway?"

"Protection," the woman said. "Sure, you can set up in an empty home—there are lots of those—but without a good family at your back, you're likely to get robbed blind, or worse."

"Rough," I said, shivering. "Anything else I should know? Isn't there a new Epic to worry about?"

"Limelight?" she said. "Yeah, I'd stay out of his way.

Any Epic's way, even more than usual. Limelight is mostly in charge now, but there are a few holdouts. Stormwind. Larcener. War is brewing. Either way, Epics like the skyrises, so stay away from downtown. Right now, the downtown is about five."

". . . Five?"

"Five days since it grew," she said. "Two more days until the skyscrapers degrade. Usually the roughest time of the week is when that happens. When the taller buildings downtown start to go, the Epics get annoyed and go looking for entertainment. Some move to midtown. Others prowl about. A day or so after, their suites will have regrown and their servants will have moved everything, and it's generally safe to emerge. Don't know how the power struggle is going to change all this though."

We reached the stack of crates at the edge of the city, and I grabbed one off the pile. I still carried my pack on my back—I wasn't going to separate from it, even if it increased my load each trip. Were there other questions I could ask this woman?

"You and your friends are good workers," the woman noted, getting a crate of her own. "We might be able to give you a place in my neighborhood. Can't speak for certain, that's Doug's call. But we're fair, only take a quarter of your rations—use it to feed the elderly and the sick."

"That sounds tempting," I said, though it wasn't at all. We would be making our own safehouse somewhere in the city. "How do I go about applying?"

"You don't," she said. "Just show up at this edge in the morning and do some hard work. We'll be watching. Don't come looking for us, or things will go poorly for you."

She hefted her box and strode off. I adjusted my own box, watching her, noting the outline of what was most likely a handgun hidden in the crook of her back, beneath her jacket.

"Tough city," Mizzy mumbled, grabbing a box and passing me.

"Yeah," I said. But then again it wasn't.

I lifted my box to my shoulder and hiked off down the road. I had been young when this had all started, only eight, an orphan on the streets. I'd lived a year on my own before I'd been taken in. I remembered hushed conversations among adults about the breakdown of society projecting horrible things like cannibalism and gangs burning whatever they could find, families breaking apart—every man living for himself.

That hadn't transpired. People are people. Whatever happens, they make communities, struggle for normalcy. Even with the Epics, most of us simply wanted to live our lives. The woman's words had been harsh, but also hopeful. If you worked hard, you could find a place in this world despite the insanity. It was encouraging.

I smiled. Right about then, I realized that the street was empty. I stopped, frowning. The kids were gone. No bicycles on the road. Curtains drawn. I turned to catch a few other workers ducking for buildings nearby. The woman I'd talked to passed me in a rush, her crate dropped somewhere.

"Epic," she hissed. She rushed to an open doorway in what had once been a storefront, following a couple other people inside.

I dumped my crate in a hurry and followed, pushing through the cloth draping the doorway and joining her and a family huddled in the dim light. One man who'd entered before us took out a handgun and looked over the two of us warily, but didn't point the weapon at us. The implication seemed clear: we could stay until the Epic passed.

The draping in the doorway flapped softly. They probably had as much trouble with doors here as we did in Newcago. I'm sure a door made of salt was hard to use, so they knocked it off and used this cloth as a replacement. Not terribly secure—but then, that was why you had guns.

The front window of the store was made of thinner salt, almost like a glass window, though too cloudy to make out details through. It gave the room some light, and I could see a shadow pass on the other side. A single figure, trailed by something glowing, in the shape of a sphere.

Green light. Of a shade I recognized.

Oh no, I thought.

I had to look. I couldn't help it. The others hissed at me as I moved to the doorway and peeked past the rippling cloth at the street outside.

It was Prof.

14

I used to think that I could pick out Epics by sight. The fact that I spent weeks in the Reckoners alongside not one but *two* hidden Epics proved me wrong on that count.

That said, there *is* a look about an Epic who is in the throes of their power. The way they stand so tall, the way they smile with such confidence. They stand out, like a burp during a prayer.

Prof appeared much as he had when I'd last seen him, clad in a black lab coat, hands glowing faintly green. He had a head of greying hair that one wouldn't expect to be paired with such a powerful physique. Prof was sturdy. Like a stone wall, or a bulldozer. You'd never call this man elegant, but you would absolutely not want to try to cut in front of him in line.

He strode down the white and grey street, a spherical forcefield trailing him with a person trapped inside. Long, dark hair obscured her face, but she wore a traditional Chinese dress. It was Stormwind, the Epic who brought the rains and caused crops to grow at hyperaccelerated rates. The woman I'd talked to earlier said she'd been holding out against Prof's rule.

Looked like that had changed. Prof stopped outside the shop I was in, then turned, looking toward the windows of the buildings along the street. I ducked back inside, heart thumping. He seemed to be searching for something.

Sparks! What to do? Run? My rifle was in my pack, disassembled, but I had a handgun stuffed into my belt, under my shirt. The guards outside had let that pass as Abraham had said they would. They apparently didn't care if people inside were armed. They seemed to expect it.

Well, guns wouldn't do much against Prof. He was a High Epic with *two* prime invincibilities. Not only would his forcefields protect him from damage, but if he did get hurt, he would heal.

I slipped the handgun from my belt anyway. The other people in the room huddled together, staying quiet. If there was another way out, they'd probably have taken it—though that wasn't a hundred percent given. Many people hid from Epics instead of running. They figured the only way to cope was to hunker down and wait it out.

I peeked through the doorway again, my heart thundering. Prof hadn't moved, but he had turned from our building, inspecting one across the street instead. I hurriedly wiped the sweat from my forehead before it could trickle into my eyes, then pulled my earpiece out of my pocket and fitted it in.

"Has anyone seen David?" Cody was saying.

"I passed him on the last round," Abraham said. "He should be near the warehouse, I think. Far away from Prof."

"Yeah, about that," I whispered.

"David!" Megan's voice. "Where are you? Get under cover. Prof is moving down the street."

"I can see that," I said. "He seems to be looking for something. What are everyone's positions?"

"I've got a spot with a good view," Cody said, "'bout fifty yards from the target, second story of a building with an open window. Have my sights on him now."

"Megan grabbed me," Abraham said, "and towed me around a corner. We're a street over to the east, watching Cody's feed on our mobiles."

"Hold your positions," I whispered. "Mizzy?"

"Haven't heard from her," Abraham answered.

"I'm here," Mizzy said, sounding breathless. "Maaan, I just about *stepped on him,* guys."

"Where are you?" I asked.

"Ran away, perpendicular to our street. I'm at a market or something. Everyone's hiding, but it's packed here."

"Stay in position," I whispered, "and tap into Cody's feed. This might not be related to us. He's obviously making a show of having captured Stormwind, and . . . *Sparks.*"

"What?" Mizzy asked.

Prof was glowing. The pale green light spread from him as he turned in place on the street. "Are you going to come out?" he bellowed. "I know you are here! Show yourselves!"

I hated hearing Prof's voice sound so . . . like an Epic. He'd always been gruff, but this was different. Imperious, demanding, *angry.* I held the handgun in a sweaty grip. Behind me, one of the children whimpered.

"I'm going to lead him away," I whispered.

"What!" Megan demanded.

"There isn't time," I said, standing up. "If he starts ripping apart the area looking for me, he'll kill people. I've got to draw his attention."

"David, no," Megan said. "I'm coming your way. Just—"

Prof thrust his arms forward, toward the building in front of him—not mine, but an apartment complex across the street. It was some eight stories high, constructed entirely of pink and grey salt.

And at Prof's gesture, it vaporized.

In Newcago, I'd seen him do incredible things with his powers. He'd faced down an Enforcement squad, destroying their weapons, bullets, and armor as he fought. But that had been *nothing* compared to this. He disintegrated an entire building into dust in an eyeblink.

Prof's powers destroyed not only the salt structure, but the furniture inside it as well, leaving people and personal effects to plummet. The people hit the ground with awful thuds and cries of pain. Except for one, who remained flying in the air about twenty feet up. He leveled a pair of uzis at Prof and fired.

The bullets had no effect, of course. In an instant, the hovering man was surrounded by a glowing green sphere. He dropped his guns, feeling at the walls of his new prison in a panic.

Prof made a fist. The sphere shrank to the size of a basketball, crushing the Epic inside into pulp.

I looked away, suddenly sick. That . . . that was what he had done to Exel and Val.

"False alarm," Cody said over the line, sounding relieved. "He's not looking for us. He's hunting Epics who still follow Larcener."

Prof released the sphere and dropped the remnants of the dead Epic to the ground with a nauseating splat. From a shop next to mine, someone else stepped out onto the street, a young man—still a teenager—in a loose necktie and a hat. He stood facing Prof for a moment, then dropped to one knee, bowing.

A sphere of light appeared around him. The young man looked up in a panic. Prof held out a single palm, as if weighing the newcomer. Then he swiped his hand to the side, and the sphere vanished.

"Remember that feeling, little Epic," Prof said. "You are the one they call Dynamo, I believe. I accept your allegiance, tardy though it is. Where is your master?"

He gulped, then spoke. "My former master?" the youth asked, his voice breaking. "He is a coward, lord. He runs from you."

"He was with you earlier today," Prof said. "Where did he go?"

The youth pointed along a street, hand shaking. "He has a safehouse one street over. He forbade us to join him. I can show you."

Prof gestured, and the youth ran past him on wobbly legs. Prof clasped his hands behind his back and started to follow at a stroll, but paused.

My breath caught in my throat. What was wrong?

Prof took a few steps in my direction, then knelt, looking at the crate I'd dropped earlier. It had cracked open at the side. He nudged it with his foot and seemed contemplative.

"Lord?" the youth asked.

Prof turned away from the crate and swept after the youth, his lab coat rippling at the motion. The forcefield carrying Stormwind followed like an obedient puppy. The woman inside didn't look up.

I relaxed, slumping against the wall, and lowered my gun.

"Mizzy," I whispered over the line, "he's coming your direction."

"Sounds like he's searching for Larcener," Megan said over the line. "We've managed to stroll right into his final throwdown with the city's former leader. How delightful for us."

"I'm following him with my scope," Cody said. "But I won't be able to see much as he moves to the next street. You want me to maintain surveillance, lad, or stand down?"

"Being this close to him is dangerous," Abraham said. "If he so much as glimpses one of us . . ."

"Yeah," Cody said, "but I sure would like to know what he's capable of before we try to bring 'im down. That thing he did with the building . . . that makes the tensors look like a child's toy by comparison."

"Nice metaphor," I said absently. "We need to know the results of his face-off with Larcener, if it happens. Cody, see if you can get in position. Mizzy, I *do* want you out of there."

"Trying," she said, grunting. "I'm pressed into a room with a lot of people, and . . . Blah. I don't know how quickly I can get out, guys. . . ."

Well, we weren't going to fall back while one of our own was in danger. "Megan, be ready for a distraction. Abraham, stay with Megan." I took a deep breath. "I'm going to tail Prof."

Nobody objected. They trusted me. I shouldered my pack—there was no time to assemble my Gottschalk—and stood up beside the doorway, peeking through the fluttering cloth draping. Before ducking out, I glanced at the room's other occupants.

All of them—the man with his children, the woman who had talked to me earlier—were staring at me with dumbfounded expressions.

"Did you say you're going *after* that Epic?" the man demanded. "Are you insane?"

"No," the woman said softly. "You're one of them, aren't you? The ones who fight. I heard you were all killed in New York."

"Don't tell anyone you saw me, please," I said. I saluted them with a lift of my gun, then slipped out onto the empty street.

I stopped to nudge the box that Prof had paused beside— the crate I'd dropped. It was filled with foodstuffs, the packaged kind you had to trade to get, that came from cities that still had factories: beans, canned chicken, soda. I nodded, then hurried in the direction Prof had gone.

15

"**ALL** right," I said, pulling up beside the wall of an alleyway, my pistol in a two-handed grip before me. "Let's play this very, *very* carefully. Our primary objective is to make sure Mizzy extracts safely. Information gathering comes second."

A sequence of "rogers" came over the line. I tapped my mobile's screen into Cody's feed. Our earpieces, which had a part that curled over the ear and pointed forward, could give any of us a view of what another one of us was doing.

He was moving down a dark hallway. Diaphanous light seeped through the wall to his right, like a flashlight shining inside someone's mouth. He reached a room that still had a salt door—I was surprised when he shoved it that it moved. He slipped inside and crept up to a window. He broke the salt there—which proved more difficult than I'd have guessed—with the butt of his rifle, then poked the gun out. When he patched through the feed from his scope instead of his earpiece, it gave us a vantage from several stories up.

The market was easy to spot—it was an old parking garage, the sides draped with colorful cloths and awnings that spread out onto the streets around it.

"Yeah," Mizzy said as Cody focused on it, "I'm in there. Got pushed down onto one of the lower levels by the crowd. I'm trying a stairwell now. Still a lot of people hiding in here."

Prof was heading right for the market, the green glow of his forcefields lighting up the street. I followed a parallel path down a smaller side street, eventually taking cover beside some bushes made of pink salt.

In fact, this bush was still growing. I stared, momentarily transfixed by the little salt leaves sprouting out of tiny branches like crystals. I'd assumed that things grew up on the leading edge of the city, stopping once they matched the way Atlanta had once been, then remained static. It seemed that parts of the inner city were still developing.

"David?" a voice whispered. I turned to see Megan and Abraham scrambling up to me.

Right, right. Friend and mentor on a murderous rampage. I should probably remain focused.

"Megan," I said, "a little more cover might be nice."

She nodded, and concentrated for a moment. In an eyeblink, the bushes in front of us became far more dense. It was an illusion, a shadow pulled from another world where those shrubs *were* more dense, but it was perfect.

"Thanks," I said, taking off my pack and quickly assembling my rifle.

Prof strode out onto the street a short distance from us. The teenage Epic I'd seen earlier led him, gesturing as they walked. Stormwind's bubble had been parked at the mouth of an alleyway and left there, hovering.

The younger Epic with Prof . . . Dynamo? I wasn't sure what his powers were. In a city like this there would be dozens of lesser Epics, and I didn't have them all memorized.

Dynamo pointed toward the ground, then toward the market. Prof nodded, but I was too far away to hear what they said.

"An underground room," Abraham whispered. "That has to be the safehouse—an office linked to the parking garage, perhaps?"

"Can there *be* basements in this city?" I asked.

"Shallow ones," Abraham said, tapping the ground with his foot. "Depending on the area, Ildithia can grow up on a mass of salt rock that's several stories high in some places; it replicates the landscape of the original Atlanta, filling in holes and creating hills. It's as shallow as a few feet elsewhere, but this is a thick portion. Did you notice the slope while we walked to the warehouse?"

I hadn't. "Mizzy," I said, "he might be coming in there. Status?"

"Trapped," she whispered. "Stairwell is packed; everyone and their dog thought to hide in here. Like, seriously. There are *four* dogs. I can't find a way out."

Prof didn't follow the young Epic toward the parking garage. He strode farther down the street and swept both hands before himself.

The street melted away. The salt became powder, and that blew off in a gust of air that Prof created by quickly pushing two concave forcefields. The rest drained away into a hollow space below, leaving behind a set of stairs that Prof walked down without breaking stride.

It was amazing. I'd studied Epics, come up with my own systems of categorization. I admit I was a little obsessed. In the same way that a million preschoolers asking questions over and over at the same time might be a little obnoxious.

Prof's power was unique—he didn't just destroy matter, he sculpted it. It was beautiful destruction, and I found that I envied him. Once, I'd held that power, gifted to me. After Steelheart's death, Prof had stopped doing that so much. I'd had the spyril to keep me entertained, but I could see that even then he'd been withdrawing from us.

It was the time he saved me from Enforcement, I realized. *That was the beginning of the problems.*

I'd started him down this path. I knew I couldn't take all the blame—Regalia's plot to turn Prof would probably have happened whether or not I had joined the Reckoners—but neither could I deny responsibility.

"Mizzy," I said over the line, "hold tight. You might be safest in there after all."

Prof stepped down into the chamber he'd uncovered, but Cody's vantage from above let us watch on our mobiles. Prof didn't descend far before turning around and striding up again, dragging someone by the collar. Back on the street, he tossed the person aside. The figure fell limply to the ground, neck at an unnatural angle.

"A decoy," Prof barked. His voice carried through the square. "Larcener *is* a coward, I see."

"Decoy?" Megan said, taking my rifle from me and zooming in on the body.

"Ooooh," I whispered, excited. "Larcener absorbed Dead Drop. I wondered if he was ever going to do that."

"Talk normal-person, Knees," Megan said. "Dead Drop?"

"An Epic who used to live in the city. He could make copies of himself—kind of like Mitosis, but Dead Drop could make only a few at a time. Three, I think? The copies each retained his other powers though. And, well, you know how Larcener is. . . ."

The other two looked at me blankly.

"He's an assumer. . . . Don't you know what one does?"

"Sure," Cody said over the line. "Makes an ass out of you and Mer. Hate that guy."

I sighed. "You people know very little, for being a specialized team trained to hunt Epics."

"Maintaining lists of Epics and their powers was Tia's job," Abraham said. "Now yours. And we haven't had our briefing."

After a few days in the city, spent investigating who was here and who wasn't, I had planned to sit them down and explain all the Epics they needed to watch for. I probably should have prepped them for Larcener early. We'd been too focused on Prof.

"An assumer," I said, "is the opposite of a gifter. Larcener steals powers from other Epics—it's his one natural ability, but he's *very* powerful. Most assumers only 'rent' the powers, so to speak. Larcener can take another Epic's abilities *permanently,* and he can keep as many as he wants. He's got an entire collection of them. If Prof found a clone, it means Larcener grabbed Dead Drop's powers—an Epic who could create a decoy of himself, imbue it with his consciousness and powers, then retreat to his real body if the decoy was threatened."

I took my gun back from Megan and studied the decoy. It was decomposing quickly now that it had been killed, the skin melting off the bones like a marshmallow slipping off its roasting stick. Undoubtedly this was how Prof had recognized that he didn't have the real Larcener.

"Larcener makes other Epics *very* uncomfortable," I explained. "They don't like the idea that someone might be able

123

to take their abilities. Fortunately for them, he's not very ambitious, and has always been content to stay in Ildithia. The Coven relied on him—or the idea of him—to keep other Epics from moving in on their territory. . . ."

Megan and Abraham were rolling their eyes at me now.

"What?" I demanded.

"You look like you just found an old hard drive," Megan said, "full of lost songs by your favorite pre-Calamity band."

"This stuff is cool," I grumbled, inspecting Prof. He seemed thoroughly displeased by what he'd discovered in that hole. Now he was contemplating the market, which I could see from out here was packed like Mizzy had said.

"I don't like that look on his face," Abraham said.

"Guys," Mizzy said, "I think I'm by a wall to the outside. I can see sunlight through it if I squint. Maybe we can get me out that way."

Abraham looked at Megan. "Can you make a portal into another dimension, where the wall isn't there?"

Megan looked skeptical. "I don't know. Most of what I can do is ephemeral, unless I've recently reincarnated. I can trap someone in another world for a time, so long as it's very similar to our own—or pull that world into ours. But they're only shadows, and sometimes things seem to reset after the shadow fades."

Prof was on the move, striding toward the marketplace. He snapped his fingers, and Dynamo hurried over to him. A moment later when Prof spoke, his voice boomed through the area, as loud as if enhanced by a speaker.

"I am going to destroy this building," Prof said, pointing at the market. "And all of those nearby."

Ah, right, a part of me thought. *Dynamo. He has sound manipulation.*

The rest of me was horrified.

"Everyone who wishes to live," Prof continued, "must come out here to the square. Those who run will die. Those who remain will die. You have five minutes."

"Oh, hell," Cody said over the line. "You want me to pop him? Make a distraction?"

"No," I said. "He'd come for you, and we'd trade one problem for another." I looked at Megan.

She nodded. If *she* created a distraction and Prof came for her, she'd reincarnate. Sparks. I hated thinking of her ability to die as some kind of disposable resource.

Hopefully we wouldn't need that.

"Abraham, fall back and support Cody," I said. "If something goes wrong, you two continue with the plan to make a safehouse in the city. Be sure he doesn't spot you."

"Roger," Abraham said. "And you two?"

"We're going to get to Mizzy," I said. "Megan, can you conjure up some temporary faces for us?"

"Not a problem." She concentrated and changed in a split second—eyes the wrong color, a face that was too round, and hair that was black instead of golden. I assumed I'd undergone a similar transformation. I took a deep breath, then handed my rifle to Abraham. Though I'd seen people in Ildithia carrying guns, mine was far too advanced. It would draw attention.

"Let's go," I said, slipping out from behind the cover and joining the groups of people who were—timidly—leaving buildings and the market to stand before Prof.

16

MIZZY was in the parking garage on the other side of the street from us, which presented a problem. "How close do you need to be to give her an illusory face?" I whispered to Megan.

"The closer the better," she whispered back as we moved into the crowd. "Otherwise, I risk catching more people in the ripple between worlds."

So we had to cross the street in front of Prof without drawing attention. He was fully in the grip of his powers, so he'd be selfish to the extreme, completely lacking the ability to empathize. It wouldn't matter who we were or what we looked like; if someone inconvenienced him, he'd kill them as easily as another man swatted a mosquito.

I slumped my shoulders and pinned my eyes to the ground.

The act was still second nature to me; they'd drilled it into us at the Factory. I used it now to become inconspicuous as I stepped away from the mass of other people and headed eastward across the street, moving purposefully, yet careful to keep my posture hunched and subservient.

I shot a furtive glance over my shoulder to see if Megan was following, and she was—but she stood out like a hammer in a birthday cake. She was obviously trying to look innocuous, hands shoved in her pockets, but she walked too tall, too unafraid. Sparks. Prof would spot her for certain. I reached out and took her hand, then whispered to her, "You need to be more beaten down, Megan. Pretend you're carrying a lead statue of Buddha on your back."

"A . . . what?"

"Something heavy," I said. "It's a trick we learned in the Factory."

She cocked her head at me, but then slouched. That was better, and I was able to enhance it by clinging to her in a frightened way, pushing the back of her head so that she bowed it farther while we walked arm in arm. My shuffling— while acting extra nervous and dodging out of the way of others when they got too close—got us about halfway across the street, but then the press of people grew too great.

"Bow!" Prof bellowed at us. "Kneel before your new master."

The people went down in a wave, and I had to tow Megan with me to follow. Never before in our relationship had the disparity between us been so obvious. Yes, she had Epic powers and I didn't—but at the moment, that distinction seemed slight compared to the fact that she obviously had *no concept* of how to properly cower.

I was strong. I fought, and I didn't accept Epic rule.

But Calamity . . . I was still human. When an Epic spoke, I jumped. And though I seethed inside, when one told me to kneel, I did it.

The crowd hushed as more people piled out of the garage, filling the street, kneeling. I couldn't see much with my head down. "Mizzy?" I hissed. "You out yet?"

"Near the back," she whispered over the line. "By a light post with blue ribbons on it. Should I run?"

"No," I said. "He's watching for that."

I glanced up at Prof, who stood imperiously before us, new Epic lackey at his side, Stormwind hovering in her prison beyond. Prof scanned the crowd, then turned sharply as someone exited a nearby building and sprinted away.

Prof didn't capture her in a globe of force; instead, he raised his hands to the sides and two long spears made of light, almost crystalline in shape, appeared and shot toward the fleeing woman. They speared her through, dropping her—crumpled—to the street.

I swallowed, brow damp with sweat. Prof stepped forward, and something glowing shot out beneath his feet. A pale green forcefield that made a path for him. His own personal roadway, it elevated him three or four feet above us, so that when he walked he didn't have to risk brushing against one of the huddled figures.

We crouched lower, and I pulled the earpiece from my ear, worried it might remind him of the Reckoners, though we weren't the only ones to use them. Megan did likewise.

"The fight for Ildithia is over," Prof said, his voice still amplified. "You can see that your most powerful Epic master, Stormwind, is mine. Your onetime leader hides as a coward from me. *I* am your god now, and with my arrival I create a new order. I do this for your own good; history has proven that men cannot care for themselves."

He stopped uncomfortably close to me on his radiant pathway. I kept my eyes down, sweating. Sparks, I could hear him breathe in before every proclamation. I could have reached out and touched his feet.

A man I loved and admired, a man I'd spent half my life studying and hoping to emulate. A man who would kill me without a second thought if he knew I was there.

"I will care for you," Prof said, "so long as you do not cross me. You are my children, and I your father."

It's still him, I thought. *Isn't it?* Twisted though they were, those words reminded me of the Prof I knew.

"I recognize you," a voice whispered beside me.

I started, turning, and found *Firefight* kneeling beside me. He wasn't aflame like he had been at the Foundry; right now he looked like a normal man, wearing a business suit with a very narrow tie. He knelt but did not cower.

"You're David Charleston, aren't you?" Firefight asked.

"I . . ." I shivered. "Yes. How did you get here? Are we in your world or mine?"

"I don't know," Firefight said. "Yours, it would seem. So in this world, you live still. Does *he* know?"

"He?"

Firefight faded before he could answer, and I found myself staring at a frightened young man with spiky hair. He seemed baffled that I'd been speaking to him.

What had all *that* been? I glanced toward Megan, who knelt on my other side, then nudged her. She looked at me.

What? she mouthed.

What was that? I mouthed back.

What do you mean?

Prof continued to walk through the crowd, a glowing field forming before his feet as he stepped. His path rounded, and he came back along on my other side. "I have need of loyal soldiers," he declared. "Who among you wish to serve me, and be lords over your inferiors?"

About two dozen opportunists in the crowd stood up. Serving Epics so directly was dangerous—merely being in their presence could get you killed—but it was also the one way to get ahead in the world. I felt sick to see how eagerly some of the people stood, though the majority of the crowd remained kneeling, too scared—or too sensible—to throw their lot in with a new Epic when he hadn't yet established total dominance.

I'd have to ask Megan more about Firefight later. For now, I had a plan. Kind of.

I took a deep breath, then stood up. Megan glanced at me, then stood as well. *What are we doing?* she mouthed.

This will let us move through the crowd, I mouthed back. *It's the only way to get to Mizzy.*

Prof stood on his glowing walkway, hands behind his back. He studied the people in the crowd, surveying them. He turned about, looking directly at the two of us, and I swallowed nervously. This *could* be a way to weed out those whose loyalty was too fleeting. His next step could be to kill those of us who had stood.

No. I knew Prof. He'd realize that in murdering those most eager to serve, he'd have trouble finding servants in the future. He was a leader, a builder. Even as an Epic, he wouldn't discard useful resources unless he considered them a threat.

Right?

"Good," Prof said. "Good. I have a task for you all." He held his hands out, and I thought I felt something vibrate. A familiar sensation from the days, months ago, when I'd worn the gloves and used Prof's power.

I towed Megan to the side as Prof released a wave of

power over the top of the crowd. The air warped, and the entire parking garage behind us exploded to salt dust. People screamed and dropped through the collapsing powder.

"Go," Prof said, waving toward the destruction of the parking garage. "Execute those still living who disobeyed my will and hid as cowards."

The twenty-something of us jumped into motion. Though the drop had already hurt, or killed, those on the upper two floors of the garage, there would be others who hadn't fallen far—or who were hiding in the underground portion.

Prof turned to resume his inspection of the crowd. That gave Megan and me our opening. We veered, using the pole Mizzy had indicated as a reference point. There she was, huddling down with a hoodie—I had no idea where she'd gotten it—covering her head. She glanced at us, and I gave her a thumbs-up.

She didn't hesitate. She sprang to her feet and joined us, and in an eyeblink Megan had changed Mizzy's features to something similar but unrecognizable.

"Megan?" I said.

"See that wall over there?" she said. "The one by the ramp leading to where the garage used to be? I'll create duplicates of us once we reach it. When they appear, drop down by the wall."

"Got it," I said, and Mizzy nodded.

We hit the location indicated, a salt ramp that now ended abruptly to our left. One version of the three of us split off and started up the ramp. The duplicates wore our clothing, and had the same fake faces we'd been wearing. Three people from another reality, living in Ildithia. It hurt my brain sometimes to wonder how all this worked. Those faces Megan had overlaid us with . . . did that mean these three were doing the same things we were? Were they versions of us, or were they completely different people who had somehow ended up living lives very like our own?

The three of us—the real three—dropped and ducked behind the wall as our doppelgangers reached the edge of the ramp and hopped off. We were shielded from Prof and the crowd by this wall, but I still felt horribly conspicuous as we army-crawled across the ground toward an alleyway.

A gust of wind carried dust across us, and it stuck to my face, tasting sharply of salt. I still wasn't used to how dry it was in this city; my throat felt ragged from just breathing.

We made it to the alley without incident, and our doppelgangers disappeared into the pits of the destroyed parking garage. I wiped the dust from my skin as Mizzy made a face, sticking out her tongue. "Yuck."

Megan settled on the ground beside the wall, looking exhausted. I knelt beside her, and she grabbed my arm and closed her eyes. "I'm fine," she whispered.

She'd still need time to rest, so I gave it to her. I didn't miss that she started rubbing her temples to try to massage away a headache. I knelt by the edge of the alleyway so I could make sure we were safe. Prof continued to walk among the crowd, passing the place where Mizzy had been hiding. He occasionally made someone look up and meet his gaze.

He must have a list of descriptions of Epics, I thought, *or other malcontents in the city.*

He was here for a purpose. I couldn't believe that Prof had randomly picked Ildithia to rule. And I was increasingly suspicious that the secrets to why he did what he did came from the things he'd found when he'd taken power from Regalia.

I didn't lure Jonathan here to kill him, child, Regalia's voice echoed in my head. *I did it because I need a successor.*

What did Ildithia hide that had drawn Prof's attention?

Behind me, Mizzy gave Abraham and Cody an update. I kept my attention on Prof. He looked not unlike Steelheart, who—though taller and more muscular—had stood frequently in that same domineering pose.

Out in the square, a baby started crying.

My breath caught. I spotted the woman clutching her baby, not far from where Prof stood. She frantically tried to soothe the child.

Prof raised his hand toward her, a look of annoyance on his face. The sound had jarred him out of his contemplations, and he sneered toward the disturbance.

No . . .

You learned quickly: Don't bother the Epics. Don't draw attention. Don't annoy them. They'd kill a man for the simplest of things.

Please . . .

I didn't dare breathe. I was in another place for a moment. Another crying child. A hushed room.

I looked into Prof's face, and despite the distance, I was certain I saw something there. A struggle.

He spun and stalked away, leaving the woman and her child alone, barking at his new Epic lackey. The forcefield sphere holding Stormwind trailed after him, and he left a bewildered crowd.

"We ready to go?" Megan asked, standing up.

I nodded, letting out a long, relieved breath.

There was still something human inside Jonathan Phaedrus.

17

"I *did* see him, Megan," I said, unzipping my backpack. "I'm telling you, Firefight was there in the crowd."

"I'm not doubting you," she said, leaning against the pink saltstone wall of our new hideout.

"Point of fact," I said, "I believe you were doing *exactly that*."

"What I said is that I didn't pull him through."

"Then who did?"

She shrugged.

"Can you be absolutely sure he didn't slip through?" I said, taking several changes of clothing out of my pack and kneeling by the trunk that was going to be my sole piece of furniture. I stuffed the clothing inside, then looked at her.

"On occasion, when I pull a shadow from another world, the fringes bleed," Megan admitted. "It usually only happens when I've just reincarnated, when my powers are at their fullest."

"What about when you're stressed or tired?"

"Never before," she said. "But . . . well, there are a lot of things I haven't tried."

I looked up at her. "Why not?"

"Because."

"Because why? You have amazing, reality-defying powers, Megan! Why not experiment?"

"You know, David," she said, "you sure can be stupid sometimes. You have lists of powers, but you don't have any idea what it's *like* to be an Epic."

"What do you mean?"

She sighed, then settled down on the floor next to me. There were no beds or couches yet—our new hideout wouldn't ever be as lush as the one in Babilar had been. But it was as secure as we could make it. We'd built it ourselves over the past few days, hiding it as one of the large "cancerous" lumps of salt that grew across Ildithia.

I'd given Megan some time at first, not wanting to push her about Firefight. She was often evasive for a few days after she used her powers strenuously, as if even thinking about the powers gave her a headache.

"Most Epics aren't like Steelheart, or Regalia," Megan explained. "Most Epics are small-time bullies—men and women with just enough power to be dangerous, and just enough taste of the darkness to not care who they hurt.

"They didn't like me. Well, Epics don't like most anybody, but me especially. My powers frightened them. Other realities? Other versions of *them*? They hated that they couldn't

135

define limits to what I could do, but at the same time my powers couldn't protect me. Not actively. So . . ."

"So?" I asked, scooting closer, putting my arm around her.

"So they killed me," she said, shrugging. "I dealt with it, learned to be more subtle with my powers. It wasn't until Steelheart took me in that I had any kind of security. He always did see the promise of what I did, rather than the threat.

"Anyway, it's like I've told you. I took what my dad had taught my sisters and me about guns, and I became an expert. I learned to use guns to mask the fact that my powers couldn't hurt anyone. I hid what I could truly do, became Steelheart's spy. But no, I didn't experiment. I didn't want people to know what I could do, didn't even want *him* to know the extent of my powers. Life has taught me that if people learn too much about me, I end up dead."

"And reincarnating," I said, trying to be encouraging.

"Yeah. Unless it's not me that comes back, but just a copy from another dimension—similar, but different. David . . . what if the person you fell in love with really *did* die in Newcago? What if I'm some kind of impostor?"

I pulled her close, uncertain what to say.

"I keep wondering," she whispered. "Is next time going to be *the* time? The time I come back and am obviously different? Will I be reborn with a different hair color? Will I be reborn with a different accent, or with a sudden distaste for this food or that? Will you know then, once and for all, that the one you loved is dead?"

"You," I said, tipping her chin up to look her in the eye, "are a sunrise."

She cocked her head. "A . . . sunrise?"

"Yup."

"Not a potato?"

"Not right now."

"Not a hippo?"

"No, and . . . wait, when did I call you a hippo?"

"Last week. You were drowsy."

Sparks. Didn't remember that one. "No," I said firmly, "you're a sunrise. I spent ten years without sunrises, but I always remembered what they looked like. Back before we lost our home, and Dad still had a job, a friend would let us come up to the observation deck of a skyscraper in the morning. It had a dramatic view of the city and lake. We'd watch the sun come up."

I smiled. It was a good memory, me and my father eating bagels and enjoying the morning cold. He'd always make the same joke. *Yesterday, son, I wanted to watch the sunrise. But I just wasn't up for it. . . .*

Some days, the only time he'd been able to make for me had been in the morning, but he'd always done it. He'd gotten up an hour earlier than he needed to get to work, and he'd done it after working well into the night. All for me.

"So, am I going to get to hear this glorious metaphor?" Megan said. "I'm twinkling with anticipation."

"Well, see," I said, "I would watch the sun rise, and wish I could capture the moment. I never could. Pictures didn't work—the sunrises never looked as spectacular on film. And eventually I realized, a sunrise isn't a moment. It's an event. You can't capture a sunrise because it changes constantly—between eyeblinks the sun moves, the clouds swirl. It's continually something new.

"We're not moments, Megan, you and me. We're events. You say you might not be the same person you were a year ago? Well, who is? I'm sure not. We change, like swirling clouds and a rising sun. The cells in me have died, and new ones were born. My mind has changed, and I don't feel the thrill of killing Epics I once did. I'm *not* the same David. Yet I am."

I met her eyes and shrugged. "I'm glad you're not the same Megan. I don't want you to be the same. My Megan is a sunrise, always changing, but beautiful the entire time."

She teared up. "That . . ." She breathed in. "Wow. Aren't you supposed to be bad at this?"

"Well, you know what they say," I told her, grinning. "Even a clock that runs fast is still right twice a day."

"Actually . . . You know what, never mind. Thank you."

She kissed me. Mmmmm.

Some time later, I stumbled from my quarters, ran a hand through my disheveled hair, and went to get something to drink. Cody was on the other side of the hallway, finishing the hideout's roof there with the crystal-growing device that Knighthawk had given us. It looked kind of like a trowel, the kind you'd use to smooth concrete or plaster. When you pulled it along the salt, the crystal structure would extend and create a sheet of new salt. With the glove that came with the device, you could mold that new salt how you wanted for a short time, until it hardened and stayed strong.

We called it Herman. Well, I called it Herman, and nobody else had come up with something better. We'd used it to grow this entire building in an alleyway over the course of two nights, expanding upon a large lump of salt that had grown there already. This place was on the northern rim of the city, which was still growing, so that the half-finished structure wouldn't look odd.

The nearly finished hideout was tall and thin, going up three narrow stories. In places, I could reach out and touch both walls at once. We'd made the outside of it look like lumps of rock to match the other growths like this in the city. All in all, we'd decided we preferred a place that was more secure, built ourselves, rather than moving into one of the houses out there.

I headed down the steep pink crystal steps to the next level, the kitchen—or at least where we'd set up a hot plate and water jug, along with a few small appliances powered by one of the jeeps' power cells.

"Finally done unpacking?" Mizzy asked me, wandering by with the coffeepot.

I stopped on the bottom step. "Uh . . ." Actually, I hadn't finished.

"Too busy smooching, eh?" Mizzy said. "You *do* realize that without doors, we can kinda hear everything."

"Uh . . ."

"Yeaaaah. I wish there were a rule against team members making out and stuff, but Prof would never have done that, considering that him and Tia were a thang."

"A thang?"

"It's a word you probably shouldn't ever say again," she said, handing me a cup of coffee. "Abraham wanted to see you."

I set the coffee aside and got a cup of water instead. I could never see why people drank that stuff. It tasted like soil boiled in mud, with a topping of dirt.

"You still have my old mobile?" I asked Mizzy as she climbed the steps. "The one Obliteration broke?"

"Yup, though it's cracked pretty good. Saved it for parts."

"Grab it for me, will you?"

She nodded. I climbed down to the ground floor, where we'd stashed most of our supplies. Abraham knelt in one of the two rooms here, lit only by the light of his mobile—the upper two floors had hidden skylights and windows, but not much filtered down this far. We'd built him a worktable here out of saltstone, and he was going over the teams' weapons one at a time, cleaning and checking them.

Most of us were perfectly willing to do it on our own, but . . . well, there was something comforting about knowing that Abraham had approved your gun. Besides, my Gottschalk was no simple hunting rifle. With electron-compressed magazines, hyperadvanced scope, and electronics systems that hooked into my mobile, I would be able to do only the basics on my own. It was the difference between putting ketchup on your hot dog and decorating a cake. Best to let an expert take over.

Abraham nodded to me, then waved toward his pack nearby on the floor, which hadn't been completely unloaded. "I brought something back for you during my trip out to the jeeps."

Curious, I walked over and rummaged in the pack. I pulled out a skull.

Made entirely of steel, it reflected the mobile's light with its eerie, smooth contours. The jaw was missing. That had been separated from it in the blast that had killed this man, the man who had named himself Steelheart.

I stared into those eye sockets. If I had known then that there was a chance of redeeming Epics, would I have pushed forward with my insistence on killing him? Even now, holding this skull made me think of my father—so hopeful, so *confident* that the Epics would turn out to be the saviors of mankind, not its destroyers. Steelheart, in murdering my father, represented the ultimate betrayal of that hope.

"Oh, I'd forgotten about that," Abraham said. "I threw it in at the last minute, because there was space."

I frowned, then set the skull on a salt shelf overhead. I dug farther in the pack and located a heavy metal box. "Sparks, Abraham. You *carried* this in?"

"I cheated," he said, snapping the trigger guard assembly onto my rifle. "Gravatonics at the bottom of my pack."

I grunted, lugging out the box. I thought I recognized it. "An imager."

"Thought you might want one," Abraham said. "To set up the plan, like we used to do." Prof would often call the team into a room to go over our plans, and he used this device to project ideas and images onto the walls.

I wasn't nearly that organized. I turned on the imager anyway, plugging it into the power cell Abraham was using. The imager scattered light through the room. It wasn't calibrated to this location, so some of the images were fuzzy and distorted.

It showed Prof's notes. Scribbled lines of text, as if made in chalk on a black background. I walked to the wall and felt at some of the scribbled writings. They smudged as if real, and my hand made no shadow on the wall. The imager wasn't like an ordinary projector.

I read through some of the notes, but there was little of relevance here. These were from when we'd been fighting Steelheart. Only one sentence struck me: *Is it right?* Three solitary words, alone in their own corner. The rest of the writing was cramped, words fighting with one another for space like too many fish in a tiny tank. But these sat on their own.

I looked back at Steelheart's skull. The imager had interpreted it as part of the room and had projected words across its surface.

"How's the plan?" Abraham asked. "I assume you have something brewing?"

"A few things," I said. "They're kind of random."

"I'd expect nothing less," Abraham said, a hint of a smile

on his lips as he affixed the stock onto the Gottschalk. "Shall I gather the others into one of the rooms so we can talk about it?"

"Sure," I said. "Grab them, but not in one of the rooms."

He looked at me, questioning.

I knelt and switched off the imager. "Maybe we'll use this another day. For now, I want to go for a walk instead."

18

MIZZY tossed me the broken mobile as she joined the rest of us on the street outside our hideout. We kept the place hidden by slipping out through a secret door into the mostly abandoned apartment building next to us. It housed no family, only loners who couldn't find their own to join, which we hoped would make them pay less attention to strangers like us.

"Security set up?" I asked Mizzy.

"Yup. We'll know if anyone tries to enter the place."

"Abraham?" I asked.

He shook his pack, which contained our data pads, our extra power cells, and the two pieces of Epic-derived equipment that Knighthawk had given us. If someone did rob our hideout, all they'd get away with were a few guns, which were replaceable.

"That was under five minutes," Cody said. "Not bad."

Abraham shrugged, but seemed pleased. This hideout was far less secure than others we'd used; that meant either leaving at least two of us behind to guard at all times, or coming up with a routine pull-out protocol when we went on operations. I liked the second idea far better. It would let us field larger teams in the city without worrying. Either way, we'd had Mizzy set up some sensors on the door that, if opened, would send our mobiles warnings.

I slung my rifle over my shoulder—Abraham had scuffed it up, then painted over a few portions to make it look both more battered and less advanced at the same time. That should help me not draw attention. Each of us wore a new face granted by Megan. It was early afternoon, and I found it odd how many people were about. Some hung laundry; others walked to or from the market. A large number were carrying possessions in sacks, having been ousted from the decaying side of the city and sent in search of someplace new to live. This sort of thing seemed constant in Ildithia; someone was always moving house.

I didn't see anyone alone—the kids playing ball in an empty lot were watched by no fewer than four elderly men and women. Those heading to market went in pairs or groups. People congregated on steps up to houses, and quite a few had rifles nearby, though they laughed and smiled.

It was a strange kind of peace. The atmosphere implied that so long as everyone stuck to their own business, everyone would get along. I was disturbed to see how many of the groups seemed segregated along racial lines though. Our group with mixed ethnicities was irregular.

"So, lad," Cody said, walking beside me with hands

shoved into the pockets of his camo pants. "Why are we out on the street again? I was planning on a wee nap this afternoon."

"I didn't like the idea of being cooped up," I said. "We're here to save this city. I don't want to sit and plan in a sterile little room, away from the people."

"Sterile little rooms are secure," Megan said from behind, where she walked with Abraham. Mizzy was to my right, humming to herself.

I shrugged. We could still talk and not be overheard. People on the street kept to themselves, and gave way when others approached them. The smaller groups actually demanded more respect—when one person did pass walking alone, everyone moved to the other side of the street in a subtle motion. A solo man or woman might be an Epic.

"This," I said as we walked, "is what passes for a functional society these days. Each group with their territory, each with an implicit threat of violence. This isn't a city, it's a thousand communities one step from war with one another. It's the best the world has to offer. We're going to change that, once and for all. And it starts with Prof. How do we save him?"

"Make him confront his weakness," Mizzy said. "Somehow."

"We have to find it first," Megan noted.

"I have a plan for that," I said.

"What, really?" Megan asked, moving up so she was walking beside Cody. "How?"

I held out the broken phone and wiggled it.

"Folks," Cody said, "looks like the lad's finally snapped and gone completely mental. I take full credit."

I got out my working mobile and wrote a text to Knighthawk. *Hey. I've got a mobile with a broken screen here. Battery is in though. Can you still track it?*

He didn't respond immediately.

"Let's assume that I *can* discover Prof's weakness," I said. "Where do we go from there?"

"Hard to say," Abraham answered. He was carefully watching everyone else on the street as we made our way down it. "The nature of the weakness often defines the plan's shape. It could take months to perfect the right approach."

"I strongly doubt that we have months," I said.

"I agree," Abraham said. "Prof has plots of his own, and he's been here for weeks already. We don't know why he is here, but we certainly don't want to wait around and see. We need to stop him quickly."

"Besides," I added, "the longer we wait, the greater the chance Prof will notice us."

"I think you're trying to do things backward, lad," Cody said, shaking his head. "We can't plot anything without the weakness."

"Though perhaps—" Abraham started.

I looked at him.

"We do have something of a trump card," he said, nodding toward Megan. "We have a team member who can make *anything* real. Perhaps we can begin planning a trap, with the assumption that whatever he fears, Megan can create it."

"That's a leap," Mizzy said. "What if he fears . . . I don't know, a sentient taco."

"I could probably make that," Megan said.

"Okay, fine. What if he fears being afraid? Or being proven wrong? Or something else abstract? Don't a lot of weaknesses come from things like that?"

Mizzy was right. The rest of us fell silent. We passed an old fast-food place on the left, crafted from a beautiful shade of blue salt. More of this region slowly bled to that color as we walked. I didn't lead us anywhere in particular yet; we'd want to do some intel gathering later today, which was standard Reckoner protocol after securing a base. For now, I wanted to be out, to be moving. Walking, talking, thinking.

My mobile buzzed.

Sorry, Knighthawk said. *Was taking a koala. What's this about another mobile?*

You said you could track mobiles, I wrote to him. *Well, I've got a broken one here. Can you pinpoint it?*

Leave it somewhere, he wrote, *then move on. Your signals are all too close together.*

I did what he said, setting the mobile on an old trash can and leading the others off a ways.

Yeah, that one is working enough to send a signal, he wrote. *Why?*

I'll tell you in a bit, I sent, jogging back to get the broken phone. From there I turned the team left, heading down a larger street. Some of the salt signs hanging above us had already been knocked down and broken, even though we were in the part of the city that was freshly grown.

"All right," I said, taking a deep breath. "We can't talk specifics about fighting Prof until we get the weakness, but there are still things to plan. For example, we need to figure out how to get him to *face* his fear, not run from it."

"In my case," Megan said, hands in her jacket pockets, "I had to enter a burning building to try to save you, David. That meant I had to be sane enough, away from the powers *long* enough, that I wanted to save you."

"That's not a lot to go on," Mizzy said. "I don't mean to be negative, but maaaan, don't you think we're leaning too much on what happened to one person?"

I remained silent. I hadn't talked to anyone but Megan about it, but something similar had happened to me. I had been . . . granted Epic powers by Regalia. It had something to

147

do with Calamity, and her relationship with him had allowed her to assert that I would become an Epic.

Those powers hadn't ever manifested. Right before that moment, I'd faced the depths of the waters in an attempt to get out and save Megan and the team. There *was* a connection there. Face your fears. And . . . what? For Megan, it had meant some control over the darkness. For me, it had made the powers never manifest in the first place.

"We should get more data," I admitted. "Cody, I still want to talk to Edmund."

"You think he went through the same thing?"

"It's worth asking."

"We've got him hidden away in a safehouse outside Newcago," Cody said. "A place we set up after you and Prof left. I'll get you in touch with him."

I nodded, and we continued in silence. If nothing else, this meeting had helped me define my goals for Ildithia. *Step one, find Prof's weakness. Step two, use it to negate his powers long enough for him to come to his senses. Step three, contrive a way that he has to confront and overcome that weakness.*

We turned another corner and then pulled to a stop. I'd been intending to wind us around toward the outer sections of town, but the path in front of us was blocked off. It must have taken a great deal of effort to move the barricade of metal chains and posts every week, but judging by the men atop the building beyond—armed with wicked-looking rifles—this force had plenty of manpower.

As a group, without needing to say a word, we turned and walked the other way. "Epic stronghold," Cody guessed. "Someone Prof has already subdued, or a neutral party?"

"That's probably Loophole's place," Abraham said, thoughtful. "She was always one of the most powerful Epics in the city."

"Size-manipulation powers, right?" I asked.

Abraham nodded. "Don't know how she fell into the conflict between Prof and Larcener."

"Look into it," I told him. But this raised another issue. "We might want a plan to deal with Larcener. I don't want to get so focused on Prof that we ignore the turf war in Ildithia."

"Well," Mizzy said, "if only we had access to someone with a freakishly large repository of knowledge about Epics, and who can't *help* but tell us about them. Like, all the time."

"Well, it is my thang."

"What did I tell you about that word, David?"

I smiled. "Larcener. By all reports, he was a teenager when Calamity rose—maybe even a kid. One of the youngest High Epics, he's probably in his early twenties right now. He's tall, with dark hair and pale skin; I'll send a photo to your mobiles when we get back. I have a couple good shots of him in my notes.

"He steals powers, and *keeps* them. All he has to do is touch someone, and he can take their powers. One of the reasons he's so dangerous is that it's impossible to tell what abilities he has, as he has likely never manifested them all. Prime invincibilities include danger sense, impervious skin, regeneration, and now the ability to project his consciousness and powers into a fake body."

Cody let out a long, soft whistle. "That's . . . quite the list."

"He can also fly, transform objects to salt, manipulate heat and cold, conjure objects at will, and put people to sleep with a touch," I added. "By all accounts, he's also incredibly lazy. He could be the most dangerous Epic alive—but he doesn't seem to care. He stays here, rules Ildithia, and doesn't bother others unless he has to."

"His weakness?" Megan said.

"I've got no idea," I replied as we reached the edge of town. "Everything I know about him is limited to a few widely accepted—but far too general—reports. He's lazy, which we can probably use. He also is reportedly slow to steal new powers; he finds it easier to let Epics who serve him keep their abilities, since they can do the hard work for him. It's said he hasn't taken a new power in years, which was why I was surprised to find he'd absorbed Dead Drop's abilities."

Abraham grunted. "I'd still rather have an idea of his weakness."

"Agreed," I said. "We should do some intel gathering. Today, if possible. I'd rather not fight Larcener if we can avoid it, but I'd like to have a plan anyway."

We walked on, passing buildings that were still growing stumps. They kind of looked like teeth. Giant, lumpy teeth. Beyond those, people worked the fields. Conflicts between Epics in the city didn't change the workers' routine: harvest the grain, give it to whoever ended up in charge. Avoid starving.

The others gave me confused looks as I settled in here to wait, checking my mobile.

You sure it's today? I typed.

The delivery? Knighthawk asked. *That's what the mobiles said. I don't know why they'd lie.*

Sure enough, a caravan of trucks soon approached, laden with goods ordered from UTC's trading network. I wasn't certain if Terms herself would be in attendance and—though it pained me, since I wanted to see her powers work—I knew I probably shouldn't try to catch a glimpse. I did, however, spot the same overseer from a few days ago, when we'd first entered.

"All right," I said to the team. "I figure this is as good a place as any to get some information. We need intel on

Larcener, if we're going to have any shot at guessing his weakness. Go do what it is you do best."

"Make stuff up?" Cody asked, rubbing his chin.

"So you admit it!" Mizzy said, pointing at him.

"Course I admit it, lass. I have seven PhDs. That kind of time spent learning makes a fellow very self-aware." He hesitated. "Course, all *seven* are in Scottish literature and culture, from different schools. A lad's got to be thorough in his approach to his expertise, you see."

I shook my head, approaching the overseer. We wore different faces now, but the man didn't care. He put us to work as easily as he had before, hauling crates from the UTC shipment. The team spread out, engaging the other workers, listening to gossip. I managed to get myself assigned to unloading crates from one of the trucks.

"This is a good place for intel," Abraham said to me softly as he stepped up to get a crate. "But I can't help thinking you have an ulterior motive, David. What are you up to?"

I smiled, slid the broken mobile from my pocket, and wrapped it in a dark cloth. I picked a specific crate, then wedged the slim mobile between the slats in the wood near one of the corners. As I'd hoped, it was practically invisible in there.

I handed the crate to Abraham and winked. "Put this with the others."

He raised an eyebrow toward me, then peeked into the crate. He grinned immediately, then obeyed.

The rest of the afternoon was consumed by work, with us carrying boxes and chatting up the other workers. I didn't learn much, as I was distracted by my plans, but I passed Abraham and Cody engaged in several relaxed conversations with other workers. Mizzy seemed to have the most talent for it.

151

It would have been nice to have Exel along. That man had been wide as a boat and as morbid as a . . . um . . . sinking boat, but he'd been good with people. And good with information.

Thinking about him made me sick. I had convinced myself Prof couldn't be blamed, but sparks . . . I'd really liked Exel.

I forced myself to chat up one of the other workers. The older man had an accent that reminded me of my grandmother's. As we walked to the warehouse—a different one this time than last—he seemed to know the city well. He didn't know much about Larcener, though he did complain that the Epic didn't rule strongly enough.

"In the old country," the man explained, "they'd have made short work of a fellow like Larcener. He lets all the Epics in town run about—he's like a grandfather without any sense to discipline his grandkids. A stronger hand, *that's* what's needed here. Police, rules, curfews. People complain about that kind of thing, but it's where we get order. Society."

We passed Cody, who was sharing a cigarette with another worker. Cody appeared to be loafing, but if you watched him you could see that he was carefully minding the locations of the other Reckoners. If you needed to know where someone was, Cody was the person you asked.

I found myself comfortably entering conversations with several other workers. I realized after some time that I was actually more at ease here than I'd been in Babilar, where the people were more open, the society less oppressive. I didn't like what was being done to Ildithia; I didn't like how scared the people were, how divided and brutal life here was proving to be. But I *was* accustomed to it.

Eventually, we accepted our grain rations and made our way to the hideout, sharing intel. Nobody knew Larcener's weakness, though we hadn't expected that it would simply be open knowledge. The problem was, nobody seemed to have *seen* Larcener either. He kept to himself, and there were a shockingly small number of rumors. Mostly about Epics whose powers he'd stolen, leaving them as common people.

I listened to it all with a growing sense of disappointment. It was evening by the time we arrived home, and Mizzy used her mobile to double-check the security sensors on the door. We piled into our narrow pencil box of a hideout and split our separate ways. Cody asked Abraham for the rtich, which he wanted to practice with. I still hadn't been able to get it to do much; maybe he'd have more luck. Megan retreated to her room, Abraham went to tinker with some of the weapons, and Mizzy went to make a sandwich.

I settled down on the ground in the main room on the bottom floor, my back against the wall. The only light was from my mobile, which eventually dimmed. I'd always chided Prof for taking things too slowly, for being too careful. Yet here I was in Ildithia, and my entire planning meeting had amounted to "Yup, we sure do need to stop Prof. And find Larcener's weakness. Anyone got any ideas? Nope? Oh well, good job anyway."

Looking back, dealing with Steelheart seemed *easy* in comparison. I'd had ten years to prepare for that. I'd had Prof and Tia to work out the details of the plan.

What was I doing here?

A shadow fell on the steps and Megan appeared, lit from the kitchen above. "Hey," she said. "David? Why are you sitting in the dark?"

"Just thinking," I said.

She continued down, eventually taking a seat on the ground beside me, lighting her mobile and setting it in front of us for illumination. "We've packed about forty different guns into the city," she muttered, "but not a one of us thought to bring a sparking cushion."

"You surprised?" I asked.

"Not in the least. Good job today."

"Good job?" I said. "We didn't come up with anything."

"Nothing is ever decided at the early meetings, David. You got everyone pointed in the right direction, got them thinking. That's important."

I shrugged.

"Nice work with the hidden mobile too," she noted.

"You saw that?"

"Had me confused until I checked in the box. You think it will work?"

"Worth a try," I said. "I mean, if . . ." I trailed off as an indicator light hanging on the wall blinked softly.

That meant someone had walked into the entryway of the apartment building beside us. Our fake door led into that entrance, and was one of our security threats. Cody had hidden it by covering some old boards—taken from cargo crates he'd scrounged up—with a thin layer of salt on one side and a black cloth backing. From the outside it looked like any other section of the wall, but you could push it in and slide it open to make a doorway. He warned that if someone was in the entryway, they might be able to hear something coming from the false section. Hence the light, and the instructions for everyone on the ground floor to be quiet if someone was outside the door.

Megan draped her arm around me, yawning, as we waited for the people to move on. We needed a pressure plate out there to let us know when they were gone, or maybe a camera or something.

Our phones flashed, and the hidden door rattled.

I blinked, then scrambled to my feet, following Megan,

who had moved a hair faster than me. Both of us had hand-guns out a second later, leveled at the door, while Abraham cursed in the room nearby. He charged out a moment later, with his minigun at the ready.

The door wobbled, scraped, then slipped to the side. "Hum," a voice said outside. I imagined Prof bursting through, having traced us. Suddenly all of our preparations seemed simplistic and meaningless.

I had led the team to its destruction.

The door opened all the way, revealing a backlit figure. It wasn't Prof, but a younger man, tall and lanky, with pale skin and short black hair. He looked us over, not a glimmer of concern in his eyes, despite facing three armed people.

"That door isn't going to do *at all*," the man said. "Far too easy to get through. I thought you people would be capable!"

"Who are you?" Abraham demanded, eyeing me, waiting to see if I gave the order to fire.

I didn't, though I knew this man. I had several pictures of him in my files.

Larcener, emperor of Atlanta, had come to pay us a visit.

19

"**OH,** put those things down," Larcener said, stepping into the hideout and pushing the door closed. "Bullets can't hurt me. You'll only draw attention."

Unfortunately, he was right. This man was invulnerable in multiple ways. Our guns might as well have been wet noodles.

None of us lowered our weapons.

"What's going on?" I demanded. "Why are you here?"

"Haven't you been paying attention?" Larcener had an unexpectedly nasal voice. "Your friend wants to *kill* me. He's been tearing the whole city apart looking for me! My servants are useless, my Epics too cowardly. They'll switch sides on me in an eyeblink."

He walked forward—making all three of us jump—and

kept right on talking. "I figured you'd know how to hide from him, if anyone does. This place looks *horridly* uncomfortable. Not a cushion in sight, and it smells like wet socks." He shivered visibly, then poked into Abraham's workroom.

We crowded around the doorway as, inside, he spun and flopped backward. A large stuffed chair materialized out of nowhere, catching him. He lounged there. "Someone get me something to drink. And try not to make too much noise. I'm tired. You have no idea how nerve-racking it is to be hunted like a common *rat*."

The three of us lowered our weapons, baffled by the slender Epic, who had started muttering under his breath as he lay, eyes closed, on his new easy chair.

"Um . . . ," I finally ventured. "And if we don't obey you?"

Abraham and Megan looked at me as if I were crazy, but it seemed a valid question to me.

Larcener cracked open an eye. "Huh?"

"What are you going to do," I said, "if we don't obey you?"

"You have to obey me. I'm an Epic."

"You do realize," I said slowly, "that we're the Reckoners."

"Yes."

"So . . . we kinda disobey Epics all the time. I mean, if we listened to what Epics said, we'd be pretty bad at our job."

"Oh?" Larcener said. "And didn't you spend your entire career doing *exactly* what an Epic told you?"

Sparks. Did *everyone* know about that? I supposed it wasn't too tough to guess, now that he'd moved into town. Still. I opened my mouth to object further, but Megan pulled me from the room by my arm, Abraham retreating with us, awkwardly hefting his gun. Cody and Mizzy were on the steps leading down, looking concerned.

We ended up in the middle-floor kitchen, arranged around a narrow saltstone table, speaking in hushed tones.

"Is that really *him*?" Mizzy asked. "Like, the big dude, the king of the city, wazzisnamemagoo?"

"He materialized a chair," I said. "That's a very rare power. It's him."

"Spaaaarks," Mizzy said. "You wanna sneak out and blow the place? I got the explosives all ready."

"Wouldn't harm him," Megan said. "Unless we can engage his weakness."

"Beyond that, this might be his decoy," I said. "Though I'm not sure how likely it is, Larcener's real body could be somewhere else. It would be basically unconscious, in a kind of trance. Breathing, heart beating, but not truly awake."

"Seems a dangerous gamble," Megan said, "considering how scared he's acting. Would he want to leave his real self unprotected like that?"

"Who knows," I said.

"I wonder either way," Abraham said, "why is he here? His claim of seeking refuge is a front, is it not? He is a most powerful Epic. He wouldn't need to—"

Footsteps in the stairwell. We all turned as Larcener climbed up to the second floor. "Where is my drink?" he demanded. "You *seriously* couldn't remember even one simple order? I can already see that my assumption of your limited capacities was a gross *over*estimation."

The team held weapons in nervous grips, subtly turning to form a unified front against the creature. A High Epic. Prowling through our base unrestrained. We were specks of mud on the window; he was a giant, vengeful bottle of spray cleaner.

Extra-strength lemon scent.

I carefully stood from my seat. The others had all been

Reckoners long before me, trained by Prof to be careful, quiet. They'd want to bolt—they'd want to distract Larcener, then flee and set up a different base.

I saw an opportunity instead. "You want to work together," I said to Larcener. "Since we have a common enemy, I'm willing to hear your offer."

Larcener sniffed. "I just want to avoid being murdered. The whole city is turning against me. The *whole city*. Me, the one who protected them, gave them food and shelter in this miserable world! Humans are thankless creatures."

Megan stiffened at that. No, she did *not* like the philosophy that considered humans and Epics to be different species.

"Larcener," I said, "my team is not going to become your servants. I'll let you stay with us, on certain conditions—but *we* are doing *you* a favor."

I could practically hear the breath catch in the throats of the others. Making demands of a High Epic was a sure way to get yourself exploded. But he hadn't hurt us so far, and sometimes this was the only option. Either you juggled the fire, or you let it burn everything down.

"He's made you insolent, I see," Larcener said. "Gave you too much freedom, let you *participate*. If you bring him down, it will be his own fault."

I stood my ground. Finally Larcener's knees bent, a stool—with a plush top—forming for him to settle upon. He slumped. "I could kill you all."

"You could *try*, kiddo," Megan muttered.

I stepped forward, and Larcener looked up at me with a sharp glance, then *cringed*. I'd never seen this behavior from an Epic of his stature. Most of them stood defiant even in the middle of a trap, confident they'd be able to escape it. The only thing that ever seemed to make them uncomfortable was the moment when their weakness exposed them.

I stooped to meet Larcener's eyes. He looked like nothing so much as a frightened child, despite being a few years older than me. He wrapped his arms around himself and turned aside. "I suppose I have no choice," he said. "He'll destroy me otherwise. What are your conditions?"

I blinked. Honestly . . . I hadn't gotten that far. I looked toward the others, who shrugged.

"Um, no killing any of us?" Mizzy said.

"What about the one in the stupid clothing?" Larcener asked, pointing at Cody, in his camo gear and old sports team T-shirt.

"Not even him," I said. Mizzy was probably right to spell it out. Epics could have . . . strange ideas about social mores. "First rule is that you don't hurt us or anyone else we bring here. You stay in the base, and don't use your powers to make our lives difficult."

"Fine," Larcener snapped, wrapping his arms around himself tighter. "But when you're done, I get my city back, right?"

"We'll talk about that later," I said. "For now, I want to know how you found us. If Prof can repeat what you did, then we'll need to pull out immediately."

"Bah, you're fine. I can smell Epics; he can't."

"*Smell* them?" I asked.

"Sure. Like food being cooked, all right? It lets me find Epics to . . . you know . . . ." Steal their powers.

So he was a dowser as well as everything else. I shared a look with Megan, who seemed troubled. We hadn't considered that someone might find us by tracking her powers. Fortunately dowsing was a very rare ability, though it certainly made sense as part of Larcener's original portfolio.

"Dowsers," I said, turning back to him. "Are there any others in the city?"

"No, though that monster who led you has some disc-shaped devices that can do it."

We were safe then. Those discs were like the one we'd had in Newcago; it had required direct contact, and Megan could fool it with her illusions. Prof shouldn't be able to sniff us out.

"There," Larcener said. "See, I'm cooperating. Will someone *finally* get me something to drink?"

"Can't you just make one?" Abraham asked.

"No," Larcener snapped, and didn't offer any further explanation, though I knew anyway. He could create only a limited mass of items, and they faded when he wasn't concentrating on them. Food or drinks he created wouldn't sate, as they'd eventually vanish.

"Very well," I said. "You can stay—but as we said, no hurting us. That includes taking powers from anyone here."

"I already promised that, idiot."

I nodded to Cody, then gestured at Larcener.

Cody tapped the front of his cap in agreement. "Now, what would y'all like to drink?" he said to Larcener. "We have lukewarm water and warm water. Both taste like salt. But on the bright side, I've tested both on old Abraham there, and I'm reasonably confident they won't give ya the runs."

He would fetch Larcener some water, keep him company, and see what he could find out about the man. I grabbed the other three, walking below while Cody distracted the Epic. As we reached the bottom floor, Megan took me by the arm. "I don't like this," she hissed.

"I'm inclined to agree," Abraham said. "High Epics are erratic and untrustworthy. Present company excluded."

"There's something odd about him," I said, shaking my head, looking back up the stairwell and listening to Cody's voice drift down as he started telling Larcener a story about

161

his grandmother over in Scotland. She'd swum to Denmark, apparently?

"I've *felt* that darkness, David," Megan said. "Keeping him in here is like snuggling up to a bomb, content that it's not going to explode simply because you can still hear it ticking."

"Nice simile," I said absently.

"Thanks."

"But inaccurate," I said. "He doesn't follow the pattern, Megan. He's scared, and less defiant than simply arrogant. I don't think he's dangerous. To us right now, at least."

"Are you willing to bet our lives on that feeling, David?" Mizzy asked.

"I've already bet your lives by bringing you here." It was discomforting to say, but it was true. "I've said it before: the only way we're going to win this war against the Epics is by using *other* Epics. Are we going to turn away one of the most powerful when he seems willing to work with us?"

The others fell silent. In the quiet, my mobile buzzed. I glanced at it, half expecting it to be Cody with some addendum to his story that he wanted me to hear. Instead it was Knighthawk.

Your crate is on the move, he wrote.

What, already? I typed back.

Yeah. Out of the warehouse, on its way someplace else. What's going on here? Who ordered that box?

"I need to chase this lead," I said, looking up to the others. "Megan, stay here. If something *does* go wrong with Larcener, you'll have the best chance of getting the others out. Be careful not to touch him, just in case. He can't take your powers without touching you and holding on a good thirty seconds, or so my reports say. Let's be careful and not let him have any direct contact with you."

"Fine," she said. "But it won't come to anything like that.

If I see a hint that he's going dark, I'm grabbing the others and we're bolting."

"Deal," I said. "Abraham, I could use some support on this mission. We'll have to go without Megan's disguises, so it could be dangerous."

"More dangerous than staying here?" he asked, looking upward.

"I don't know, honestly. Depends on how bad a mood our target is in."

20

AFTER we slipped from the hideout, I showed Abraham my mobile, which displayed a map of the city. A red dot from Knighthawk showed the location of our target.

"With it moving like that, it could take hours to chase down," Abraham said with a grunt.

"We'd better get going then," I said, tucking my mobile into my pocket.

"David, in all kindness and peace," Abraham said, "your plans have already made me exhaust myself today, and now you want to walk across the city again. *Ç'a pas d'allure!* One wonders if you have determined I am getting fat. Wait here." He shoved his large bag into my hands—it held his gun, and was way heavier than I'd expected. As I stumbled, he strode across the street toward a vendor who had set up under a small awning.

You going to tell me what this is about? Knighthawk texted me as I waited.

You're a smart man, I wrote back. *Guess.*

I'm a lazy man. And I hate guessing. Despite that, a moment later, he sent me something. *Is this about the caverns, somehow? Like . . . you think maybe Larcener is hiding in them, and you're trying to track him?*

That was a clever guess. *Caverns?* I wrote. *What caverns?*

You know. St. Joseph?

The religious figure?

The city, idiot, Knighthawk sent. *The one that used to be in this area. You really don't know?*

Know what?

Wow. And here I was beginning to think you were some kind of omniscient super-nerd when it came to Epics. I actually know something about them you don't? I could sense the self-satisfaction oozing from the screen.

There's an Epic from St. Joseph, I wrote, *that you think I should know about?*

Jacob Pham.

Drawing a blank.

Give me a moment. I'm reveling.

I looked up toward Abraham, eager to be on with things, but the Canadian man wasn't finished with his haggling yet.

You called him Digzone.

I started, feeling a shock of recognition.

The one who created the Diggers, I wrote. *Back in Newcago.*

Yup, Knighthawk sent. *Before he was driving people mad for Steelheart, he came from a sleepy town out there. Half that side of the state is pocketed with the crazy tunnels and caverns he made. But if you didn't know that, then your little plot with the mobile today couldn't be about finding Larcener in them.*

Digzone. He'd been behind the strange labyrinths underneath Newcago. It felt distinctly odd to think about similar tunnels being out here, cut into the ground.

No, what I'm doing today isn't about finding Larcener, I wrote to Knighthawk. *We don't need to find him. He showed up on our doorstep.*

WHAT?

Sorry. Abraham is back with our bikes. Talk to you in a bit.

Let him chew on that. I pocketed the mobile again as Abraham returned, wheeling two rusty bicycles. I regarded them, dubious. "Those look older than two guys in their sixties."

Abraham cocked his head.

"What?" I asked.

"I'm still surprised, sometimes, at the things that leave your mouth," he said, reclaiming his pack. "These bicycles are old because that was all I felt I could pay for without raising suspicion. These should get us where we want to go. You . . . can ride a bike, can't you?"

"Sure I can," I said, getting onto one of the squeaky things. "At least I used to be able to. Haven't done it in years, but it's like riding a bike, right?"

"Technically, yes."

He watched me with skepticism, which was unwarranted. My hesitance hadn't come from inability, as I proved by riding around on the bike to get used to it.

Bikes reminded me of my father.

I checked my mobile's map—and sent a quick explanation to Knighthawk to keep him from freaking out about Larcener—and we set out, joining a smattering of other cyclists on the street. I hadn't seen these often in Newcago;

in the overstreets, the rich had prided themselves on using working automobiles. On the understreets, things had been too twisty and uneven to make bikes practical.

In Ildithia they made perfect sense. Here, the sides of the streets were lined with cars made of salt, but there was open space in the road. Many of the salt cars had been pushed out of the way—they didn't fuse to the roadway, like things had in Newcago—leaving an open and wide road. It was easy, even when you had to weave around a traffic jam nobody had cleared out. These things must grow again each week.

I enjoyed our ride for a short time, though I couldn't help remembering earlier days. I'd been seven when my father had taught me to ride. Way too late to be first learning; all my friends could already do it, and had started to make fun of me. Sometimes I wished I could just go back and slap myself around. I'd been so timid, so unwilling to act.

After I'd turned seven, Father had decided I was ready. Though I'd whined the whole time, he'd never seemed frustrated. Perhaps teaching me to ride had been a way to distract himself from the eviction notices and an apartment that felt too empty, now that it had only two occupants.

For a moment I was there with him, on the street in front of our building. Life hadn't been good then. We'd been in the middle of a crisis, but I'd had *him*. I remembered his hand on my back as he walked with me, then ran with me, then let go so I could ride on my own for the first time.

And I remembered feeling, suddenly, that I *could* do it. A swelling of emotion had overwhelmed me, one that had almost nothing at all to do with riding a bike. I'd looked back at my father's tired grin and had started to believe—for the first time in months—that everything was going to be okay.

That day, I'd recaptured something. I'd lost so much with

Mom's death, but I still had him. I'd known I could do anything, so long as I still had him.

Abraham pulled up to a street corner and halted, yielding to a couple of horse-drawn wagons bearing grain from the harvest, men with battle rifles riding alongside. I stopped beside him, my head lowered.

"David?" Abraham asked. "David, are you . . . crying?"

"I'm fine," I rasped, checking my mobile. "We turn left here. The crate has stopped moving. We should be able to catch it soon."

Abraham didn't press further and I took off again. I hadn't realized that the pain was still so close to the surface, like a fish who liked to sunbathe. Probably best not to dwell on the memories. Instead, I tried to enjoy the breeze and the thrill of motion. The bikes certainly did beat walking.

We took another corner at an eager speed, then were forced to slow as a group of bikes ahead of us stopped. We pulled to a stop too, and my skin prickled, hairs standing on end. No people on the sidewalks. Nobody carting their possessions toward a new home, as had been prevalent on the other streets. No one leaning out windows they'd broken open.

This roadway was quiet, save for the rattling of bike pedals and a voice, farther up the street.

"Now, this'll just take a minute." A British accent of some flavor I didn't recognize. I grew cold as I caught a glimpse of a man with a shaved head wearing spiked black leather. A little neon sphere hovered to his side, changing colors from red to green. A tag, they sometimes called it. Epics who could manifest their powers visually would sometimes walk around with an obvious display—a glow about them, or a few spinning leaves. Something that said, *Yes, I'm one of* them. *So don't mess with me.*

"David," Abraham said softly.

"Neon," I whispered. "Minor Epic. Light-manipulation powers. No invisibility, but he can put on quite a show—and drill you dead with a laser." Weakness . . . Did my notes have a weakness for him?

He spoke further with the group in front of us while some men in long jackets approached, carrying a device that looked like a plate with a screen on one side. One of the dowsers that Larcener had mentioned. It was indeed identical to the one I'd seen the team use in Newcago.

Neon's team scanned each person in the group ahead of us, then waved them on. *Prof's hunting Larcener,* I thought. *He wouldn't use one of those to try to find us. He knows Megan can beat them.*

Neon's team motioned us forward.

"Loud noises," I whispered, remembering. "If this goes south, start screaming. It will negate his powers."

Abraham nodded, looking far more confident as the two of us wheeled our bikes forward. There was a chance this team had our descriptions—depending on how worried Prof was about the Reckoners. I was relieved when Neon yawned and had his team scan Abraham, with no look of recognition in his eyes.

The dowser approved Abraham, and the team waved him forward. Then they wrapped the scanner's strap around my arm.

And we stood quietly on the street. It took forever, long enough that Neon stepped over, looking annoyed. I started to sweat, preparing to yell. Would he decide to burn me away out of frustration for slowing him down? He wasn't that important an Epic; the minor ones had to be more careful about wanton murder. If they ruined the working population of a city, the High Epics wouldn't have anyone to serve them.

Finally, lethargically, the machine gave a response. "Huh,"

169

Neon said. "Haven't had it take that long before. Let's search the nearby buildings. Maybe someone's in them, making our machine flip." He unhooked the device and waved me away. "Get outta here."

I moved, noticing as I passed that the dowser had given me a negative reading, as it should. I was no Epic.

No matter what Regalia claimed.

I spent the rest of the ride feeling sick, remembering those moments confronting my reflection in the water. Listening to her awful promise.

You were angry at Prof for hiding things from the team, a voice inside me whispered. *Aren't you doing exactly the same?*

That was stupid. There was nothing to hide.

We reached the location where the crate had stopped moving: a street lined with three- and four-story apartment buildings. After two days in the city, I was well aware that the powerful clans looked for locations like this, while what had once been rich suburban homes were now widely ignored. In a world of Epics and rival gangs, living space was far less valuable than security.

The two of us stopped at the mouth of the street. A group of young men no older than me lounged here holding an assortment of old weapons, including one teenager with a crossbow of all things. A large flag flying the emblem of a stingray fluttered above one of the buildings.

"We're not recruiting," one of the youths said to me. "Beat it."

"You have a visitor among you," I said to them, hoping my guess was correct. "An outsider. Give this person our descriptions."

The youths shared a few looks, then one ran off to do as I ordered. Within moments I knew I'd guessed *something* right, because a good number of older men and women with really *nice* guns came stalking down the street toward us.

"Uh . . . David?" Abraham asked. "Do you want to say something more, perhaps? That we . . ."

He trailed off as he spotted one person among the group wearing a hoodie, rifle slung over her arm. The hood made her face difficult to see, but several locks of red hair poked out next to her chin.

Tia.

21

ABRAHAM didn't say anything as the two of us were quickly surrounded by armed people and hustled off the street toward one of the apartment buildings. He simply gave Tia a friendly salute, one finger tapping the middle of his brow. He'd obviously figured out what we were doing long ago.

Tia's people shuffled us into a room with no windows, lit only by a row of candles that were slowly melting onto the countertop of an old kitchen bar. Why bother with candlesticks when your home would be dissolving anyway? Though the room did have an actual wooden door on it, which was rare in this city. It would have to be carted each week to the next location and reattached.

One of the armed Ildithians relieved us of our weapons, while another shoved us down into chairs. Tia stood at the back of the group, arms folded, her face shrouded by that hood. She was slender and short, and her lips—which I could see within the hood's shadows—were drawn into a line of disapproval. She was the Reckoners' second in command, and one of the smartest people I'd ever met.

"David," she said calmly, "in Babilar, you and I met together in our hideout, after you'd gone out to deliver supplies. Tell me what we discussed."

"What does that matter? Tia! We need to talk about—"

"Answer the question, David," Abraham said. "She is testing to see if we are ourselves."

I swallowed. Of course. Any number of Epics could have created doppelgangers of the Reckoners at Prof's command. I tried to recall the event she was talking about. Why hadn't she picked something more memorable, like when I'd first joined the Reckoners?

She needs something Prof wouldn't know about, I realized.

I started to sweat. I'd been out on the submarine, and . . . *Sparks,* it was hard to think with those armed men and women staring at me, each as angry as a cabdriver who'd discovered I'd ralphed all over his back seat.

"I met with Prof that day," I said. "I came to the base to report, and we talked about some of the other Epics in Babilar."

"And what . . . interesting metaphor did you make?"

"Sparks, you expect me to *remember* those?"

"I've heard a few that were rather hard to forget," Abraham noted. "Despite a great deal of time trying."

"Not helping," I muttered. "Uh . . . mmm . . . Oh! I talked about using toothpaste for hair gel. No, wait. Ketchup. Ketchup for hair gel, but as I think about it, toothpaste would have been a *way* better metaphor. It hardens stronger, I think, and—"

"It's him," Tia said. "Put your guns down."

"How did you know she was with us, kid?" said one of the Ildithians, a stocky older woman with thinning hair.

"Your shipments," I said.

"We get shipments twice a week," the woman said. "As do most of the sizable families in the city. How would *that* have led you here?"

"Well . . . ," I said.

Tia groaned, putting her hand to her face. "My cola?"

I nodded. I'd spotted it in the crate that day when I'd first seen Prof. Not just any cola; the brand she loved. It was expensive, unique, and worth playing a hunch on.

"I told you," said another Ildithian, a bulky man with a face like a barbecue grill. In that it was ugly. "I told you that accepting this woman among us would be trouble. You said we wouldn't be in danger!"

"I never said that," replied the woman with thinning hair. "I said that helping her was something we needed to do."

"This is worse than you think, Carla," Tia said. "David is smarter than he might first seem, but it's hardly outside of reason that something *he* discovered might be discovered by someone else."

"Uh . . . ," I said.

They all looked at me.

"Now that you mention it," I said, "Prof might know about the cola. At least, he spotted some of it in the boxes the other day."

The people in the room froze, then started shouting to one another, sending messengers, warning their lookouts. Tia pulled off her hood, exposing her short red hair, and rubbed her forehead. "I'm a fool," she said, barely audible over the shouted orders from Carla. "They put in their supply order

174

and asked if I needed anything. I barely gave it any thought. A few cans of cola would be nice. . . ."

Nearby, the ugly Ildithian man entered with the crate that had held the cola and dug through it, discovering the broken mobile. "A Knighthawk mobile?" he said. "I thought these were untraceable."

"It's only a shell," I said quickly. "Convenient to put the bug in, since it had a power supply and antenna." I wasn't giving everything up.

The man accepted that and tossed the mobile to Carla. She removed the battery, then moved to the side of the room with several other people, where they held a quiet conference. When I stood up, ugly-face glared at me, hand on his pistol, so I sat back down.

"Tia?" I asked. It was odd to see her like this, with a rifle slung over her shoulder. She had always run operations for us from positions of relative safety; I didn't think I'd ever seen her fire a weapon. "Why didn't you contact us?"

"Contact you how, David?" she asked, sounding tired. She stepped closer to me and Abraham. "Jonathan had access to our mobile network and knew every one of our hideouts. I didn't even know if you'd survived."

"We tried contacting you in Babilar," I said.

"I was in hiding. He . . ." She sighed, sitting down on the table next to us. "He was hunting me, David. He came directly to where I'd been set up during the Regalia hit, pulled the sub out of the water, and crushed it. I was out by then, thankfully. But I heard him calling for me. Pleading, begging me to help him with the darkness." She closed her eyes. "We both knew that if this day came, I'd be in more danger than anyone else in the Reckoners."

"I . . ." What did I say to that? I could imagine how it would feel to have the one you loved begging for your help, all the while knowing it was a trap. I imagined struggling to not give in, to ignore their pleas.

I wouldn't have been strong enough. Sparks, I'd chased Megan halfway across the country, despite her threatening to kill me.

"I'm sorry, Tia," I whispered.

She shook her head. "I'm prepared for this. Jon and I talked about it, like I said. I can do him one last favor." She opened her eyes. "I see you had the same instinct."

"Not . . . exactly," Abraham said, sharing a look with me.

"Tia," I said. "We've cracked it."

"It?"

"The secret," I said, growing eager. "The weaknesses, the darkness—they're tied together. Epics all have nightmares about their weaknesses."

"Of course they do," Tia said. "The weaknesses are the only thing that can make them feel powerless."

"It's more than that, Tia," I said. "Way more! The weaknesses are often tied to something the person feared *before* getting their powers. A phobia, a terror. It seems . . . well, I haven't talked to enough of them, but it seems like becoming an Epic makes the fear worse. Either way, stopping—or at least managing—the darkness *is* possible."

"What do you mean?"

"Fears," I said quietly, only to her. "If the Epic confronts their fear, it drives back the darkness."

"Why?"

"Um . . . does it matter?"

"You're the one who kept saying that this should all make sense. If there really is a logic behind the weaknesses, then shouldn't there be a logical reason for the darkness?"

"Yeah . . . yeah, there should be." I sat back. "Megan says—"

"Megan. You brought *her*? She's one of them, David!"

"She's why we know this works. Tia, we can save him."

"Don't give me that hope."

"But—"

"Don't *give me that hope*." She glared at me. "Don't you *dare* do that, David Charleston. You don't think this is hard enough? Planning to kill him? Wondering if there isn't something more I should do? He made me promise. I'm going to keep that promise, damn you."

"Tia," Abraham said softly.

She looked at him as I sat there, stunned by her tone.

"David is right, Tia," Abraham said in his calm way. "We must try to bring him back. If we cannot save Jonathan Phaedrus, then we might as well give up this fight. We cannot kill them all."

Tia shook her head. "You believe he's found the secret, after all this time?"

"I believe he has a good theory," Abraham said. "And Megan *has* learned to control the darkness. If we do not test David's theories, we are fools. He is right. We cannot kill them all. We've been trying the same thing for too long; it is time to do something different."

I suddenly felt very, *very* smart for having brought Abraham along. Tia listened to him. Heck, a rabid Chihuahua having a seizure would stop and listen when Abraham spoke.

The door burst open, and a frantic young woman scrambled into the room. "Sir!" she said to Carla. "Crooknecks. The whole family, three hundred strong, and then some. All armed, and coming this way. He's with them."

"He?" the woman, Carla, asked.

"The new Epic. Sir, we're surrounded."

The room fell silent. The ugly man who had disagreed

with Carla earlier turned to her. He didn't speak, but the implication was there in his dark expression. *You've doomed us.*

Abraham stood up, drawing all eyes. "I will need my gun."

"Like hell," Carla said. "You caused this."

"No, I did," Tia said, rising. "We're just fortunate that David got here first."

Carla growled, but then barked for her people to prepare for battle. For all the good it would do. Prof could destroy this neighborhood on his own.

Someone tossed Abraham's pack to him as others rushed out the door. Carla moved to follow them, perhaps to get a look at the foe herself.

"Carla," Tia said. "You can't fight them."

"I doubt they'll give us a choice."

"They might if you give them what they want."

Carla looked at her companions, who nodded. They'd been thinking the same thing.

"No!" I said, standing up. "You can't turn her over."

"You have five minutes to prepare, Tia," Carla said. "I'll send runners to talk to the oncoming force, see if I can get them to demand you. We can act like we didn't know who you were."

She left us in that windowless box of a room, posting two conspicuous guards at the door.

"I can't believe—" I began.

Tia cut me off. "Don't be a child, David. The Stingray Clan was good enough to take me in, listen to my plans. We can't ask them to die protecting me."

"But . . ." I looked at her, pained. "Tia, he'll kill you."

"Eventually," she said. "I might have some time."

"He murdered Val and Exel immediately."

"Yes, but me he'll want to interrogate first."

"You *do* know it, don't you," I said softly. "His weakness."

She nodded. "He'd rip apart this entire city to get at me. We'll be lucky if he doesn't murder everyone in this district, to be certain the secret hasn't gotten out."

It made me sick. Steelheart had done something similar on that day, so long ago, when my father and I had seen him bleed.

Tia pressed something into my hand. A data chip. "My plans," she said. "For bringing Jon down. I've had variations on this in mind for years, just in case. But I've tailored it specifically to this city and what he's doing here. David, there's something bigger going on with him. I've been able to get people in to scout near him. I think Regalia must have given him something—some kind of intel on Calamity. I think she *sent him here*."

"Tia," I said, looking to Abraham for support. "I suspect some of the same things. But you can't go with Prof. We *need* you."

"Then stop him," she said, "before he kills me."

"But—"

She crossed the room quickly and grabbed the broken mobile from a table. "You can track this if I stick the battery back in?"

"Yeah," I said.

"Good. Use it to see where he takes me. I didn't tell any of the Ildithians his weakness, and I can hide behind that truth for a time. They might be safe, and if he asks about you all, I can say I got separated from you in Babilar. He'd spot a lie from me, but I won't be lying."

"He will break you eventually, Tia," Abraham said. "He is nothing if not persistent."

She nodded. "Yes, but he'll act kindly at first. I'm certain of it; he'll try and bring me to his side. Only after I refuse will he get brutal." She grimaced. "Trust me, I have *no intention* of being some kind of noble martyr. I'm counting on you. Stop him, and get me out."

Abraham saluted again, more solemn this time. Sparks. He was going to let it happen.

People were calling outside the room. Carla ducked back in. "They've said we have five minutes to turn over the outsider. I think they believe that we didn't know who you were. They also don't seem to know about the other two."

"Jon's paranoia works for us," Tia said. "If *he'd* been hiding here, he'd never have told you who he really was. He'll believe that I was trying to blend in." She looked toward me. "Are you going to make this difficult?"

"No," I said, resigned. "But we *will* get you out."

"Good." She hesitated. "I'll see if I can dig up what he's working on here, what his plot is for this city."

"Tia," Carla said from the doorway. "I'm sorry."

Tia nodded, turning to leave.

"Wait," I said, then continued in a whisper. "The weakness, Tia. What is it?"

"You know it."

I frowned.

"I don't know if your theory is correct," she said. "But . . . yes, he has nightmares about something. Think, David. In all our time together, what is the one thing you've truly seen him fear?"

I blinked, and realized she was right. I did know. It was obvious. "His powers," I whispered.

She nodded, grim.

"But how does that work?" I demanded. "He can obviously use his own powers. They don't . . . negate themselves."

"Unless someone else is using them."

Someone else . . . Prof was a gifter.

"When we were younger," Tia whispered urgently, "we experimented with Jon's powers. He can create lances of light, forcefield spears. He gifted the ability to me. And I—by accident—launched one of those lances at Jon. David, the wound he took that day *didn't regenerate*. His powers couldn't fix it; he took months to recover, healing like a normal person. We never told anyone, not even Dean."

"So someone gifted with one of his powers . . ."

"Can negate the rest. Yes." She glanced at Carla, who was waving urgently, then leaned in to me, continuing to speak very quietly. "He fears them, David. The powers granted him, the weight they bring. And so he lives his life with a great dichotomy—he takes every opportunity he can to gift his powers away, to let the team use them so he doesn't have to. But each time he does, he gives them a weapon that could be used against him."

She gripped my arm. "Get me out," she said, then turned and rushed to Carla, who led her from the room.

They let us watch. From a distance, using scopes atop one of the apartment buildings, where they'd hollowed out a nice little hidden sniper nest. We were attended by a couple of guards who—we'd been promised—would let us go, assuming that Prof took Tia and left without demanding more.

Again I had to watch a man I loved and respected act like someone else. Someone proud and imperious, bathed in a faint green glow from the forcefield disc he stood upon.

I felt so powerless as the Ildithians led Tia up to him, then forced her down on her knees. They bowed and retreated from Prof. I waited, sweating.

Tia was right. He didn't kill her immediately. He surrounded her in a forcefield, then turned and stalked away, her orb trailing behind him.

He never gifted us that power, I thought. *He gifted us forcefield protection in the form of the "jackets," but only in small amounts. The globes, those spears I saw him use the other day . . . He didn't let us know about those abilities.*

For fear that someday they might be used to kill him. Sparks, how were we going to get him to give away his abilities? I knew his weakness, but approaching it still seemed impossible.

As Tia and Prof left, I closed my eyes, feeling like a coward. Not because I'd failed to save Tia, but because of how badly I'd been wanting her to come with us.

She would have taken over, been in charge. She'd have known what to do. Unfortunately, that burden was now back on me.

22

I was somewhere dark and warm again.

I had memories . . . voices, like my own, that spoke in harmony. Together we were one. I'd lost those voices somehow, but I wanted them, needed them. I felt an ache, being separated from them.

At least I was warm, and safe, and comfortable.

I knew what to expect, though I could not brace myself in the dream. So the crashes of thunder still shocked me. The peals of terrible, blaring sound, like a hundred raging wolves. Garish, cold, harsh light. Snapping, attacking, assaulting, *smothering*. It came at me, and sought to destroy me.

I shot bolt upright, suddenly awake.

I was back on the floor of the upper room of our hideout. Megan, Cody, and Mizzy slept nearby. Abraham was on watch tonight. With an unknown Epic in the hideout, none of us were comfortable sleeping on our own or in pairs, and we were certain always to post a guard.

Sparks . . . that nightmare. That *terrible* nightmare. My pulse was still racing and my skin was clammy. My blanket was soaked in sweat; I could probably have wrung out an entire bucketful.

I'm going to have to tell the others, I thought as I sat there in the dark, trying to catch my breath. Nightmares were directly tied to Epics and their weaknesses. If I was having a persistent one . . . well, it might mean something.

I kicked off my blankets and realized that Megan wasn't in her place. She got up in the night a lot.

I picked my way around the others toward the hall. I didn't like this fear. I wasn't the coward I'd been as a child. I could face anything. *Anything.*

I reached the hallway and checked the room across from ours. Empty. Where had Megan gotten to?

Abraham and I had returned from the Stingray Clan's base late enough that we'd decided to call it a night and save digging into the new information Tia had given us for tomorrow. I'd told them Prof's weakness, which had set them thinking. That was enough for the moment.

I continued to the steps, my feet bare on the saltstone floor. We had to be very careful with water; spill it, and the ground started to rub off on your feet. Even as it was, I woke up in the mornings with salt crust on my legs. Building a city out of something that could dissolve was decidedly *worse* than building one out of steel. Fortunately I didn't much notice the smell any longer, and even the dryness was starting to feel normal.

I found Abraham on the middle floor, in the kitchen. He

was bathed in the light of his mobile, the rtich on his hands and a large globe of mercury hovering in front of him. The mercury certainly had an otherworldly cast: perfectly reflective, it undulated as Abraham moved his hands around it. He drew his palms apart, which caused the large globe of mercury to elongate like a loaf of French bread. The way reflections distorted and shifted on its mirrored surface made me imagine it was showing us a different, distorted world.

"We must be careful," Abraham said softly. "I think I've learned to contain the fumes this metal releases, but perhaps it would be wise for me to find another place to practice."

"I don't like splitting us up," I said, getting myself a cup of water from the large plastic cooler we kept on the counter.

Abraham spread his palm out, and the mercury made a disc in front of him, like a wide plate—or a shield. "It is marvelous," he said. "It conforms perfectly to my commands. And look at this."

He brought the disc down, flat portion facing the ground, then hesitantly stepped *onto* it. It held him.

"Sparks," I said. "You can fly."

"Not exactly," Abraham said. "I cannot move it far while I'm standing on it, and it needs to be nearby for me to manipulate it. But watch this."

The disc of mercury rippled, and a piece of it siphoned off, forming *steps* in front of Abraham. Very thin, very narrow, reflective metal steps. He was able to walk up them, stooping down as he got closer and closer to the ceiling.

"This will be of great use against Prof," Abraham said. "It is very strong. Perhaps I could use it to counteract his forcefields."

"Yeah."

Abraham glanced at me. "Not enthusiastic?"

"Just distracted. Is Larcener still awake down there?"

"Last I checked," Abraham said. "He does not seem to sleep."

We'd discussed what to do with him, but had come to no conclusions. So far though, he hadn't posed much of a threat.

"Where's Megan?" I asked.

"Haven't seen her."

That was odd. If she'd left, she would have had to pass this way—and I hadn't seen her on the top floor, which was pretty small. Maybe Abraham hadn't noticed her slipping by.

He continued to work with the rtich, climbing down his steps and creating other shapes. Watching him was hard, but mainly for juvenile reasons. We'd all agreed that Abraham should practice with the device, with Cody or Mizzy as backup. Abraham was our primary point man now.

But sparks, that device looked *cool*. Hopefully it would survive our activities here. Once we had Prof and Tia back, I could return to running point, where I belonged.

I left Abraham and walked down to the bottom floor to check on Larcener. I stopped in the doorway to his room.

Wow.

The once-bare walls were now draped with soft red velvet. A set of lanterns glowed on mahogany tables. Larcener lay on a couch as elegant as any we'd had in the Babilar hideout, wearing a pair of large headphones, with his eyes closed. I couldn't hear what, if anything, he was listening to—the headphones were likely connected wirelessly to a mobile.

I stepped into the room. Sparks, it seemed way larger than it had before. I paced it off, and found that it *was* bigger.

Spatial distortion, I thought, adding that to his list of powers. Calamity, that was an incredible power. I'd only heard *rumors* about Epics having it. And his ability to materialize objects from thin air . . .

186

"You could beat him," I said.

Larcener said nothing, remaining on his couch, not opening his eyes.

"Larcener," I said, more loudly.

He started, then ripped off his headphones and shot me a glare. "What?"

"You could beat him," I repeated. "Prof . . . if you were to face him, you might be able to win. I know you have multiple prime invincibilities. Add on top of those the ability to create anything, to distort space . . . you could beat him."

"Of course I couldn't. Why do you think I'm *here* with you useless idiots?"

"I haven't figured that out yet."

"I don't fight," Larcener said, moving to put his headphones back on. "I'm not allowed."

"By who?"

"By myself. Let others do the fighting. *My* place is to observe. Even ruling this city is probably inappropriate for me."

People, including me, tended to work under the assumption that all Epics were essentially the same: selfish, destructive, narcissistic. But while they *did* share these traits, they also had their own individual levels of strangeness. Obliteration quoted scripture and sought—it seemed—to destroy all life on the planet. Regalia channeled her darkness toward greater and greater schemes. Nightwielder, in Newcago, insisted on working through lesser intermediaries.

Larcener seemed to have his own psychosis. I reached into a bowl on a little marble pedestal beside the door. Glass beads trickled between my fingers. No—diamonds.

"I don't suppose," I said, "you could make me a—"

"Stop."

I glanced at Larcener.

"I should have made this clear at the start," he said. "You

get nothing from me. I am not here to give you gifts, nor to make your life easier. I will *not* become some servant."

I sighed, dropping the diamonds. "You don't sleep," I said, trying a different tack.

"So?"

"You gained that power from another Epic, I assume. Did you take that one specifically because of the nightmares?"

He stared at me for a moment, then suddenly tossed his headphones aside and leaped to his feet. He took a single step, but crossed the wide distance between us in an instant.

"How do you know about my nightmares?" he demanded, looming in front of me. Larger. Taller.

I gaped, my heart racing again. Before this, he'd been *determinedly* lazy with us. Now—dwarfed by Larcener, who stood seven feet tall, with a terrible sneer and wild eyes—I felt I was a moment from being destroyed.

"I . . ." I swallowed. "All Epics have them, Larcener. Nightmares."

"Nonsense," he said. "They are mine. I am unique."

"You can talk to Megan," I said. "She'll tell you she has them. Or you can go find any Epic and beat it out of them. They have nightmares, which are tied to their weaknesses. What the person fears becomes—"

"Stop your lies!" Larcener shouted, then growled at me and spun on his heel, stalking back to his couch and throwing himself down. "Epics are weak because they are fools. They will destroy this world. Give men power, and they abuse it. That is all one needs to know."

"And you've never felt it?" I asked. "The sudden darkness that comes from using your powers, the lack of empathy? The desire to destroy?"

"What are you talking about?" he said. "Silly little man."

I hesitated, trying to read him—and having a tough time

of it. Maybe he was constantly consumed by the darkness. He certainly acted arrogant enough.

But he hadn't hurt any of us. He liked to order us around, but not in the way of an Epic, I realized. In the way of a spoiled child.

"You faced it young," I guessed. "You grew up as an Epic, able to get whatever you wanted, but you never felt the darkness."

"Don't be stupid," he said. "I *forbid* you to speak of this idiocy anymore. Darkness? You want to blame the terrible things that Epics do on some nebulous idea or feeling? Bah. Men destroy themselves because that's what they deserve, not because of some mystical force or emotion!"

He has to be facing it continually, I thought. *Whatever his fear is, he must see it every day, and defeat it.* That was what we'd learned with Megan; if she didn't stay vigilant, the darkness crept back toward her.

I slipped from his palace of a room.

"I *do* hate you, you understand," Larcener called from behind.

I glanced in again. He lounged on his couch, and like that he really did look like a kid. A teenager with his headphones on, trying to ignore the world.

"You deserve this," he continued. "People are evil to the core. That's what the Epics prove. That's why you're dying out." He closed his eyes and tipped his head back, away from me.

I shivered, then checked the other room—which was now packed with supplies—for Megan. Not there. Above, Abraham was still practicing in the kitchen. On the top floor, I knocked outside the small bathroom—we'd resorted to using buckets again, unfortunately. Finally I peeked into the other bedroom once more.

Empty. Where—

Wait. Something about that dark room seemed too . . . um . . . dark? I frowned and walked into the room, passing through a veil of something. Megan sat cross-legged on the floor on the other side, a small candle on the floor beside her. She was staring out the wall.

Which was now gone.

The wall of the hideout was simply . . . gone. And there was no city beyond either. Megan looked out upon a nighttime landscape of blowing fields beneath a billion stars. She was rubbing her hand.

She noticed me as I walked up, first reaching for the gun on the floor beside her, then relaxing when she realized who it was. "Hey," she said. "I didn't wake you, did I?"

"Nah," I said, settling down beside her. "That's quite the view."

"Easy to make," she said. "In so many of the branching possibilities, Ildithia didn't come this direction. It was simple to find one where it isn't here, and the field is empty."

"So what is this, then?" I asked, reaching out. "Is it real?"

My hand felt something—the saltstone wall, though it looked like I was touching empty space.

"Just a shadow, for now," she said.

"But you can go further," I said. "Like you did when saving me from Knighthawk."

"Yes."

"You brought Firefight through," I continued, feeling again at the invisible wall. "Not just his shadow, not just a . . . projection of the other world. He himself was here."

"I see your brain working, David," she said, cautious. "What are you thinking?"

"Is there a reality where Prof hasn't given in to his powers?"

"Probably," Megan said. "That's a little change, and very recent."

"So you might be able to bring him here."

"Not for very long," Megan said. "What? You want to replace him in the team? My solutions are temporary. It . . ." She trailed off, eyes widening. "You don't want a new Prof as a replacement. You want one to *fight ours*."

"His fear is his powers, Megan. I initially tried to think how to trick him into gifting his abilities to someone—but there's no reason we have to do that when we have you. If you can bring a version of Prof in from another world, we can make them face off, and *bam* . . . we engage Prof's weakness. Make him confront his own powers in the most direct way possible, and therefore help him defeat the darkness."

She looked thoughtful. "We could try it," she said. "But David, I don't like relying on the powers. My powers."

I looked to where she was rubbing her hand. A fresh burn. I glanced at the candle.

"This might be the only way," I told her. "He certainly won't be expecting it. If we're going to save Tia . . ."

"You still want me to practice," she said. "Go further than I've gone before."

"Yes."

"That's dangerous."

I didn't reply. I knew it was, and I knew I shouldn't be asking this of her. It wasn't fair. But sparks . . . Tia was in Prof's hands. We had to do something.

"All right," Megan said. "I'm going to try to alter reality a little further. You might want to move back from the wall."

I did so. Megan's face darkened in concentration.

And the entire building vanished, leaving me alone, hanging in the sky, in an unfamiliar world.

23

MY stomach lurched as I dropped a good twenty feet before crashing into some thick brush. The growth broke my fall, but the landing knocked the wind out of me. I lay there, trying to gasp but unable to draw in breath. Finally, painfully, I managed to suck air into my lungs.

A star-filled sky spun and wavered above me, my watering eyes making it difficult to see. Sparks . . . there were so many stars, and in such strange patterns. Clusters, ribbons, fields of light upon the black. I still wasn't used to it. In Newcago the sky had been veiled in darkness by Nightwielder, so I'd had to imagine stars. Over the years my memories had grown fuzzy, and I'd started to imagine the stars spaced evenly, like in my vague recollections of picture books.

The reality was far messier. More like cereal spilled on the floor. I groaned and managed to sit up. *Well,* I thought, look-ing around, *I probably deserved that.* What had happened? Had I been sucked into Megan's shadow dimension?

It seemed that way at first, though I was confronted with an oddity: Ildithia was here, off in the distance. Hadn't Megan said that in her shadow world, it hadn't come this way?

Something else was wrong. It took me an embarrassingly long time to figure it out.

Where was Calamity?

The stars were all there, sprinkling the sky, but the omni-present red spot was gone. That was discomforting. Calamity was *always* there at night. Even in Newcago it had pierced the darkness, glaring at us.

I climbed to my feet, staring upward, trying to find it. And as I stood, everything around me fuzzed.

I found myself in our hideout again, near Megan, who was shaking me. "David? Oh, sparks, *David!*"

"I'm fine," I said, trying to take it all in. Yes, I was back, right where I'd been standing when I'd fallen. The wall was no longer transparent. "What happened?"

"I sent you through by accident," Megan said. "You van-ished completely, until you popped back out. Sparks!"

"Interesting."

"Terrifying," she said. "Who knows what you might have found on the other side, David? What if I'd dropped you into a world where the atmosphere was different, and you suf-focated?"

"It was like our world," I said, rubbing my side and look-ing around. "Ildithia was there, except in the distance."

"What . . . really?" she asked. "Are you sure? I specifi-cally picked a world where this region was empty, so I'd have a good view."

I settled down. "Yeah. Can you reach out to the same world again, on purpose?"

"I don't know," she said. "The things I do, they just kind of *happen*. Like bending your elbow."

"Or eating a bagel," I said, nodding.

"Not . . . actually like that, but whatever." She hesitated, then settled down on the floor beside me. A moment later, Cody peeked in on us—apparently she'd been too loud when she'd cried out to me. Megan's veil of dark fog had vanished, and he could see us.

"Everything all right?" he asked, rifle in hand.

"Depends on your definition," Megan said, lying back on the floor. "David convinced me to do something stupid."

"He's good at that," Cody said, leaning against the doorframe.

"We're testing her powers," I said to Cody.

"Ach," he said. "And y'all didn't warn me first?"

"What would you have done?" I asked.

"Gotten up and eaten some haggis," Cody said. "Always nice to have a good haggis before someone accidentally destroys your hideout in a burst of unexpected Epic power."

I frowned. "What's haggis?"

"Don't ask," Megan said. "He's just being silly."

"I can show him," Cody said, thumbing over his shoulder.

"Wait," Megan said. "You actually have some?"

"Yeah. Found it in the market the other day. Guess they believe in using the whole animal round here, eh?" He paused. "The stuff's *nasty*, of course."

Megan frowned. "Isn't it like a Scottish national dish or something?"

"Sure, sure," Cody said, sauntering into the room. "Being nasty is what *makes* it Scottish. Only the bravest of men dare eat it. Proves you're a warrior. Like wearing a kilt on a cold, windy day." He settled down with us. "So what's up with the powers?"

"Megan sent me into an alternate dimension," I said.

"Neat," Cody said, digging in his pocket and pulling out a chocolate bar. "You didn't bring me a mutant bunny or something, did ya?"

"No mutant bunnies," I said. "But Calamity wasn't there."

"Now that's even *stranger*," Cody said, taking a bite of the chocolate bar. He grimaced.

"What?" I asked.

"Tastes like dirt, lad," he said. "I miss the old days."

"Megan," I said, "can you bring up an image of that world again?"

She looked at me, skeptical. "You want to keep going?"

"By the measuring stick of Epic powers," I said, "this doesn't seem *too* dangerous. I mean, you dropped me into another world, but I popped back in under a minute."

"And if that's a result of lack of practice?" Megan asked. "What if, in doing it more, it gets more dangerous?"

"Then that means you're learning to affect things more permanently," I said. "Which is going to be a huge advantage to us. It's worth the risk."

She drew her lips to a line, but seemed persuaded. Maybe I *was* a little too good at getting people to do stupid things. Prof had accused me of that on more than one occasion.

Megan waved at the wall she'd changed before, and it vanished, once again providing the view of an empty plain of grass.

"Now the other side," I said, pointing at the wall with the doorway Cody had come through.

"That's dangerous," she warned. "Trapping us between

two shadows means that the other dimension is more likely to bleed into . . . But you don't care, do you? All right. You owe me a back rub for this, by the way."

The opposite wall vanished, and it now seemed like the three of us were in a solitary building on the plains, with two walls cut out. The new perspective gave us a view of what I'd seen before: Ildithia in the distance.

"Huh," Cody said, standing up. He unslung his rifle and used the scope to inspect the city.

"The city is in a different place in this dimension," Megan said. "Not surprising. It's easier to view dimensions that are similar to ours, so I should have guessed."

"Nah, that's not it," Cody said. "Ildithia is in the same place in that dimension. But your window isn't opening where our hideout would be there."

"What?" Megan said, standing up.

"See those fields? Those are the eastern side of Ildithia, marked by that stand of trees. Same as in our dimension. The city's in the same place; we're merely looking at it from the outside."

Megan seemed troubled.

"What's the problem?" I asked her.

"I always assumed that my shadows had a direct location connection," she said. "That if I pulled something through, it was because that was what was happening in another dimension, right where I was."

"We're talking about altering the shape of reality," Cody said with a shrug. "Why should location matter, lass?"

"I don't know," she said. "It just . . . it's not what I've always thought. It makes me wonder how much I've been wrong about."

"No Calamity," I said, walking as close to the invisible wall as I dared. "Megan, what if the shadows you grab are always from the *same* world, a parallel one to ours? I keep seeing Firefight during moments when you use your powers. That seems to indicate that the shadows you're pulling are always from his world."

"Yeah," she said, "that or there are hundreds upon hundreds of different versions of him, and each world has one."

Cody grunted. "This sounds like a headache."

"You have no idea," Megan said. She sighed. "I've done things that your theory can't explain, David. Though perhaps there *is* one similar parallel world that I reach into most often—but if my powers can't find what I need there, they reach farther. And right after I reincarnate, they go anywhere, do anything."

I stared at that distant Ildithia for as long as Megan kept the shadow active. A world parallel to our own, a world without Calamity. What would it be like? How were there still Epics, if there was no Calamity to give them powers?

Eventually Megan let the images vanish, and I gave her a neck rub to try to deal with the headache all of this had given her. She kept glancing at the candle, but didn't reach for it. Before long, all three of us returned to our beds. We needed sleep.

Tomorrow we would dig into Tia's plan and try to figure out how to save her.

PART THREE

24

I rubbed my hand along the saltstone shelf, disconcerted to find that my fingers left gouges. I dusted my hand off, sprinkling pink sand to the floor. As I stood there, the shelf on the wall *split* in the middle, crumbling away. Salt ran down like sand through an hourglass.

"Uh, Abraham?" I said as he passed.

"We have a day left before we need to leave, David," he said.

"Our hideout is *literally* disintegrating."

"Accessories and ornaments crumble first," he said, ducking into our third-floor spare bedroom—the place where Megan and I had experimented with her powers the night before. "The floors and walls will hold for a time yet."

I didn't find this very comforting. "We'll still have to move soon. Find a new hideout."

"Cody's been working on that. He says he has a few options to talk to you about later today."

"What about the caverns?" I asked. "Under the land the city is passing over? The ones made by Digzone? We could hide there."

"Perhaps," Abraham said.

I followed Abraham into the room, where Cody was whistling and sweeping salt into a pile. Apparently the saltstone we'd grown disintegrated at the same rate as the stone around it. Soon this entire region would collapse, and the salt would vanish.

Morning light shone through the thinning saltstone roof above. I settled in on a stool, one of the ones Cody had purchased during a scrounging mission. It was strange to be in a city where there wasn't trash to pick through; Ildithia just moved away, leaving behind anything people discarded. It left a sparseness I hadn't seen in Newcago or Babilar.

Megan came in but didn't sit. She leaned against the wall, arms folded, wearing her jacket and jeans. Abraham knelt by the wall, fiddling with the imager, which he'd calibrated earlier. Cody lifted his old broom and shook his head. "Ya know, I think I might be making more salt than I'm cleaning up." He sighed, walking over and settling down on a stool beside me.

Finally Mizzy entered, bearing one of the team's rugged laptops. She tossed a data chip to Abraham, who plugged it into the imager.

"This isn't going to be pretty, guys," Mizzy noted.

"Cody is on the team," Abraham said. "We are accustomed to things that are not pretty."

Cody tossed the broom at him.

Abraham engaged the imager, and the walls and floor went black. A three-dimensional projection of Ildithia appeared on them, but one drawn as a red wireframe. We seemed to be hovering above it.

At one time this had been disorienting to me, but I was used to it now. I leaned forward, peering down through the floor toward the large city. It seemed to be growing and disintegrating at an accelerated rate in this illustration, though the details weren't terribly specific.

"It's a time-lapse computer model from Tia's data," Mizzy said. "I thought it was cool. The city moves at a constant rate, so you can predict what its shape and look will be for any given day. Apparently whoever controls the city can steer it using a big wheel that grows in one of the buildings downtown."

"What happens if it hits another city?" I asked, uncomfortable. In the time-lapse model, the city looked *alive*—like some kind of crawling creature, buildings shooting up like stretching spines.

"Collisions are messy," Abraham said. "When I scouted here years back, I asked that very question. If Ildithia intersects a city it grows into the cracks, buildings squeezing between buildings, streets covering streets. In times past, people got trapped inside rooms while sleeping and died. But a week later the salt crumbled, and Ildithia moved on basically unaffected."

"Aaanyway," Mizzy said, "this ain't the ugly part, kids. Wait until you see the plan."

"The plan looked well developed when I glanced at it," I said, frowning.

"Oh, it's developed," Mizzy said. "The plan is awesome. But we're never going to pull it off." She turned her hand, using the motion to zoom us down toward the wireframe city.

In Newcago this had all been done with cameras, and it had felt like we were flying. Here it seemed more like we were in a simulation, which made it a lot less disorienting.

We stopped near the downtown, which was—in the simulation—currently on the growing edge of the city, fresh and new. A particularly tall building sprang up, cylindrical, like a giant thermos.

"Sharp Tower," Mizzy said. "That's its new name—used to be some fancy hotel in Atlanta. It's where Larcener made his palace, and it's where Prof has set up. Upper floors are occupied by whatever lackeys are most favored at the moment, with the reigning Epic living in the large room near the very, very tippy top."

"They climb all those steps?" I asked. "Prof can fly. Do the rest take the stairs?"

"Elevators," Mizzy said.

"Made of *salt*?" I asked, looking up.

"They swap in a metal one and use new cables—salt ones don't work, go figure—and bring in a motor. The shafts are perfectly reasonable though."

I frowned. Still seemed like a lot of work, especially since you had to redo it each week. Though a little slave labor and heavy lifting for their minions was hardly a bother.

"Tia's plan," Mizzy said, "is pretty good. Her goal was to kill Prof, but she had decided she needed more intel before trying that. So the first part of her plan includes a detailed plot for infiltrating Sharp Tower. Tia intended to raid Prof's computers to figure out what he was up to in the city."

"But we," I said, "can use that same plan to rescue Tia instead of raiding his computers."

"Yup," Mizzy said. "Judging by the signal from the broken mobile, Tia's been stashed near the top of this building, on the seventieth floor. She's in some kind of old hotel room. It's a nice suite, judging by the maps. I'd have expected something more prisonlike."

"She said Prof would at first try to persuade her he was rational," I said, feeling cold. "Once she refuses to give him the information he asks for, he'll grow impatient. That's when things will start going badly."

"So what is this plan?" Megan said. She was still leaning against the wall, which was obscured by the imager's blackness. We hovered, looking up at the red lines of Sharp Tower. A stupid name, since it was basically round and had a flat top.

"Right," Mizzy said. "Two teams will run the mission. First one will infiltrate a party at the top of the building. Larcener let one of the town's most important people—an Epic named Loophole—throw parties in Sharp Tower. Prof hasn't stopped the tradition."

"Infiltrate?" Abraham asked. "How?"

"Heads of important communities in the city get an invitation to Loophole's parties in exchange for sending specialist workers to help throw the shindig," Mizzy explained. "Tia planned to join with members of the Stingray Clan who were already attending."

"That's . . . going to be tough," Abraham said. "Will we be able to do the same? We don't have the trust of any of the clans."

"It gets worse," Mizzy said pleasantly. "Watch."

"Watch?" Cody asked.

"There are *animations,*" Mizzy said. A group of people—represented by bouncing stick figures—hopped along the road and joined a larger group thronging the tower. The two "teams" were represented in blue. One group bounced their way into the elevators at the rear. Another team slipped in through a back door and entered a different elevator shaft. They somehow shot up along the shaft, toward the roof.

"Huh?" I asked.

"Wire climbers," Mizzy said. "Devices you hook to a cable, then ride up by holding on. See, there's a service elevator, since the *reaaal* important folk need other folk to do stuff for them. And who wants to ride up in the elevator with stinky servants, right? The second team sneaks up that shaft to position themselves on the top residential floor."

"And we get these wire climbers . . . how?" I asked.

"No idea," Mizzy said. "There certainly aren't any for sale in the city. I think the community that took Tia in must have been planning to buy them somehow."

I sat tight, seeing what Mizzy meant by "ugly." When we'd departed the Stingray Clan, Carla and her companions had been very clear in explaining to me that they wouldn't help rescue Tia. They were too frightened by their close call with Prof, and were determined to get their people out of the city. Over the next week, they'd covertly pull out of Ildithia and run.

"That's not the whole of it," Mizzy said. "To pull off Tia's mission, we'd need a whole ton of other stuff. Advanced hacking devices, parachutes, kitchen mixers . . ."

"Really?" Cody asked.

"Yup."

"Sweet," he said, settling back.

It didn't seem sweet to me. I watched the plan play out, as animated by the little bouncing figures. Two teams, operating independently to distract, infiltrate, and steal—all without Prof knowing what had happened. It *was* a good plan, and we could use it to get to Tia instead of the computers.

It was also impossible.

"It would take months to gather this equipment," Abraham said as we watched figures parachuting off the building. "Assuming we could pay for it."

"Yeah," Mizzy said, arms folded. "Warned ya. We're going to have to come up with something else—and we have less time and fewer resources. Which sucks."

The simulation of stick figures ended, and the building hovering in front of us eventually reached the edge of Ildithia and disintegrated, melting away like a lonely ice cream sundae with nobody to eat it.

We don't have time to come up with something better, I thought, glancing at the list of required and suggested supplies that hovered in the air nearby. *Or even something worse.*

I stood and walked from the room.

Megan was first to chase after me, and she caught up quickly. "David?" she asked, then scowled as she saw that her jacket was covered in salt from leaning against the wall. She brushed it off as we headed down the steps to the second floor.

The others followed as well. I didn't speak, leading the group to the first floor. Here, we could hear voices from the buildings next to us. Our neighbors were moving out in preparation for their homes falling apart.

I turned and walked into Larcener's room, where the Epic was sitting wrapped in blankets, though it wasn't that cold, in a chair beside a fireplace—which he hadn't lit.

I needed to play this cool, careful, like a true leader.

I flopped down on one of Larcener's couches. "Well, it's over. We're totally screwed. Sorry, great one. We failed you."

"What are you babbling about?" he demanded, perking up in his blankets.

"Prof captured a member of our team," I said. "He's

probably torturing her right now. He'll soon know anything he wants about us. We'll all be dead by the end of the day."

"Idiot!" Larcener said, standing up.

The rest of the team gathered outside the room.

"You might want to simply kill us yourself," I said to Larcener. "So that you get the satisfaction, instead of Prof."

Megan gave me a *What are you doing, you slontze?* look. I was pretty used to that one.

"How did this happen?" Larcener demanded, pacing. "Aren't you supposed to be skilled, efficient? Adept! I see that you're as utterly incapable as I'd guessed all along!"

"Yup," I said.

"I will be alone in the city," he continued. "Nobody else would dare stand against a High Epic. You've *thoroughly inconvenienced* me, human."

To an Epic, that was a major insult.

"I'm sorry, my lord," I said. "But there's nothing we can do now."

"What, you aren't going to even *try* to kill your friend?"

"Well, there's a plan that . . ." I trailed off. "Kill?"

"Yes, yes. Murder her, so she can't speak. The rational course."

"Oh, right." I swallowed. "Well, we've got this plan, and it's a good one, but we'll never make it work. It requires all kinds of things we don't have. Parachutes. Mannequins. Technology." I made a good show of it. "Of course, if someone could *make* that stuff for us . . ."

Larcener spun on me, and his eyes narrowed.

I smiled innocently.

"Impudent peon," he muttered.

"All you Epics use language like that," I said. "Do you take some kind of evil dictator language course or something? I mean, who *talks* like—"

"This is a ploy to get me to be your servant," Larcener interrupted, stepping over to me. "I expressly told you that I would *not* use my powers to serve you."

I stood up, meeting his eyes. "Tia, a member of our team, has been captured by Prof. We have a plan to save her, but without resources we won't be able to make it work. Either you summon the objects we need, or we'll have to pull out of the city and abandon this cause."

"I do *not* get involved," Larcener said.

"You're already involved, bub. You can start working as a member of this team, or you're out. Good luck surviving in the city. Prof has every thug and two-bit Epic here searching for you. Random stops on the streets with a dowser, huge bounties, your likeness being distributed . . ."

Larcener clenched his jaw. "I thought I was supposed to be the evil one."

"No. You beat the darkness somehow. You're not evil; you're just spoiled and selfish." I nodded toward the others. "We'll bring you a list. It should all be within your powers. You can make . . . what, anything up to about the size of a couch, right? Range of three miles, if I recall. Maximum mass limit shouldn't be an issue."

"How . . ." He focused on me, as if seeing me for the first time. "How do you know *that*?"

"You got your conjuration powers from Brainstorm. I had a whole file on her." I walked toward the doorway.

"You're right about one thing," Larcener said after me. "I'm not evil. I'm the only one. Everyone else in this filthy, horrible, *insane* world is broken. Evil, sinful, revolting . . . whatever you want to call it. *Broken*."

I looked over my shoulder, meeting his eyes again. In those eyes, I swear I saw it. The darkness, like an infinite pool. Seething hatred, disdain, overwhelming lust for destruction.

I was wrong. He hadn't overcome it. He was still one of them. Something else held him back.

Disturbed, I turned and left the room. I told myself I needed to get him a list as soon as possible, but the truth was that I couldn't look into those eyes any longer. And I wanted to be as far from them as I could get.

25

"**WELL,** yes," Edmund said over my mobile, "as I think about it, something like that *did* happen to me."

"Tell me," I said, eager. I wore the mobile stuck to my jacket on the shoulder, earpiece in my ear, as I put together things for the mission tonight. I was alone in a room of our new, interim hideout. It had been five days since Tia's capture, and we'd moved as planned. I'd talked to Cody about using the caverns under the city, but we'd eventually decided they hadn't been explored well enough and might be unstable.

Instead, we'd used one of his suggestions, a hidden location under a park bridge. As eager as I was to get to Tia, we hadn't been able to move immediately. We'd needed the time to set up somewhere new and practice. Beyond that, Tia's plan required a party to be happening at Sharp Tower, and the soonest one was tonight. We had to hope that Tia had been able to hold out.

"It must have been . . . oh, two, three years ago now," Edmund said. "Steelheart was told by my previous masters that dogs were my weakness. He would occasionally lock me up with them. Not for any specific punishment though. I never could figure it out. It seemed random."

"He wanted you to be afraid of him," I said, going through the contents of a pack and checking it against my list. "You're so even-keeled, Edmund. Sometimes you don't seem afraid of anything. You probably worried him."

"Oh, I'm afraid," he said. "I'm an ant among giants, David! I'm *hardly* a threat."

That wouldn't have mattered to Steelheart. He'd kept Newcago in perpetual gloom and darkness, all to make certain that his people lived in fear. Paranoia had been his middle name. Except he'd had only one name—Steelheart—so Paranoia had been more like a last name for him.

"Well," Edmund continued over the line, "he'd lock me in with dogs. Angry, terrible ones. I'd huddle against the wall and weep. It never seemed to get better, maybe even worse."

"You were afraid of them."

"Why wouldn't I be?" he said. "They negated my powers. They ruined me, turned me into a common man."

I frowned, zipping up the backpack and then taking off my mobile so I could look at the screen and see Edmund, an older man with brown skin and a faint Indian accent.

"You gave away your powers anyway, Edmund," I said. "You're a gifter. Why would being powerless bother you?"

"Ah, but my value to others has let me live in luxury and relative peace, while other men starve and scramble for life. My powers make me important, David. Losing them terrified me."

"Dogs terrified you, Edmund."

"That's what I just said."

"Yes, but you might have the cause wrong. What if you weren't afraid of dogs because they negated your powers; what if they negated your powers because you were afraid of them?"

He looked away from me.

"Nightmares?" I asked.

He nodded. I couldn't see much of the room he was in; a safehouse outside Newcago, one Prof didn't know about. We hadn't been able to contact Edmund until Knighthawk had delivered him a new mobile, via drone. He'd turned the old one off at our request, and had neglected to ever turn it on again. He'd claimed he was merely being careful, in case our attack on the Foundry had gone wrong. Another one of his little rebellions.

"Nightmares," he said, still looking away from the screen. "Being hunted. Teeth gnashing, rending, ripping . . ."

I gave him a moment and turned back to my work. As I knelt to the side, something slipped out of my T-shirt at the top. My pendant, the one Abraham had given me, marked with a stylized S shape. The sign of the Faithful, those who believed good Epics would come.

I wore it now. After all, I *did* have faith in the Epics. Kind of. I tucked it into my shirt. Three packs checked over; two left. Even Cody, who would run ops on this mission, needed an emergency pack in case things went wrong. Our new hideout—a hastily constructed set of three rooms beneath the bridge in a rarely traveled park—wasn't as secure as our other one, and we didn't want to leave much behind.

I needed to finish this, but I wanted to be able to see Edmund, not just hear him. This was an important conversation. I thought for a moment, then spotted one of Cody's camo baseball caps sitting atop a stack of supplies we'd carted from the previous hideout.

I smiled, grabbed some duct tape, and hung my mobile from the front of the bill—it took about half a roll of the tape, but whatever. When I put the cap on, the mobile hung down in front of me like a HUD on a helmet. Well, a very sloppy HUD. Either way, it meant I could see Edmund while keeping both hands free.

"What are you doing?" he asked, frowning.

"Nothing," I said, getting back to work, mobile dangling near my face. "What happened with the dogs, Edmund? The day things changed. The day you faced them down."

"It's silly."

"Tell me anyway."

He seemed to weigh the situation. He didn't have to obey, not with all of us so distant.

"Please, Edmund," I said.

He shrugged. "One of the dogs went for a little girl. Someone opened the doors to let me out, and . . . well, I knew her. She was a child of one of my guards. So when one of the beasts lunged for her, I tackled it." He blushed. "It was her dog. It didn't want to attack her. It was just excited to see its master."

"You faced your fear," I said, digging into the next pack, comparing its items to my list. "You confronted the thing that terrified you."

"I guess that's one possibility," he said. "Things did change after that. These days, being around dogs still dampens my powers, but it doesn't completely negate them. I assumed I'd been wrong all along—I thought maybe my weakness was actually pet dander or something like that. I couldn't experiment though, without alerting everyone to what I was doing."

Would that happen to Megan too? Over time, would fire

stop negating her powers? Her weakness still worked on her, but she could make the darkness retreat. Perhaps what Edmund experienced was the next stage.

I zipped up the pack and set it with the others beside the wall.

"Tell me," Edmund said. "Why is it that, if dogs are my weakness, devices with power cells charged by my abilities don't fail when they're around dogs?"

"Hmm?" I said, distracted. "Oh, the Large Dispersal Rule."

"What?"

"An Epic's weakness has less and less influence on their powers the farther you get from the Epic's presence," I said, zipping up the fourth pack. "Like in Newcago—if Steelheart's powers had been negated in all places where someone didn't fear him, then he wouldn't have been able to turn the whole city to steel. Most of the people in the city didn't know who he was, and couldn't fear him. There would have been pockets of non-steel all over the place."

"Ah . . . ," Edmund said.

I stood up, setting the pack with the others. This hat was not working as well as I wanted it to—it was too front-heavy, and kept slipping down.

Needs ballast, I decided. I grabbed the duct tape and used what was left to attach a canteen to the back of the cap. *Much better.*

"Are you . . . all right?" Edmund asked.

"Yup. Thanks for the information."

"You can repay me," he said, "by agreeing to give me to another master."

I stopped in place, the empty cardboard roll from the duct tape in my hand. "I thought you liked helping us."

"You've grown weak." He shrugged. "You can't protect me any longer, David. I'm tired of hiding in this little room;

I'd rather serve a High Epic who can make sure I'm cared for. I hear Night's Sorrow is still dominant."

I felt sick. "You can go free, Edmund. I won't stop you."

"And risk being murdered?" He gave me a thin-lipped smile. "It's dangerous out there."

"You've escaped the darkness, Edmund," I said. "You stumbled on the secret before anyone else. If you don't want to run off, why not come join us? Be a member of the team?"

He picked up a book, turning away from the screen. "No offense, David, but that sounds like an awful ruckus. I'll pass."

I sighed. "We'll send you another supply drop," I said. "Knighthawk might want you to charge some power cells for him though."

"Whatever I am commanded to do," Edmund said. "But David, I do think you're wrong about one aspect of the powers. You claim my fear of dogs created my weakness originally, but before Calamity, I wasn't so afraid of them. I didn't *like* them, mind you. Might even have hated them. But this fear? It seemed to bloom alongside my powers. It's like the powers . . . *needed* something to be afraid of."

"Like water," I whispered.

"Hmm?"

"Nothing." That was silly. Calamity couldn't have been watching me then. "Thanks again."

He nodded to me, then switched off the mobile. I knelt down and went over the contents of the last pack, then set it with the others. Right as I was doing so, Megan peeked in on me. She hesitated in the doorway, looking at me with a befuddled expression, mouth half open, as if she'd forgotten what she was going to say.

The hat, I realized. Pull it off or play it cool? I decided to play it halfway, and reached up to yank my mobile out of the duct tape but left the hat on. I calmly strapped the mobile to my arm. "Yes?" I asked, ignoring the metric ton of silvery refuse hanging at eye level.

The hat slipped backward, now too heavy in the rear because of the canteen. I caught it and yanked it into place.

Yup. Smooth.

"I'm not even going to ask," she said. "You done in here?"

"Just finished the last one. Had a nice chat with Edmund too. His experiences match yours."

"So there's no getting rid of the weakness for good."

"Well, the potency of his weakness seems to have decreased over time."

"That's something, at least. We're ready out here."

"Good." I stood, gathering up the packs.

"You're . . . not going to wear the hat on the mission, are you?"

I casually removed the hat—though I had to yank it hard, as the tape was stuck to my hair—then took a drink from the canteen. With the hat still attached to it.

I put the hat back on and tugged it into place. "Just testing some ideas."

So smooooth.

She rolled her eyes as she left. I tossed the hat aside as soon as she was gone, then carted the packs out.

The team was gathered in the main room, lit by glowing mobiles in the waning light. This base had only one story. On either side of the large, round main room was a smaller room. Mizzy and Abraham wore our stealth suits, sleek and form-fitting, with heat sinks at the waists and goggled hoods that could be pulled up and over their faces.

"Team Hip, ready to go," Mizzy said as I handed her and Abraham their backpacks, which were the heaviest.

"What happened to 'Team One'?" I asked.

"Obviously not hip enough," she said. "I considered

'Team Black' instead, but figured that was like, kinda racist or something."

"Isn't it all right if you call *yourselves* black though?" Megan asked, leaning against the wall, arms folded. "Since you're both African American?"

"*Canadian,*" Abraham corrected.

"Yeaaah," Mizzy said. "Maybe it's okay if I pick the name? Honestly, I can never remember. Pre-Calamity folks cared a lot about race. Like, it's good to remember that not everything sucks worse now than it did then. Some stuff sucked in those days too. It's like, without the Epics, everyone had to find other things to argue about. Race, nationality . . . oh, and sports teams. Seriously. If you go back in time, do *not* bring up sports teams."

"I'll try to remember that," I said, handing Cody his pack. I wished the things she mentioned were confined to the past, but the way Ildithians seemed to have segregated themselves indicated that even with the Epics, we were still perfectly capable of arguing about race.

Cody took his pack. He was wearing camo, his sniper rifle over his shoulder, and Herman—the crystal grower—attached to his belt. He would use it to create a hiding place out of salt for running ops from the top of a building near Sharp Tower. With the rifle, he might be able to give us some emergency cover.

I'd suggested myself as ops, but Mizzy and Abraham would need someone on ops who could dig into files and schematics and coach them on technological details. That left me on Megan's team, which I wasn't complaining about. We would be sneaking into the party, though we'd had to alter Tia's plan, picking one of her backup options as our method of getting in.

I handed Megan her pack. "Everyone ready?"

"Ready as we can be," Abraham said, "with less than a week to practice."

"What about me?" a voice asked. We turned to find Larcener standing in the doorway to the hideout's last room. He'd decorated it in his preferred fashion, though with fewer sofas. Some of the mass he could use in manifesting objects was dedicated to maintaining the tools he'd made for the team.

"You want to come?" I asked, surprised.

He glared at me. "What if someone shows up here while you're gone?" he said. "You're abandoning me."

"Sparks," I said. "You're worse than Edmund. If someone shows up, project yourself into a decoy and lead them away. That's one of your powers, right?"

"It's painful," he said, folding his arms. "I don't like doing it."

"Oh for the . . ." I shook my head, turning to the rest of the team. "Let's do this."

26

SHARP Tower rose, a dark form in the night save for the top floors, which glowed from the inside. The salt was a dusty grey in this area, so that the top floors seemed somehow both light and dark at once. Like a black hole wearing a silly birthday hat.

Megan and I approached, packs slung over our shoulders, wearing new faces courtesy of another dimension. This sort of little illusion was easy for her, and she could maintain it indefinitely so long as I didn't stray too far from her. I couldn't help trying to work out the mechanics of it. Were these the faces of some random people? Or were they people who, in their dimension, were going the same place we were?

A large number of people gathered on the ground floor of the building. The old windows, made of thinner salt, had a warm glow to them, and several doors had been opened up to let the elite gather. I stopped, watching another group arrive, conveyed in bicycle rickshaws.

They were dressed like people in Newcago: short, sparkling 1920s-style dresses and bright lipstick on the women; pinstriped suits and sharp hats, like in old movies, on the men. I half expected them to be carrying tommy guns in violin cases. Instead, their bodyguards were armed with Glocks and P30s.

"Darren?" Megan asked, using my fake name.

"Sorry," I said, breaking out of my thoughts. "Reminds me of Newcago." Memories of my youth carried a lot of baggage.

The guests were being entertained on the ground floor while they waited for their turn in the elevator up to the party. Music poured out of the lobby, the type Mizzy would have liked: lots of thumping and rattling. It seemed at odds with the elegant formalwear. Martinis and caviar were being passed around, more signs of favor and power.

I'd never even tasted a martini. For years I'd assumed it was a brand of car.

Together, Megan and I took a sharp right outside and rounded the building toward a smaller door at the back. Instead of trying to fake our way up the elevator with the rich people, we'd decided to try an avenue where we'd be under far less scrutiny. Tia's plan had included a backup option of sending Team Two up with the servants.

With the images in Tia's notes, we'd been able to fake an invitation here—and a quick check with the Stingray Clan verified that they weren't going to be sending anyone to this party. They'd be expected, but were too busy with their preparations to leave the city.

That left a hole we would hopefully be able to wiggle

through. Around the rear of the tower, we found a less privileged class of people gathering to be carted up a smaller service elevator.

"Ready?" I said.

"Ready," Megan said. Her voice was echoed by those of Mizzy and Abraham, who spoke over my earpiece—I had it tucked up under the illusory hair Megan had granted me. Knighthawk was confident our lines would be secure; Prof had bugged our phones in Babilar, but he'd needed to physically place those bugs in the actual handsets, and we'd replaced that equipment.

"Engaging," I said.

Megan and I started running. We jogged up to the crews working the back door and pulled to a stop, struggling to catch our breath as if exhausted.

"Who are you two?" the guard demanded.

"Cake decorators," Megan said, proffering the invitation—which for workers like us was more an order to appear. "Stingray Clan."

"About time," the guard growled. "Get searched and I'll put you on the next load up."

Loophole loved fancy cupcakes. The Stingrays always sent a pair of cake decorators, even when they didn't send Carla or other important people to attend the party.

My heart was thumping as we stepped over and relinquished our backpacks. A stern woman began unzipping pockets.

"Step one, pass," Megan said quietly into the line as the guard pulled out our electric mixers and placed them on the table with a thump. Various cake-decorating paraphernalia followed. I didn't even know the names of most of the stuff, let alone how it was used. All of this had taught me one thing: cake decorating was *serious* business.

After a quick frisk, we repacked and were ushered ahead of other workers into a dark, salt-walled room with an elevator shaft. The shaft didn't have doors, which seemed terribly unsafe.

"We're in too," Abraham said, "one floor up."

They'd snuck up using the rtich—Abraham had created steps out of mercury up to the second floor—then they'd melted their way in through a window using a specialized pressure washer that delivered a small jet of water strong enough to cut stone. They had used it on one of the windows turned to salt.

Megan and I were loaded onto the elevator, which was a small, ramshackle thing lit by a single lightbulb. The two of us were joined by three other workers, servers in white uniforms.

"Go," I whispered.

I thought I felt our elevator shake as Abraham and Mizzy latched on to the cables above. They zipped up the lines, using the devices Larcener had made for us.

A few seconds later, some distant machine started whirring, and we began to rise. The climb was slow and tedious, with nothing to see—most of the levels still had doors on them, indicating the floors weren't used. Mizzy and Abraham would have to slow their climb before each of the upper floors to peek out and make sure nobody was in the hallway beyond.

The elevator quivered and shook, occasionally grinding against the sides of the shaft, gouging out chunks of salt. What if Mizzy's or Abraham's device slipped, and they fell? What if they spotted someone in one of the upper hallways—where the elevator shafts didn't have doors—and were forced to wait while the elevator approached, threatening to push them into the open? I wiped my brow, and my hand came away grimy with salt dust and sweat.

"We're safe," Abraham said into our ears. "No problems. Unhooking on the sixty-eighth floor."

I relaxed with a sigh. It took us another few minutes to pass the open doorway where Mizzy and Abraham had climbed out, but we saw no sign of them. They still had a couple of floors to climb before reaching their target on the seventieth floor, but Tia's plan indicated this floor would be less likely to be guarded, something Larcener had confirmed.

I let out a prolonged breath as light flooded us from the seventy-first floor. An old restaurant filling the top of the tower, and our target.

We piled out, the servers rushing to join others who were already delivering trays of food to the partygoers. Megan and I carted our packs into the kitchens, where a veritable legion of cooks used hot plates and skillets to prepare dishes. Large lamps had been clipped to parts of the ceiling, bathing the place in sterile white light, and they'd set out plastic over the floor and most of the old countertops. I wondered what they did when they wanted to salt a dish. Scrape some off the wall?

It was all powered by several thick cords that ended in a set of overtaxed power strips. Seriously, there were a ton of them. To plug in something new, you'd have to unplug *two* other cords, which I was pretty sure violated some law of physics.

Megan tried to get information out of a passing server, but was interrupted by a call of "There you are!"

We turned to face a towering chef who had to be nearly seven feet tall. The man stooped as he walked, to not bang his head on an old salt light fixture. His face was so pinched, he looked like he'd been drinking a lemon-juice-and-pickle smoothie.

"Stingrays?" he bellowed.

We nodded.

"New faces. What happened to Suzy? Bah, never mind." He grabbed me by the shoulder, dragging me through the busy room to a smaller pantry on the side where they'd set out ingredients. A helpless-looking woman in a small chef's hat stood here, overlooking a single tray of unfrosted cupcakes. Her eyes wide, she held a small tube of frosting in sweaty hands and regarded the cupcakes as someone might a row full of tiny nuclear warheads, each labeled *Do not bump.*

"Pâtissier is here!" the lurchy chef said. "You're off the hook, Rose."

"Oh, thank heavens," the young woman said, tossing aside the tube of frosting and scrambling away.

The tall chef patted me on the shoulder, then retreated, leaving the two of us in the little pantry.

"Why do I get the feeling there's something they aren't telling us?" Megan said. "That girl was looking at these cupcakes like they were scorpions."

"Yeah," I said, nodding. "Right. Scorpions."

Megan eyed me.

"Or tiny nuclear warheads," I said. "That works too, right? Of course, you could *strap* a scorpion to a nuclear warhead, and that would make it even more dangerous. You'd have to try to disarm the thing, but wow—*scorpion.*"

"Yes, but why?" Megan said, setting her pack on the plastic-topped counter.

"Hmm? Oh, Loophole has executed three different pastry chefs so far for creating substandard desserts. It was in Tia's notes. The woman *really* likes her cupcakes."

"And you didn't mention this because . . ."

"Not important," I said, getting my own pack out. "We aren't going to be around long enough to deliver any pastries."

"Yes, because our plans *always* go *exactly* as they're supposed to."

"What? Was I supposed to take a crash course in decorating?"

"In fact," Cody said over the line, "I'm not too bad at cake decorating, if you must know."

"I'm sure," Megan said. "You going to tell us about the time when you had to fix cupcakes for the Scottish high king?"

"Don't be silly, lass," Cody drawled. "It was the king of Morocco. Cupcakes are too dainty for a Scotsman. Give him one, and he'll ask why didn't you shoot the wee cake's parents instead and serve that."

I smiled as Megan unhooked the side of her mixer and quietly retrieved the pair of Beretta subcompacts hidden inside, along with a pair of suppressors. Her mixer wouldn't work—its innards had been sacrificed to give us storage. That had seemed a reasonable risk to Tia, since the team doing the searching down below wasn't likely to have access to electricity.

We each screwed a suppressor in place, then tucked our handguns into underarm holsters. I plugged in my mixer, which did work; the loud *wrrr* it put out gave us covering sound. I threw some ingredients into the mixing bowl just in case, then laid out the decorating tools.

Advantageously, our little pantry had its own door into the main room. I moved over to peek out while Megan tore apart her mixer's power adapter and removed a small, boxy device much like a mobile.

I cracked the door to do a quick survey of the party. The kitchens were in the absolute center of the seventy-first level, which was important, since a portion of the floor outside *rotated*.

A revolving restaurant: one of those strange ideas from pre-Calamity that I sometimes had trouble believing were real. Once upon a time, ordinary people could have come up here for a nice meal while they looked over the city. The tower's pinnacle restaurant was like a wheel, with the hub remaining stationary and the floor rotating in a ring outside. The outer walls were stationary as well. The ceiling rose in places two more floors to the tower's roof; the partial levels above us were now being used only to position lighting.

The transformation into salt had positively ruined the machinery for the floor, particularly the motors and wires. Getting the place rotating again apparently required the effort of a work crew, engineers, and a minor Epic named Helium who had levitation powers. Loophole went through the hassle every week though, to make something special—something that would stand out. A very Epic thing to do.

I spotted the woman herself sitting at one of the tables on the rotating portion. She had a pixie cut and a slender build. A nice complement to the 1920s-style outfit she wore.

The party up here was more subdued than the one on the first floor; no loud music, just a string quartet. People sat at tables draped in white, waiting for food. In other areas, the salt tables and chairs had been moved aside to allow dancing, but nobody was bothering with that. Instead each table was its own little fiefdom, with an Epic holding court, surrounded by sycophants.

I picked out a series of minor Epics, noting which ones were still alive—meaning they'd thrown their lot in with Prof rather than fleeing the city. Stormwind was there, surprisingly: a young Asian woman sitting on a dais. She had obviously weathered her time in Prof's prison and been released. Prof had apparently paraded her around as he had in order to show that *he* was now dominant in Ildithia. But ultimately, he needed her. Without her powers the crops wouldn't grow, and luxuries—and even basic necessities—in the city would dry up.

I shook my head. I couldn't see the entire room from my vantage, as it was shaped like a ring, but Prof wasn't in this half—and I doubted he was in the other half. He wasn't likely to attend a party like this.

"We're in position," Mizzy said softly over the line. "We've made it to the seventieth level."

That was where Tia was being held, and was also where Prof's rooms would be. The two were on opposite sides of the building though, so hopefully we'd have Tia in hand and be gone before he even realized we'd been here. Her original plan had included luring him out of his rooms with a distraction so she could grab his information without him knowing, but we didn't have to worry about that now.

"Roger," Cody said. "Nice work, Team Hip. Wait for David's or Megan's go-ahead before continuing."

"Yeaaah," Mizzy said. "No risk of us doing otherwise. This place is *littered* with security cameras. Infiltration suits won't be enough to get us any farther."

"We'll get ready for step three," I said. "Just let us . . ."

I trailed off, my jaw dropping as I spotted something out in the main room.

"David?" Cody asked.

Someone had rotated into view, sitting on a salt throne and surrounded by women in tight dresses. A man in a long black coat, with dark hair that tumbled past his shoulders. He sat imperiously, hand resting on the hilt of a sword, which stood point-down beside him like a scepter.

Obliteration. The man who had destroyed Houston and Kansas City and tried to blow up Babilar. The tool that Regalia had used to push Prof into darkness. He was *here*.

He met my eyes and smiled.

27

I ducked back into our pantry room, heart thumping, palms sweating. It was all right. I was wearing a false face. Obliteration wouldn't recognize me. He was just a creepy guy who would give that look to—

Obliteration appeared next to me. Like always with his teleportation, he materialized in a flash of light. Megan cursed, stumbling backward, as Obliteration rested his hand on my shoulder. "Welcome, killer of demons," he said.

"I . . ." I licked my lips. "Great Epic, I think you have mistaken me for someone else."

"Ah, Steelslayer," he said. "Your features may change, but your eyes—and the hunger within them—are the same. You have come to destroy Limelight. This is natural. 'For I am come to set a man at variance against his father, and the daughter against her mother . . .'"

Megan's gun clicked as she rested it against the side of Obliteration's head. She didn't shoot. It would draw attention to us, ruining the plan. Besides, he'd simply teleport away before the bullet hit.

"What are you doing here?" I demanded.

"I was invited," Obliteration said, smiling. "Limelight sent for me, and I could not but agree to appear. His calling card was . . . demanding."

"Calling card . . . ," I said. "Sparks. He has a motivator based on your powers." Knighthawk had said that if you tried to build a device using a living Epic's powers, it would work—but would cause them pain, and draw them to it.

"Yes, he did use one of those . . . devices to summon me. He must wish for death, Steelslayer. As we all do, in the depths of our souls."

Sparks. Regalia must have made at least one more bomb from Obliteration's powers—one other than the ones for Babilar and Kansas City. A bomb Prof now had. Prof would have had to charge his with sunlight. I assumed that was what had drawn Obliteration.

That meant that somewhere in this city was a device capable of destroying it in an instant. How terrible would it be if Prof gave up his humanity to protect Babilar, only to inflict the exact same destruction on Ildithia?

Obliteration watched us, relaxed. When we'd parted last, it had been after a long chase in which he'd tried his best to kill me. He didn't seem to bear a grudge, fortunately.

But before we'd parted, I'd been forced to reveal something to him. "You know the secret of the weaknesses," I said.

"Indeed," he answered. "Thank you very much for that.

Their dreams betray them, and so my holy work may proceed. I need only discover their fears."

"You mean to rid this world of Epics," Megan said.

"No," I said, holding Obliteration's eyes. "He means to rid this world of *everyone*."

"Our paths align, Steelslayer," Obliteration said to me. "We will need to face one another eventually, but today you may proceed with your task. God will make of this world a glass, but only after the burning has come . . . and *we* are his fires."

"*Damn,* you're creepy," Megan said.

He gave her a smile. " 'And there shall be no night there; and they need no candle, neither light of the sun; for the Lord God giveth them light.' " With that, he vanished. As always, when he teleported away, he left a statuelike image of himself created from glowing white ceramic that shattered a second later, then quickly evaporated.

I sagged against the doorway and Megan caught me by the arm, propping me up. Sparks. As if there weren't enough to worry about already.

"Where are those pastries!" a voice shouted outside. "Move, you slontzes. She's demanding cupcakes."

The tall chef burst into our pantry. Megan spun toward him, tucking her gun behind her back. And suddenly, the pan full of cupcakes from earlier had intricate frosting on the tops.

The tall chef let out a relieved breath. "Thank heavens for that," he said, grabbing the pan. "Let me know if you two need anything."

He moved away. I watched, horrified, worried that once it got too far from Megan, the frosting would vanish. She rested her hand on the counter, then slumped, and it was my turn to grab her.

"Megan?" I asked.

"I . . . think I managed to make those permanent," she said. "Sparks, that's more than I've done in a long time. I can feel the headache coming on already." Her skin felt clammy under my fingers, and she'd gone pale.

That said, it was *remarkable*. "Imagine what you could do with more practice!"

"Well, we'll see." She paused. "David, I think I found a dimension where you're not an expert in guns, but in *pastries*."

"Wow."

"Yeah," she said, righting herself. "Yet—in all of infinity—I don't think I've ever found a dimension where you can kiss worth a hill of beans."

"That's unfair," I said. "You didn't complain last night."

"You stuck your tongue in my ear, David."

"That's way romantic. Saw it in a movie once. It's like . . . a passionate wet willie."

"All y'all *do* realize your line is open to me, right?" Cody asked.

"Shut up, Cody," Megan said, tucking her gun back into its place under her arm. "Warn Abraham and Mizzy we had a run-in with Obliteration. We're moving on step three now."

"Roger," Cody said. "And David . . ."

"Yeah?"

"Y'all ever stick your tongue in *my* ear, and I'll shoot ya in yer bagpipes."

"Thanks for the warning," I said, then proceeded to undress.

I was wearing slacks under my bulky jeans and a button-up shirt underneath my jacket. Megan tossed me her jacket; I pulled out the lining, which reversed the jacket into a tuxedo coat.

Her sweater came off next, revealing the gown she had

bunched up around her waist. Off came her trousers—she wore tight biker shorts beneath—and then she yanked down the gown's skirt, covering her legs.

I tried not to gawk. Or, well, I tried to gawk covertly. Megan's sleek red gown was all sparkly and gorgeous and . . . well, it really accented her curves. Like how a nice cheekpiece with shadow lines accents a perfect rifle stock.

Unfortunately, she wasn't wearing her own face. That ruined the effect. But still, that neckline . . .

I caught her looking at me and blushed. Only then did I realize she didn't seem to have noticed my ogling, but was instead nodding to herself, a faint smile on her lips.

"Are you . . . staring at my chest?" I asked.

"What?" she said. "Stay focused, Knees."

Awesome, I thought, tossing on my jacket.

"Take this," she said, handing me the small box she'd removed from her mixer's power adapter. "Dresses like this don't have much in the way of storage."

"Don't you usually . . ." I nodded toward her cleavage.

"I've already got my mobile stuffed in there," she said. "And before you ask, no, there wasn't more room for any mini-grenades. I strapped those to my thigh. A girl's got to be prepared."

Sparks, I love this woman.

I tucked the box into a pocket, and the two of us stepped to the door. Megan concentrated, transforming our features again. I felt a warping as it happened. A blink of another world, another reality. In it, the people we'd been disguised as walked away—a woman with the face Megan had been wearing, and a man with a solemn expression and wide lips.

Gone were the two pastry chefs. What stepped out into the main room was instead a pair of rich dinner guests wearing a different pair of false faces. For a moment there, I'd seen

233

what Megan must when she used her powers—the ripples of
time and space that made up our reality.

Megan slipped her arm through mine and we started to
stroll through the large disc of a room, on the upper walkway,
a portion that didn't rotate. I noted that Obliteration had returned to his throne, a *coconut* in hand, of all things. He'd
probably teleported somewhere and fetched one. So far as I'd
been able to discover, there was no distance limitation to his
teleportation—he simply had to have seen the place, or at
least had it described, to get there.

He glanced toward me and nodded. Sparks. He saw
through this disguise too? I didn't buy his line about my eyes;
he had some kind of power he was keeping hidden. Maybe he
was a dowser and could sense Epics. Though this room was
filled with Epics. How would he recognize the two of us?

Troubled, I tried to keep my mind on our task.

"Nice work," Cody said in my ear. "Keep it up. A quarter
rotation through the room to go."

"Team Hip still good?" I asked.

"Ready and waiting," Cody said.

We continued, passing close to Loophole's table. The lean,
short-haired woman was shrinking servers and making them
dance on her table for the amusement of her gathered crowd.
I'd always wondered . . .

Megan steered me onward as I started to linger.

"Her powers are awesome," I whispered to her. "She has
incredible control of what she can shrink and how she does it."

"Yeah, well, ask for an autograph later," Megan said.

"Um . . . are you jealous? Because your powers are way
better than—"

"Focus, David."

Right. We walked around the room until we approached a
small door marked with a restroom sign. It was in the central

234

hub, same as the kitchens. We stepped in, and as Tia's plans indicated, beyond was a small service hallway, with a restroom on either side. Straight ahead was our goal. A nondescript white door, obviously important—the other doors were still salt, heavy and awkward to move. This one was wood, with a silvery doorknob.

I got out a set of lockpicks. "This would be easier if you could swap the door for one that wasn't locked," I said, working on the knob.

"I might be able to do that," she said. "But I don't know if I could make it permanent. Which would mean that you'd enter through the door, step into another dimension, and change things there—then it would all swap back once you stepped out."

"You fixed the cupcakes," I said.

"Yeah," she said softly, looking over her shoulder. "This is new territory for me, David. Always before, if I pushed this far I lost myself. I often ended up dead. It's not a good mix, knowing that you're immortal and having no sense of responsibility. Perfect recklessness."

I got the door unlocked. It was an easy one, nowhere near as difficult as what Abraham and Mizzy would have to deal with. This door wasn't locked to keep out determined interlopers; it was here to prevent the casual passerby from getting hurt. I swung the door open.

Beyond were a large generator and an engine that turned the floor. Megan and I slipped into the chamber before anyone entered the hallway to use the restrooms, and I took out my mobile for some light. It was cramped, and the floor was coated with powdery salt.

"Sparks," Megan said. "How do they get this all in here? They redo this every week?"

"It's not as tough as it sounds," I said. "Loophole shrinks

all this and carries it up in her pocket. She then shrinks some workers and sends them into the walls and floor with drills to place the wires she needs. With Helium levitating the floor just enough to keep it from grinding, they can get it spinning again."

I knelt beside the machinery, picking out the engine. It was connected to some wires and metal gears below.

"That's the power cell," Megan said, pointing at one part of the machine, "with a backup diesel generator."

"We didn't plan on a backup," I said. "Is that going to be a problem?"

"Nah," she said, holding out her hand. I placed the box from earlier into it. "We're fooling with the cords, not the generator itself. We should be good."

I held out my mobile, the instructions for clipping on the device pulled up. I held this for her as she attached our little box to the proper wires. When we stepped back, I could barely tell it was there.

"Step three complete," I announced, satisfied. "We're pulling out of the generator room."

"Roger," Cody said. "Tapping Abraham and Mizzy into the main line. Be ready, you two. Let Megan and David extract, and we'll move to step four."

"Roger," Abraham said.

"Groovy," Mizzy said.

"There's that word again," I said, pushing out into the restroom hallway. "I tried looking it up. Something to do with record grooves? It—"

I broke off, suddenly face to face with a serving girl leaving one of the restrooms. She gaped at me, and then at Megan. "What are you two doing here?" she asked.

Calamity! "We were looking for the restrooms," I said.

"But they're right—"

"Those are the *peasant* restrooms," Megan said from behind. I stumbled out of her way as she strode past me. "You expect me to use the facilities of the common *servants*?"

Megan wore the mantle of an Epic like it had been designed with her in mind. She stood up taller, eyes wide, and *flames* began to flicker in the hallway.

"I didn't—" the server began.

"You question me?" Megan demanded. "You *dare*?"

The server shrank down, lowering her eyes, and fell silent.

"Better," Megan said. "Where might I find the proper rooms?"

"These are the only ones that are maintained. I'm sorry! I can—"

"No. I've had enough of you. Away, and be glad I don't want to upset our great lord by leaving a body for him to deal with."

The woman scampered out into the main party room.

I cocked an eyebrow at Megan as the flames faded. "Nice."

"It was too easy," she said. "I've been abusing my powers. Let's get Tia and pull out."

I nodded, leading the way back into the restaurant proper. "We're out," I said as the two of us stepped down onto the rotating floor. I couldn't sense anything; it was moving too slowly to be noticeable. We took up position near a table, doing our best to look as innocuous as possible.

"In position," Abraham said. "On your mark."

"Cody?" I said.

"All looks good. Proceed."

"Give us a count of three," Abraham said.

I took a deep breath and pressed the mobile in my pocket, activating the device attached to the generator. Any of us could do it, as it was connected to all of our mobiles, but we'd decided that Megan and I should be in charge of it. It would be easier for Mizzy and Abraham to vocalize what they wanted than to get out their mobiles, risk the light involved, and activate the device on their own.

As soon as I pushed the button, the lights flickered off and the revolving restaurant ground to a stop. Voices murmured and dishes clattered as I counted to three, then removed my finger.

The lights came back on, and the machinery whirred to life. We started to move again. Nervous, I watched for a sign of alarm.

None came. Apparently one of the difficulties in working with machinery that had been hacked together a day ago was that breakages and brownouts were common. Tia's plan made use of this.

"Perfect!" Abraham said. "We're past the first bank of cameras."

"No alarm on any radio frequency I can find," Cody said. "Only some security guards grumbling and hoping Prof doesn't blame them for the brownout. Tia, lass, you're a genius."

"Let's hope you can give her the compliment in person soon," I said to Cody. "Abraham, let us know when your team is at the next camera. We're on a timer now. The chefs are going to start wondering where their pastry makers went, and people are eventually going to go inspect the generators."

"Roger."

Megan and I remained in position. From here on out, the plan was supposed to take under ten minutes. It was tough to wait. Mizzy and Abraham were crawling through guard-infested hallways, while the two of us were supposed to stand up here and look innocent. We'd tried—and failed—to work out a way to get down and meet them, so Megan could use her powers to help with the last portions of the infiltration.

Perhaps that was for the best. Megan was looking haggard,

rubbing her forehead, growing testy. I fetched us some drinks from a servant standing near the bar, but then realized that they probably had alcohol in them, which was a very bad idea right now. We needed to be alert. Instead, I grabbed a cupcake off a passing tray. Might as well sample an alternate-dimension David's handiwork.

I stopped halfway to our table. Had I heard . . .

I turned around, trying to pick the voice out of those chattering in the crowd. Yes. I did know that voice.

Prof was here.

I was mildly surprised; socializing wasn't exactly a Prof thing. Yet that deep voice was unmistakable.

There was ample reason to stay far away from him, but at the same time I was wearing a new face—and our experiences on the first day showed that he was fooled by Megan's illusions. Maybe it would be worth scouting to find out where exactly he was and what he was saying.

"Prof's here," I said over the line.

"Sparks," Cody said. "You sure?"

"Yes," I said, moving to where I could see him standing beside one of the windows. "I'm going to approach with care and watch him. If the guards spot Abraham and Mizzy, he'll be alerted first. Thoughts?"

"I agree," Megan said over the line. "The two of us aren't doing anything else useful up here. This could give us important intel."

"Yes," Cody said. Then he paused. "But be careful, lad."

"Sure, sure. I'll be careful as a diabetic slug in a candy factory."

"Or, you know," Megan said, "a slug in Ildithia."

"That too. You going to back me up?"

"On your tail now, Knees."

I took a deep breath, then crossed the room toward Prof.

28

I slid up to a tall table near where Prof was speaking. A cluster of people surrounded him—lesser Epics, judging by the ones I recognized. Prof had a notepad out, and had settled down at a table.

Others gave the group a wide berth. I leaned on the tall table, trying to look nonchalant. I scratched at my ear, flipping on the directional audio amplification on my earpiece.

"Larcener must be found," Prof said. I could barely pick him up. "Until we accomplish this, we can do nothing."

The others in the group nodded.

"I want Fabergé and Dragdown to spread rumors," Prof said, writing on his notepad. "Claim there is an underground resistance movement against me, and it's looking for a leader. Surveillance is your duty, Inkwell. You'll watch the various powerful family neighborhoods. One of them has to be sheltering him, like the Stingrays were doing for our captive below.

"We attack in two ways: the promise of a rebellion to draw him out, mixed with the threat of discovery. Fuego, I want you to keep working with your dowser, doing sweeps through the city. We'll make a big show of where we're looking and expect Larcener to move—we flush him out like dogs in a field scaring pheasants."

I leaned against my table, suddenly feeling as if I'd been punched in the gut.

Prof had put together a team.

It made sense. Prof had years of practice organizing and leading teams of Reckoners, and he was *very* good at hunting Epics. But hearing him talk to these people like he'd once talked to us . . . it was heartbreaking. How easily he'd replaced his friends and freedom fighters with a team of tyrants and murderers.

"We're at the next corner," Abraham whispered through my earpiece. "Tia's maps show hidden cameras here."

"Yeah, I spot 'em," Mizzy said. "Conspicuous pictures hung on the wall, to hide a hollowed-out section of saltstone. Hold this one until we give word."

"Roger," Megan said. "Dimming on Cody's mark."

"Proceed," Cody said.

The lights flickered, dimmed, and went out.

"Again?" Prof demanded.

"Engineers must have messed up the installation," one of the Epics said. "Could be grinding against the old salt gears and machinery."

"Through," Abraham said.

Megan let go of the button and the lights returned. Prof stood up, seeming dissatisfied.

"My lord Limelight," said a young female Epic. "I *can* find Larcener. Just give me leave."

Prof turned to study her, then settled back down in his chair. "You were slow to come to my service."

"Those quick to give allegiance are quick to change it, my lord."

Do I recognize her? "Cody," I whispered, "is there anything in my notes about a female Epic in Ildithia with blonde hair? Wears it in a braid. She may be twenty to twenty-five years old."

"Let me see," Cody said.

"And what would you do," Prof said to the woman, "if you found him?"

"I'd kill him for you, my lord."

Prof snorted. "And in so doing, destroy everything I'm working toward. Fool woman."

She blushed.

Prof reached into his pocket, taking something out and setting it on the table. A small cylindrical device, perhaps the size of an old battery.

I recognized it. I had one in my own pocket; Knighthawk had given it to me. I reached in and felt it, to reassure myself it was still there. A tissue sample incubator.

"You have my leave to hunt him," Prof said, "but if you *do* find him, do not kill him. Get me some of his blood or skin in this. He dies only after I know that the sample is good. If anyone kills him before that, I *will* destroy them."

I shivered.

"You there," he said louder.

I jumped, looking to find that he was pointing *right at me*.

He waved me over. I checked behind me, then looked back at him. He *was* looking at me.

Calamity!

He waved again, more impatiently, expression darkening.

"Guys, this could be bad," I whispered, rounding my table and walking toward Prof.

"What are you doing?" Megan demanded. She'd set up nearby, leaning against a railing and sipping at a drink.

"He called for me."

"We're at Tia's door," Abraham said. "Two guards. We're going to have to engage them."

"Prepare for another blackout," Cody said. "David, what's your status?"

"Crapping my pants," I whispered, then stepped up to Prof's table.

He gave me a brief glance, then pointed at my hand. I frowned and looked down. Only then did I realize that I was still holding the uneaten cupcake. I blinked, then handed it over.

Prof took it, then dismissed me with a wave.

I was all too happy to obey. I scuttled back, then leaned against the table, trying to relax my strained nerves.

"Situation stable," Megan said, sounding relieved. "False alarm. Abraham, you ready?"

"Yes. I'll give a mark."

"Proceed," Cody whispered.

The lights went out again, causing Prof to curse. I closed my eyes. This was the moment. Would Tia be behind those doors?

"We're in," Abraham said. "Both guards are down. Dead, I'm afraid."

I breathed out softly as Megan restored the lights. Two dead guards. Reckoner protocol was to minimize such things, as Prof had always said we wouldn't get far killing our own. The guards weren't innocent; they implicitly condoned Tia's capture, and likely her torture. But in the end, two normal people—just trying to survive in the new, terrible world—were dead because of us.

Let the prize be worth the cost.

"Tia?" I whispered.

"She's here," Mizzy said. "Abraham's freeing her from her bonds right now. Doesn't look too bad."

A short time later, a familiar female voice spoke over the line. "Huh. You slontzes actually did it."

"How are you?" I asked, sharing a relieved look with Megan.

"He said that some members of his team were 'growing impatient' and had me tied up to think about my answers. But he didn't hurt me." She paused. "There's still a lot of Jon there. I wouldn't have assumed . . . I mean . . ."

"I know," I said, turning to watch Prof interact with his Epics, though I wasn't angled right to catch what he was saying.

"I almost believed him, David. Believed that he hadn't turned, that this was all part of some necessary ploy to fight the Epics . . ."

"He knows what to say," I told her. "He's not fully gone, Tia. We'll get him back."

She didn't reply as Megan and I started toward the elevators. If anyone questioned us, I'd pretend to be feeling ill, and we'd take the next ride down. They wouldn't check us against the guest list down there, like they would have if we'd tried to go up that way.

Easy up, easy down. I almost felt like I'd been slacking through the mission, with Abraham and Mizzy doing the difficult work. "Objective achieved," I said. "Full extraction, everyone."

"You have the data already?" Tia asked.

"Data?" I said.

"From Jon's computers."

"No," I said. "We came for you, not for that."

"And I appreciate it. But David, I've been talking to him, and I got some things out of him. We were right. Regalia left a plan for Jon to follow. He's here at her bidding. Coming to Ildithia, it's part of some kind of master plan. One we *need* to discover."

"I agree, but . . . Wait."

Behind me, the room had suddenly hushed. Megan's hand tightened on my arm, and we turned around.

Prof had stood up, quieting everyone around him.

Tia started to object to what I'd said, but I cut her off. "Something's wrong. What did you do?"

"Nothing," Mizzy said. "We just stepped out of Tia's rooms. We're on our way to the elevator shaft."

Prof gestured sharply toward the elevators, saying something I couldn't make out. The urgency in his motions was unmistakable.

"Abraham, Mizzy," I said. "You've been discovered. Repeat, you've been discovered. Get to an exit, *right now.*"

29

I pushed toward the main guest elevators, but was surprised when Megan held me back. I looked at her, and she in turn nodded toward Prof's team of lackeys. They were moving in the same direction. They'd have priority; we'd be shouted out of the way.

Stairs? Megan mouthed.

I nodded. They were in the hub of the circular chamber, so we began to move in that direction, trying not to look conspicuous. If Abraham's team had been spotted, then it was even more imperative that Megan and I remain hidden.

"Backtracking for emergency escape," Abraham said, breathing heavily. "Those cameras are going to spot us. Even if they've been alerted, I'd rather they not know which hallways we're in."

"Killing the lights," I said. "Move to night vision."

"Roger."

I turned off the lights with the mobile, causing a general outcry in the restaurant.

"What tipped him off?" Mizzy asked.

"He must have planted a bug of some sort on me," Tia said. "One set to trigger if I left my room."

"He could be tracking you!" I said.

"I know," she said. "Little we can do about that right now though."

I felt so helpless. Megan and I sidled up to the room's inner ring, moving toward the stairwell.

"David," Tia said, "Jonathan's chambers are on this level. I'm going to take Abraham and Mizzy and go get that data. We can grab it during the blackout confusion; they'll never expect us to be going that way."

I stopped in place. "Tia, no. Abort. *Get out.*"

"Can't do that."

"Why?" I said. "Tia, you've always been the *careful* one! This mission is going to hell. We need to extract."

"You do realize what's in that data, David."

"Regalia's plans?"

"More than that. She saw Calamity, David. Regalia interacted with him, or her, or whatever it is. Jon boasted to me of what he'd seen. David, there are *pictures.*"

Sparks. Pictures of Calamity? The Epic?

"All the secrets we've been hunting could be on that data drive," Tia said. "The answers we've been chasing all our lives. Surely you, of all people, can see it. My plan got you this far; we need to take the last step. That data is worth the risk."

From this angle I could see through a glass window on the outside rim of the building. Calamity was there, of course. It was always there, heaven's bullet hole. Calamity . . . an Epic. The ultimate gifter? Would we find answers in that spot of garish light? Would we find out why all this had begun?

The meaning of Epics . . . the truth?

"No, Tia," I said. "We've been discovered, and my team is in serious danger. We can't grab that data right now. We'll get it later."

"We're *so close*," she said. "I'm not leaving it, David. I'm sorry. This team is mine, and as the senior Reckoner, I—"

"Senior Reckoner?" Megan cut in. "You abandoned us."

"Says the traitor."

Megan stiffened. She stood beside me, my hand on her shoulder, but I couldn't see much of her. The room was completely black, with partygoers knocking into things, voices raised in confusion. Across the room, an Epic burst into red lightning, giving the place a glow. Soon a second Epic started glowing with a calmer, blue light.

"Tia," I said, trying to be rational, "I'm in command of this mission, and I'm telling you to extract. That information isn't worth risking my team. Abraham, Mizzy, get out of there."

Deathly silence came over the line. I could imagine them one floor down, looking Tia in the eye, considering.

"Roger that, David," Abraham said. "Team Hip extracting."

"I'm with him," Mizzy said. "This isn't the time for a power struggle, Tia. Let's get *out* of here."

Tia muttered something inaudible but made no further argument. Megan tugged on my arm, leading me the last distance toward the door to the stairwell, which we could now make out by the light of several glowing Epics. Unfortunately, with the power out, Prof's team was gathering there as well, and blocked the way.

"David?" Mizzy asked over the line a short time later. "What about you two?"

"Keep on with your emergency extraction plan," I said quietly. "We have false identities. We're safe up here."

"We're ready," Abraham said. "Won't need the inflatables. Regrettably, we have something superior."

"Go," Cody said. "You should be clear."

I thought I heard a window being blown open below, or at least felt the vibrations.

"Parachutes!" someone in our room shouted. "Outside!"

People rushed for the windows; Megan and I backed away. Prof's Epics shoved past us to a window, and then the blonde woman I thought I recognized waved over several guards. She glanced at Prof, who stood with arms folded, lit by the glowing Epics nearby. He nodded.

"Bring them down," the woman said, pointing.

The guards started shooting. The window shattered amid the cacophony of indoor weapons fire. It was like firecrackers, if they'd been stapled to your head and stuffed in your ears.

Muzzles flashed, illuminating the dark room like strobe lights. I winced, backing away as the guards filled Abraham's parachutes with holes. Fortunately, the action at the window had drawn everyone's attention that way. Megan and I were able to retreat toward the stairwell at the center of the room.

"Parachutes down, my lord," the blonde Epic said, turning to Prof.

We didn't have long until they discovered that the chutes were attached to the corpses of the dead guards. Abraham, Mizzy, and Tia would be using the distraction to reach the elevator doors, then ride their wire climbers down the cables and exit the building.

"We're at the elevators," Abraham said.

"Go!" Cody said.

"Right."

I waited a tense few moments.

"We've hit the second floor," Abraham finally said, out of breath. "Stopping here."

"That was *quuuuiiite* the ride," Mizzy added. "Like a zip line, except straight down."

"At least the wire didn't break on you halfway," I noted.

"What?" Mizzy asked.

"Nothing."

"David," Abraham said, composed again. "There is a problem. Tia didn't come with us."

"She *what*?"

"Tia remained above," Abraham said. "When we jumped into the elevator shaft, she ran the other way."

Toward Prof's room. Calamity's *shadow*, that woman was stubborn. After all the work we'd done, she was going to get herself killed.

"Continue your extraction," I said. "Tia is on her own now. Nothing we can do."

"Roger."

After all the work we'd gone through to get to her, she did *this*. Part of me couldn't blame her; I was tempted by that information too. The rest of me was irate with her for forcing me into this position, where I had to make the call to leave a team member behind.

The lights suddenly came on again.

The ground lurched under the dining tables—Megan and I, near the hub, were on the nonrotating portion. To our left a short, balding Epic from Prof's team approached around the hub, triumphantly raising the dampening device we'd attached to the generator.

Prof looked at it, then shouted, "They're here! Secure both the elevators and the steps. Wiper, sweep the room!"

Wiper . . . That was a name I recognized.

"Oh!" Cody said. "Right, Wiper. I found that Epic for you, David. Sorry, lad. Had it in hand right as everything went to Wales in a handbasket. Wiper. Her powers—"

"—are to disrupt other Epics' abilities," I whispered. "Short them out for a second."

A flash of light pulsed through the room. In that moment, I turned and found Megan looking at me. Not the false face she'd created, but Megan herself. Beautiful though that was, it wasn't what I'd wanted to see at all.

Our disguises were gone.

30

FOR better or worse, my time with the Epics had seriously helped me deal with being surprised. I was almost as quick as Megan was in pulling out my handgun.

Pointedly, while we both moved by instinct, neither of us fired on Prof. Megan gunned down the three armed soldiers who had been firing out the window. Our little popguns acquitted themselves well, for compacts.

I shot Wiper.

She died a lot more easily than most Epics I'd killed—in fact, watching her drop in a spray of blood almost surprised me more than losing our disguises. I'd grown used to Epics being exceptionally tough; it was sometimes difficult to remember that the majority of them had only one or two powers, not a full suite.

Prof roared in outrage. I didn't dare look at him; he'd been intimidating enough when he *hadn't* been trying to kill me. Instead, I sprinted for the open stairwell door and gunned down the surprised Epic standing inside.

Megan followed me. "Duck!" she shouted at me as people in the room behind us pulled out guns. A few fired.

I dove through the doors. Nobody outside got off more than two or three shots before an explosion rocked the room, cracking saltstone walls and sending a shower of dust raining down.

I coughed, blinking salt from my eyes, and struggled to my feet. It had been one of Megan's grenades. I managed to grab her outstretched hand and join her in running down the steps.

"Sparks," she said, "I can't believe we're alive."

"Wiper," I said. "Her bursts negate Epic powers, specifically external usages, like Prof's forcefields. Her burst left him momentarily unable to trap us."

"Could we have . . ."

"Killed him?" I asked. "No. Wiper would have been executed by one High Epic or another long ago if her powers were that strong. She can't . . . well, couldn't . . . remove an Epic's innate protections, just fiddle with manifestations for a second or two. Forcefields, illusions, that sort of thing."

Megan nodded. The stairwell was dark—nobody had thought to hang lights in here—but we heard when people ventured in from above. Megan pulled back against the wall, looking up. I could make her out by the light trickling down from above.

I nodded to her unasked question when she glanced at me. We needed time to plan, and that meant keeping the pressure off us. She pulled her other mini-grenade from her thigh case, then activated it and tossed it upward.

The second explosion sent chunks of saltstone tumbling down on us, and seemed to have broken an entire section of steps above. I nodded to her, and we looked down the stairwell. There was no way we'd be able to take this stairway down seventy floors without finding ourselves trapped at the bottom. We needed another way out.

"David?" Cody's voice. "I spotted some explosions up there. Y'all all right?"

"No," I said over the line, "we've been compromised."

Abraham swore softly in French. "We left the backup equipment, David. Where are you?"

David and Mizzy had brought extra wire climbers, in case there were more prisoners than Tia—or in case Megan and I joined them. Mission parameters called for emergency equipment to be left behind, just in case.

"We're right by the door to floor seventy," I said. "Where's the equipment?"

"Black backpack," Abraham said, "hidden in the air vent near the service elevator. But David, that level was flooding with guards when we were leaving."

It would also be the same floor where Tia had given them the slip to go after Prof's data. I wasn't sure I could save her though. Sparks. I wasn't sure I could save *myself* at this point.

"Radio chatter went silent right after Abraham was spotted," Cody said. "They must have some kind of secure signal to use in emergencies. And they won't be using Knighthawk mobiles, you can bet your kilt on that."

Great. Well, at least with that pack, Megan and I had a chance. My back to the wall beside the door onto the seventieth floor, I took out my mobile. Its light bathed us as we examined the map that Cody helpfully sent of this level. We were marked as a green dot; the elevator, red.

That red dot was halfway across the sparking building. Lovely. I memorized the route—noticing Prof's chambers. We'd travel close to it, down a hallway right outside his suite.

I glanced at Megan, and she nodded. We slid the door open and Megan leaped out, gun ready, checking right and then left. I followed, keeping watch down the right hallway as she scouted ahead to the left. A string of lightbulbs hung along the ceiling, revealing absurdly beautiful waves of red salt shot through the otherwise black and grey walls. It looked like a pigeon on fire.

I exhaled. No guards yet. The two of us continued down the left hallway, passing closed doors that I knew led into luxurious apartments. By the time we'd reached the end of the hall, I was feeling pretty good about our chances. Maybe the guards had all been pulled out to search other floors or to protect Prof upstairs.

Then the wall about ten feet in front of us disintegrated.

We stumbled back as the night wind whipped in through a new gap in the outside wall of the building, blowing in more salt dust from seventy floors up in the air. I raised my hand against the salt, blinking.

Prof hovered outside on a glowing green disc. He stepped off it and into the building, feet crunching on salt dust. Megan cursed, backing away, gun out in front of her. I remained in position and searched Prof's face, hoping for some sign of warmth; pity, even. I found only a sneer.

He raised his hands at his sides, summoning lances of green light—spears of forcefield to impale us. In that moment, I felt something unexpected.

Pure anger.

Anger at Prof for not being strong enough to resist the darkness. The emotion had been hidden within me, tucked away behind a series of rationalizations: He'd saved Babilar. Regalia had manipulated him into his fall. The things he did weren't his fault.

None of that stopped me from being angry—*furious*—at him anyway. He was supposed to be better than this. He was supposed to have been invincible!

Something trembled inside me, like an ancient leviathan stirring in its slumber within a den of water and stone. The hair on my arms stood up, and my muscles tensed, as if I were straining to lift something heavy.

I looked into Prof's eyes and saw my death reflected back at me, and something within me said *no.*

That sense of confidence was gone in a moment, replaced with sheer terror. We were going to die.

I leaped to the side, dodging a spear of light. I rolled as Megan jumped back against the wall, managing to get out of the way of another razor-sharp lance of forcefield.

I tried to scramble down the hallway, but smashed right into a glowing green wall. I groaned, turning to see Prof studying me with a look of disdain. He raised a hand to destroy me.

Something tiny hit him in the side of the head. He started, then turned, and another one smacked him in the forehead. Bullets?

"*Oh* yeah," Cody said over the line. "Did y'all see that? Who just sniped a guy at a thousand yards? I did."

The bullets didn't penetrate Prof's defensive powers, though they did seem to annoy him. I scrambled over to Megan. "Can you do anything?" I asked.

"I . . ."

A forcefield sprang up, surrounding both me and Megan, gouging out a large chunk of the saltstone floor as well.

Sparks. This was it. We were going to be crushed like Val and Exel.

I reached for Megan, wanting to be holding her as it happened. She had adopted a look of concentration, teeth clenched, eyes staring sightlessly.

The air shimmered. Then someone *else* appeared inside the globe with us.

I blinked in surprise. The newcomer was a teenage girl with red hair worn short in a pixie cut. She had on a plain pair of jeans and an old denim jacket. She gasped and looked up at the forcefield globe surrounding us.

Prof closed his hand into a fist to make the globe shrink, but the young woman thrust her hands to the sides. I felt a *thrumming* vibration, like a voice with no sound. I knew that sound. The tensors?

Prof's forcefield disintegrated, dropping us to the ground. I lost my balance, though the young woman landed easily on two feet. I was utterly baffled, but I was alive. I'd take that exchange. I grabbed Megan, pulling her away from the girl. "Megan?" I hissed. "What did you do?"

Megan continued to stare sightlessly.

"Megan?"

"*Shhh,*" she snapped. "This is *hard*."

"But . . ."

Prof cocked his head.

The girl stepped forward. ". . . Father?" she asked.

"*Father?*" I repeated.

"I couldn't find an uncorrupted version of him in a close enough reality," Megan muttered. "So I brought what I *could* find. Let's see if your plan works."

Prof regarded his "daughter" contemplatively, then waved his hand, summoning another forcefield around Megan. The girl destroyed it in a flash, hands forward, releasing a burst of tensor power.

"Father," the girl said. "How are you here? What's happening?"

"I have no daughter," Prof said.

"What? Father, it's *me*. Tavi. Please, why—"

"I have no daughter!" Prof roared. "Your lies will not fool me, Megan! Traitor!"

He thrust his hands to the sides and spears of green light appeared there, shaped like glass shards. He flung them down the hallway toward us, but Tavi waved her hand, releasing a burst of power. That *was* the tensor power—as Tavi destroyed the spears of light, she vaporized the wall nearby as well. It fell to dust.

A set of blue-green spears appeared around Tavi, just like Prof's. Sparks! She had his same power portfolio.

Prof's eyes widened. Was that fear in his expression? Worry? Megan hadn't brought a version of him into this world, but this was apparently close enough. Yes, he was afraid of her powers. *His* powers.

Face your fears, Prof, I thought, desperate. *Don't flee. Fight!*

He bellowed in frustration, sweeping his hands before him, destroying the hallway in a long swath and sending a wave of salt dust over us. Forcefields flashed into existence— shards of light that struck at Tavi, walls that swept in to crush, a cacophony of destruction.

"Yes!" I shouted. He wasn't running.

Then, unfortunately, the floor disappeared beneath me.

31

PROF'S wave of destructive power had ended right about as it hit me, and though I fell into the hole in the floor, I was able to reach out and grab the edge to stop myself. Megan knelt by the ledge, oblivious to the hole that had opened beside her.

The drop was about ten feet, but that was a little far for me to want to risk. I started to pull myself up.

"David," Tia's voice suddenly said in my ear, "what are you doing?"

"Trying not to die," I said with a grunt, still dangling. "You still here on the seventieth floor somewhere?"

"In Jon's chambers, trying to get into his office. Can you cut the power for me, maybe? There's an electronic lock on the security door here."

A tensor wave hummed above, and I heard an ominous groan from the ceiling.

"Dampener is gone, Tia," I said, getting to my feet—and finding myself in a war zone. "And we have bigger troubles than getting into Prof's rooms. He's *here*."

"Sparks!" Tia said. "What's going on? Are you all right?"

"Yes and no."

In the moments I'd been down, Prof and Tavi had leveled walls separating rooms, creating a much larger field of battle. They exchanged bursts of light and tensor powers, leaving rips and craters in the floor.

That ceiling wasn't going to last much longer. I sought out Megan, who knelt beside the remnants of a wall. She hissed between clenched teeth, watching the contest with unblinking eyes. I stepped toward her, but when she looked at me, her lips curled, teeth clenched. A sneer.

Uh-oh.

This was dangerous. She'd pulled too many things through to our world too quickly.

But sparks, it was *working*. Prof was backing down the hallway before an assault by Tavi—flying spears of blue light, which he was able to vaporize with his tensor power. The outer wall to his left was in shambles, wind howling through. To his right, rooms were pocked with holes, the floor and walls almost completely destroyed.

I threw myself toward Megan as the ceiling to Prof's right fell in. Blinking—sparks, that salt made a scrape I'd gotten on my arm *sting*—I saw spears of glowing green launch toward Tavi, their light illuminating the dust around them. She deflected those, barely.

Prof had lost his air of uncompromising confidence; he was sweating and cursing as he fought, and—to my surprise— I saw a few scratches on his arm.

They weren't healing.

Her powers were indeed negating his. But why hadn't he turned good? Hadn't he confronted his fears?

"David," Tia said, anxious. "It sounds like the entire *building* is coming down. Are you all right?"

"For now. Tia . . . Megan summoned a version of him from another world. Someone with his powers. They're fighting."

"Sparks!" Tia cursed over the line. "You're insane." She grew silent for a moment as I stared at Prof, mouth agape, awed by the use of power. "All right," Tia said, sounding reluctant. "I'm coming to you."

"No," I said. "Stay hidden. I don't think there's anything you can do. Anything *any* of us can do."

I looked at Megan, her teeth clenched, and started toward her.

She looked at me, angry. "Stay back, David," she growled. "Just . . . stay back."

I stopped, then sighed and scuttled farther down the corridor—toward Prof and Tavi. Stupid, perhaps, but I needed to watch this. I passed the room where the ceiling had collapsed on my right, then came up toward the two combatants. The corridor turned here, but they'd continued on, vaporizing the wall and stepping into a lavish suite.

Prof unleashed a wave of tensor power toward Tavi, melting tables and chairs and hitting her full force. Buttons on her shirt disintegrated to dust, though the shirt didn't. Only dense nonliving materials were affected.

Her forcefields vanished. She jumped for cover, narrowly dodging lances of light. It took a count of three before she was able to summon a forcefield to block oncoming blasts. It was *working*. She seemed to have the same weakness as Prof: the powers themselves, wielded by someone else. Getting hit

261

by the tensors negated her abilities for a time, like fire did to Megan.

Could I do something? Explain this to her? I stepped forward, then hesitated as the air warped near me.

I was drawn into a momentary vision of another world: Firefight standing on a rooftop, hands clenched at his sides, fire rising from his fists. A night sky. Cold air punctuated by bursts of heat from the Epic.

The vision passed, and I was on the skyscraper battlefield again. I stepped away from the warping air, then took cover behind a broken saltstone wall, outside the room where Prof and Tavi were fighting. A few spears of light shot overhead, slamming into the wall above me like forks into a cake.

Now that I knew to look, I spotted other places where the air twisted and warped. They dotted the corridors and rooms; Megan's powers were tearing our reality apart, interweaving it with Firefight's.

That seemed to me like a very, very bad thing.

The lights suddenly dimmed, went out—then almost immediately came back on. Prof and Tavi didn't even pause in their contest, but I did notice that the young woman looked far more haggard than he did. She was sweating, her teeth clenched, and tears streaked her face, washing through the prevalent salt dust there.

"Sparks," Tia cursed over the line. "Still can't get through this door. Jon has a backup generator in his rooms somewhere. It turned on when I cut the wires; I can hear it chugging inside."

"You're still going on about that?" I demanded.

"I'm not just going to *sit* here," she said. "If he's distracted, then—"

She cut off as Prof released a wave of tensor power—intended to stop a sweeping forcefield—and it blasted the wall of the suite he was fighting in. The wall fell in, revealing another suite of rooms beside it—where Tia was kneeling on the floor.

She cursed and ducked beside the broken wall. "Didn't realize you'd gotten so close," she said through the line. "Wait. That girl looks familiar. Is that . . ."

Oh boy . . .

"Lad," Cody said over the line, "I can't make out what's going on up there. Are y'all *fighting* him somehow?"

"Kind of," I said, sliding my gun from its holster. Prof was consumed by his conflict with Tavi. A spike hit the girl, pinning her arm, spraying blood against the wall in a gruesome display. She fell to her knees, and moments later the wound started to heal. She deflected further spears of light with tensor power, clutching her arm. She then wobbled to her feet, flesh scabbed over, blood stanched.

Still hiding near the hole into the room, I gaped. She healed. And her powers had come back far quicker than Megan's did after touching fire.

Like Edmund. Her weakness doesn't affect her as much as it does Prof or the others. She's faced her fears, overcome them long ago, perhaps?

Prof still bore the cuts where she'd hit him. Yet I couldn't help feeling that I was missing something *big* about the nature of powers and weaknesses. Prof was fighting her. Wouldn't that mean facing his fears himself? Why was he still so obviously consumed by the darkness?

Inside the room, and through the broken wall on the west, Tia had finally managed to get into Prof's office. I could barely make her out in there, moving past a generator like the one we'd found above. She sat down at his desk and began furiously working at the computer there.

But Tavi . . . poor Tavi. I didn't know her, but my heart

wrenched to see her being driven back by Prof's blasts of power. She still fought, but she was obviously less experienced with combat than he was.

I stood up, gripping my little pistol in two hands. Over my shoulder, I saw Megan approaching down the hallway, actively weeping, her face a mask of pain and concentration.

I had to stop this. It wasn't working, and it was destroying Megan. I leveled my gun at Prof while he was focused on Tavi; I breathed out and fell still. I waited for a wave of Tavi's tensor power to wash over him, destroying a forcefield.

Then I fired.

I can't say if I pulled to the side on purpose, or if it was an effect of the floor shaking. The ceiling here was straining like the one in the other room; too many walls gone.

Either way, my shot clipped Prof on the side of the face instead of drilling him right in the back of the head. The bullet ripped off a chunk of his cheek, spraying blood. His innate forcefield protections were down. Maybe I could have killed him.

The moment passed. Prof tossed up a forcefield wall behind him to prevent other shots—an almost absent gesture, as if I were an afterthought. Calamity . . . what if he killed Tavi? We'd pulled her from her reality and thrust her into our war. I looked again at Megan.

Fire, I thought. That was another way to end this. I fished in my pocket, searching for my lighter. Where was it? I hadn't even noticed how ragged my clothing had become, the nice coat covered in salt, the trousers ripped. I couldn't find my lighter; I'd lost it somewhere.

I did find something else in my pocket though. A small cylinder. Knighthawk's tissue sample incubator.

I looked up, toward where I'd shot Prof. Dared I? Could Megan hold out a little more?

I made my decision and dashed across the room, ducking around the forcefield and hopping over the remnants of a sofa that had been half melted by the tensor. This put me in the middle of the battle, Prof and Tavi fighting near the lush room's wet bar. Waves of dust blew over me, getting into my eyes. Salt forced its way into my mouth, making me want to gag. The ground rocked, and I threw myself to the floor, rolling out of the way as an invisible tensor blast gouged a large hole nearby. Dust rained down from a hole in the ceiling.

I came up, skirting very close to Prof as I made for the bloodstain on the floor. He turned on me, eyes wide with fury. Sparks, sparks, *sparks!*

I skidded across the floor and—in the bloody patch— found a loose chunk of skin from his cheek. He'd already healed from the shot. Apparently the cuts remained unhealable only if he was hit by one of the spikes of light. An ordinary wound would start healing as soon as his powers reasserted themselves.

I scooped up the piece of flesh into Knighthawk's device, too panicked to worry about the morbidity of it. Prof summoned spikes of light, a dozen or more. He roared, flinging them toward me.

I threw myself sideways.

Right into one of the shifting ripples in the air.

32

THIS time I didn't drop twenty feet after transitioning to the other world, which was a plus. I instead rolled onto the top of a roof in a quiet section of the city. This wasn't a skyscraper, just some apartment building, though an admittedly tall one.

Nothing was dissolving, no gunfire sounded, and there was a complete absence of the disconcerting hum of Prof's tensor power. Only the serene night sky. Beautiful . . . with no red spot to glare down upon me.

I clutched the tissue sample, lying there, and stared up at the sky, drawing in a few calming breaths. That might have been the craziest thing I'd ever done, and my life so far had set a pretty high bar.

"You," a voice said from behind me.

I rolled over to a kneeling position, holding Prof's cells closer with one fist while raising my handgun with the other. Firefight hovered beside the rooftop, alight and burning, skin and clothing consumed by his curling flames. Bullets wouldn't hurt a fire Epic; they'd simply melt away. Had I traded one deadly situation for another?

I have to stall until I'm pulled back into my own world, I thought. Except . . . how long would I stay, if Megan wasn't actively trying to pull me back? I couldn't have slipped over permanently, right?

Firefight was inscrutable, his aura of heat and flame warping the air around him. Eventually he stepped up onto the rooftop and, surprisingly, his flames dampened. Clothing emerged, a jacket over a tight T-shirt, a pair of jeans. The fire continued to burn along his arms, but it was subdued, like the last flames of a campfire before they gave themselves up to the embers. His face was the same as the other times I'd seen him.

"What have you done with Tavi?" he demanded. "If you've hurt her . . ."

I licked my lips, which were extremely dry and salty. "I . . ." Again, the morality of what we'd done smacked me upside the head, like the fist of the Factory's lunch lady after I'd tried to steal an extra muffin. "She's been sucked into my world."

"So Tia *is* right. You are actively looking to pull us into your dimension?" He strode forward, his fires flaring up again. "Why are you doing this? What is your plot?"

I scrambled backward on the rooftop. "It's not that! Or, well, we didn't know—Megan didn't, at first, know what—I mean, we didn't—"

I had no idea what I was trying to say.

Fortunately Firefight stopped, then dampened his flames once more. "Specks, you're terrified." He took a deep breath. "Look, can you bring Tavi back? We're in the middle of something. We need her."

"Tia . . . ," I said, lowering my gun as I put it together. "Wait. You're one of the Reckoners?"

"Is that why you keep pulling me into your world?" he asked. "Is there no version of me there?"

"I . . . think you might be a girl," I said. *And dating me.* I'd noticed the similarities before; Firefight was blond and had a face that, if you ignored its masculinity, was reminiscent of Megan's.

"Yes . . . ," he said, nodding. "I've noticed her. She's the one who pulls me through. Odd to think that I might have a sister, in another place, another world."

A flash of light ignited a building nearby—a tall, round building. Sharp Tower? For the first time I realized that I was still in the same district of Ildithia. But outside the tower, on top of a building like the one where Cody had set up.

Firefight spun toward the explosion, then cursed. "Stay here," he said. "I'll deal with you later."

"Wait," I said, scrambling to my feet. That flash . . . it felt familiar. "Obliteration. That light was caused by Obliteration, wasn't it?"

"You know him?" Firefight said, spinning back to me.

"Yeah," I said, trying to make sense of what I was seeing. "You could say that. Why are—"

"Wait," Firefight said, putting his hand to his ear. "Yes, I saw it. He's come to Sharp Tower. You were right." He squinted, looking up at the taller building. "I want to engage. I don't care if he's trying to lure me, Tia. We have to face him eventually."

I hesitantly walked over beside Firefight, who stood at the edge of our building. There was so much that was different here, but so much was the same. Obliteration, Ildithia itself. *Tia,* apparently? And Tavi . . . her daughter?

The flash of heat from Obliteration returned, a deep pulsing heat. The salt couldn't catch fire, but Obliteration continued radiating it. Shadows moved up there. I squinted, and then—silhouetted against the flames—I saw figures leap from the windows.

"Specks!" Firefight said. "Tia, there are people up there. Jumping out to avoid the heat he's creating. I'm going."

Firefight burst alight and streaked into the air—though I could see that he wouldn't reach the people in time. It was too far, and they were falling too quickly. My heart lurched. What a terrible decision: be burned by Obliteration, or fall to your death? I wanted to tear my eyes away, but couldn't. Those poor souls.

Someone else leaped from the room atop the burning building. A figure with glowing hands—a magnificent form that shot downward, trailing a silvery cape. Like a meteor, he made a brilliant, powerful streak of light as he rocketed toward the falling people. My breath caught as he seized the first person, then the second.

I stumbled backward. *No.*

Firefight turned around and landed by me again. "Never mind," he said to Tia, his flames partially dampening. "He got here in time. Should have known. When has he ever been late?"

I knew that figure. Dark clothing. Powerful build. Even at a distance, even in the gloom of night, I *knew* that man. I'd spent my life studying him, watching him, hunting him.

"Steelheart," I whispered. I shook myself, then grabbed

Firefight, completely forgetting he was on fire. The flames vanished on contact, fortunately, and I wasn't burned. "Steelheart is *helping* you?"

"Of course he is," Firefight said, frowning.

"Steelheart . . . ," I said. "Steelheart's not *evil*?"

He raised an eyebrow at me as if I'd gone insane.

"And no Calamity," I said, looking at the sky.

"Calamity?"

"The red star!" I said. "That brought the Epics."

"Invocation?" he said. "It vanished a year after it arrived; it's been gone a decade."

"Do you feel the darkness?" I demanded. "The drive toward selfishness that strikes every Epic?"

"What are you *talking* about, Charleston?"

No Calamity, no darkness, a *good* Steelheart.

Sparks!

"This changes everything," I whispered.

"Look, I've told you before that you must meet him," Firefight said. "He refuses to believe what I've seen, but he *needs* to talk to you."

"Why me? What does he care about me?"

"Well," Firefight said, "he killed you."

In my world, I killed him. Here, he killed me. "How did it happen? I have to . . ."

I felt a lurch. A shimmering. "I'm going," I said, starting to disappear. "I can't stop it. We'll send Tavi back. Tell him . . . tell him I'll return. I have to—

"—figure out what happened here," I finished, but Firefight was gone. The rooftop was gone. In its place was a room of dust and glowing light. Two Epics at battle. They'd moved into the hallway again, skirting Prof's chambers. That left them to my right—where most of the hallway's walls were gone.

Guards had arrived during my absence, and they'd set up at the corner in the hallway, near where I'd been hiding. They'd begun ganging up on Tavi, firing barrages down the hallway in her direction.

No Calamity . . .

I had to tell someone! I spotted Tia easily, working furtively at a computer station inside the next apartment over—in front of me and a little to my left. A stream of salt trickled down onto my head, and the ceiling groaned.

I looked over my shoulder to see Megan striding through the suite toward me. Tall, deliberate, her head thrust back and hands at her sides, each finger trailing a ripple in reality. A High Epic in her glory.

She looked at me, and *snarled*.

Right. I had a bigger problem to deal with.

33

FIRE. I needed *fire*.

It seemed a cruel irony that mere moments ago I had been standing next to a man literally made of flame, yet now I couldn't find even a spark.

I shoved Prof's captured cells into my pocket, then scrambled to my feet and crossed the suite, doing my best to stay low. The guards were falling back. As I frantically searched for some way to create a flame, I spotted Tavi out in the hallway on her knees, surrounded by several layered bubbles of light. Presumably the innermost was her own. She huddled there with head bowed, skin plastered with salt dust streaked by sweat, trembling.

My heart lurched, but I ran for Tia, hoping she might have a lighter. Megan reached for me, but I dodged her. The air still rippled around me. I caught glimpses of other worlds, of alien landscapes, of places where this plain had become a jungle. Another where it was a barren wasteland of dust and stone. I saw armies of glowing Epics, and piles of the dead.

A large portion of the ceiling behind me caved in, crashing down with a cacophony of stone grinding against stone. It collapsed a section of the floor and knocked my feet from under me. I hit the ground shoulder first, skidding through salt.

When I finally came to a stop, I blinked away dust, coughing. Sparks. My leg hurt. I'd twisted my ankle in the fall.

The debris settled to reveal that most of the floor of the suite was gone. I had ended up inside Prof's chambers, near Tia, who had taken cover beside the desk, her mobile gripped tightly in her fist. It was connected by wires to the data drive of a computer powered—along with the swinging lightbulbs—by the small generator that puttered in the corner.

Megan hadn't so much as flinched. She turned toward me. Behind her, on the other side of the hole in the floor, Prof's guards called to one another and pulled themselves out of the rubble. To her right, Prof loomed over Tavi, who was crumpled on the floor. Her forcefield was gone. She stirred, but didn't rise.

Megan met my eyes, hands raised before her. Her lips curled in a sneer, but she held my gaze, then gritted her teeth. I sensed a plea in her expression. Still lying on the broken floor, I yanked my gun from its holster, then leveled it and fired.

At the generator.

Like the one above, it had a gas tank. It didn't explode as I'd expected, but the shots punctured it and sparked a fire, sending up jets of flame.

The lights immediately went out.

"No!" Tia cried.

Megan stared into the fire, and it danced in her eyes.

"Face it, Megan," I whispered. "Please."

She stepped toward it, as if drawn by its heat. Then she screamed and ran forward, passing me and thrusting her arm into the flames.

Megan collapsed. Tavi vanished. The rents in the air shrank away. I let out a relieved breath and managed to crawl over to Megan, dragging my pained foot behind me.

She trembled, clutching her arm, which she'd burned severely. I pulled her farther from the generator, in case it flared up, and folded her into my arms.

In the pitch-black room, there were only two lights: the dwindling fire . . .

And Prof.

Megan squeezed her eyes shut, shaking from her ordeal. She'd saved our lives, had put my plan into motion, and it hadn't been enough. I could see that easily as Prof strode toward us. He stepped up to the lip of the broken hole in the floor, then across it, a forcefield forming under his feet. Lit from beneath, he looked like a specter, his face mostly in shadow.

Prof had always possessed a kind of . . . unfinished look. Features like a stack of broken bricks, his face usually accented by stubble. Today though, I could spot signs of exhaustion as well. The slowness of his step, the streaks of sweat on his face, the slump to his shoulders. His fight with Tavi had been difficult. He was practically indestructible, but he *did* get tired.

He studied me and Megan. "Kill them," he said, then turned his back on us and walked off into the shadows.

Two dozen guards lowered their weapons to fire. I pulled Megan close, close enough to hear her whisper.

"I die as me," she said. "At least I die as me."

Fire. Her powers were negated. She was always without them for a minute or two after deliberately burning herself.

If she died now, would it be permanent?

No.

No . . . What have I done?

I twisted, sheltering her as the guards opened fire in a terrible barrage. The walls exploded in sprays of salt chips. The computer monitor shattered. Bullets pelted the area, accompanied by the earsplitting sound of weapons fire.

I clutched Megan close, my back to the assault.

Something stirred again within me. Those depths lurking in my soul, the blackness below. Shadows moving around me, screams, emotions like spikes piercing me, the sudden and overpowering sensation from my dreams. I threw back my head and screamed.

The gunfire stilled, a few last pops sounding as the magazines fell empty. With an enemy Epic in their sights, these people had not hesitated or held back. Several flipped on lights attached to their guns, to inspect their handiwork.

I awaited the pain, or at least the numbness, that came from having been shot. I felt neither. Hesitant, I turned to look behind me. Destruction surrounded us—floor, walls, furniture splintered, pocked, broken . . . all except in my immediate area. The ground here wasn't broken at all. In fact, it was glassy and reflective. A deep, burnished silver-black. Metallic.

I was alive.

Regalia's voice whispered from my memory. *I have been assured that you will be . . . thematically appropriate.*

"Impressive," Prof said from the shadows. "What did

she do? Open a door to another world and send the bullets through?" He sounded tired. "I will have to do this myself. Don't think it doesn't pain me."

"Jonathan . . . ," a voice whispered.

I frowned. It had come from nearby. Who—

I'd forgotten about Tia.

She slumped against the saltstone desk, lit by the fluttering firelight. She had been hiding there, but the bullets had gotten her. She bled from multiple hits, mobile clutched in her fingers. It had been shot straight through.

"Jon," she said. "You bastard. You feared it would come to . . . this." She coughed. "I was wrong, and you were right. As . . . always."

Prof stepped into the light of the soldiers' weapons. That haggard, broken face seemed to change, his jaw dropping. He seemed to *see* for the first time that night. So he got to watch as Tia breathed a last ragged breath and died.

I knelt, stunned, and barely heard Prof's roar—his sudden, shocked cry of agony and regret. He tore across the hole in the floor on a field of light, charging past me and Megan, ignoring us as he grabbed Tia.

"Heal!" he commanded her. "Heal! I gift it to you!"

I held on to Megan, deadened, disbelieving. Tia's figure remained limp in his hands.

The floor vaporized. The walls, the ceiling, the *entire tower*. It all shattered to dust in the face of Prof's tormented scream. Soldiers dropped like stones, though a bubble sprang up around Prof and Tia.

My stomach lurched as Megan and I also began to plummet through salt dust seventy stories toward the ground. "Megan!" I shouted.

Her eyes had drooped closed. I held on to her, tumbling.

No. No. *NO.*

Bodies fell around us in the night, sprays of dust and furniture, scraps of cloth. They passed us.

"Megan!" I screamed again, over the sound of wind and terrified soldiers. "Wake up!"

Her eyes flared open and seemed to burn in the night. I jerked, barely keeping hold of her—as suddenly I was in a parachute's harness.

We smacked the ground mere moments later, hitting with a distressing *crunch*. Then the pain arrived. I gasped at its intensity, like a wave of electricity running up my body from my legs. It was so overpowering, I couldn't move. I suffered it, staring upward into the black sky.

And at Calamity, who stared back.

Time passed. Not much, but enough. I heard footsteps. "He's here," Abraham's voice said, urgent. "You were right. Sparks! That *was* a parachute. One of ours, but I didn't leave any behind. . . ."

I turned my head, blinking away salt dust to find him, a hulking form in the night.

"I've got you, David," Abraham said, taking me by the arm.

"Megan," I whispered. "Under the chute." It had drifted down over her after we hit.

Abraham moved over, picking at the parachute. "She's here," he said, sounding relieved. "And she's breathing. Cody, Mizzy, I need your help. David, we're going to have to move you. We can't wait. Prof's up there, glowing. He could come down at any moment."

I braced myself as Abraham hefted me over his shoulder. The other two arrived, pulling Megan out of the rubble. There was no time to worry whether they were doing more damage than good.

They dragged us off into the night, leaving behind the wreckage of a mission we had failed, utterly and completely.

34

I didn't sleep, though when Cody had us pause in an alley to see if we were being tailed, I let Abraham give me something for the pain. Mizzy worked on a litter to help carry Megan and me while Abraham inspected me. Turned out I'd snapped both legs when I hit the ground.

The sky had turned sour by the time we left that alley, and a misty rain started falling on us, making the roadway slick with salty water. The saltstone held up better than I'd have expected though. No mass melting of the city.

The rain felt good at first, washing some of the dust from my skin as I lay in the litter beside Megan. But by the time we approached the bridge in the park, I was soaked through. The lumpish sight of our base, growing under the bridge ahead like some strange fungus, was a beautiful thing.

Megan was still unconscious, but she seemed to have fared better than I had. No broken bones that Abraham could find, though she was going to have some serious bruises, and her arm was burned and blistered.

"Well, we're alive," Cody said as we stopped at the doorway to the hideout. "Unless of course we didn't spot a tail and Prof is lurking out there, waiting for us to lead him to Larcener."

"Your optimism is so encouraging, Cody," Mizzy said.

It took a little work to navigate our litter through the entrance, which we'd made as a small tunnel covered in rubble on one end. I was able to help by pushing with my hands. My legs still hurt, but it was more a "Hey, don't forget about us" kind of hurt than the "HOLY HECK, WE'RE BROKEN" it had been before.

The hideout smelled of the soup Larcener liked—a simple vegetable broth with almost no taste. Abraham lit the place with his mobile.

"Turn that off, idiot," Larcener snapped from his room.

He must be meditating again. I sat up in my litter as Mizzy crawled in, then sighed and dropped her equipment into a pile. "I need a shower," she called to Larcener. "What's a girl got to do to get you to conjure one?"

"Die," Larcener called back.

"Mizzy," Abraham said softly, "check over the equipment, and return to Larcener the things he created for us, with our thanks. It probably does not matter, as they will just fade away, but perhaps the gesture will mean something to him. Cody, watch outside for any signs of pursuit. Now that we have more time, I want to check these two over more thoroughly."

I nodded dully. Yeah. Orders. Orders needed to be given. But . . . the trip here was something of a blur to me. "We need a debriefing," I said. "I've discovered things."

"Later, David," Abraham said gently.

"But—"

"You're in shock, David," he said. "Let us rest first."

I sighed and lay back. I didn't feel like I was in shock. Sure, I was clammy and cold—but I'd been rained on. Yes, I was trembling, and hadn't been able to think of much during the trip here. But that was because of how thoroughly *draining* it had all been.

I doubted he'd listen to my arguments. Despite the fact that he agreed I was in charge, Abraham could be downright motherly. I did convince him to see to Megan first, and with Mizzy's help he carried her away to change her out of the wet, ripped evening gown and make sure she hadn't suffered any unnoticed wounds. Then Abraham returned to splint my legs.

About an hour later Abraham, Mizzy, and I huddled together in the smallest of the rooms in our new base—far enough from Larcener to speak privately, we hoped. Megan lay bundled up in the corner, asleep.

Abraham kept eyeing me, expecting me to doze off. I remained stubbornly awake, seated against the wall with my splinted legs stretched before me. They'd given me some industrial-strength painkillers, so I was able to confidently stare back at him.

Abraham sighed. "Let me check on Cody," he said. "Then we will talk."

That left me and Mizzy. She sipped some hot cocoa she'd bought at the market a few days ago. I couldn't stand the stuff. Way too sweet.

"So," she said, "that . . . wasn't a *complete* disaster, right?"

"Tia's dead," I said, my voice hoarse. "We failed."

Mizzy winced, looking down into her cup. "Yeah. But . . .

I mean . . . you got to test one of your theories. We know more than we did yesterday."

I shook my head, sick with worry over Megan, frustrated that we'd gone through so much to save Tia only to lose her for good. I felt adrift, and defeated, and pained. I'd looked up to Tia; she'd been one of the first of the team to treat me like someone useful. Now I'd failed her.

Could I have done more? I hadn't said anything about how I'd survived the gunfire. Truth was, I didn't know the answer myself. I mean . . . I suspected. But I didn't *know*, so what use was there in talking about it?

Lying to ourselves, are we? a piece of me asked.

"That parachute," Mizzy said, glancing at Megan. "She made it, didn't she?"

I nodded.

"She put it on you, instead of on herself," Mizzy said. "She's always like that. I suppose if you're reborn when you die, it makes sense. . . ." She trailed off.

Abraham stepped back in. "He's as happy as a jackrabbit in its den," he said. "Hunkered up on the bridge in his raincoat, chewing on beef jerky and looking for something to shoot. Nothing so far. We may actually have escaped."

He settled down, sitting cross-legged. Then he carefully removed the pendant he wore, the symbol of the Faithful, and held it before himself. It sparkled, silvery, in the light of the mobiles we'd set out.

"Abraham," I said. "I know that . . . I mean, Tia was a friend. . . ."

"More than a friend," he said softly. "My superior officer, and one I disobeyed. I believe we made the right call, and she the wrong one, but I cannot take her loss lightly. Please. A moment."

We waited, and he closed his eyes and said a quiet prayer in French. Was it to God, or to those mythical Epics he believed would save us someday? He wrapped the chain of his pendant into his hand and held it close, but as usual I couldn't get a good feel for his emotional state. Reverence? Pain? Worry?

Finally, he took a deep breath and put the necklace back on. "You have information, David. You feel it important to share. We will mourn Tia properly when the war is through. Speak. What happened in there?"

He and Mizzy looked at me expectantly, so I swallowed, then started talking. I'd already told them about Tavi, but now I explained what had happened when I'd been sucked into Firefight's world. The things I'd seen. Steelheart.

I rambled a lot. In truth, I *was* tired. They probably were as well, but I couldn't go to sleep. Not before unloading the burden of what I'd seen, what I'd discovered. I told them everything I could before eventually trailing off. Any more, and I'd have to talk about what I suspected regarding my own . . . development.

"He killed you?" Abraham said. "In their world, Steelheart killed you? Is that what they said?"

I nodded.

"Curious. That world is similar to our own, yet different in such important ways."

"You didn't ask him about me, did you?" Mizzy asked.

"No. Why? Should I have?"

She yawned. "I dunno. Maybe I'm, like, some kinda super-awesome ninja thing over there."

"I'd say you were a super-awesome ninja thing today," Abraham said. "You performed that mission well."

She blushed, taking a drink of her cocoa.

"A world with no Calamity," Abraham said. "But what

does that—" His mobile started buzzing. He frowned, looking at it. "I do not know this number." He turned it around toward me.

"Knighthawk," I said. "Answer it."

He did so, lifting it to his ear, then moved it away as Knighthawk started talking loudly. Abraham lowered the phone. "He is excited about something," he said.

"Obviously," Mizzy said. "Speaker that sucker."

Abraham pressed the requisite buttons. Knighthawk's face appeared on the mobile and his voice projected into the room.

"—can't believe the *balls* on that woman. What happened to David's mobile? Did he get it vaporized? I haven't been able to track the thing for hours."

I pulled mine out. It had survived the fight, barely—with a cracked screen and a ripped-off back, battery gone.

"It . . . has seen better days," Abraham said.

"He really needs to be more careful," Knighthawk said. "Those things aren't free."

"I know," I said. "You made us pay for them."

"Heh," Knighthawk said. He was shockingly, even annoyingly, chipper. "I'll send you a replacement on the house after this, kid."

"This?" I asked.

"Regalia's data," he said. "It's incredible. Haven't you been reading it?"

"The data?" I said. "Knighthawk, that was on Tia's . . . mobile. You *copied* it?"

"Of course I copied it," he said. "You think I built a nationwide network of data links for fun? Well, it *is* fun. But that's because I get to read people's mail."

"Send us a complete dump," Abraham said.

Knighthawk fell silent.

"Knighthawk?" I said. "You're not—"

"Hush," he said. "I'm not ditching you. I just got another call." He swore sharply. "One second."

Silence. The three of us regarded one another, uncertain. If Knighthawk *had* grabbed that data, then perhaps the mission wasn't a complete write-off.

He came back a few minutes later. "Well, hell," he said. "That was Jonathan."

"Prof?" I said.

"Yeah. Demanded that I track you. I don't know how he figured out I can do that. I've always told him I can't."

"And?" Mizzy asked.

"I sent him to the other side of the city," Knighthawk replied. "Nowhere near you guys. Which means that once he's done with you, he's basically *guaranteed* to come murder me. I should have turned you idiots away at my door."

"Um . . . thank you?" Mizzy said.

"I'm sending you a copy of Regalia's plans," Knighthawk said. "Keep in mind that it references a few photos that aren't in the folder. That's not because I'm holding out on you; it's because the mobile died before finishing the full download of the files. Tell Tia she did great though."

"Tia got shot," I said, subdued. "He killed her."

The line fell silent again, though I heard Knighthawk breathe out after a short time. "Calamity," he whispered. "I never thought he'd go that far. I mean, I knew he would . . . but *Tia*?"

"I don't think he meant to," I said. "He turned his goons loose on us, and she ended up dead."

"Your transfer is working," Abraham said, holding up his mobile. "Does this data explain what Prof is *doing* here?"

"Sure does," Knighthawk said, growing excited again. "He—"

"He's here for Larcener," I broke in. "He's here to make a motivator from Larcener's assumer abilities, then use that to absorb Calamity's powers—all of them—thereby becoming the ultimate Epic."

Mizzy blinked in shock, and Abraham looked up at me.

"Oh," Knighthawk said. "So you *did* read the data?"

"No," I said. "It just makes sense." The pieces were falling into place. "That's why Regalia brought Obliteration to Babilar, isn't it? She could have come up with a hundred different ways to threaten the city and force Prof to use his powers. But she invited him because she wanted to make a motivator out of his destruction powers to hide what she was *really* doing."

"Making a teleporter," Knighthawk said. "So she could get to Calamity, once she had Larcener's abilities. But she died before putting her plan into motion, so Prof is doing it instead. Sharp guess, kid. You've been holding out on me; you're nowhere near as stupid as you act. As a side note, I'm abandoning my base here. Manny is already carting me to the jeep. I'm *not* going to hang around here when the most dangerous Epic in the world can likely teleport anywhere he wants in an eyeblink."

"He'd alert Obliteration if he did that," I said. "Part of the reason for the bomb in Babilar was to keep Obliteration from knowing that his powers were being stolen."

"Still leaving, at least until Jonathan cools off from my little goose chase."

"Knighthawk," Abraham said. "We need your harmsway. We have wounded."

"Tough," he said. "It's the only one I've got right now. I love you guys—well, I don't actively dislike you guys—but my skin is more important than yours."

"And if I could give you something to make another one?" I asked, digging in my pocket. I pulled out the tissue sample container and held it up. Abraham obligingly turned his mobile around to give Knighthawk a view.

"Is that . . . ," Knighthawk's voice said.

"Yes. From Prof."

"Everyone else get out of the room. I want to talk to the kid alone."

Abraham raised an eyebrow at me, and I nodded. Reluctantly, Abraham handed me his mobile, and he and Mizzy left. I slumped back against the wall, looking at Knighthawk's face on the screen of the mobile. His own mobile seemed to be secured before him with some kind of device he wore around his neck, as Manny carried him through one of his tunnels.

"You did it," Knighthawk said softly. "How? His force-fields should have protected him from harm."

"Megan reached into an alternate dimension," I said, "and pulled out a version of Prof. Kind of."

"Kind of?"

"His daughter," I said. "His and Tia's, I think. She had his same powers, Knighthawk. And . . ." I took a deep breath. "And that's his weakness. His powers. At least, so Tia claimed."

"Hmm . . . ," he said. "Makes sense, knowing Jonathan. Odd that his daughter has his powers. Children of Epics here have been born without powers. Anyway, she got past his abilities?"

"Yeah," I said. "I managed to blow a chunk of skin off him and bag it for you."

"Man," Knighthawk said, "we are *really* asking for it here, you realize. If he knows you have that . . ."

"He does."

Knighthawk shook his head, rueful. "Well, if I'm going to get murdered, might as well let an old friend do it. I'll send you that harmsway via drone, but you send me back that sample. Deal?"

"Deal, with one condition."

"Which is?"

"We need a way to fight Prof," I said. "And make him face his powers."

"Have your pet Epic summon another version of him."

"No. It didn't work; we were able to bypass his powers, but he didn't turn. I need to try something else."

That was true, but only halfway. I glanced at Megan, unconscious and breathing softly. Doing what she'd done tonight had nearly destroyed her; I wouldn't ask her to do something like that again. It wasn't fair to her, and it certainly wasn't fair to the person we brought through into our world.

"So . . . ," Knighthawk said.

I held up the sample container. "There's another way to make him confront someone using his powers, Knighthawk."

The man laughed. "You're serious."

"Serious as a dog about to be given treats," I said. "How long would it take? To make devices for all three powers. Forcefields, regeneration, disintegration."

"Months," Knighthawk said. "A year even, if any of the abilities are tough to crack."

I'd worried about that. "If that's the only way, we'll have to do it." I did not relish being on the run for a year, keeping Larcener out of Prof's hands.

Knighthawk studied me. His mannequin set him into his jeep, then did up the seat belt. "You've got guts," Knighthawk said. "You know how I said we did testing on early Epics and discovered that a living Epic was pained by a motivator created from them?"

"Yeah?"

"Did I tell you *who* we tested on?"

"You have them already," I said. "That's why you're so

eager for Prof's cells. You've already *built* devices to replicate his powers."

"We built them together," he said. "He and I."

"In your room," I said. "The one with the mementos of fallen Epics. One didn't have a plaque. A vest and gloves."

"Yeah. We destroyed all his tissue samples after we discovered how much it hurt him. I think that all along he's been worried I would get another sample from him. He's certainly kept his distance from me." Knighthawk's mannequin rubbed his chin, as if in thought. "Guess he was right to worry. You send me those cells, and I will be able to get you devices mimicking his powers almost instantly. But I'm going to try his healing powers on my wife first."

"You do that, and he'll know immediately," I said. "And he'll come kill you."

Knighthawk gritted his teeth.

"You're going to have to gamble on us, Knighthawk," I said. "Send us the devices. We'll turn him, and then we can try to save your wife. It's the only chance you have."

"Fine."

"Thank you."

"It's self-preservation at this point, kid," Knighthawk said. "The drone I send will reach you in six hours. The return trip with your tissue sample will take another six to reach me at my safehouse. Assuming the cells are good, I can get to work on a full set of motivators for you. Forcefield projection, healing powers, and tensor abilities."

"Will do."

"And David," Knighthawk said as his mannequin started the jeep. "Don't get cute. This time if he doesn't turn, do what we both know you need to. After killing Tia . . . sparks, what kind of life is he going to live going forward? Put him out of his misery. He'd thank you for it."

The line went dead, Knighthawk's face vanishing. I sat there, trying to process everything that had happened tonight. Tia, Firefight, Prof's face in the shadows. A patch of dark grey metal on the floor.

Eventually I put aside the mobile, then turned and—ignoring the protest of my splinted legs—pulled myself across the room until I was beside Megan. I rested my head on her chest and wrapped my arm around her, listening to her heartbeat until I finally, at long last, fell asleep.

PART FOUR

35

I woke up in a sweat. Again.

Those same images haunted me. Sounds garish and terrible. Harsh lights. Fear, terror, abandonment. None of the normal relief that came with waking from a nightmare. No comfort from the realization that it was only a dream.

These nightmares were different. They left me panicked. Raw, flayed, bruised, like a slab of meat in a boxing movie. After I awoke, I had to sit there on the floor—broken legs aching—for what seemed like an eternity before my pulse recovered.

Sparks. Something was *very* wrong with me.

At least I hadn't woken any of the others. Abraham and Cody slept on their pallets, and during the night sometime

I'd found my way from Megan's pallet to my own, which the others had set out for me. Mizzy's was empty; she'd be on watch. I reached beside my pillow, where I was pleased to find my mobile—repaired by Mizzy—waiting for me.

Checking the mobile showed that it was six in the morning, and its light revealed a glass of water and several pills on a box set beside my pallet. I gulped them down, eager to get some painkillers into my system. After that, I pulled myself to a sitting position beside the wall, noticing for the first time that my side and arms ached as well. I'd done some real damage to my body during that mission.

I felt at my back and found a set of strange bruises shaped—best I could tell—like quarters. The growing pain of my legs and accumulated wounds was bad enough that I had to sit there for I don't know how long until the meds started to kick in. Once I could think clearly, I started searching through my mobile. Abraham had forwarded the entire team the data package Tia had recovered, so I dug into it, trying not to worry whether I'd eventually have to wake up Abraham or Cody to take me to the restroom.

Regalia's writing was clear, careful, straightforward. I felt like I could hear her voice as I read. So certain, so calm, so *infuriating*. She'd stolen Prof from us in a deliberate, destructive act—just to sate her own lust for an immortal legacy.

Still, the reading was good. Regalia's plan was incredible. Audacious even; I couldn't help but feel a growing respect for her. As I'd guessed, Regalia had summoned Obliteration not because of his ability to destroy cities, but for his teleportation powers.

Her plot reached back some five years, but she'd eventually run up against a final and unanticipated deadline: her own mortality. Epic powers could not cure natural diseases. She had found herself terminal, and so she'd looked for a successor in Prof. Someone who could travel to Ildithia, make a motivator from Larcener, then teleport to Calamity and do the unthinkable.

Despite the plan's insane brilliance, it was filled with holes. By our best assumptions, Calamity was the source of all Epic powers. But who was to say that you could even steal his abilities in the first place? And if you did, wouldn't that simply replace Calamity with another host who acted exactly the same?

Still, at least this plan had been something to try—something to do other than accepting the world as it was. For that I respected Regalia, though I had been the one to kill her in the end.

Once done with Regalia's notes, I opened a set of photos. Past the maps of Ildithia, I found several shots of Calamity. The first three were pictures through a telescope. These were indistinct; I'd seen shots like them before. They made Calamity look like some kind of star.

The final image was different. I'd worried about what Knighthawk had said, that not all the images had made the transfer. I'd worried there wouldn't be any real pictures of Calamity.

But here one was, staring at me from the glowing screen in my hand. It wasn't a terribly good shot—I got the distinct impression of a covert photo snapped with a mobile—but it was obviously the Epic. A figure made of red light, though I couldn't tell if it was male or female. It seemed to be standing in a room, and all around it light reflected off odd angles and surfaces.

I searched through the files for anything similar, to no avail. Other shots of Calamity, if there had been any, were lost. Curiously, however, it appeared that Knighthawk had copied the *entire* memory of Tia's mobile, not just the new files from

Regalia. Indeed, a folder simply labeled *Jonathan* glowed on my screen. I knew that I should probably leave it alone, that it was private, but I couldn't help myself. I thumbed into it and tapped on the first media file.

It was a video of Prof in a classroom.

I kept the sound low, but could still hear the enthusiasm in his voice as he took a lighter and moved down a line of eggs with holes in the top, setting them on fire. Students laughed and jumped as each egg popped in turn, exploding from the hydrogen Prof explained he'd filled them with.

Balloons went next, each flashing and popping in a different way as he went down the line. I didn't care much about the science involved; I was too focused on Prof. A younger Prof, with jet-black hair, only a few strands of grey. An enthusiastic Prof, who seemed to be enjoying every moment of this demonstration, despite the fact that he'd likely done it a hundred times.

He seemed like an entirely different person. I realized that in all our time together, I couldn't remember seeing Prof *happy*. Satisfied, yes. Eager. But truly happy? Not before this moment, watching him interact with students.

This was what we'd lost. I struggled to hold back my emotions as the video ended. The coming of Calamity had broken this world in more ways than one. Prof should have still been there, teaching those children.

Footsteps outside caused me to quickly wipe my eyes. Mizzy peeked in a moment later, then held up something the size of a basketball, with rotor blades on top. One of Knighthawk's drones.

"The guy works fast," she said, setting it down. Abraham and Cody stirred; they'd likely asked to be woken up when the thing arrived. Megan turned over, and for a moment I thought she was going to wake too. But she fell back asleep, snoring softly.

As Mizzy set down the drone, Cody and Abraham turned on their mobiles, lighting the room further. I watched as Mizzy twisted the top half of the device off, revealing a compartment, and pulled out a box that looked a lot like the harmsway we'd used in Newcago. Prof had apparently developed his fake to look like the real thing.

"Nice," Abraham said, rubbing his eyes.

"I'm surprised you convinced him to send it, David," Mizzy said as she set it aside.

Cody yawned. "Either way, let's get that puppy hooked up and running. The sooner David's legs are working, the sooner we can be out of this city."

"Out of this city?" I said.

The other three looked at me.

"You . . . intend to stay, then?" Abraham said, careful. "David, Tia is dead, and your theory—smart though it was—proved false. Confronting Prof with his weakness did not turn him away from his current course."

"Yeah, lad," Cody said. "It was a good run, but we know what he's trying to accomplish here, and we *do* have a way to stop it. We slip away with Larcener, and his plot can never work."

"That's assuming we *want* it not to work," Mizzy added.

"*Mizzy,*" I said, surprised. "He's trying to become the ultimate Epic!"

"So?" she said. "I mean, how does our life change if he takes Calamity's place? There's no doomsday coming—no 'Imma destroy the world, kids' or anything like that. So far as I can see, all he wants to do is kill a couple of Epics. Sounds toasty to me."

"I suggest," Abraham said softly, "that you do not say such things where we might be overheard."

Mizzy winced and checked over her shoulder. "All I'm saying is that there isn't a *reason* for us to be here, now that we know what Prof's up to."

"And where do we go, Mizzy?" I asked.

"I don't know. How about we start with a place *other* than the city inhabited by a guy determined to kill us?"

I could see that the other two agreed, at least in part.

"Guys, the reason we came here in the first place hasn't changed," I said. "Prof still needs us. The *world* still needs us. Have you forgotten the point of our mission? We *need* to find a way to convert Epics, not just kill them. Otherwise we might as well give up now."

"But, lad," Cody said, "Abraham is right. Your plan to turn Prof didn't work."

"*That* attempt didn't work," I said. "But there are logical reasons why it might be the case. Maybe he didn't see Tavi as having *his* powers—he saw them as belonging to another Epic; similar, but different. So confronting her wasn't confronting his abilities."

"Or," Abraham said, "Tia was wrong about his weakness."

"No," I said. "The fight with Tavi did negate his powers. She could destroy his forcefields, and he couldn't heal from wounds her attacks caused. Like Steelheart could be hurt only by someone who didn't fear him, Prof can be hurt only by someone wielding his own powers."

"This is all irrelevant, regardless," Abraham said. "You said that Megan summoned this woman because she could not find an actual version of Prof. Her powers are limited then, and this was our sole method of making him face himself."

"Not necessarily," I said, fishing in my pocket and taking

out the cell incubator device. I rolled it across the ground to Mizzy, who picked it up.

"Is this . . . ," she said.

"Tissue sample from Prof," I said.

Cody whistled softly.

"We *can* make him face himself, Abraham," I said. "We can do it literally by creating motivators using his own cells. Knighthawk already has a prototype ready from years ago."

The others fell silent.

"Look," I said. "We *need* to give this another try."

"He's going to persuade us," Mizzy said. "It's kinda what he does."

"Yes," Abraham agreed, motioning for her to roll him the tissue sample. He picked it up. "I won't argue with you further, David. If you believe it worth another attempt, we will support you." He turned the tissue sample over in his fingers. "But I don't like giving this to Knighthawk. It feels like . . . like a betrayal of Prof."

"More of a betrayal than him killing members of his own team?"

The comment quieted the room, like a sudden shout of "Who wants extra bacon?" at a bar mitzvah.

Mizzy took the tissue sample back from Abraham, then placed it in the drone. "I'll go release this while it's still dark," she said, standing. Cody joined her; he was next on watch. The two slipped out, while Abraham picked up the harmsway, then walked over to me.

"Megan first," I said.

"Megan is unconscious, David," he said. "A state that might not be caused merely by her wounds from the fire and the fall. I suggest that we first heal the person we know will return to fighting readiness."

I sighed. "All right."

"Very wise."

"You should be leading this team, Abraham," I said as he wrapped the diodes of the harmsway around the exposed skin of my feet and ankles. "We both know it. Why did you refuse?"

"You do not ask this question of Cody," Abraham said.

"Because Cody is a loon. You have experience, you're calm in a fight, you're decisive. . . . Why put me in charge?"

Abraham continued working, switching on the device, which caused a fuzzy feeling in my legs, like I'd slept on them wrong. If my wound back at the Foundry was any guide, this device—created from some unknown Epic—wouldn't be as efficient as using Prof's powers had been. It might take some time to heal me fully.

"I was JTF2," Abraham said. "Cansofcom."

"Which is . . . what exactly? Other than a strange jumble of letters."

"Canadian special forces."

"I knew it!"

"Yes, you are very smart."

"Was that . . . sarcasm?"

"Smart again," Abraham said.

I eyed him. "If you were military," I said, "that makes it even *stranger* you haven't taken command. Were you an officer?"

"Yes."

"High rank?"

"High enough."

"And . . ."

"You know Powder?"

"Epic," I said. "Could cause gunpowder and unstable materials to explode just by looking at them. He . . ." I swallowed, remembering a point from my notes. "He tried to conquer Canada, second year A.C. Attacked their military bases."

"Killed my whole team when he hit Trenton," Abraham said, standing up. "Everyone but me."

"Why not you?"

"I was in the stockade awaiting court-martial." He eyed me. "I appreciate your enthusiasm and your grit, but you are young, yet, to understand the world as much as you think you do." He raised his fingers to me in salute, then walked away.

36

I scraped the wall of our under-bridge hideout, easily breaking off salt and rubbing it between my fingers. Time to move again. Though we'd always considered this to be an interim hideout, it felt like we'd barely gotten here. It left me feeling transient. How could anyone get a sense of *home* in this city?

I crossed the room, stretching my now-healed legs. They still ached—though I hadn't admitted that to the others—but I felt sturdy and strong. It had only taken a few hours in the night; I'd been ready by the time dawn arrived.

Megan's arm and bruises had also been healed. The harmsway worked on her, blessedly. I'd been worried about that since in Newcago, she couldn't be healed or use the tensors. Both of those abilities, however, had secretly come from

Prof—and as Knighthawk had said, sometimes the abilities of specific Epics interfered with one another.

Well, this harmsway had worked, but she still hadn't woken up. Abraham told me not to be concerned; he said it wasn't uncommon for someone to spend a day or two in bed following something so traumatic. He was trying to comfort me. How could anyone know what was or wasn't normal when it came to an Epic overextending their powers?

Mizzy's head popped out of the storage room. "Hey, slontze. Knighthawk is ticked at you. Check your phone."

I dug out my mobile, which had been muffled from being in the bottom of my bag. Forty-seven messages. Calamity! What had gone wrong? I scrambled to open the messenger. Maybe the cells hadn't taken. Or the drone had been shot down by a wandering Epic. Or Knighthawk had decided to switch sides on us.

Instead, I was treated to the sight of forty-seven messages of Knighthawk saying things like *Hey* or *Yo* or *Hey, you. Idiot.*

I quickly messaged him. *Is something wrong?*

Your didgeridooing face, the message came back.

The cells, I sent. *They're broken?*

Exactly how does one BREAK cells, kid?

I don't know, I sent back. *You're the one sending emergency texts to me!*

Emergency? Knighthawk sent. *I'm just bored.*

I blinked, holding my phone and rereading that text.

Bored? I sent. *You're literally spying on the entire world, Knighthawk. You can read anyone's mail, listen to anyone's phone calls.*

First, it's not the whole world, he wrote. *Only large chunks of North and Central America. Second, do you have any idea how mind-numbingly DULL most people are?*

I started a reply, but a flurry of messages came at me, interrupting what I was going to say.

Oh! Knighthawk wrote. *Look at this pretty flower!*

Hey. I want to know if you like me, but I can't say that, so here's an awkward flirtation instead.

Where are you?

I'm here.

Where?

Here.

There?

No, here.

Oh.

Look at my kid.

Look at my dog.

Look at me.

Look at me holding my kid and dog.

Hey, everyone. I took a huge koala this morning.

Barf. The world is ruled by deific beings who can do stuff like melt buildings into puddles of acid, and all people can think of to do with their phones is take pictures of their pets and try to figure out how to get laid.

Well . . . I wrote to test if his diatribe was done yet. *The people who can afford your mobiles are the privileged rich. You shouldn't be surprised they're shallow.*

Nah, he wrote back. *There are more than a few cities like Newcago, where the ruling Epics are clever enough to realize that a population with mobiles is a population they can propagandize and control. I can tell you, the poor are just as bad. Except their pets are mangier.*

Is there a point to this? I asked.

Yeah. Entertaining me. Say something stupid. I've got popcorn and everything.

I sighed, tucking away the mobile and returning to my work—going over the list of Epics who, according to rumors in the city today, had died as a result of Prof's tantrum at Sharp Tower. There had been dozens of them at the party, and very few of them had flight powers or prime invincibilities. He'd killed off half of Ildithia's upper class.

My mobile buzzed again. I groaned, but glanced at it.

Hey, Knighthawk said. *My drones did a flyby on your city. You want the pictures or what?*

Pictures? I wrote back.

Yeah. For the imager. You've got one, right?

You know about the imager?

Kid, I MADE that thing.

It's Epic technology?

Of course it is, he said. *What, you think projectors that magically render near-three-dimensional images on irregular surfaces, without causing shadows from the people inside, are NATURAL?*

I honestly had no idea. But if he was offering a scan of the city, I'd take it.

It's one of the few I managed to mass-produce, like the technology for your mobiles, Knighthawk added. *Most tech like this, it degrades significantly if you make more than one or two motivators from the cells. Not imagers though. Sparks—mobiles don't even NEED motivators, except the ones I keep here in the hub. Anyway, you want this imager file or not?*

I do, thanks, I wrote. *What's the progress on the motivators from Prof's cells?*

I've got to grow the culture a little first, he said. *Will take at least a day before we know if it all worked, and if I've made Jonathan into my motivator dingo or not.*

Great, I said. *Keep me up to date.*

Sure. So long as you promise to record yourself the next time you say something stupid. Damn, I miss the internet. You could always find people doing stupid stuff on the internet.

I sighed, pocketing the mobile. It, of course, beeped at me again a short time later. I grabbed it, annoyed and ready to tell off Knighthawk, but it was a notification saying my mobile had received a large data package. The scan of the city.

I didn't know much about technology, but I was able to tether the phone to the imager in the storage room, then transfer the file. When I turned on the machine, I found myself hovering above Ildithia. The grandeur of this was spoiled by the piles of supplies in the room, which also hovered in the sky, like I was some kind of magical space hobo who flew about with my possessions in tow.

I did a quick sweep through the city, using my hands to adjust the perspective, reacquainting myself with the controls. The imager faithfully reproduced Ildithia, and for a moment I let the illusion of it run away with me. I swooped past a skyscraper, the windows a blur on my right, then pulled up to soar down a street, passing saltstone trees. I wove between them in rapid succession, then shot through a park past our hideout.

I felt alive, thrilled, awake and alert. My incapacitation with broken legs had been brief, but it had still left me confined, controlled, *powerless*. Sparks . . . it felt like it had been years since I'd been able to walk in the open without fear of exposing my team.

I delighted in the freedom of flying around the city. Then I hit a building. I continued through it, the scenery blurring to a black jumble of nothing until I emerged from the other side.

That reminded me that this was a fabrication, a lie. Objects warped when I drew too close to them, and I could see the corners of the room if I looked hard.

Worse, no wind greeted me upon my leaps. No lurch in my stomach marked gravity's disapproval. I might as well have been watching a movie. There was no fun to this, no power. And it wasn't nearly wet enough.

"That looked fun," Cody said from the doorway, which opened like a portal in the middle of the air. I hadn't seen him approach.

I flattened my hands, lowering the camera view so I settled in place atop the small apartment building. "I miss the spyril."

In all the running around, fighting, and fleeing we'd done lately, I hadn't thought much about the device that had let me fly through the watery streets of Babilar. Now I recognized a hole inside me. For a short time in that drowned city, I'd known true freedom, powered by twin jets of water.

Cody chuckled, sauntering in. "I remember the first time you saw the imager work, lad. You looked like you were about to show us all what you'd eaten for lunch."

"Yeah," I said. "I took to it pretty quick though."

"I suppose you did," Cody said, joining me on the rooftop, then turning to look over the city. "You have a plan for us yet?"

"No," I said. "Any thoughts?"

"Coming up with plans has never been my strong point."

"Why not? Seems like you're pretty good at making things up."

He pointed at me. "I've punched men for wisecracks like that." He paused. "Of course, most were Scots."

"Your own kind?" I asked. "Why would you fight other Scots?"

"Lad, you don't know much about us, do you?"

"Only what you've told me."

"Well, I guess you know a heap of things then. Just none of them useful." He smiled, looking out over the city, thoughtful. "Back when I was in the force, if we had to bring in someone dangerous, first thing we did was try to catch them alone."

I nodded slowly. Cody had been a cop—that much about his stories I believed. "Alone," I said. "So he wouldn't be able to get help as easily?"

"More so we didn't put people in danger," Cody said. "Lots of people in this city. Good people. Survivors. What happened at Sharp Tower, that's partly our fault. Sure, Prof melted the place, but *we* pushed him to do it. That'll weigh on me the rest of my life—another brick in a pile that's way too big."

"So we try to fight him outside the city?"

Cody nodded. "If that idiot with the mannequin is right, then as soon as we use Prof's powers, he'll know where we are. We can pick the place to fight, draw him to us."

"Yeah," I said. "Yeah . . ."

"Except?" Cody asked.

"That's what we did with Steelheart," I said softly. "Drew him to our trap, away from the populace." I raised my hands to control the imager, moving us through the city toward the remnants of Sharp Tower. The drone flybys had happened right after dawn, and corpses still littered the site.

"Lifeline," I said, counting off the fallen Epics I spotted. "Minor electricity powers and telepathy. Darkness Infinity— that was her fourth name, by the way. She kept coming up with 'something better' and it was always worse. She could jump between shadows. Inshallah and the Thaub, from Bahrain. Both had linguistic powers—"

"*Linguistic* powers?" Cody asked.

"Hmm? Oh. One could force you to speak in rhyme. The other could speak in any made-up language anyone anywhere had imagined."

"That's . . . very strange."

"We don't talk much about the odd powers," I said absently. "But there are a lot of minor Epics whose abilities are very specific. It—" I froze. "Wait."

I spun us in the air, fast enough that Cody stumbled and reached out to touch the wall. I zoomed us down toward the rubble, picking out a bloodied face, the body trapped beneath the remnants of the tower's large generator. Prof's blast had vaporized only the salt. It was the first confirmation I'd had that he, with exquisite control over his powers, could release a blast that vaporized some dense materials but not others.

That wasn't important now. That face *was.*

"Oh, Calamity," I whispered.

"What?" Cody demanded.

"That's Stormwind."

"The one who . . ."

"Makes this city grow food," I finished. "Yeah. Ildithia's food production supplied dozens of other cities, Cody. Prof's little tirade might have some very lasting consequences."

I dug out my mobile and typed a message to Knighthawk.

How soon after an Epic dies do you need to freeze their cells?

Soon, he wrote back. *Most cells die quickly. CO2 poisoning, without the heart pumping blood. Epic DNA melts fast, in addition. We don't know the reason yet. Why do you ask?*

I think Prof just started a famine, I wrote to him. *He killed an Epic last night who was vital to the economy.*

You can try to harvest me a sample, Knighthawk replied. *Some cells last longer than others. Skin cells . . . some stem cells . . . The DNA problem works on a kind of weird half-life, with most of it being gone in seconds, but some individual cells could linger. But kid, it's REALLY hard to get a culture going from old Epic cells.*

I showed the messages to Cody.

"It'll be dangerous to go out," he noted. "We don't have Megan to give us new faces."

"Yeah, but if we can prevent starvation, isn't it worth the risk?"

"Sure, sure," Cody said. "Unless we expose ourselves to Prof—who could very well have people watching those bodies—and then get ourselves killed. Which would leave only three Reckoners, instead of five, to confront him. Assuming he didn't torture our secrets out of us and then go kill the rest of the team. Which he probably would. All for a very, *very* slight chance that we might be able to make a motivator that *might* feed people."

I swallowed. "Right. Fine. You laid it on a bit thick."

"Yeah, well," he said. "Y'all've got a history of not listening to logic."

"Like your logic of modern rock and roll being derived from bagpipes?"

"That one's true, now," Cody said. "Look it up. Elvis was a Scot."

"Yeah, whatever," I said, walking over to switch off the imager and the view of Stormwind's face. It hurt, but today I would hold myself back.

A moment later, Mizzy poked her head into our room. "Hey," she said. "Your girlfriend's awake. Do you want to go smooch or—"

I was already on my way.

37

MEGAN was sitting up, holding a bottle of water in both hands, her back to the wall. I passed Abraham on my way in, and he nodded. According to his—admittedly limited—medical knowledge, she was fine. We'd unhooked the harmsway from her hours ago.

Megan gave me a wan smile and took a pull on her water bottle. The others left us alone, Abraham steering Cody away by the shoulder. I let out a long sigh of relief as I reached Megan. Despite Abraham's assurances, a piece of me had been terrified she wouldn't wake up. Yes, she could reincarnate if killed, but what if she didn't die, just slipped into a coma?

She cocked an eyebrow at my obvious relief. "I feel," she said, "like a barrel of green ducks at a Fourth of July parade."

I cocked my head, then nodded. "Oh, yeah. Good metaphor."

"David. That was supposed to be nonsense . . . a joke."

"Really? Because it makes perfect sense." I gave her a kiss. "See, you feel healed, and that's not right—like the ducks, thinking they're out of place. But *nobody's* truly out of place at a parade, so they simply fit in. Like you fit in here."

"You're absolutely mental," she said as I settled down beside her, my arm around her shoulders.

"How do you feel?"

"Awful."

"So the healing didn't take?"

"It did," she said, staring at the water bottle.

"Megan, it's all right. Yes, the mission went awry. We lost Tia. We're recovering from that. Moving forward."

"I went dark, David," she said softly. "Darker than I've been in a long time. Darker than when I killed Sam . . . darker than I've been since before meeting you."

"You pulled out of it."

"Barely," she said, then glanced at her arm. "I was supposed to be past this. We were supposed to have figured it *all out*."

I pulled her close, and she rested her head on my shoulder. I wished I knew what to say, but everything I thought of was stupid. She didn't want false reassurances. She wanted answers.

So did I.

"Prof killed Tia," Megan whispered. "I could end up doing the same to you. Did you hear her? At the end?"

"I'd hoped you were unconscious for that part," I admitted.

"She said he'd warned her and she hadn't listened.

David . . . I'm warning you. I can't control this, even with the secret of the weaknesses."

"Well," I said, "we'll merely have to do the best we can."

"But—"

"Megan," I said, lifting her head to look her in the eyes. "I'd rather die than be without you."

"You mean that?"

I nodded.

"Selfish," she said. "Do you know what it would *do* to me to know that I'd killed you?"

"Then let's see that it doesn't happen, all right?" I said. "I don't think it will—but I'll risk it, to stay near you."

She breathed out, then rested her head on my shoulder again. "Slontze."

"Yeah. Thanks for trying my idea with Prof."

"Sorry I wasn't able to make it work."

"Not your fault. I don't think we want to try another dimensional version of him."

"What then?" she asked. "We can't just give up."

I smiled. "I've got an idea."

"How crazy is it?"

"Pretty darn crazy."

"Good," she said. "The world's gone mad; joining it is the only solution." She was quiet a moment. "Do . . . I have a part in it?"

"Yes, but we shouldn't need you to overextend your powers."

She relaxed, snuggling against my side, and we sat there together for a time. "You know," I finally said, "I really wish my father could have met you."

"Because he'd be curious to meet a good Epic?"

"Well, that too," I said. "But I think he'd like you."

"David, I'm abrasive, cocky, and loud."

"And brilliant," I said, "and an awesome shot. Commanding. Decisive. My dad, he liked people who were straightforward. Said he'd rather get cussed out by someone who meant it than be smiled at by someone who didn't."

"Sounds like a great man."

"He was." The kind of man others ignored or talked over because he was too quiet, and not quick with something clever—but also the kind of man who would run to help others when everyone else fled for safety.

Calamity, I missed that man.

"I've been having nightmares," I whispered.

Megan sat up, looking at me with a sharp motion. "What kind?"

"Persistent," I said. "Terrible. Something about loud noises, jarring sensations. I don't get it—I don't think it's something I'm afraid of."

"Any . . . other oddities?" she asked.

I met her gaze. "How much do you remember from Sharp Tower?"

She narrowed her eyes. "Tia's words. And before that . . . gunfire. Lots of it. How did we survive that?"

I drew my lips to a line.

"Sparks!" she said. "How likely do you think . . . I mean . . ."

"I don't know," I said. "Could be nothing. There were a lot of powers being flung around that room—maybe there was a leftover forcefield, or . . . or maybe some pocket of another reality . . ."

She rested her hand on my shoulder.

"Sure *you* want to stay around *me*?" I asked.

"I'd rather die than do otherwise." She squeezed my shoulder. "But I don't like this at all, David. It feels like we're holding our breath, waiting to see who explodes first. Do you think Prof and Tia had conversations like this, where they decided it was worth the risk of remaining together?"

"Maybe. But I don't see that we have any option but to proceed. I'm not going to leave you, and you're not going to leave me. It's like I said. We have to accept the danger."

"Unless there's another way," Megan said. "A way to make sure I'm not a danger to you, or to anyone else, ever again."

I frowned, uncertain what she meant. But she seemed to decide something, looking at me, and she lifted her hand to caress my face. "You can't say you haven't considered it," she said softly.

" 'It'?"

"The entire time he's been here," Megan said, "I've wondered. Is this my way out?"

"Megan, I don't understand."

She stood up. "It's not enough to make promises. It's not enough to *hope* I won't end up hurting you." She turned and strode, unsteadily at first, from the room.

I scrambled to my feet and followed, trying to sort out what she was planning. Salt scuffed under our feet as we walked past a table in the main room where the others sat; this building's time had come, as it was too near to the trailing edge of Ildithia. It wouldn't last the night.

Megan crossed the room and walked into Larcener's smaller chamber. Sparks! I jogged after her, stumbling into the room. There was a way to make sure Megan never hurt anyone with her powers again. It was here, inside our base.

"Megan," I said, seizing her by the arm. "Are you sure you want to do something so drastic?"

She studied Larcener, who lay on a plush couch with his headphones on. He didn't notice us.

"Yes," she whispered. "During my time with you, I've

started to lose my hatred of the powers. I started to think it could be controlled. But after the things that happened last night . . . I don't want this anymore, David."

She looked to me questioningly.

I shook my head. "I won't stop you. This is your choice. But maybe we should think about it some more?"

"This from you?" she said with a grim smile. "No. I might lose my nerve." She strode up to Larcener, and when he didn't notice her, she kicked at his foot, which was dangling over the side of his couch.

He immediately pulled off his headphones and scrambled up. "You *drudge*," he snapped. "Useless peasant. I'll—"

Megan thrust her arm toward him, wrist upward. "Take my powers."

Larcener gaped, then backed away from her, regarding the arm like one might regard a ticking box with the words NOT A BOMB stenciled on it. "What are you babbling about?"

"My powers," Megan said, stepping toward him. "Take them. They're yours."

"You're insane."

"No," she said, "just tired. Go ahead."

He didn't reach for her arm. I strongly suspected that no Epic had ever *offered* to give him their powers before. I stepped up to Megan.

"I spent months in Babilar serving Regalia," Megan said to Larcener, "all because of the implication that she could make Calamity remove my powers. I wish I'd known about you; I would simply have come here. *Take them*. They'll make you immortal."

"I'm already immortal," he snapped.

"Then be double immortal," Megan said. "Or quadruple, or whatever. Take them, or I'll reach into another dimension, and I'll—"

He grabbed her arm. She gasped, jerking upright, but didn't pull her arm away. I steadied her by her shoulders, worried. Sparks. Watching her was one of the hardest things I'd ever done. Should I have persuaded her to wait? To think it over?

"Like ice water," she hissed, "in my veins."

"Yes," Larcener said. "I've heard it is unpleasant."

"Now it's become *fire*!" Megan said, trembling. "Pouring through me!" Her eyes went glassy and unfocused.

"Hmm . . . ," Larcener said, his tone like that of a careful surgeon. "Yes . . ."

Megan jerked, growing tense, staring into the distance.

"Perhaps you should have thought this through before prancing in here and making demands," Larcener said. "Enjoy being even *more* of a peasant. I'm sure you'll fit in brilliantly with this crew, if you can even think straight when this is done. Most can't, you see—"

The room caught fire.

I ducked as ribbons of flame lanced across the ceiling, then down the walls. The heat was distant, subtle, but I *could* feel it.

Megan stood up straight, and her trembling ended.

Larcener let go, then looked at his hands. He seized Megan again, sneering, and she met his eyes. There was no trembling this time, no jerk of pain, though her face tightened as she clenched her jaw.

The flames didn't go away. They were a phantom burning. She'd said that she'd learned to create those dimensional shadows to help hide her weakness and her fear of fire. They came out by instinct.

The room started to grow very hot.

Larcener let go of her hand and backed away.

"You can't take them, it seems," Megan said.

"How?" he demanded. "How do you defy me?"

"I don't know," Megan said. "But I was wrong to come here."

She turned and strode from the room. I followed her, confused. Abraham and Mizzy stood at the doorway, and Megan brushed past them. I gave them a shrug as I followed her into the communal bedroom.

"You really still have the powers?" I asked her.

She nodded, looking tired. She slumped down onto her pallet. "I should have guessed it wouldn't be so easy."

I knelt beside her, hesitant, but also relieved. That had been a roller coaster of emotions—the type that was old and rickety and didn't have proper seat belts.

"You . . . all right?" I asked.

"Yeah," she said. "I don't understand it either. It was strange, David—in that moment, with him sucking my abilities out in that wave of ice, I realized . . . that the powers are as much *me* now as my personality." She closed her eyes. "I realized I couldn't give them to him. If I did, I'd become a coward."

"But how did you defy him?" I said. "I've never heard of something like that happening."

"The powers are *mine*," she whispered. "I claim them. *My* burden, *my* task, *my self*. I don't know why that mattered, but it did." She opened her eyes. "So what now?"

"When we were at Sharp Tower," I said, "I visited the other world. The one where Firefight lives. There's no darkness there, Megan. *Steelheart* is a hero."

"So we got born one dimensional degree away from paradise."

"We'll just have to bring paradise here," I told her. "Regalia's plan was for Prof to travel to Calamity and, once there, steal his powers. If we can get Prof back, he'll give us the

318

teleportation device she developed. Seems like that would give us a pretty good opportunity to kill Calamity and free us all."

She smiled and took me by the arm. "Let's do it. Rescue Prof, bring down Calamity, save the world. What's your plan?"

"Well," I said, "it's not fully formed yet."

"Good," she said. "You have great ideas, David, but your execution is crap. Go grab some paper. We're going to come up with a way to pull this off."

38

I set down my pack in the center of the large, open building. The place had a sharp salty scent. Newly grown. The floor reflected my mobile's light; polished white saltstone. After leaving behind a hideout that had literally been decomposing around us, this place felt almost *too* clean. Like a baby the moment before it barfed on you.

"This feels wrong," I said, my voice echoing in the large chamber.

"In what way?" Mizzy said, passing with a sack of supplies over her shoulder.

"It's too big," I said. "I can't feel like I'm hiding if I have a whole *warehouse* to live in."

"One would think," Abraham said, setting down his

supplies with a clink, "you would be happy to escape the tight confines of our previous dwellings."

I turned around and felt distinctly creeped out that—by the frail light of my mobile—I couldn't see the edges of the room. How could I explain that sensation without sounding silly? Every Reckoner hideout had been tucked away and secure. This empty warehouse was the opposite.

Cody claimed it would be secure anyway. Our time in Ildithia had let him and Abraham do some investigating, and they'd come up with this warehouse as a spot nobody used, and one that was convenient to a spot I wanted to use in our plan to attack Prof.

I shook my head, grabbing my pack and lugging it across the room to the far wall, where Abraham and Mizzy had set theirs. Nearby, Cody had already started growing a smaller room inside the warehouse. He worked carefully with a gloved hand, stroking the salt outward like he was sculpting clay, using the trowel to make smooth surfaces. His glove hummed softly, making the crystal structure of the salt extend behind his motions. He'd only been working for about an hour, but he already had a good start on the smaller chamber.

"Ain't nobody gonna bother us here, lad," Cody said in a reassuring voice as he worked.

"Why not?" I asked. "Seems like a perfect place to hole up a large group of people." I could imagine the warehouse filled with families, each around their own trash can fire. That would transform it. Rather than being tomblike and empty, it would be full of sounds and life.

"This place is too far away from the city center—it's from the northern edge of the section of old Atlanta that became Ildithia. Why pick the cold warehouse when you can have a group of townhomes for your family?"

"I suppose that makes sense," I said.

"Plus, a whole bunch of people got murdered in here," Cody added. "So nobody wants to be near the place."

"Um . . . what?"

"Yeah," he said, "tragic event. Bunch of kids started playing here, but it was too close to another family's territory. The other family got spooked, thought rivals were moving in on them, so they tossed some dynamite through the door. They say you could hear the survivors crying under the rubble for days, but a full-on war had started by then, and nobody had time to come help the poor kids."

I regarded him, stunned. Cody started whistling and continued to work. Sparks. He had to be making that story up, right? I turned and took in the vast, empty room, then shivered.

"I hate you," I muttered.

"Ach, now, don't be like that. Ghosts are drawn to negative emotions, you see."

I should have known better; talking to Cody was generally among the *least* productive things you could do. I went looking for Megan instead, passing Larcener, who—of course—had refused to help carry anything to the new base. He swept into Cody's unfinished chamber and flopped down, an overstuffed beanbag materializing beneath him.

"I'm tired of being interrupted," he said, pointing at the wall. A door appeared, propped up against it. "Work that into your construction, and I'll put a lock on the thing. Oh, and make the walls *extra* thick so I don't have to listen to the lot of you squeaking and babbling all the time."

Cody gave me a long-suffering look, and somehow I could tell that he was contemplating walling the Epic up.

I found Megan with Mizzy, near where Abraham was unpacking his guns. I held back, surprised. Megan and Mizzy sat on the floor surrounded by our notes—some in my careful hand, others in her . . . well, Megan's handwriting could be mistaken for the aftermath of a tornado in a pencil store.

Mizzy nodded as Megan pointed at one page, then gestured wildly at the sky. Megan thought a moment, then huddled over the paper and started writing.

I sidled up to Abraham. "The two of them are talking," I said.

"You expected maybe clucking?"

"Well, shouting. Or strangulation."

Abraham turned back to unloading equipment from his bags.

I started toward the women, but Abraham took me by the arm without looking up. "Perhaps it would be best to simply let them be, David."

"But—"

"They are adults," Abraham said. "They do not need you to work out their problems."

I folded my arms, huffing. What did their being adults have to do with it? Plenty of adults *did* need me to work out their problems—otherwise Steelheart would still be alive. Besides, Mizzy was seventeen. Did that even count as an adult?

Abraham removed something from one of the packs and set it down with a soft thump. "Instead of poking where you aren't needed," he said to me, "how about helping where you *are*? I could use your aid."

"Doing what?"

Abraham lifted the top of the box, revealing a pair of gloves and a jug of sparkling mercury. "Your plan is daring, as I would expect. It is also simple. The best often are. But it *does* require me to do things I am not sure I can do."

He was right; the plan was simple. It was also *exceptionally dangerous.*

Knighthawk had used drones to explore a few of the caverns underneath Ildithia, the ones Digzone had created long ago. There were many under the region, tunneled into the rock here. Ildithia was passing over a large set of them, and we'd chosen this warehouse in part because here we could dig down into one of the caverns and practice there.

Our plan was to train for a month. By then Ildithia would have left these caverns behind—but they would still make a perfect location for a trap. Lots of tunnels, places to set up explosives or to plot escape routes. We'd be familiar with the tunnels, which would give us an edge in the fight.

Once we were ready, we'd sneak from the city and go back to the caves. From there we could lure Prof out. All it would take was using the motivators based on his powers, and he'd come right to us. Ildithia would be miles away, and safe from whatever destruction happened during our fight.

Abraham and Megan would hit him first. The idea was to wear him down before revealing Cody, wearing the full "tensor suit," as we were calling the set of devices that mimicked Prof's power portfolio. It hadn't arrived yet, but Knighthawk claimed it was on its way. So once Abraham and Megan had worn Prof down a little, Cody would appear, manifesting all of Prof's powers.

We had to hope that Tavi's power hadn't been recognized by Prof as being "his." After all, her forcefields had been a different color.

A piece of me whispered that there might be a larger problem. Prof had been wounded by Tavi's forcefields, but they hadn't shut down his powers completely, like what happened with Megan and most Epics.

Could Tia have been wrong? I'd decided that she wasn't, but now—confronted with one last shot at stopping

Prof—I wavered. Some things about Prof and his powers didn't add up.

What *was* it that Prof feared?

"For this to work," Abraham said from beside me, snapping me out of my introspection, "I will need to be able to use the rtich to face Prof. And facing him will require not getting squished by his forcefields."

"The rtich should be enough," I said. "The structural integrity of the mercury will be—"

"I believe your notes," Abraham cut me off, pulling on the gloves. "But I'd still rather do some testing, followed by *much* practice."

I shrugged. "What did you have in mind?"

What he "had in mind," apparently, was to put me to work. Our warehouse had a little loft inside it. I spent the next hour working with Cody, who created some large slabs of saltstone in the loft. I then lashed these together and positioned them, in several bunches, ready to push them off the loft.

Finally, I wiped my brow with a rag that was already soaked through, then settled down with my legs hanging over the ledge.

Below, Abraham practiced.

He'd developed his own training regimen with the rtich, based on some old martial art. He stepped into the center of a ring of lights he'd set out on the ground, thrust his hands to one side, then pulled them back and thrust them the other way.

Mercury danced around him. At first it covered his arm, like a silvery sleeve and glove. As he thrust his hands forward, it sprayed outward, becoming a disc connected to his palm. When he moved back into his martial arts motions, it withdrew and covered his arm again, then shot into the shape of a spike as he thrust his hands the other way.

I watched hungrily. The metal moved with a beautiful, otherworldly flow, reflecting light as it snaked around Abraham's arms—first one, then across his shoulders to the other, like something alive. He turned and ran, then leaped—and the mercury coursed down his legs, becoming a short pillar that Abraham landed upon. It held his weight, though it looked spindly and frail.

"Ready?" I called from above.

"Ready," he called.

"Be careful," I said. "I don't want this crushing you."

He gave no response, so I sighed, then stood and used a crowbar to pry one of the large, lashed-together slabs of saltstone off the loft and send it tumbling toward him. The idea was for him to create a thin line of mercury in the path of the falling slabs, then see how much the impact twisted the mercury.

Instead, Abraham stepped directly into the path of the stones and raised his hand.

My view was obstructed, but best I could figure, Abraham caused the mercury to run up his side and arm—becoming a long ribbon that extended from his palm, down his side, and to his feet to form a kind of brace.

My breath caught as the saltstone plummeted toward him. I craned my neck to look down, and the pile hit *hard,* bouncing off Abraham, the lashings snapping. The slabs crashed to the sides, revealing Abraham grinning below, his hand still raised, his palm coated with mercury. The brace had been enough to deflect the weight of the slabs.

"That was foolhardy," I called to him. "Stop trying to put me out of a job!"

"Better to know now if this will work," he called back to me, "than to find out in the middle of a fight with Prof. Besides, I was relatively certain."

"Still want to try this next part?" Cody asked, coming up beside me, sniper rifle on his shoulder.

"Yes, please," Abraham said, thrusting his hand toward us and making the shield. It grew as large as he was, shimmering and incredibly thin.

I looked at Cody, then shrugged and put my hands over my ears. A series of shots followed; fortunately they were suppressed, so the ear-holding wasn't as necessary as it might have been.

The mercury puckered, *catching* the bullets. Or, well, it stopped them—which upon consideration wasn't all that impressive, as bodies technically did *that* all the time. Mine had done so on occasion.

Still, the mercury didn't tear or split, so it was an effective shield, though unfortunately the application was limited. Abraham didn't have superhuman reflexes; he wouldn't be able to stop bullets already fired.

He turned and the mercury flowed back to him, scattering the bullets to the floor. It ran down his arm and then his leg before streaking from his feet to form a series of steps rising toward me. He walked up them, grinning widely.

I shoved down my envy. I doubted I'd ever stop wishing I had been able to make this device work, but I *could* avoid acting childish about it. Cody and I clapped Abraham on the shoulder, giving him a thumbs-up. The Canadian man bore an uncharacteristic smile of pleasure, which was good to see. It wasn't that he never smiled, it was just that his smiles always seemed so controlled. He rarely seemed to enjoy life. It was more that he let it pass around him, regarding it curiously, like a rock watching a river.

"Maybe this will actually work," he said to me. "Maybe we won't all end up dead." He held up his hand and the mercury ran up his arm, pooling in a sphere above his gloved palm. It rippled and shook like a miniature ocean with waves and a tide.

"Do a puppy next!" Mizzy called from below. "Oh! Then a hat. Make me a silver hat. A *tiara*."

"Shut it, you," Abraham called.

My pocket buzzed. I pulled out my mobile, finding yet another text from Knighthawk. The guy considered me his personal entertainment factory. I flipped the message open.

Jonathan contacted me again today.

He's discovered you sent him on a wild rat chase?

Rat?

I've never seen a goose, I wrote back to him. *Don't know why you'd chase one. But Newcago has lots of rats.*

And you'd chase those instead? . . . Never mind. Kid, Jonathan sent a message to me. For you.

I felt cold, then waved for Abraham and Cody to step over and read along with me.

He said, Knighthawk continued, *that you have two days to turn over Larcener to him, or he'll destroy Newcago. Every single person in it. Then Babilar the next day.*

Abraham and I shared a look.

Do you think he could actually do that? Knighthawk wrote. *Destroy a whole city?*

"Yes," Abraham said softly. "If he killed Tia, he's capable of anything."

"I think he's asking if Prof has the *power* to do it," I said.

"Didn't you say you talked to Obliteration at the party?" Abraham asked.

"Yeah. And he implied that Prof had summoned him by using a device linked to Obliteration's powers. Even though

Regalia made the bombs to hide her true goal—the teleportation device—I think it's safe to assume Prof has access to at least one bomb."

"He has the capability," Abraham said. "And we have to assume he'll do it. Which means . . ."

". . . we have a new deadline," I said, tucking away the mobile.

So much for our month of preparation.

39

THE drone landed on our warehouse roof that night. Four of us waited in a silent huddle, cloaked in darkness, while Cody scanned the city from inside a sniper nest he'd made on the rooftop nearby.

I reached into my pocket and clicked a button on my mobile; its screen went dark. The click sent a message I'd prepared earlier: *Drone has landed the prize. We're inspecting it now.*

We knelt over the drone, night-vision goggles in place, looking at a world painted green. Mizzy pulled the drone open.

Inside, packed in straw mixed with old newspapers, was a glorious sight: a vest, a small metal box, and a pair of gloves. I breathed out. Those gloves looked exactly like the tensors—black, with lines of metal running like tiny rivers up the fingers and pooling at each tip. Those would glow green when engaged.

"Niiiice," Mizzy whispered, poking at the vest. "Three different motivator casings. The first one offers healing, judging by the sensors you attach to the skin; it probably activates automatically upon injury. This one is connected to the tensors. Last one for forcefields."

She turned over one of the gloves. I couldn't help feeling that this suit represented something new, a different step in the creation of Epic-derived technology. Instead of one lone power, this replicated everything Prof could do. A complex network of wires and multiple motivators, combined in an imitation of an enhanced human. Should I be disturbed or impressed?

Heroes will come, son. My father's words. I thought of that as I ran my fingers along the sleek metal of the suit's motivators. *But sometimes, you have to help them along. . . .*

"There is a problem with this," Abraham said. "Cody cannot practice with this device without alerting Prof that he's using it, and therefore revealing ourselves to him."

"I've got an idea for that," I said. "Though it will require Megan to use her powers."

She looked up at me, curious.

"I doubt Prof can sense Cody practicing," I said, "if he's in another dimension."

"Clever," she said. "He'll only be able to stay a short time though. Ten, maybe fifteen minutes, if I push it."

"Don't push it," I said. "It might not give us much time, but at least we'll be able to make sure the motivators are working."

Everyone seemed to like this plan, and together we dug out the tensor suit. Beneath were some other supplies that we'd managed to beg off Knighthawk: some explosives, some tiny drones that were little more than cameras with feet, and some technological gizmos Mizzy had suggested as additions to Megan's and my plan.

The others carted all this away, Mizzy placing the old harmsway in the drone—the one that had healed Megan and me—and sending it off to return to Knighthawk. We had something better now, though we'd have to be careful about using it lest we alert Prof.

I caught Megan by the arm as the team passed, carrying the goodies. She nodded to me. She felt all right about using her powers. I didn't follow her into the warehouse below, but instead walked over to Cody's sniper nest. It was my turn to be on watch.

The nest was shaped like a wide, shallow box near the center of the roof. Cody had devised a ceiling for it with the crystal grower that merged right into the roof and made the structure look like another normal building feature. It had slits on all sides, however, and a large enough hole at the rear for you to crawl in and lie down.

I peeked in; the lanky Southerner was cuddled into the hole like a joey in its mother's pouch—though people really shouldn't let baby kangaroos play with a Barrett .50 cal with armor-piercing rounds.

"Has my new toy arrived?" Cody asked, setting aside the gun and wriggling backward out of the nest.

"Yeah," I said, stepping out of his way as he stood up. "It looks great."

"You sure you don't want to pilot it, lad?"

I shook my head. "You have more experience with the tensors, Cody."

"Yeah, but you were way more talented with them."

"I . . ." I swallowed. "No, I need to be running the mission from behind."

"Right, then," he said, turning toward the steps down to the building.

"Cody?" I said, and he stopped, turned back. "The other day I was talking to Abraham and . . . well, he kind of bit my head off."

"Ah. You were poking around, were you?"

"Poking around?"

"In his past."

"No, of course not. I just asked why he didn't want to be in charge."

"Close enough," Cody said, patting me on the arm. "Abraham's a strange one, lad. The rest of us, we make sense. You fight for revenge. I fight because I was a cop, and I took an oath. Mizzy, she fights because of her heroes, people like Val and Sam. She wants to be like them.

"Abraham though . . . why does he fight? I couldn't tell you. Because of his fallen brothers and sisters in the special forces? Maybe, but he doesn't seem to be holding a grudge. Maybe to protect the country? But if that's the case, why's he down here in the Fractured States? All I've been able to figure is that he doesn't want to talk about it—and you shouldn't assume he's gentle because he's in control, lad." Cody rubbed his jaw. "Learned that the hard way once."

"He *punched* you?"

"Broke my jaw," Cody said with a laugh. "Don't poke, kid. That's what I learned!" He seemed not to care much, though a broken jaw sounded like a pretty big offense to me.

But then, who *hadn't* wanted to punch Cody on occasion?

"Thanks," I said, sitting down to begin wiggling into the sniper nest. "But you're wrong about me, Cody. I don't fight for revenge, not anymore. I fight for my father."

"Isn't that the same as revenge?"

I reached into my shirt and took out the small S-shaped

symbol of the Faithful that I wore around my neck. The mark of one who awaited a day when the heroes would come. "No. I don't fight because of his death, Cody. I fight for his dreams."

Cody nodded. "Good on ya, lad," he said, turning to walk to the steps. "Good on ya."

I crawled into the sniper nest, head brushing the low ceiling, and lifted Cody's rifle, patching my mobile into it. I pulled off my night-vision goggles and used the gun's scope instead—it had an overlaid map of the area, as well as thermal imaging. Better than either, the rifle had an advanced sound-detection system. It would alert me if it heard anything nearby, creating a small blip on my map.

At the moment, nothing. Not even pigeons.

I lay there positioned on cushions Cody had left. Occasionally I would twist about in the square enclosure, poking my rifle out one of the other sides.

Sounds came from below, inside the warehouse. I checked in with the others, and Mizzy said that my idea—sending Cody into the parallel dimension to practice—was working. Said he had to frighten some kids away over there, who were living in the warehouse in that dimension, but otherwise he hadn't encountered anyone.

I checked on an oddity after that—noise the rifle had picked up—but it turned out to be a few scavengers moving through the alleyway. They didn't stop at our warehouse. Instead they continued on toward the outskirts of the city. This let me have an extended period alone to think. My mind wandered in the silence, and I realized something was nagging at me. I was dissatisfied, though annoyingly I couldn't figure out exactly *why*. Something bothered me, either about the place we'd set up or the plan we'd made. What was I missing?

I mulled it all over for about an hour—only a fraction of

my shift—and was actually glad when the alarm on my gun buzzed again. I zoomed in on the source of the disturbance, but it was just a feral cat scampering along a rooftop nearby. I watched it carefully, in case it was some kind of shape-shifting Epic.

By this time light had dawned on the horizon, and I yawned, licking my lips and tasting salt. I wouldn't be sad to be away from this place. Unfortunately my watch was a full eight hours, which would include another six hours of dullness until noon arrived.

I yawned again and rubbed my fingernail on the rooftop's saltstone rim in front of me. Curiously, our warehouse was still growing. The changes were minute, but looking closely I could see that vines as thin as pencil lines were growing along the saltstone, as if carved by an invisible hand.

The city's major changes happened on the first and last days of a building's life, but the times between weren't static. Tiny ornamentations often popped up, ones that would be gone in another day or two, weathered away by the inevitable decay that was this city's infinite cycle.

The alarm on my rifle buzzed again, and I looked through the scope at the map. The sound was coming from on top of our warehouse, and a moment later I heard footsteps grinding on the saltstone. They came from the direction of the staircase from the building below, the one that led from the loft to the roof. It was likely one of my team. Still, I carefully slipped my mobile out the side of the sniper hole, using its camera—which had a feed to the scope—to see who was up there.

It was Larcener.

I hadn't been expecting *that*. I couldn't recall him setting foot outside his room at any of the three bases, except during times when we'd needed to transition from one to the other.

He stood with his hand shading his face, scowling at the distant sunrise.

"Larcener?" I asked, crawling back out of the sniper hole, rifle in tow. "Is everything all right?"

"People enjoy these," he said.

"What?" I asked, following his gaze. "Sunrises?"

"They always talk about the sunrise," he said, sounding annoyed. "How beautiful it is, blah blah. Like each one is some unique wonder. I don't see it."

"Are you crazy?"

"I'm increasingly certain," he said dryly, "that I'm the only one on this planet who *isn't*."

"Then you must be blind," I said, looking toward the sunrise. As sunrises went, it wasn't much. It didn't have clouds to reflect off, and today it was pretty much uniformly one color instead of spanning the spectrum.

"A ball of fire," he said. "Garish orange. Harsh light."

"Yeah," I said, smiling. "Amazing." I thought of the years in Newcago's darkness, when we'd judged the time of day by the dimness of the lights. I thought of emerging to an open sky for the first time since my childhood, watching the sun come up and bathe everything in warmth.

The sunrise didn't need to be beautiful to be beautiful.

"I come look at them sometimes," Larcener said, "just to see if I can pick out what everyone else seems to see."

"Hey," I said. "How much do you know about the way this city grows?"

"Why does it matter?"

"Because it's interesting," I said, kneeling down. "Do you see this vinework? It's still growing. Is that because the original warehouse had this pattern in its brick and wood? I mean, it wouldn't make much sense if it did, but the other option would be that the *powers* are making art here. Isn't that odd?"

"I really couldn't say."

I looked at him. "You don't know, do you? You absorbed this power when you took over the city, but you don't know how it works."

"I know that it does what I want. What else matters?"

"Beauty," I said, rubbing my finger along one of the vines. "My father always said that the Epics were wonderful. Amazing. A glimpse of something truly divine, you know? It's easy to pay attention to the destruction, like what Obliteration did to Kansas City. But there's beauty too. It almost makes me feel bad to kill Epics."

He sniffed disdainfully. "I see through your act, David Charleston."

"My . . . act?" I stood back up and turned toward him.

"The act of despising Epics," he said. "You hate them, yes, but as the mouse hates the cat. The hate of envy. The hate of the small who wishes to be great."

"Don't be silly."

"Silly?" Larcener asked. "You think it isn't obvious? A man does not study, learn, obsess as you have because of *hatred*. No, these are the signs of lust. You have sought a father among the Epics, a lover among them." He stepped toward me. "Admit it. You want nothing more than to be one of us."

"I loved Megan before I realized what she was," I said, teeth clenched, shocked at the sudden anger I felt. "You don't know anything."

"Don't I?" he said. "I've watched people like you so many times—you see the truth of men manifest in those first moments, David. New Epics. They murder, they destroy, they show what every man would do if his inhibitions were re-moved. Men are a race of monsters, inefficiently chained. That's what's inside *you*. Deny it, I dare you. Deny it, man who presumes to know Epics better than he knows himself!"

I didn't dare. I spun from him and climbed back into the sniper nest to finish my shift. Eventually, he grumbled be-hind me and left.

Hours passed. I couldn't shake the things Larcener had said, though I tried. As noon approached, and the time for my shift to end, I found myself fixating on something he'd said to me.

Man who presumes to know Epics better than he knows himself . . .

Did I really know them? I knew their powers, yes, but not the Epics themselves; they weren't all of one mind. That was one of the easy mistakes people made. Epics felt an over-whelming sense of arrogance, so you could predict some of their actions, but they were still people. Individuals. No, I didn't know them.

But I did know Prof.

Oh, Calamity, I thought.

It finally came together. The thing that had been bother-ing me. I pulled out of my sniper nest and dashed down the steps into the warehouse.

I stumbled out of the stairwell into the loft, running to the edge to look at the warehouse floor below. Mizzy sat on a table, spinning her keys around her finger, while Megan sat cross-legged on the floor, concentrating. Near Megan, the air shimmered and Cody appeared.

"Well," Cody said, "I think I'm getting the hang of this. It seems way more powerful than the tensors were back in Newcago. Full-blown forcefield walls work too."

"Guys!" I shouted.

"David, lad?" Cody called up. "This dimensional deal is working great!"

"*Why,*" I shouted, "would Prof give us a two-day deadline?"

They all regarded me in silence.

"To . . . make us panic?" Mizzy asked. "Force us to give in? That's why you usually give deadlines, right?"

"No, look at it like a Reckoner," I said, frustrated. "Assume that Prof is plotting, like we are. Assume he's formed his own team, his own plan to attack. We're thinking of him like some faceless despot, but he's not. He's one of us. That deadline is way too suspicious."

"Sparks," Megan said, standing up. "Sparks! In this case, you'd only give a *two*-day deadline . . ."

". . . because you're planning to attack in *one* day," Abraham finished. "If not sooner."

"We need to pull out," I said. "Out of this location, out of the *city*. Move!"

40

THE subsequent mad scramble had *some* order to it, as we never set up a base without first preparing to pull out. The team knew what to do, even if there was a lot of cursing and some chaos.

I dashed down the steps, almost colliding with Mizzy, who was on her way up to the loft to get our extra ammunition and explosives, which we kept far from where we slept. Abraham went for our power cells and guns, where he'd set them out along the wall.

Cody went running toward the door. I stopped him with a barked "Wait!"

He froze and turned toward me, still in the tensor suit.

"Megan," I said, "you're on scouting duty instead of Cody. Cody, you do her job and get the food rations ready. That suit is too valuable to risk out there, in case there's some sort of trap waiting for a scout."

Megan obeyed immediately, and I tossed her Cody's rifle as she passed. Cody hiked back, looking a little sullen, but started gathering our packs together—checking to make sure each one had food, water, and a bedroll.

I hurried to text Knighthawk. *Our location might be compromised,* I sent him. *We are pulling out. Would you mind lending me one or two of the drones you have patrolling the area?*

He didn't reply immediately, so I hurried to help Mizzy with the ammo and explosives. She nodded in gratitude as I took the armful from her.

"Goodbye gift?" she asked.

"Yes," I said. "But only if you can do it quickly. I want out of here in five."

"Got it," she said, scrambling up to the loft. She'd have an explosive charge set and ready to blast the entire warehouse to dust by the time we were done packing.

"Make sure there's a remote way to disarm it," I called after her, remembering Cody's story about the dead kids— which I was *almost* certain was made up.

I placed the ammo in the backpacks—which Cody had set out in a row, bedrolls attached at the top—then zipped each one. There were packs for all of us but Abraham, who would be carrying a larger duffel with gravatonic lifts, filled with our guns and power cells.

My mobile buzzed.

How do you know I still have drones in the area? Knighthawk wrote.

Because you're paranoid, I wrote back, *and you want to keep an eye on Prof?*

I slung one pack over my shoulder, then set a second one

at my feet—I'd be carrying Megan's until she could meet up with us.

You really are smarter than you seem, he wrote me. *Fine. I'll do a sweep of your area and send you the video.*

I waited, anxious, as Abraham finished his packing. Mizzy hurried down to grab her bag, and nodded at me. Cody already had his on his shoulder. Under five minutes. Nearby, Larcener wandered out of the little room Cody had made for him.

"Did I miss something?" he asked.

"Crap," Megan said over the line.

I put my hand to my earpiece. "What?"

"He's got an entire army working its way through the streets toward us, Knees. Our primary exit points are both blocked. By the time we picked up on this from the sniper nest, we'd have been surrounded. We might be already."

"Pull back," I said. "I'm going to get intel through Knighthawk."

"Roger."

I looked to the others.

"False faces?" Mizzy asked.

"Whatever our faces are, we're going to look *sparking* suspicious with all this equipment," I said.

"Then we leave it," Abraham said. "We're not ready for a fight."

"And we'll be more ready in twenty-four hours?" I asked. "When he destroys Newcago?"

My phone buzzed; Knighthawk was actually calling me, which was rare. I picked up, dialing his feed into our communal line so everyone could hear him through their earpieces.

"You guys are screwed," he said. "I'm sending you footage in infrared."

Abraham stepped over, lowering his mobile, and we crowded around to look. A map of our area showed hundreds, maybe thousands of people descending on our position, each an infrared dot. They formed a complete circle.

"East Lane," Knighthawk said. "See those corpses? Bystanders who tried to run. They're gunning down anyone who attempts to escape that circle. They're sending a team into every building, holding the people there at gunpoint and—best I can tell from the shot I got through a window— feeling their faces."

"Feeling their faces?" Mizzy asked.

"To see if any part is illusory," I said. "Prof knows that Megan can fool a dowser, but the overlays she creates *are* still illusions. They feel a nose that doesn't fit the image of its face, something like that, and they'll know they've found us."

"Like I said," Knighthawk added. "Screwed."

Megan rushed in through the door and closed it behind her, back up against the saltstone. "Surrounded?" she asked, reading our expressions.

I nodded.

"So what do we do?" she asked, joining our little huddle.

I looked at the others. One at a time, they nodded.

"We fight," Abraham said softly.

"We fight," Mizzy agreed. "He'll be expecting us to try to punch out; it's Reckoner protocol when surprised or outmatched."

I smiled, feeling a sudden swell of pride. "If this were one of Prof's teams," I said, "we'd run."

"We're not his team," Cody said. "Not anymore. We're here to change the world; we ain't going to do that without a fight."

"It's stupid," I noted.

"Sometimes stupid is right," Megan said, then paused. "Hell. I hope nobody ever quotes me on that one. So where's our battlefield?"

"Same place it was always going to be," I said.

Then I pointed down. That tunnel and cave complex was beneath us. "Cody, cut us a path. We go in full gear, exactly as we planned. We won't have as much of an edge as we hoped, but we've still got those caverns mapped, and they'll allow us to fight him with the least chance of causing harm to people nearby."

"Wait," Megan said. "If Cody uses the tensors, that will call Prof right to us—he'll know that we have the device."

"Yeah," Knighthawk said over the line. "He's hovering at the rear of his little army right now, but that won't last long. Years ago, when we tested it, using a motivator drove him into a rage. He'll come for you immediately."

Cody looked at his hands. "I . . . Lad, I just started practicing with these tensors. They're stronger than the ones we had before, but it could take *hours* for me to cut an escape hole."

"It shouldn't," I said. "You've seen what Prof can do—level buildings, vaporize huge swaths of ground. You hold that power, Cody."

Cody set his jaw. The tensors started glowing green.

None of us asked how Prof had located us. It could have happened in one of any number of ways—our bases here in Ildithia weren't terribly secure. Maybe we'd been spotted by an informant, or perhaps Prof did have an Epic who could dowse for us, or maybe he'd noticed the drone deliveries.

"All right," Cody said. "Everyone get ready, and then I'll do the deed. Time to fight."

41

THE team loaded up. Weapons in hand, mobiles strapped to arms, earpieces in. Mizzy tossed a small box to each of us: a compressed rappelling cord. I affixed mine to my belt.

We left our packs, only grabbing some ammo. The packs were for long-term survival. After this, one way or another, we wouldn't need them.

Tension laced the air, like the distant scent of smoke that signaled a fire. We weren't ready, but the battle had arrived anyway. Right now it was all up to Cody. He stood in the center of our warehouse base, eyeing the dusty saltstone floor. He'd always seemed lanky in an almost comical way to me, but now—wearing the tensor suit, with its glowing greens and dramatic, futuristic vest, he cut an imposing profile.

I stepped up to him. "It's down there, Cody," I said. "An

entire cave complex. The battlefield *we* have chosen. All we need is a pathway."

He took in a deep breath.

"Remember what you said when you were first training me in the tensors?" I asked.

"Yeah . . . you've gotta use them like you're caressing a beautiful woman."

"I was thinking more the other thing you said. You've got to have the soul of a warrior, like William Wallace."

"William Wallace got murdered, lad."

"Oh."

"But he didn't go down without a fight," Cody said, steeling himself. "All right. Hold on to yer haggis, everyone." He raised his hands before himself, and a green glow ran down the wires strapped to his arms and into his hands. He thrust his hands forward, and I felt a distinct hum that seemed to vibrate all the way down to my soul without actually making a sound.

A three-foot-by-three-foot section of ground vaporized, maybe ten feet deep. That was very impressive on the old scale of the tensors, but nowhere near what we needed to reach those caverns.

"Jonathan's moving!" Knighthawk said over the lines. "Sparks. You people are in trouble. He does *not* look happy!"

Cody swore under his breath, regarding the patch of floor that had been reduced to fine grains of sand. Wind from the open door of the loft curled some of the powder up in the draft.

I grabbed Cody's arm. "Try again."

"David, that's as big as I can make it!" he said.

"Cody," I said. "*Concentrate*. Soul of a warrior!"

"If I keep screwing this up, lad, we're dead. Trapped in here. Gunned down. Hell of a lot of pressure to work under."

"Sure," I said, frantic. "But . . . um . . . no more pressure than when you stopped those terrorists from launching the nukes at Scotland that one time, right?"

He glanced at me, brow beading with sweat. Then he grinned. "How'd y'all know about that?"

"Lucky guess. Cody, you *can do this.*"

He focused again on the floor in front of him. His suit started glowing once more, ribbons of emerald coursing along his arms, pulsing like a heartbeat. Being so near made me feel something familiar, like hearing the voice of an old friend. It reminded me of days in the caverns of Newcago, of innocence and conviction.

Cody raised his hands over his head, and the thrumming grew louder. "Like caressing a woman," he whispered. "A very, very *large* woman." He released the power with a defiant shout, and it blasted into the floor with such force that it sent me to my knees.

Inches before me, the ground disintegrated into a large hole filled with grains of salt. I watched as the grains siphoned away to reveal a hole a good five feet across. It curved downward, with smooth, glassy sides, traveling through salt-stone and then actual rock. The vanishing salt indicated that it opened into something much larger below.

"Remind me," I said to Cody, "never to let you caress me."

He grinned, holding up hands that glowed bright green.

"He'll be there any second, you slontzes," Knighthawk said over the line. "He's taking it more slowly than I'd have expected; he's a careful one, to be sure, but he's still almost upon you. I'd vacate if I were you."

"Down," I said, catching my Gottschalk as Abraham tossed it to me. "Remember starting positions!"

Mizzy skidded to the side of the hole and, using a large, tubelike gun, planted a series of spikes into the floor there.

She hooked her rappelling cord to one, then jumped in. Megan hooked on to another spike, then followed, sliding down the hole like it was a ride in an old amusement park.

I glanced at Larcener, gesturing for him to go.

"I'll remain," he said.

"He wants to kill you!" I said.

"And he'll be drawn to you people," Larcener said, folding his arms. "I'll be safer hiding in my room up here."

"Not with the explosives Mizzy left behind. Look, we could use your help. Join us. Change the world."

He sniffed and turned away.

I felt it like a punch to the gut.

"David," Cody said, watching the ceiling. "Let's move, lad!"

Teeth clenched, I pulled the end of the rappelling cord from the box at my belt and hooked it on to an empty spike, then threw myself into the hole. I slid down smooth stone in the darkness, trying to contain my frustration. My expectations were foolish, but part of me had still assumed that Larcener would join us for this battle.

I'd always intended to speak with him further, but we'd constantly been frantic with some other preparation. Should I have done anything else? *Could* I have done anything else? If I'd been cleverer, or more persuasive, could I have found a way to bring him to our side?

My mobile automatically engaged the box at the correct depth, putting resistance on my cord until I slowed, then popped out into a larger chamber, lurching to a stop a mere two or three feet above the ground. I cut and dropped into an enormous pile of salt and rock dust. I pushed through, getting out of the way of the opening.

Mizzy and Megan shined their mobiles about, lighting a series of natural caverns covered with an impressive amount of graffiti. The caverns tended to be low-ceilinged—about ten feet high, though this wasn't uniform—and connected by tunnels with lots of nooks. It didn't look quite natural, but it was far more organic than the tunnels beneath Newcago. Had Digzone been as mad as the Diggers he gifted his powers to? Judging by the crazy number of caverns down here, that seemed likely.

Abraham came down into the pile of salt next, the rtich coating one arm. Finally Cody entered, and he hadn't bothered with a cord—he dropped out of the hole onto a forcefield that sprang into existence under his feet.

"Cody, disengage the powers," I said, and pointed down a turn in the cavern. "Find a spot in that direction and be ready. We won't be able to surprise him with your abilities, but I still want you to be hidden at first. Mizzy, be ready to blow your present up above on my mark."

"Larcener?" she asked.

"He knows about the blast," I said. "He'll get out of the way." And if he didn't, well, that was purely on his head.

I grabbed my mobile and scrambled across the cavern's uneven floor to a side passage. The complex was intricate, but my mobile's map noted a few relatively safe nooks from which I could run ops. This wasn't the exact side of the cavern complex where we'd originally planned to pull our trap, but it had to work.

Megan joined me. "Nice job with the Scotsman up there."

"He just needed a little nudge," I said, "to become what he always pretends to be."

"He's not the only one," she said. We stopped at an intersection of tunnels, and she pulled me close for a quick kiss. "You always thought you wanted to be in charge, David. You had good reason."

She turned to go the other direction. I held her arm, then

hand, as she slipped away from me. "Don't push yourself too hard, Megan."

She smiled—sparks, what a smile—and held on to my fingers with hers. "I own it, David. It's *mine*. I don't fear it anymore. If it takes me, I'll find a way back."

She let go, crossing the cavern as I ducked into my chosen nook. It was a tight squeeze, requiring me to wriggle through some rock, but would shelter the light of my mobile from Prof's eyes, and shelter *me* from explosions. Inside, I was in a small bubble of a room with no other exits.

I reached to my belt and detached a headset with a dome of glass attached to its front. A grudging gift from Knighthawk in the same shipment as the tensor suit, multiple screens could be projected onto it.

"Mizzy," I said, "cameras in place?"

"Sticking the last one," she said. "Knighthawk, these things are *waaay* creepy."

"She says to the man who built them using a mannequin he controls with his mind," Abraham added under his breath.

"Shut it," Knighthawk said, though his voice was somewhat difficult to make out over noise on his end.

"Knighthawk," I said, "your line has some kind of static or interference on it."

"Hmm? Oh, don't worry. The popcorn is almost done."

"You're making *popcorn*?" Abraham demanded.

"Sure, why not? Should be quite the show. . . ."

One by one, four screens blinked on on my headset's display, giving me a sequence of views of the main cavern and its nearby tunnels. Mizzy had set out glowsticks, though the cameras had thermal and night vision. These things had come from Knighthawk, little crablike drones with cameras in their bodies. I used my mobile to turn the camera of one drone, and it worked perfectly.

"Nice," Knighthawk said. He and Mizzy would be watching the screens also, though Mizzy would be busy with her explosives. Megan and I had been desperate when we'd faced our weaknesses; I hoped that if we could drive Prof to exhaustion, if we presented a real danger, we'd make it easier for him to do the same.

"Knighthawk," I said, cycling through the cameras to get a view from Cody's eyes, then Megan's, "Prof's ETA?"

"Just landed on your building," he said.

"Any other Epics with him?"

"Negative," Knighthawk said. "All right, he's vaporized the roof and he's dropping through."

"Mizzy," I said, "blow the present."

We felt the shock of it, and some debris rolled down the hole we'd made. I waited, tense, trying to watch all of the different screens at once. Which direction would he come from?

The roof of the cave trembled, then fell in, dumping practically a *ton* of salt dust into the main chamber. Light shone down in streaks. Prof wasn't content with a little hole like we'd made. He'd ripped the top off an entire cavern.

He floated down on a glowing disc of light, dust swirling around him, goggles on his face and his dark lab coat fluttering. My breath caught.

I didn't see a monster. In my mind's eye, I remembered a man who had come down through another roof amid falling dust. A man who had run for all he had—breaking through to face an Enforcement team, risking his life and his own sanity—to save me.

It was time to return the favor.

"Go," I whispered over the line.

42

ABRAHAM engaged him first, bringing out the big gun—his gravatonic minigun. I always got a little thrill when I watched it fire, because *man*—it could unload bullets faster than a pair of drunk hicks visiting a varmint factory.

"Everyone stay under cover," I warned as Abraham's gun flashed from the darkness, spraying Prof with a couple hundred rounds.

Prof's forcefields were up, and the bullets deflected—but those forcefields weren't invincible. Using them took effort. We could wear him down.

He sneered at Abraham, then flung his hand to the side, forming his trademark forcefield globe around the Canadian man. Prof clenched his fist to shrink it, but the forcefield caught as Abraham used the rtich to brace it on either side.

I had a good view of Prof's startled face through one camera.

"Cody, go," I said.

A flash of light shot from the shadows, and the forcefield around Abraham shattered. Good. As before, the tensor could negate forcefields. Though we had to be careful not to vaporize Abraham's gun as a byproduct.

Prof roared and pointed at Cody, though nothing seemed to happen. I frowned at the gesture, but didn't have time to think on it as Cody and Abraham engaged Prof. Cody wasn't practiced with forcefields—while perhaps trying to throw a globe around Prof, he instead made a wall between them. That accidentally protected him as Prof sent spears of light Cody's way. They slammed into the wall, piercing it and getting stuck.

"Abraham, wind around to his left," I instructed. A blip appeared on my map of the caverns, a location where Mizzy had set up a pack of explosives. "Megan, see if you can draw him down that tunnel to the right, toward Mizzy's surprise."

"Roger," Megan said.

My little cubby of a cave shook as Prof and Cody clashed, tensor blasts vaporizing one another's forcefields. Abraham held his own with the rtich, forming it into a shield and catching spears of light. Cody wasn't very useful with his own forcefields, unfortunately. A few hours of practice did not an expert make.

However, he did have tons of practice with the tensors from back in the day, and he was able to work those easily. He kept vaporizing Prof's forcefields, protecting himself and—most importantly—Abraham. Cody's suit had a harmsway attached to it, but Abraham didn't have such a blessing.

I directed the team as best I could, and for once I didn't have time to wish I were with them. I was too busy leading the team to push Prof toward the set explosions—we blasted him several times, staggering him and keeping him from bringing down Cody and Abraham. I also kept watch on Prof as he occasionally ducked through caverns at a run, trying to loop around and gain an advantage.

On my mark, Megan entered the fray, creating illusory versions of herself and Firefight to draw Prof's attention and his attacks. So long as she didn't push too hard, these would just be shadows from other dimensions, like the false faces we'd worn. It wouldn't put anyone in any other dimension in danger, and hopefully wouldn't risk her sanity. Only shadows and feints—anything to keep Prof distracted and off-balance.

I watched all of this with a sinking feeling. The longer they fought, the more obvious it became that Cody's powers—though aligned more closely with Prof's own abilities than even Tavi's had been—would not immediately force Prof to change.

I zoomed my cameras in on Prof's face, watching his expressions. His sneers and condescension soon gave way to a look of fierce determination. In that, I saw the man I knew.

Face it, Prof! I thought, huddled in my cocoon of stone, snapping orders and directing cameras. *Come on.* Why wasn't it enough? Why wouldn't his powers give way before his fears?

"Megan, Cody," I said, "I want to try something. The tensors disrupt his forcefields, even the ones protecting his skin. Find a way to catch him in a blast of tensor power, Cody. Then, Megan, I want you to shoot him."

"Roger," Megan said. "Do you care where I hit him?"

"No," I said. "His powers are strong enough that he

should be able to heal from anything a handgun can dish out." I paused. "But maybe make the first hit or two someplace non-lethal, just in case."

"Roger," they said as one.

Cody was panting. "Hitting him with the tensors is going to be tough, lad. He's been trying to do the same to us, to melt my motivators away. We've been keeping our distance."

I focused a camera on him. Seemed like using the tensor suit was exhausting. He and Megan maneuvered into position while Mizzy set up some more explosives farther down the corridor.

"We'll have to risk it," I said. "I—"

"Ach!" Cody interrupted. "What the . . ."

"Cody?" I asked. He didn't seem hurt, but he'd stumbled back against the cavern wall and had managed to surround himself with a box of glowing green forcefields.

"Was that a squirrel?" he said. "It was running across me. A *bloody* squirrel?"

"What are you talking about?" Mizzy asked.

Cody seemed confused. "Maybe it was a rat or something. I didn't get a good look."

I frowned as he dismissed his forcefields and ran to join Abraham, who had moved in close to Prof after forming the rtich into a gauntlet covered in spikes.

"Knighthawk, Mizzy," I said, "did either of you happen to see that thing? Whatever it was that was attacking Cody?"

"I saw a blur," Knighthawk said. "I'm rewinding the footage now. I'll send you a still if I spot something."

Prof pushed past Abraham, leaving him tripping over a forcefield rod created right before his legs. Prof slammed his hand to the floor of the cavern and vaporized it in a large swath, dumping Cody into a river of dust. Cody stumbled, slowing down.

Prof summoned a spike of light in each hand and shot them across the room, pounding them into Cody's shoulders. Cody screamed and fell into the dust.

Sparks. It was obvious who knew these powers better.

"Megan!" I cried.

"On it," she said, and the ceiling of the cavern rumbled and collapsed, making Prof jump back in alarm. Merely a shadow of another world, but hopefully it would buy Cody enough time to heal.

"Prof started speaking into a mobile," Knighthawk said, surprised. "He must know we're monitoring his line. . . . Sparks. He's talking to you, I think."

"Patch it through to me," I said, "but don't let him hear what we're saying."

". . . think to beat me with my own curse." Prof's familiar voice, gruff and deep, startled me even though I'd been expecting it. "I have borne this viper for years, felt it poisoning me day by day. I know it like a man knows his own heartbeat."

"David, lad," Cody said, coughing. "I'm . . . I'm not healing. . . ."

I felt an icy chill. I focused on Cody, and it was true. He crawled through dust in the trench Prof had made, bleeding from both shoulders, where he'd been struck by light made solid. Why wasn't the harmsway working?

"Got it," Knighthawk said. "Kid, this is trouble." He sent to my screen an image from the camera footage from moments earlier. It showed a blur moving away from Cody, small like a mouse. Or a tiny person.

"Loophole is here!" I said over the line. "He didn't come alone! Warning, there's *another Epic* in the cavern." I hesitated. "Sparks, she unhooked one of the motivators from Cody's vest and ran off with it."

"Cameras have infrared," Knighthawk said, taking control of several of them. He sounded excited. Engaged, even. "Overlaying now . . . There! I've got her. Ha. Think you can hide from my all-seeing eyes, little Epic? You don't know who you're dealing with."

Knighthawk zoomed one of our cameras toward a tiny figure hiding in the shadows near one of the cavern's many broken chunks of rock. She wore jeans, goggles, and a tight shirt. I didn't spot the motivator, but she'd likely shrunk it to a size small enough to carry.

"Megan!" I said as Prof rounded the false cave-in. "You and Abraham are going to have to handle him on your own for a time. Keep him distracted; he's going to try to finish off Cody. Mizzy, go help get Cody bandaged. Don't let him bleed out!"

A series of "rogers" sounded. I started wriggling out of my stone confines.

"Should have known," Knighthawk said over the line. "Of course Jonathan came with a plan. He may not have realized I used multiple motivators on this version of the suit though, so his orders to Loophole weren't complete enough."

"I need you to run ops, Knighthawk."

"Fine," he said, reluctant. "You're going to take on the mini-Epic by yourself?"

I squeezed out of my cubby and rolled to my feet, Gottschalk to my shoulder. "She's not a High Epic. A single bullet will kill her."

"Yeah. Hit her with a bullet the same size as she is—I'm sure that won't harm the motivator she's carrying."

I grimaced as I crept down the hallway. It was a valid point. "Keep an eye on her for me."

"Already done. One of the cameras is set to auto-track her. Jonathan's talking again."

"Patch him through to me, but not the others. I don't want them distracted. And Knighthawk . . . keep them alive for me, please."

"I'll try. Get that motivator, kid. Fast."

43

"I didn't want to be here."

I had to listen to Prof as I crept back up the tunnel, lit by the sickly green light of glowsticks.

"I wanted to remain quiet," Prof continued, grunting as he fought. "I didn't want to push myself, or my teams, too hard. This is your fault, David. Everything that happens here is because of *you*."

I couldn't see the battle. I still wore the domed headset, but my task was now Loophole and that motivator. I had one screen fixed on the map of the caverns with her location pinpointed; another showed the view from the camera watching her. They hovered at the edges of my vision; I needed the area right in front of my eyes clear.

I walked carefully, as if preparing to join the battle with Prof. I didn't want to alert Loophole.

"Tia . . . ," Prof whispered. "You drove me to this, David. You and your idiot dreams. You upset the balance. You should have accepted that I was *right*."

I gritted my teeth, face flushing. I couldn't let him get to me. But his words were dangerous for reasons he likely didn't know. Last time I'd been in a fight, back in Sharp Tower . . . things had happened.

Something lurked inside me. And so, while Prof's belittling voice in my ears was abrasive, Larcener's taunts from the rooftop earlier were what truly dug into me.

You see the truth of men manifest in those first moments, David . . . New Epics. They murder, they destroy, showing what every man would do if his inhibitions were relaxed. Men are a race of monsters, inefficiently chained. . . .

Loophole. I had to focus on Loophole. She was the problem right now! What could she do?

She . . . she had slightly augmented speed and could alter the size of things, herself included. She had to touch them first though. Her size manipulation lasted a few minutes if left unchecked—she couldn't do it permanently, but she could shrink something and leave it. It would return to normal on its own later, or if she touched it and changed its size again.

Fortunately, unlike other similar Epics, when she shrank she didn't retain her strength or mass. She was fast, clever, and dangerous—but not a High Epic. And her weakness . . . I strained trying to remember . . . her weakness was sneezing. Her powers disappeared if she sneezed. I had explicit records of that.

Well, just because she wasn't a High Epic didn't mean she wasn't dangerous. I reached the part of the corridor where she was hiding, then continued down it toward the others, pretending I didn't know she was there. Light shone down from the hole Prof had made in the ceiling. I grabbed a handful of rock dust off the ground, shoving it into my pocket. Distant crashes and shouts echoed from ahead. I resisted the urge to switch camera views and check in.

"And where are you, David?" Prof said in my ear. "You let the others die fighting me, but you hide? I never would have figured you for a coward."

On the screen hovering to my right, Loophole was beside her rock, waiting with her back pressed against it. She didn't seem concerned; she was a mercenary, known for giving her loyalty to whichever powerful Epic paid her. Prof had likely hired her only to steal the motivator. She'd want nothing else to do with this fight.

Too bad for her.

Go.

I leaped toward the rock where she was hiding, shoving it against the wall of the cavern, hoping to pinch her in place. Halfway through my push the rock vanished, shrinking to the size of a pebble. I hit the ground, scrambling to grab the tiny figure as it sprinted away.

I got ahold of her but immediately felt a lurching jolt. Loophole was my size again, but she was halfway down the tunnel from me. Why was the tunnel so much larger now?

Aw, didgeridoo, I thought, *she shrank me!*

I scrambled to my feet between pebbles that were now the size of boulders. In front of me, a small crack in the floor had become a chasm—though granted, it was only about twice as deep as I was tall. I'd been shrunk, as had everything I'd been holding.

Loophole, also tiny, had gotten a good fifty feet in front of me, or at least what seemed fifty feet at my current size. Her augmented speed let her run quickly, but it wasn't true super speed. Just a little edge on a regular person.

That meant she couldn't outrun bullets or anything like that. I unslung my tiny Gottschalk, took aim, and released a burst, intentionally missing. I could still easily pierce the motivator, effectively killing Cody. I'd take that chance if she didn't stop, but a warning shot seemed appropriate.

"I've got you, Loophole!" I shouted to her. "Give me the motivator and leave. You don't care about this fight, and I don't care about you."

She stopped in the corridor and glanced at me.

Then grew to normal size.

Uh-oh . . .

She came stomping toward me, each footfall shaking the floor like an earthquake. I yelped and threw myself into the nearby crack, sliding down onto a ledge as Loophole loomed overhead. She reached down for me, and I unloaded with the Gottschalk. Apparently even a tiny gun on full auto doesn't feel good. She pulled her fingers back and cursed—a sound like a thunderstorm.

Bits of rock dust tumbled into my chasm, falling like a shower of hail. I reached in my pocket and pulled out some of the dust I'd grabbed earlier; it had shrunk with me.

I had to get it into her face. Great. It would be like climbing Everest to get up there. Also, noses look really strange from below. I did notice a small pouch hanging from a strap around her neck. The motivator, maybe?

She came at me with a knife next, jabbing it into the crack. I grabbed hold of the back of it with one hand, letting the Gottschalk hang from my shoulder by its strap. I was able to ride the knife out as she lifted it, but my plans of climbing up her arm were ruined as she shook the knife, dropping me some twenty feet to the floor.

I braced myself and hit . . . but it didn't hurt much. Huh. Being little had its advantages. I rolled to my feet as she stomped at me. I barely avoided being squished by a footfall. Blast, I'd lost my handful of dust in the fall. In fact . . .

In fact . . . I . . .

I sneezed, and thumped my head against the wall of the cavern as I crashed up against it. I'd increased in size again. Loophole and I regarded one another with similar expressions of shock.

"Sneezing works on either of us, eh?" I said. "Nice to know."

She growled, reaching for the holster at her side and the handgun there. I kicked it from her grip as soon as she got it free, then slung the Gottschalk around. "Sure you don't want to give me the motivator?"

She reached for me. So, reluctantly, I fired.

Each bullet, as it hit her, shrank to the size of a gnat. They still seemed to hurt, judging by her winces, but they certainly didn't do the whole "killing you dead" thing I'd been hoping for.

She had a hold on the rifle a second later, and it vanished in my hands, shrinking to minuscule size and falling off its strap. I gaped at Loophole. She'd shrunk bullets *as they were hitting her.*

"That was awesome," I said.

She decked me, knocking my head against the wall of the cavern again and smashing my headset. I cursed, kicking at her, then scrambled to my feet. "Seriously," I said to Loophole, "I might have to reevaluate. You could be a High Epic after all."

"What is *wrong* with you?" she asked, coming at me swinging.

I brought my hands up and managed to block. Unfortunately my return jab at her missed, and she clocked me across the face a second time. Sparks. When she came in again, I grabbed hold of her, as Abraham had taught me. I was bigger, so grappling seemed smart.

She shrank my shirt.

It just about strangled me, but fortunately it ripped before doing that. I still let go of the woman, gasping. Loophole slammed her hand into my chest, and I grew to twenty feet tall, smashing my head into the roof of the cavern.

"David!" Mizzy said over the line. "Hurry! He's in a bad way."

"Trying," I croaked as Loophole shrank me down to normal size, then punched me in the face again. The cavern shook and rattled, chips of rock falling from the ceiling, and shouts came from the direction of Prof, Megan, and Abraham.

I stumbled away from Loophole, then brought up my arms to block, my hand-to-hand training—and my brain— kind of fuzzy at the moment. Her flurry of punches backed me against the wall, where she continued to quite liberally beat on my face, then stomach, in turn. I had one chance to reach for my handgun, which I wore strapped to my leg, but she knocked it out of my grasp.

She seemed to have grown a few inches, and she towered over me. As my gun clattered away, the only thing I could think to do was jump for her and throw my weight against her, which worked well enough—in that it tumbled us both to the ground.

She got up first. I was pretty dizzy, my shirt in tatters. I groaned, rolling over, and found her picking up her fallen handgun.

Something dropped from the ceiling onto her back. A mechanical crab? Another one jumped at her from the side, then a third fell from above. They didn't look particularly dangerous, but they startled her, causing her to spin around and grab at her back.

The breather was a lifesaver for me, giving me enough time to stop the room from spinning. I dug in my pocket, getting out some more dust. Guns wouldn't work on her. I'd have to be cleverer.

"Thanks, Knighthawk," I mumbled as Loophole shrank to get out of the grip of the crabs.

I reached for her, and—like before—she shrank me as soon as I touched her tiny form. I was ready for it this time, and lunged for her as soon as I was tiny. I crashed into her again, grabbing at the pouch around her neck. I felt the thin metal rectangle through the leather inside. The motivator!

"Persistent little idiot, aren't you?" she growled at me as the two of us, still tiny, grappled across the floor.

I grunted, managing to roll us up beside the crack-chasm in the ground. Then she head-butted me—and it *stung*. The room shook and I gasped, letting go—of both her and the pouch.

She rose, standing before me, the crack in the ground behind her. "I know his plan," she said. "Epic of all Epics. Sounds like a great deal to me. I let him gather the pieces, then I make off with them. Go up and pay a visit to old Calamity myself."

I looked up at her, dazed, my nose bleeding.

"I . . . ," I said, gasping.

"Yes?"

I panted. "I . . . suppose this . . . would be an awkward time to ask for an autograph."

"What?"

I threw the dust into her face, then—as she cursed—I slammed my shoulder into her, grabbing the pouch while simultaneously knocking her backward. The cord snapped, leaving the pouch in my fingers. She fell into the chasm-crack, and I rocked there, on the edge, almost following her in.

She dropped to the bottom, where she hit with a soft thump. "You idiot!" she called up. "You realize that at this size"—she stopped, sniffling for a second—"at this size, a fall isn't harmful at all. You could fall off a building, and—and—Oh, *hell*—"

I jumped away from the crack. A very faint sneeze came from behind.

Followed by a gut-wrenching splat. I winced, peeking at the mess of pulped flesh and broken bones that Loophole had become by growing too quickly inside far too small a space. Parts of her burbled out the top of the crack, like rising dough that had outgrown its bowl.

I swallowed, nauseous, then stumbled to my feet and pulled the motivator from the pouch. A bit of dust and one sneeze later, both it and I were back to regular size—though my Gottschalk was nowhere to be found.

I grabbed my handgun instead. "Mizzy, I've got the motivator," I said over the line. "Where are you?"

44

I stumbled through the caverns underneath Ildithia, passing walls blasted open with the tensors, leaving scattered piles of sand. The glowsticks gave the tunnels a radioactive cast. I stopped, steadying myself during another tremor, then continued toward the nook where Mizzy had dragged Cody. Was that them ahead?

No. I pulled up short. Light poured through a rent in the air, like cut flesh where the skin had curled to the sides. Through it I saw another cavern, this one lit by a lively orange light. Inside, Firefight struggled against Loophole.

I gaped, watching the woman I'd just killed shrink and run from him while causing a set of falling rock chips to become boulders. Firefight zipped backward, his flames heating the rocks to a reddish orange.

I looked down the passage and glimpsed other rents in the air. Megan had been pushing herself, it seemed. I gulped and continued toward Mizzy. A flash of light to my left illuminated figures struggling in the shadows—a section of the cavern network beyond where Mizzy had placed her glowsticks.

Prof suddenly appeared a little ways down the cavern, forming like light coalescing. He was using Obliteration's powers to teleport. Sparks! Even as he appeared, a section of the roof collapsed. Not an illusion this time, an actual rockfall, which Prof was forced to catch with a forcefield above his head. He bellowed with rage, holding up the fallen rocks, then sent a few lances of light off into the distance.

They'd both been forced, it seemed, to grasp for dangerous resources. Prof using his hidden teleportation device; Megan reaching further and further into other realities. How far had she gone? What if I lost her, as I'd lost Prof?

Steady, I thought at myself. She'd been certain she could handle it. I had to trust her. I ducked my head and scrambled down a side tunnel, eventually spotting bloodstains on the stones. I rounded another corner, then stumbled to a halt as I almost tripped over Mizzy and Cody.

He lay on the ground with eyes closed, his face pale. Mizzy had needed to pull off most of the tensor suit to get at his wounds; it was piled in a heap nearby, the harmsway portion detached, but with wires extended to his arm. Mizzy yelped when she saw me, then snatched the motivator from my limp fingers. She plugged it back into the vest.

"Knighthawk," I said over the line, "you really need to secure those motivators better."

"It's a prototype," he grumbled. "I built it to have quick access so I could tweak motivators as needed. How was I to know Jonathan would yank the things out?"

Mizzy glanced at me as the harmsway glowed softly. "Sparks, David! You look like you fell off a cliff or something."

I wiped my nose, which was still bleeding. My face was starting to swell from the beating I'd taken. I slumped down next to Mizzy, exhausted. "How's the fight going?"

"Your girlfriend is kinda amazing," Mizzy said grudgingly. "Abraham keeps getting locked up in forcefields, but she gets him out. Together they're keeping Prof busy."

"Does she seem . . ."

"Crazy?" Mizzy said. "Can't tell." She looked to Cody, whose wounds were—blessedly—closing. "He'll be out for a while yet. Hope the other two can last. I'm out of boom-packs too, I'm afraid. So maybe—"

Someone exploded into existence next to us. A sudden burst of light, silent, but stunning if you watched it. I shouted, falling backward, and reached for the handgun strapped to my leg. It wasn't Prof. Unfortunately, that left only one other option.

Obliteration turned, his trench coat sweeping the side of the cavern. He looked from Mizzy to Cody to me, studying us with bespectacled eyes. "I've been summoned," he said.

"Um, yeah," I said, hands trembling as I held my gun on him. "Prof. He has a motivator built from your flesh."

"To destroy the city?" Obliteration asked, head cocked. "She made a bomb beyond those she gave me?"

"Those she gave you?" I asked. "So . . . you do have more?"

"Of course," Obliteration said calmly. "You are fallen, David Charleston." He shook his head, then disappeared, leaving behind an image made of ceramic that broke apart and faded.

I relaxed. Then Obliteration appeared beside me, hand on

my gun. It was suddenly hot, and I shouted, fingers singeing as I dropped the weapon. Obliteration kicked it aside, kneeling next to me.

"'And there are seven kings: five are fallen, and one is, and the other is not yet come,'" he whispered. He flinched as, distantly, Prof must have teleported. Then he grinned, closing his eyes. Sparks. He seemed to *like* the feeling. "The hour has come for you to die and for this city to be destroyed. I regret that I cannot give you more time." He placed his hand against my forehead, and I felt warmth coming from his skin.

"I'm going to kill Calamity," I blurted out.

Obliteration opened his eyes. The heat dampened. "What did you say?"

"Calamity," I said. "He's an Epic, and he's behind all of this. I can kill him. If you want to bring about Armageddon, wouldn't that be the perfect way? Destroy this terrible . . . um, angel? Creature? Spirit?"

That sounded religious, right?

"He is far away, little man," Obliteration said, contemplative. "You will never reach him."

"You can teleport there though, right?"

"Impossible. Calamity is too distant for me to form a proper picture of its location in my mind, and I cannot go to a place I haven't seen or cannot visualize."

How did you get in here, then? Sparks. Had he been watching us somehow? That didn't matter. Hand still trembling, I reached into my pocket and unhooked my mobile. I brought it out and turned to him, displaying Regalia's image of Calamity. "What if you have a picture?"

Obliteration whispered softly, eyes wide. "'And the beast that was, and is not, even he is the eighth, and is of the seven, and goeth into perdition. . . .'" He blinked, looking at me.

"Again you surprise me. If you defeat your former master, and impress me in so doing, I will grant your desires."

He exploded into a flash again—and this time he didn't immediately return. I groaned, leaning against the wall, shaking my burned hand.

"Calamity! What is *up* with that man?" Mizzy asked, sliding her sidearm into its holster. It took her three tries, her hand was trembling so much. "I thought we were dead."

"Yeah," I said. "I half expected him to murder me for the audacity of claiming I wanted to kill Calamity. I figured it was even odds that he worshipped the thing instead of hating it." I peeked around the corner, looking down a tunnel that shone with rents and rips into other dimensions.

"Abraham just went down!" Knighthawk said in my ear. "Repeat, Abraham is *down*. Jonathan sheared his arm off—rtich attached—with a forcefield."

"Sparks!" I said. "Megan?"

"Hard to see," Knighthawk said. "I've only got two crab cameras left. I think you're losing this fight, guys."

"We were losing it before we started," I said, turning and crawling to the tensor suit. "Mizzy, some help."

She looked at the suit, then at me, eyes widening. She scrambled over, then helped me start putting it on. "Cody should be stable now; that harmsway is something."

"Unhook it and attach it back to the tensor suit," I said. "Knighthawk, how much can your drones lift?"

"About a hundred pounds each," he said. "I work them in tandem for heavier things. Why?"

"Bring some down, grab Cody, pull him out. Is Abraham still alive?"

"Don't know," Knighthawk said. "His mobile is still on him though, so I can show you his location."

I looked at Mizzy and she nodded, plugging the wires from the harmsway into the vest of the tensor suit, which I was now wearing. "I'll find him," she said, "and stabilize him until you can get back with this."

"Get the drones hooked to Cody first."

"Assuming I can get drones in to you," Knighthawk said. "Jonathan's military has the place surrounded up above. They don't seem too eager to come down and join the fight."

"And get between two High Epics?" I said. "They'll stay back unless directly ordered. They know what happened to the soldiers at Sharp Tower. I'm surprised he was able to get even Loophole to come down here, after that."

"Yeah," Mizzy said. She looked overwhelmed, hand still trembling. I didn't feel much better myself, though with a jolt I felt the harmsway engage. My pains faded.

"Get out of here, Mizzy," I said. "You've done what you can. Try to get Abraham and Cody to safety; I'll bring the harmsway for Abraham as soon as I can. If I don't make it, set up with Knighthawk."

She nodded. "Good luck, David. I'm, um, glad I didn't shoot you in Babilar."

I smiled, yanking on first the right tensor glove, then the left.

"You going to be able to make it work?" Mizzy asked. "Without practice?"

The lights on the gloves lit up a deep green. I felt their hum course through me, a distant melody that had once been precious to me, yet one I'd somehow forgotten. I released it, reducing the stone wall nearby to a wave of dust.

"Feels like coming home," I said.

In fact, I felt almost good enough to face a High Epic.

45

I sprinted through the tunnel, passing shimmering rips on either side—windows to other worlds. Several were to Firefight's realm, but others—fainter, misty and less distinct—looked farther away. There were worlds where unfamiliar figures fought in these tunnels, or where the place was completely dark, and even worlds where there *were* no tunnels here, just rock.

The tensors hummed on my hands, eager. It was as if . . . as if the powers themselves knew I was trying to save Prof. They sang me a battle hymn. As I reached the chamber where I'd seen Prof earlier, I let out a burst of vibrating energy, dispelling the rock of a ledge before me, creating a set of dust-covered steps that I strode down.

Prof glowed green in the center of the chamber, the sleeves

of his coat rolled back to expose forearms covered with dark hair. He turned on me, then laughed. "David Charleston," he said, his voice booming in the chamber. "Steelslayer! Come to finally take responsibility for what you began in Newcago? Have you come to *pay*?"

The floor here was pocked with tensor holes, and those alternated with piles of rubble and dust that had collapsed from the ceiling. Sparks. This place was a few breaths and a modest bass beat away from a cave-in.

I stepped up before him, hoping I could make the suit's forcefields work. Where was Megan? She'd be reborn if she'd died, so that didn't worry me as much as the existence of all these tears in reality.

One of them hovered nearby. Darkness visible only because of the shimmering at its sides.

Megan stepped out of it.

I jumped. Sparks, it was her, but a . . . strange version of her. Blurry.

Because it's not just one of her, I realized. I wasn't looking at one Megan, but hundreds. Overlapping one another, each similar but somehow individual. A freckle in a different place, hair that parted another way. Eyes too pale here or too dark there.

She smiled at me. A thousand smiles.

"I've got Abraham," Mizzy said. "He's alive, but it would be reaaaal nice if you kept the harmsway safe, David. If you want Abraham back to one piece, at least. Pulling out now."

"Roger," I said, looking at Prof. His clothing was dusty, ripped. He'd bled—and healed—from multiple cuts on his face. One hadn't healed, a place where Cody had hit him with the powers somehow.

Beleaguered though he was, Prof didn't seem afraid. He

stood tall, confident. Four glowing lances of light appeared around him.

"The price, David," Prof said softly.

He released the lances, driving them toward me. I was able to vaporize them with the tensors, which shattered the forcefields to tiny specks. They sprayed across me before twinkling away. Not content to get pushed around, I charged Prof, trying to summon forcefields of my own.

All I got were a few shimmers of green, ripples like light reflecting off a pond. Crud.

Prof sent a second set of spikes, but—like Cody—I was familiar enough with the tensors to stop these as well. I leaped over a pit in the ground, then slammed my hand on the floor, opening up a gap with a blasting *humm*.

Prof dropped a mere inch before landing on a disc of green light. He shook his head, then flung his hand toward me, sending a gout of tensor energy that dropped the ground out from beneath me, as I'd done to him.

I frantically tried to create a forcefield to land on, but only got another shimmer of light. Then an instant later the hole wasn't as deep—and I hit bottom three feet down.

Megan stood beside the hole. "There are many worlds where he did not dig deep enough with that blast," she said, her voice overlapped by a hundred whispers.

Prof growled, charging me and summoning spears of light, one after another. I hopped out of the hole, falling in beside Megan, destroying the spikes where I could.

Each time I did so, Prof winced.

"So, how do we fight him?" Megan asked in overlapping voices. "All I've been able to do is distract him. Is the plan still to make him confront his fears somehow?"

"Not sure, honestly," I said, thrusting my hands in front

of me and straining. Finally I produced a forcefield wall. It was kind of like using the tensors in reverse. Instead of releasing a hum, I let it build up inside me until it coalesced.

"How much can you alter?" I asked, looking at Megan.

"Little things," she said. "Reasonable things. My powers haven't changed, I just know them. David, I can see worlds . . . so many worlds." She blinked, an action that seemed to trail infinite shadows of eyelids. "But they're all ones that are nearby. It's amazing, yet frustrating. It's like I can count as many numbers as I want, but only if they happen to be between zero and one. Infinity, yet still bounded."

Prof shattered our forcefield, then raised his hands, causing the ceiling to shake. I summoned the tensor powers as I anticipated his move—indeed, he tried to bring the ceiling down on us by vaporizing a ring of rock, dropping a large stone in the center.

I vaporized the chunk right above us. We were showered with dust, and the way it fell on Megan proved she was here and real, not a shadow as a piece of me had feared.

Prof winced again.

I'm using his power. And it hurts.

"All right, I have a plan," I said to Megan.

"Which is?"

"To *run*," I said, turning and dashing out of the main chamber into a side tunnel.

Megan cursed, following. We ran side by side and I engaged the tensors, vaporizing ribbons of stone along our path. I wasn't sure what I could do to change him or make him return to us. All of my plans had failed so far; the best thing I could do at the moment was keep the suit working and keep *him* in pain.

Behind us, Prof roared. He teleported in front of us, but I simply grabbed Megan by the hand and turned the other direction while disintegrating the forcefield Prof tried to use to trip us up. We ran into a tunnel without any light, but glowsticks appeared a second later, summoned by Megan from a realm where Mizzy had lit this place.

When Prof teleported in front of us again, red-faced and snarling, I turned us back the other way, unrelentingly using the suit's powers on random stones we passed. Each use of the tensors was driving him further into a fury.

I've been here before, I thought, feeling the echoes of another event. Another fight. Driving an Epic to anger . . .

Prof appeared again, and this time Megan reacted first, yanking me to the side as spears of light—faster than I could track—struck like blades around us. Sparks! I barely stopped them. Maybe this wasn't such a good plan.

"This is always how you are!" Prof shouted. "No thought! No concern for consequences! Don't you worry about what will happen? Don't you ever think about *failure*?"

He teleported in front of us as we tried to flee, but a second later a rock wall created by Megan separated us.

"This isn't working," she said.

"Well, technically it is. I mean, my plan was just to run."

"Okay, I revise: this isn't going to work for very long. Sooner or later he'll trap us. What's your endgame?"

"Make him mad," I said.

"And?"

"Hope . . . um . . . that makes him afraid? We were desperate, scared, frantic when we faced our weaknesses. Maybe he has to be in the same state."

She gave me a skeptical look that—reflected through all of her shadows—was even more formidable than usual.

The wall near us melted away to powder. I gathered the energy of the tensors, preparing to be attacked by a series of forcefield spears, but Prof wasn't behind the wall anymore.

Huh?

He crashed into existence behind us and seized me by the arm with one hand. With the other, he tried to vaporize the motivators on my vest. I yelped and let out a blast of tensor power—directly down, carving out the rock beneath me and dropping me lower a few feet. The sudden motion lurched me out of Prof's grip and made his blast pass over my head.

I vaporized the ground below him, and by reflex he created a forcefield to stand on, so I wriggled through the dust underneath him. He had to twist to see me, but that left him open to Megan. Who, of course, shot him.

It didn't have much effect; he was protected—as always—by thin, invisible forcefields around his whole person. Her shots did distract him long enough for me to crawl out from underneath the disc on the other side. There, I raised my handgun and started firing as well.

He turned on me, annoyed, and I hit him with a blast of tensor power, dissolving his forcefields. Megan's gunshots began to chew chunks out of him, and he cursed, flashing away.

Megan stepped up to me, her face blurred by a hundred different identities. "We don't have the weakness right, David."

"His own powers *could* hurt him," I said. "And the tensor leaves him able to be shot."

"He heals from those shots immediately," she said, "and getting hit with tensor power doesn't disrupt his abilities as much as it should. It's like . . . we have *part* of the weakness right, but don't grasp the entire thing. And that's why he's not turning—confronting the powers must not be enough."

I couldn't argue. She was right. I sensed it inside, with a sinking feeling.

"So what now?" I asked. "Any ideas?"

"We have to kill him."

I drew my lips to a line. I wasn't sure we could do that. And even if we could kill him, it felt like in so doing, we might win the battle but lose the war.

Megan glanced at my gun. "You're reloaded, by the way."

My gun suddenly felt a bit heavier. "That's convenient."

"Can't help thinking there should be more I can do than reload guns and replace walls. I can see so much. . . . It's overwhelming."

"We need to pick one thing for you to change," I said, holding my gun and watching for Prof to reappear. "Something very useful."

"A weapon," she said, nodding.

"Abraham's minigun?"

She smiled, then that smile became an almost girlish grin. "No. That's thinking too small."

"That gun is too *small*? Woman, I love you."

"Actually," she said, turning her head to look at something I couldn't see, "there is a very close world where Abraham ran ops for our team. . . ."

"What does that have to do with guns? You—"

I cut off as the cavern shook. I spun, then stumbled back as the entire *wall* of the tunnel—dozens of feet along— turned to dust in an incredible burst of power. Prof stood beyond, and he'd been busy. Hundreds of spears of light hovered around him.

We'd been talking. He'd been planning.

I shouted, thrusting my hand forward and releasing tensor power as the spears came for us. I got the first wave, and most of the second, but my blast ran out as the third bore down upon us.

They got caught in a reflective, silvery metallic surface that formed a shield in front of us. Megan grunted, holding the mercury steady, blocking the next two waves of impact.

"You see?" she said, now bearing the glove that controlled the rtich. "In a world where Abraham leads the team, someone else has to learn to use *this*." She grinned, then grunted at another impact. "So . . . we going to bring him down?"

I nodded, feeling sick. "At the very least, we need him afraid. That's the path that led us to change—we were terrified, facing death. Only when we were in serious danger did confronting our fears work."

It felt wrong, like I was still missing something, but in the chaos of the moment it was the best I could do.

"Time to be a little brash?" she said, holding out the rtich in one hand, gun in the other.

"Foolhardy," I agreed, hefting my own gun. "Reckless."

I nodded to her, took a deep breath.

And we attacked.

Megan lowered her shield, letting the rtich crawl back up her arm. I sent out another wave of tensor power, and we ran through it, firing like madmen. The guns seemed mundane compared to the deific powers spinning about us, but they were familiar. Dependable. Solid.

We interrupted Prof in the middle of raising another wave of light spears. His eyes widened and his jaw lowered, as if he was befuddled to see the two of us coming right at him. He swept his hand forward, summoning a large forcefield to block us, but I crashed through it with a tensor burst, and Megan followed.

"Fine," he said, pounding his hand into the ground. Rock vaporized around it, and he pulled out a large rod of stone. He stepped forward, slamming it toward Megan, who caught it on her arm with the rtich.

The mercury ran down onto Prof's arm, holding him in place as I arrived to send a burst of tensor power at him, intending to follow it with a few shots to the face. Prof, however, matched my invisible blast with one of his own. They canceled one another out, crashing together with a sound that made my ears pop.

I skidded to a halt, then shot him in the face anyway. I mean, it had to be distracting, right? Even if the bullets bounced off? Maybe I could get one stuck in his nose or something.

He growled, yanking his fist free of the rtich and shoving Megan away. He swung his bar toward me, but I managed to vaporize it. Then I dumped about half a ton of dust on him from the cciling, making him slip and stumble.

When he righted himself, Megan came in with the rtich coating her hand, arm, and side to give power—then slammed her fist into his face. Even with the forcefields, Prof cursed and stumbled backward. Megan came in, and he vaporized the ground in a deep hole that must have emptied into a cavern far beneath us, but Megan formed the rtich into a long rod and caught herself with it spanning the hole.

I slammed into Prof shoulder-first, sending him skidding through dust. I knelt, giving Megan a hand, and yanked her out of the hole.

Together, we went at him again. She'd apparently reloaded our guns, because I didn't run out of bullets. And when Prof vaporized my gun, she tossed me another one, almost identical, that she'd pulled from an alternate dimension.

She was amazing with the rtich, commanding it along her body like a rippling second skin, blocking, attacking, bracing herself at other times. I kept Prof's footing uneven and—when I could—vaporized his forcefields, letting us pound him with bullets.

The fight felt strangely perfect, for a time. Megan and I working side by side—voicelessly, each anticipating the other's moves. Incredible powers at our disposal, weapons in our hands. Together we forced a much more experienced Epic to retreat. For a moment I let myself believe we would win.

Unfortunately, Prof's healing powers kept spitting our bullets out. We weren't negating those, not well enough. Megan shot for his head, not holding back, and I didn't stop her. But that attack failed like the others.

We ended up in one of the main chambers, dust dribbling around us. I withstood an assault by Prof's spears, grunting as one stabbed me in the shoulder. My motivator-aided healing powers let me recover. Megan stepped in, shielding me, but judging by the sweat dripping down her face, she was wearing down. I felt it too. Using the powers like this was taxing.

We braced ourselves, waiting for another attack from Prof. My gun clicked as Megan reloaded it, and I looked to her.

"Another attack?" she whispered.

I wasn't sure anymore. I tried to force out a reply, but then the ceiling caved in on us.

I stumbled, looking up, but Megan managed to turn the rtich to stop the sudden torrent of stone and dust. Garish sunlight streamed down out of the hole Prof had made, as wide as the entire cavern. I blinked, unaccustomed to the light, and looked at Prof, who had stepped out of the way of the downpour and now stood under the lip, in shadow.

"Fire," he said.

Only then did I notice that surrounding the perfect hole about thirty feet above was a squadron of fifty men and women.

They carried flamethrowers.

46

FLAMES rained down toward us. They'd been prepared for this—we hadn't been forcing Prof to retreat. He'd been leading us by the nose!

The rtich vanished as the flames surrounded us. Megan's images and shadows all snapped together and there was suddenly one crisp version of her, lit by firelight. She threw herself to the ground as the sheets of flame fell.

"No!" I screamed, thrusting my hand toward her, my glove flashing. I couldn't afford to be bad at forcefields. Not now! I strained, like I was stretching to carry too heavy a weight.

Blessedly, a glowing protective dome appeared around Megan, blocking the flames. She pressed her hands against the shield I'd created, eyes wide as the entire thing was bathed in fire.

I stumbled back from the heat, my hand in front of my face. The fires got awfully close, but the burns I took healed.

Up above, men and women began firing automatic weapons. I screamed, releasing the tensor power and vaporizing the weapons in a wave of dust. Guns and flamethrowers crumbled. The gap above widened, raining down salt—and then people as their footing vanished beneath them.

The fires stopped falling, but the damage was done. Pools of liquid flame burned in the now-open cavern floor, curling black tongues of smoke toward the sky. It was so hot, sweat beaded on my forehead. Megan's powers would be worthless in here. I blinked against the dust and smoke as Prof emerged from the shadows—grim, bloodied, but still not afraid.

Sparks. Still not afraid.

"Did you think I wouldn't have a plan?" he said to me softly. "Did you think I wouldn't prepare for Megan and her powers?" His feet ground against salt dust as he walked past a groaning soldier. "That's what you forget, David. A wise man *always* has a plan."

"Sometimes the plans don't work," I snapped. "Sometimes careful preparation isn't enough!"

"And so you storm in, taking no care?" he shouted, startlingly angry.

"Sometimes you just have to act, Prof! Sometimes you don't know what you need until you're in the thick of it!"

"That doesn't give you an excuse to upend another man's life! Doesn't give you an excuse to ignore everyone else to follow your own stupid passions! Doesn't excuse your complete *lack of control*!"

I roared, building a crescendo of tensor power. I didn't aim it toward the ground or the walls. I hurled it toward him: a charge of raw *power,* a vessel for my frustration, my anger. Nothing was working. Everything was falling apart.

It hit him, and he leaned back as if struck by something physical. Buttons on his shirt disintegrated.

Then Prof yelled and sent a blast of tensor power at me in return.

I hit it with my own. The two slammed against one another, like discordant sounds, and the cavern *shook,* stone rippling as if it were made of water. Vibrations washed over me.

The gun in my hand crumbled to dust, as did the tensor glove on the hand holding it. But the blast didn't reach the rest of me. Still, the shock of it knocked me off my feet.

I groaned and rolled over. Prof was there, looming above me. He reached down and grabbed the three boxes on the front of my vest, ripping them free of the fabric—removing the motivators from the tensor suit. "These," he said, "belong to *me.*"

No . . .

He backhanded me, a powerful blow that sent me sprawling across the rock and dust.

I came to rest near Megan, who was out of her protective dome—I was no longer holding the power to maintain it. She stood in the firelight, raised her gun in two hands, and shot at Prof.

A meaningless popping. Prof didn't even seem to care. I lay there with my arm buried in the mottled dust of the floor.

"You're fools," Prof said, tossing the motivators aside. "Both of you."

"Better a fool than a coward," I hissed. "At least I've tried to do something! Tried to change things!"

"You've tried and you've failed, David!" Prof said, stepping forward as Megan ran out of bullets. I could hear the anguish in his voice. "Look at you. You couldn't defeat me. You've *failed.*"

I rose to my knees, then settled back, feeling suddenly drained. Megan sank down beside me, burned, exhausted.

Perhaps it was the lack of the harmsway to prop me up. Perhaps it was the knowledge that at last we were done. But I didn't have the energy to rise. I barely had the energy to speak.

"We've been beaten, yes," Megan said. "But we haven't failed, Jonathan. Failure is refusing to fight. Failure is remaining quiet and hoping someone *else* will fix the problem."

I met his eyes. He stood about five feet before us in the cavern, which was now more of a crater. Ildithia's creeping salt crystals had begun to crawl over the rim of the hole, crusting over the sides. If other soldiers were up there, they'd wisely taken cover.

Prof's face was a network of cuts—injuries from debris blown by our violent explosion of tensor power, which had temporarily negated his forcefields. As if in defiance of my hopes, those wounds started to heal.

Megan . . . Megan was right. Something glimmered in my memories. "Refusing to act," I said to Prof, "yes, *that's* failure, Prof. Like . . . perhaps . . . refusing to enter a contest, even though you dearly wanted the prize?"

He stopped right in front of me. Tia had told me a story about him, when we were in Babilar. He'd wanted desperately to visit NASA, but wouldn't enter the contest that might have won him the chance.

"Yes," I said. "You never entered. Were you afraid to lose, Prof? Or were you afraid to *win*?"

"How do you know about that?" he demanded with a roar, summoning a hundred lines of light around him.

"Tia told me," I said, climbing to my knees, placing my hand on Megan's shoulder for support. It was starting to click. "You've always been like this, haven't you? You founded the

Reckoners, but refused to push them too far. Refused to face the most powerful Epics. You wanted to help, Prof, but you weren't willing to take the last step." I blinked. "You were afraid."

The lines around him faded.

"The powers are part of it," I said. "But not the whole story. Why *do* you fear them?"

He blinked. "Because . . . I . . ."

"Because if you are so powerful," Megan whispered, "if you have all of these resources, then you don't have any excuses left for failing."

He started weeping, then gritted his teeth and reached for me.

"*You've* failed, Prof," I said.

The forcefields faded and he stumbled.

"Tia's dead," Megan added. "You failed her."

"Shut up!" The wounds on his face stopped healing. "Shut up, both of you!"

"You killed your team in Babilar," I said. "You failed them."

He lunged forward and seized me by the shoulders, knocking Megan aside. But he was trembling, tears streaming from his eyes.

"You were strong," I told him. "You have powers no others can match. And still you've failed. You've failed so deeply, Prof."

"I can't have," he whispered.

"You did. You know you did." I braced myself in his grip, preparing for the lie I spoke next. "We killed Larcener, Prof. You can't complete Regalia's plan. It doesn't matter if I die. You've *failed*."

He dropped me. I stumbled up to my feet, but he sank to his knees. "Failed," he whispered. Blood dripped from his chin. "I was supposed to be a hero. . . . I've had so much power . . . and I *still failed*."

Megan limped up beside me, ashen-faced, rubbing her cheek where Prof had hit her. "Hell," she whispered. "It worked."

I looked at Prof. He still wept, but when he turned his face toward me, I saw pure loathing in his eyes. Hatred for me, for this situation. For being made a weak, common *mortal*.

"No," I said, my stomach sinking. "He didn't face it."

We'd found the true weakness. Tia had been wrong. His fear was something deeper than just the powers, though they—and his competence as a whole—were certainly part of that. He was afraid of stepping up, of becoming everything he could be—not because the powers themselves frightened him. But because if he tried, then the failure was far, far worse.

At least if he held something back and failed, he could tell himself it wasn't completely his fault. Or that it was part of the plan, that he'd always intended for it to go this way. Only if he gave his all, only if he was using every resource he had, would the failure be complete.

What a terrible burden the powers were. I could see how they'd become a focus for him, how they represented the whole of his competence—and how they also represented his potential for true failure.

Megan pressed something into my hand. Her gun. I regarded it, then—my arm feeling like lead—I raised it to Prof's head.

"Do it," he growled. "Do it, you *bastard*!"

My hand was steady, my aim unwavering, as I rested my finger on the trigger—and *remembered*.

Another day, in a steel room, with a woman I'd driven to rage.

Me, kneeling on a gridiron battlefield.

My father, his back to the bank pillar, in the shadow of a deity.

"No," I said, turning away.

Megan didn't object. She joined me. Together, we walked away from Prof.

"Who's the coward now?" he demanded, kneeling in shadows and flickering firelight. Weeping. "David Charleston! Killer of Epics. You're supposed to *stop me*."

"That," a new voice said, "can be arranged."

I turned, completely astonished, as *Larcener* strolled from the shadows of a stone overhang nearby. Had he been there all along? It defied reason. But—

He reached Prof and lightly rested his fingers on the man's neck. Prof screamed, going stiff.

"Like ice water in the veins, I'm told," Larcener said.

I charged toward them across the open cavern. "What are you doing?"

"Ending your problem," Larcener said, holding on to Prof. "You wish me to stop?"

"I . . ." I swallowed.

"Too late anyway," Larcener said, pulling his fingers away and inspecting them. He looked into Prof's eyes. "Excellent. It worked this time. I *did* need to check, after our little . . . problem with your girlfriend." He looked up at the sky, then glared at the sunlight, stepping back into the shadows. Sparks. The sun was low on the horizon; it had to be at least five by now. I hadn't realized we'd been fighting so long.

I knelt down beside Prof. He was staring ahead, looking stunned. I prodded him softly, but he didn't move, didn't even blink.

"It's a good solution, David," Megan said, joining me. "It's either this or kill him."

I looked into those sightless eyes and nodded. She was

389

right, but I couldn't help feeling that I'd failed in some monumental way. I'd fought Prof to a halt, figured out his weakness, and negated his powers. Yet he hadn't pushed back the darkness.

We could have found another method, right? Kept his weakness engaged until he came to himself? I wanted to weep—but strangely, I felt too tired even for that.

"Let's go find the others," I said, rising. I pulled off the vest, still with wires attached for the motivators. We'd need to get the harmsway running again to heal Abraham. I set it beside the metal boxes that held the motivators, then I scanned the sky, hoping to spot one of Knighthawk's drones.

A flash of light.

Obliteration's hand fell on my shoulder. "Well done," he said. "The beast is vanquished. It is time for me to make good on my promise."

We vanished.

47

WE appeared on a barren cliff overlooking a scrub desert with sweltering air that smelled of baked earth. Red rocks peeked from the soil, displaying a variety of strata, like pancakes piled high.

Behind me, something glowed brightly. I turned and raised my hand, squinting at it.

"A bomb," Obliteration said. "Made of my own flesh. My son, you might say."

"You used one of these to destroy Kansas City."

"Yes," he said, subdued. "I cannot travel well when full of energy. I must sun myself in the place I am to destroy, but that creates a conundrum. The more my notoriety grows, the more people flee my presence. And so . . ."

"And so you took Regalia's offer. Your flesh in exchange for a weapon."

"This one was for Atlanta," he said, then rested his hand on my shoulder in an almost paternal way. "I give it to you, Steelslayer. For your hunt. Can you use this to destroy the king above, the Epic of Epics?"

"I don't know," I said, eyes watering against the light. Sparks . . . I was so tired. Drained. Wrung out, like a thread-bare dishrag so full of holes it was good for nothing more than propping up the corner of your wobbly kitchen table. "But if anything can do it, that will." Even powerful High Epics had been known to fall to overwhelming outpourings of energy like nukes, or Obliteration's own destructive force.

"I will take you, and it, to the palace above," he said. "The new Jerusalem. Detonate the bomb with this." He handed me a small rod, kind of penlike, which was startlingly familiar. A universal detonator. I'd had one of these once.

"Could I . . . maybe do it from down here?" I asked.

Obliteration laughed. "You ask if you may set aside your cup? Only natural. But no, you must face this in person. I have extended your life to perform this act because I know its result. The detonator has a short range."

I gripped the detonator in a sweaty palm. A death sentence then. Perhaps the bomb could have been rigged with a timer, but I doubted Obliteration would agree to that.

I didn't even get to say goodbye to Megan, I thought, feeling sick. Yet here was the chance I'd insisted I sought. An ending.

"Can I . . . think about it?"

"For a short time," he said, checking the sky. "But not long. He will soon rise, and we cannot let him see what we are planning."

I sat down, trying to clear my mind, trying to recover some strength and confront the opportunity I'd been handed.

I tried to sort through it. Prof defeated, but drained of powers. He'd seemed so numb when I'd looked at him, as if he'd been hit by some strong blow to the head. He'd recover, right? Some assumers left their prey stunned, even brain-dead, after their powers were taken. Those people recovered when the powers were restored, but Larcener never gave back what he stole. How had I never considered that?

Sparks, how had I missed Prof's weakness? His timid planning, the way he looked for excuses to give away his powers and mitigate failures—it all pointed to his fears. All along, he'd been unwilling to fully commit.

"Well?" Obliteration finally asked. "We have no more time."

I didn't feel any more rested, despite the breather. "I'll go," I whispered, hoarse. "I will do it."

"Well chosen." He led me to the bomb that, I assumed, had been placed here in this wasteland to gather heat from the sun. I moved closer to it and got a sense of its shape—a metal box about the size of a footlocker. It wasn't hot, though it seemed as if it should be.

Obliteration knelt and put one hand on it; the other he placed on my arm. " 'You shall eat the fruit of the labor of your hands; you shall be blessed, and it shall be well with you.' Farewell, Steelslayer."

My breath caught as I was seized in the flash of light. A second later, I found myself looking down at Earth.

I barely heard the crash behind me as Obliteration left, abandoning me. I was in *space*. I knelt on what appeared to be a surface of glass, looking down at a gloriously stomach-twisting sight: the Earth in its splendor, surrounded by a haze of atmosphere and clouds.

So peaceful. From up here, my daily concerns seemed insignificant. I tore my eyes away from that sight to look around, though I had to put my back to the bomb and squint to make anything out over its light. I was in some kind of . . . building, or ship? With glass walls?

I stumbled to my feet, noting the walls' rounded corners, and a distant red light somewhere in this glassy structure. Then I realized that despite the fact that I was all the way up in space, my feet remained planted on the surface beneath me. I would have expected to float.

The bomb shone like a star behind me. I fingered the detonator. Should I . . . do it now?

No. No, I needed to see him first. Up close. He glowed crimson, bright as the bomb, but was somewhere ahead of me in the ship, his light refracting through corners and surfaces of glass.

My eyes were gradually adjusting, and I noticed a doorway. I stumbled toward it, as the floor was uneven, lined with ladderlike grips and bars. The walls were also uneven, made of different compartments filled with wires and levers—only it was all glass.

I passed through a corridor, with difficulty. There was something etched into one wall, and I ran my hand over it. English letters? I could read them—some kind of company name, it seemed.

Sparks. I was in the old international space station, but it had been transformed into glass.

Feeling an unreal disconnect, I continued toward the light. The glass was so clear, I could almost believe that it wasn't there. I stumbled through room after room, my arm out to make sure I didn't walk into a wall, and the red light grew larger.

I eventually stepped into one last room. It was bigger than the others I'd passed through, and Calamity waited on the far side—facing away from me, I thought, though he was so bright it was difficult to make out much about him.

Arm raised against the light, I clutched the detonator tighter. I was being stupid. I should have blown the bomb. Calamity might kill me the moment he saw me. Who knew what powers this being had?

But I *had* to know. *Had* to see him with my own eyes. I had to meet the thing that had ruined my world.

I walked through the room.

Calamity's light dimmed. My breath caught in my throat, and I tasted bile. What would the people below think? Calamity going out? The light lowered to a faint glow, revealing a young man in a simple robe, with red glowing skin. He turned to face me . . . and I knew him.

"Hello, David," Larcener said.

48

"YOU," I whispered. "You were down below! With us, all along!"

"Yes," Larcener said, turning to regard the world. "I can project a decoy of myself; you know this. You even mentioned the power on several occasions."

I reeled, trying to connect it all. He'd been with us.

Calamity had been *living with us.*

"Why . . . What . . ."

Larcener sighed, a shockingly human sound. Annoyance. An emotion I'd felt from him quite often. "I keep looking at it," he said, "trying to find what you see in it."

I hesitantly stepped up beside him. "The world?"

"It's broken. Terrible. *Horrid.*"

"Yeah," I said softly. "Beautiful."

He looked at me, narrowing his eyes.

"You're the source of it all," I said, resting my fingers on the glass in front of me. "You . . . all along . . . The powers you stole from other Epics?"

"I simply took back what I once gave," he said. "Everyone was so quick to believe in an Epic who could steal abilities, they never realized they'd had it backward. I'm no thief. 'Larcener,' they called me. Petty." He shook his head.

I swallowed, blinking. "Why?" I asked Calamity. "Please, tell me. *Why* have you done this?"

He mused, hands clasped behind him. It *was* Larcener. Not only the same face, but the same mannerisms. The same way he sniffed before speaking, as if forming words to speak with me were beneath him.

"You are to destroy yourselves," he said quietly. "I am but the harbinger; I bring the powers. You use them and orchestrate your own end. It is what we have done in countless realms. I'm . . . told."

"You're told? By who?"

"It is a wonderful place," he said, as if he hadn't heard me. "You wouldn't be able to comprehend it. Peace. Softness. No terrible lights, no lights at all. We don't sense with horrid appendages like *eyes*. We live there, as one, until our duty arrives." He sneered. "And this is mine. So I came here and left it all. And exchanged it for . . ."

"Harsh lights," I said. "Loud sounds. The pain of heat, of sensation."

"Yes!" he said.

"Those aren't *my* nightmares," I said, raising my hand to my head. "They're *yours*. Sparks . . . they're *all* yours, aren't they?"

"Don't be foolish. Babbling about your silly notions again."

I stumbled back, catching myself on a boxy protrusion

from the wall. I could see it in my nightmares. Visions of being born in this world, a place so foreign to Calamity. To his senses, a terrible place.

The harsh lights of my nightmares were no more than common ceiling lights.

The clatter and yells? People talking, or the thumps of furniture moving.

The terrible nature of it was all in comparison to where he'd lived before. Another place, one I couldn't comprehend, one that lacked such intense stimuli.

"Were you supposed to leave us?" I asked.

Calamity didn't reply.

"Calamity! After you granted our powers, were you supposed to leave?"

"Why would I remain in this terrible place longer than I had to?" he said, dismissive.

"In Megan's parallel world," I whispered. "There you *did* leave, and the darkness never claimed the Epics. Here, you remained . . . and you *infected* us somehow. Your hatred, your loathing. You turned each Epic into a copy of you, Calamity."

Megan had said that her fear of flames hadn't been nearly as pronounced before her powers arrived. My fear of the depths had started once his eyes turned upon me. Whatever Calamity did, whatever he was, when he wormed his way into someone, he *magnified* their terrors to an unnatural level.

And when people were exposed to those fears—the things he hated—Calamity withdrew. Gone were the powers, and gone was the darkness.

Confronting the fears, that worked into it too somehow. It had to. When you confronted your fears, what happened?

They are mine, Megan had said. *I claim them.*

Sparks. Did that mean she had seized the powers and cast out Calamity fully? Separated them from the darkness?

"You all make so many excuses," Calamity said. "You refuse to see what your people are, once they get a little power." He looked at me. "What *you* are, David Charleston. You have hidden it from the others, but you cannot fool the source himself. I know what you are. When will you release it? When will you *destroy,* as is your destiny?"

"I never will."

"Nonsense! It is your nature. I've seen it over and over again." He stepped toward me. "How did you do it? How did you hold me off so long?"

"Is that why you came to us?" I asked. "In Ildithia? Because of me?"

Calamity glowered at me. Even now, even seeing him in his glory, I had the same impression of him I'd always had: that of a great spoiled child.

"Calamity," I said, "you have to go. Leave us."

He sniffed. "I am not allowed to go until my work is done. They made that clear, after I—"

"What?"

"I do not see *you* answering the questions I gave you," he said, then turned back to look out his window. "Why have you denied your powers?"

I licked my lips, heart thumping. "I can't be an Epic," I said. "My father was waiting for them. . . ."

"So?"

"I . . ." I trailed off. I couldn't voice it.

"Eleven years, and still your kind lingers," Calamity muttered. "Dwindling, yes, but also *lingering.* Ten years as a child I lived among you, until I fled to this place."

That's when Calamity rose, I thought. *When he was ten— and when he decided to start giving away powers.*

"This place," Calamity said, "which is closer to my home than anything else in this rotten realm. But . . . I found I had to start going down again, among you. I had to know. What did you see in all of this? Eleven years more, and I haven't been able to find it. . . ."

I looked down at the thin detonator rod still clenched in my hand. I had my answers. They raised more questions, true. What *was* the place he had come from? Why did his kind seek to destroy us? He acted like it was predetermined, but by who, and why?

Questions I would probably never see answered. My single regret was that I hadn't said goodbye to Megan. I would have liked one last, farewell kiss.

My name is David Charleston.

I clicked the button.

And I kill Epics.

The bomb detonated.

49

THE explosion ripped through the glass space station, shattering it to pieces. The heat and force hit me in an instant, then *curved* around me. It streamed into Calamity's outstretched palm, sucked like water through a straw.

It was over in an eyeblink. Behind me, the station reknit itself, glass forming back together, resealing.

I stood like an idiot, clicking the button again and again.

"You thought," Calamity said without looking at me, "that my own power could destroy me? I suppose there would be a poetry to that. But I am master of the powers, David. I know them all, in their intricacy. Yes, I could tell you how Ildithia works. Yes, I could explain what Megan does in jumping to other realms—both core possibilities and ones ephemeral.

But I am *truly* immortal. None of the powers could harm me, not permanently."

I sank to the floor. The strain of it all overwhelmed me. The fight with Prof. Being stolen away by Obliteration. Pressing that button and being prepared to die.

"I've wondered if I should simply tell them," Calamity mused, and turned to me. "You should understand that you need to destroy yourselves. But you see, I am not supposed to interfere. Even the small infractions—like being forced to make devices for your assault on Sharp Tower—worry me. It is against our way, though maintaining my cover required it."

"Calamity, you're *already* interfering. Deeply. You make them go mad! You make them destroy!"

He ignored me.

Sparks . . . how could I get him to see? How could I show him that *he* was causing the darkness and destruction, that men wouldn't take to it as naturally as he claimed?

"You are worthless, as a whole," he said softly. "You *will* destroy yourselves, and I will bear witness. I will not shirk my duty as others have. We are to watch, as is our calling. But I must not interfere, not again. The acts of youth can be forgiven. Though I was never truly a child, I *was* new. And your world is a shock. A dreadful shock." He nodded, as if convincing himself.

I forced myself to stand. Then I slipped my gun from its holster on my leg.

"Your answer to everything, David Charleston?" Calamity said with a sigh.

"Worth a try," I said, raising the gun.

"I contain the very powers of the universe. Do you understand that? They are *all mine*. I am what you call a High Epic a thousand times over."

"You're a monster either way," I said. "Divine powers

don't make you a god, I guess. They make you a bully who happens to have the biggest gun."

I pulled the trigger. The gun didn't even fire.

"I removed the powder," Calamity noted. "Nothing you can possibly do—whether the result of Epic powers or the craftiness of men—can hurt me." He hesitated. "You, however, have no such protections."

"Um . . . ," I said.

Then I ran.

"Really?" he asked after me. "This is what we're doing?"

I tore out of the room, scrambling back the way I'd come, which was tough considering that this place had been made for people who moved in freefall, not people who walked.

I reached the room where I'd first arrived. Dead end.

Calamity sprang into existence near me.

I swallowed, my mouth dry. "Noninterference, right?"

"Of course, David," Calamity said. "Though you did break the station. I needn't save you from . . . the natural result of your actions. This place can be so fragile." He smiled.

I lunged for a handgrip on the floor—just in time, as a large hole opened in the side of the room. The wind howled.

"Goodbye, David Charleston," Calamity said, strolling over to kick at my fingers.

Light flashed in the room.

Then someone *punched* Calamity square in the face, sending him sprawling. The rushing of air stopped, and I gasped in a huge breath, looking up at the newcomer.

Prof.

He wore his black lab coat and no longer bore the vacant look that had been in his eyes when I'd left him. It was replaced by an expression of determination and sheer grit.

"You," Calamity said, sprawled on his back. "I reclaimed the powers from you!"

Prof pulled apart his lab coat. There, strapped to his chest, was the vest that Knighthawk had made, quickly repaired, motivators replaced.

"Useless!" Calamity said. "If I reclaimed them, that shouldn't work. It . . . I . . ." He looked, befuddled, at the forcefield on the wall, which glowed green.

Prof offered me his hand.

I let out a long sigh of relief. "How do you feel?" I asked, taking the hand.

"Haunted," he whispered. "Thank you for bringing me back. I hate you for it, David. But *thank you*."

"I didn't bring you back," I said. "You faced it, Prof." I suddenly understood—in strapping on the motivators and trying to take up his powers again after what had happened, he'd faced them. He'd come to risk failure. He'd *done* it.

He'd claimed the powers. Like Megan, he'd ripped the darkness from the abilities, and sent one sprawling away while seizing the others.

Prof's powers were now his, and not Calamity's. The motivator boxes were meaningless.

Prof grabbed me, perhaps intending to teleport us away, but a sudden wave of *something* slammed into us, sending us sprawling. Calamity started glowing again, a harsh red light, and he spoke. . . . Sparks, that *voice*. Inhuman, unreal.

Something tumbled from Prof's hand, and it vaporized as Calamity pointed.

"What was that?" I asked over the terrible screeching that was now Calamity's voice, speaking a language I couldn't conceive.

"That *was* our way out," Prof said. "Run."

The teleporter. Hell. I scrambled to my feet as Prof placed a forcefield between us and Calamity, but it was gone in a heartbeat. Fighting him was impossible, it—

Some unseen force tossed me to the ground. Calamity glowed and raised his hands, a beam forming, then shooting right toward me.

Light flashed again, and the beam missed.

Megan stood in the room, holding Obliteration by the throat. He appeared to be choking. I gaped in surprise as she tossed the man aside—he vanished a moment later, not in his customary fashion, but just fading away. Megan raised her gun and started firing at Calamity. It still didn't do any good, though Calamity screamed again in that strange language.

Megan cursed and dropped down to a crouch beside me. "Plan?" she asked.

"I . . . Megan, how did you . . ."

"Easy," she said, firing again. "Grabbed the Oblitcration from the other dimension, showed him the picture of this place, and made him take me up here. He's still a slontze there, I'll have you know. Now . . . plan?"

Plan.

Sometimes you don't know what you need until you're in the thick of it.

"Send us both," I said, stumbling to my feet. "Send Calamity and me into Firefight's world—but not out in space, please. Send us to Firefight, wherever he is."

"David, Calamity will kill you!"

"Please, Megan. Please. Trust me."

She drew her lips to a line, and as I lurched toward Calamity in the shaking room, she released her powers.

I grabbed him, and together the two of us slipped into another place.

50

WE stumbled onto a rooftop in Ildithia, near a gaping hole smoldering in the ground. Night had fallen; darkness covered the salt city, but I recognized the location. It was above where I'd faced down Prof at the end.

At first I thought something had gone wrong. Had we really entered another dimension? But there *were* differences. Here, the hole looked like it had been made by an explosion rather than by the tensors. There were also far fewer bodies.

I turned and found that Calamity was standing there growling at me. He raised his hands, summoning light.

"I can show you," I whispered, "what it is we see in the Earth. You say you're curious. I can show you something you will wish to see. I *promise*."

He sneered at me. But as I watched, his rage seemed to

subside. Like . . . well, like an Epic when their powers re-treated.

"You're curious," I said. "I know you are. Don't you want to understand, finally, so that your curiosity will stop nagging at you?"

"Bah," he said, but lowered his hands and transformed into Larcener. Well, he'd always been Larcener, but he'd stopped glowing, his skin had returned to a human tone, and his robe had transformed to the shirt and slacks he often wore.

"What do you think to do here?" he demanded, looking around. "This is another Core Possibility, isn't it? One adjacent to yours? You realize I can just send us back."

"Specks!" Firefight's voice said. I twisted to find him on the next rooftop over, standing near Tavi. Shc remained behind, studying me while Firefight jumped, gliding across the open space, trailing flames. "He's here!" Firefight said, obviously speaking into a mobile. How had he found one that didn't burn up? "Yes, *him*."

"Can you summon the person who wants to meet me?" I asked Firefight, glancing toward Calamity.

"Oh, don't worry," Firefight said. "He's coming."

"There *is* something strange about this place," Calamity said, looking up and squinting at the sky. "Something wrong . . ."

"It's a world that you left, Calamity," I said. "It's a world where some Epics don't destroy. Where some protect and fight against those who would kill."

"Impossible." He spun on me. "Lies."

"You know your powers," I said. "You know what Megan does. You told me yourself, you are their master. Before, you demanded that I deny what I was. Well, I don't, not anymore. I'm one of you. Now *you* do it! I dare you to deny what you're seeing. *Deny* that this place, this possibility, exists!"

"I . . ." He seemed bewildered. He looked up at the dark sky, where Calamity should have been. "I . . ."

Powerful spotlights lit the area nearby, where people searched for survivors in the aftermath of whatever conflict Firefight and his team had faced. Down below, when people saw him standing near me, they cheered.

Sparks, they *cheered* an Epic.

"No . . . ," Calamity said. He looked at Firefight, then the people. "This one must . . . he must be an anomaly . . . like your Megan. . . ."

"Is that so?" I said, scanning the area. I spotted a figure rising from the city, the figure I'd been waiting for. He streaked toward us, cape fluttering behind. An outfit I knew all too well.

I seized Calamity by the front of his clothing. "Look at it!" I said. "Look at a place where the Epics are free from your corruption. Look at the one who comes, the most terrible of them all. A murderer in our world, a destroyer. Look and see that here, Calamity, *Steelheart himself is a hero!*"

I thrust my hand to the side as the figure landed on the rooftop.

"That . . . ," Calamity said. "That is not Steelheart."

What?

I looked at the figure again. Magnificent silver cape. Baggy black pants, a shirt stretched taut across a powerful physique. It was Steelheart's costume, though it now bore a symbol on the chest. That was the only difference in the clothing.

But his face . . . his face was that of a kindly man, not a tyrant. Round features, thinning hair, a wide smile, and such understanding eyes.

Blain Charleston.

My father.

51

"MY David," Father whispered. "My little *David* . . . "

I couldn't speak. I couldn't move. It was him. In this world, my father was an Epic.

No, in this world, my father was *the* Epic.

He took a hesitant step forward, such a timid action for one who bore the musculature, stature, and regal air of a powerful Epic. "Oh, son. I'm sorry. I'm so sorry."

I released Calamity, stunned. Father took another step forward, then I seized him in an embrace.

It all came out. The worry, the terror, the frustration and mind-numbing exhaustion. It poured out in heaving sobs.

I released over a decade of pain and sorrow, a decade of loss. He held me tight, and he smelled like my father, Epic or not.

"Son," he said, clutching me, weeping. "I killed you. I didn't mean to. I tried to protect you, to save you. But you died. You died anyway."

"I let you die," I whispered. "I didn't help you, didn't stand up. I watched him murder you. I was a coward."

Our words became a jumble as we spoke. But for a moment, somehow, everything was all right. I was in my father's arms. Impossible, yet true.

"But . . . it *is* him," Calamity whispered from behind. "I can see the powers. The same powers."

I finally released my father, though he kept a grip on my arm, protective. Calamity stared at the sky again.

"You brought him here?" my father said.

Calamity nodded absently.

"Thank you, hero," my father said, speaking with a confidence I hadn't known in him since before Mother's death. "Thank you for giving me this gift. You must be a mighty man of compassion in your realm."

Calamity looked at us, frowning. From my father, to me, and back.

"By the Eternal Sparks," Calamity whispered. "I *see* it."

I felt the fading sensation. Megan's power was running out, and we would soon return.

I grabbed my father again. "I'm going," I said. "I don't have a choice. But . . . Father, I forgive you. Know that I forgive you." It didn't need to be said, yet I knew that I *had* to say it.

"I forgive you," Father said, tears in his eyes. "My David . . . it is enough to know that somewhere, you still live."

The world faded, and with it my father. I anticipated pain, a lurching, a tearing away—but I felt only peace.

He was right. It was enough.

Calamity and I reappeared on the glass space station. Megan and Prof stood at the ready, her with her gun, Prof with spears of light. I raised my hands to still them.

Calamity remained in his human form. He didn't change back; he simply knelt on that glass floor, staring sightlessly. A small red glow finally started to rise from him, and he looked at us.

"You are evil," he said, almost a plea.

"I am *not,*" Megan said.

"You will . . . you will destroy everything . . . ," he said.

"No," Prof said, his voice rough. "No."

Calamity focused on me, standing with the other two.

"Your corruption isn't enough," I said. "Your fears are not enough. Your hatred is not enough. We won't do it, Calamity."

He wrapped his arms around himself and began to rock.

"Do you know what made the difference?" I demanded of him. "The reason our powers separated from yours? The same thing happened with all of us. Megan running into a burning building. Me entering the ocean. Edmund with the dog. And Prof coming here. It wasn't only confronting the fears . . ."

". . . it was pushing through them," Calamity whispered, looking from me to the others, "to save someone."

"Do you fear that?" I asked him softly. "That we aren't what you've thought? Does it terrify you to know that deep down, men are not monsters? That we are, instead, inherently good?"

He stared at me, then collapsed, curling up on the glass floor. The red light within him dimmed, and then—just like that, he faded away. Until there was nothing.

"Did we . . . kill him?" Megan asked.

"Close enough," I said.

The station rumbled, then lurched.

"I *knew* this thing was too low for such an orbital speed!"

Prof shouted. "Sparks. We need to call Tia and . . ." He grew pale.

The entire station lurched, throwing us to the ceiling. Calamity had been holding it in place. It started to crack, glass all around spiderwebbing from the internal pressure. In seconds we were plummeting toward the Earth, the station shattering around us.

But I was calm.

For in that other world, my father's shirt had borne a symbol. A symbol I recognized—a stylized S shape. A symbol that meant something.

The symbol of the Faithful.

There will be heroes. Just wait.

I seized the power within me.

Epilogue

I sat on the hillside, resting in the shadow of the fallen space station—which I'd transformed to steel as we fell. I'd made the transformation, then exited through one of the holes in its side. I'd grabbed hold, slowing it, then guided it out of its death spiral and eventually placed it here.

Well . . . *crashed* it here. Turns out flying is way harder than people think. In the air, I was about as adroit as seventeen geriatric walruses trying to juggle live swordfish.

Might need to work on that one.

Megan walked over, looking radiant as always, despite the bruises from the, um, smoothness-challenged landing. She sat down and squeezed my arm.

"So," she said, "you going to get super buff?"

"Dunno," I said, flexing. "Steelheart was, and my father is. Might come with the portfolio."

"Should make up for the terrible kissing."

"Hey, all you have to do to fix that is let me practice."

"Noted."

We were somewhere in Australia, according to Knighthawk, who was sending a copter for us. It would be hours before it arrived. I wasn't about to trust my flying skills to get us back to North America.

I nodded toward the other hillside. "How is he?"

"Bad," Megan said, looking toward Prof's silhouette, where he sat staring into the sky. "He'll have to live with it, as I do. The things we've done while consumed by the darkness . . . well, they *feel* like our own actions. Dreamlike, sometimes, but still our choice. You can remember enjoying it too. . . ."

She shivered, and I pulled her close. After this, Prof would never be the same. But then, would any of us?

"His powers still work?" I said. "Like yours do?"

She nodded, glancing at her mobile. "Abraham and Cody are doing well, though Prof will need to regrow Abraham's arm. And . . . um . . . you should read this." She showed me a message she had pulled up from Knighthawk.

"Mizzy?" I asked.

Megan nodded.

"Sparks. I wonder how she'll take to being an Epic."

"Well, without the darkness . . ." Megan shrugged.

It was well and truly gone, so far as we could tell. Megan still thought Calamity might return. I didn't.

A flash of light appeared in front of us, resolving into a man with spectacles and a goatee, wearing a trench coat.

"Ah!" Obliteration said. "You *are* here." He tucked away the mobile he'd been carrying.

Hmm, maybe we wouldn't need that copter after all. I took a deep breath and stood, hopeful. I gave Obliteration a smile and reached out my hand to him.

He slid his sword from its sheath—yes, he still had a sword—and pointed it at me. "You have done well, and blessed are you, for you have cast the dragon from his heaven. I will give you a week to recover. My next target is Toronto. You may face me there, and we shall see what comes of our clash, horseman."

"Obliteration," I said, pleading. "Calamity is gone."

"Yes," he said, sheathing his sword.

"The darkness is gone," I said. "You don't have to be evil."

"I'm not," he said. "I thank you for giving me the secrets you know, Steelslayer. I know why the darkness left me five years ago, when I faced my fear. I have been free of it ever since." He nodded to me. " 'And he placed at the east of the garden of Eden Cherubims, and a flaming sword which turned every way, to keep the way of the tree of life.' "

He flashed into white ceramic and vanished.

"Calamity," I said, slumping back down, frustrated. *"Calamity."*

"You know," Megan said, "we might need to think of new curses."

"I had hoped, maybe, on our side he would be good. Once Calamity was gone."

"They're people," Megan said. "Free to be people, David. As it should be. And that means some of them are still going to be selfish, or messed up, or whatever."

She settled closer to me. "I'm feeling rested, and am up for some exertion."

I grinned. "Practice!"

She rolled her eyes. "Not that I'm averse, Knees, but I was referring to my powers."

Oh, right. I knew that.

"You still want to try this?" she asked.

"Yeah, absolutely. He'll be waiting."

"All right. Sit still."

A moment later, I was back in the other world. I'd returned once already. Just after we'd landed the space station, I'd popped in to let them know that my visit before hadn't been the end—but I'd stayed only for a moment. Megan had been tired.

Before I'd left though, I'd arranged this meeting place. My father stood on top of a building. Sharp Tower, which hadn't been destroyed in his world. I walked up to him, noting his fluttering cape. *Look what those comic books have done to you.* Wearing a symbol and everything? Sparks, he was such a nerd.

Like father, like son, I guess.

He saw me, and turned around with a wide smile of his own. I stepped toward him, hesitant. Eleven years—a long time to catch up on. How did one begin?

"Um," I said, "Megan feels she's getting better at this, and the darkness is gone, so she can last longer. Now that she's rested, and isn't in the middle of a catastrophe or anything, she thinks she can give us a good fifteen minutes. Maybe as long as a half hour."

"Good, good," Father said. He shuffled awkwardly. "Uh, Firefight tells me that you and I share a power set."

"Yeah," I said. "Power blasts, invulnerability. Oh, and turning stuff into steel. Not sure how useful that last one will be."

"You'd be surprised," he said.

"It's still going to take some getting used to. And by the way, flying is kind of kicking me in the face."

"Flying is tricky at first."

We stood in front of one another, uncertain, until Father nodded toward the railing. "Do you . . . maybe . . . want me to teach you?"

I smiled, feeling a sudden warmth deep inside. "Dad, I can think of nothing I'd like more."

ACKNOWLEDGMENTS

Writing the acknowledgments tends to be the last thing I do for a book. As I sit here, late in the night in November, I'm left reflecting on the series as a whole. *Steelheart* has one of the most random origin stories among my canon of fiction, conceived—almost in its entirety—during a long drive on the East Coast while on tour for one of the Mistborn novels.

That was 2008. It's now 2015, seven years later, and the journey of bringing this series to you has been exceptionally satisfying. The people listed below have had no small hand in that. But I also want to take a special moment to thank all of you for following me along this crazy journey. Readers—both old and new—who took a chance on this series, you have my most sincere thanks. You give me the means to keep on dreaming.

So let the thanks roll on, my own personal team of Reckoners who make my life awesome. Krista Marino was the editor at Delacorte Press on this project, as she was on the other two books. You owe the success of these novels to her, one of the very early proponents of the series. I'd also like to thank

Beverly Horowitz for her wisdom and guidance; she has been an advocate for these books at the publisher.

Other people at Random House deserving my thanks are Monica Jean, Mary McCue, Kim Lauber, Rachel Weinick, Judith Haut, Dominique Cimina, and Barbara Marcus. The book's copy editor was Colleen Fellingham.

My agent Joshua Bilmes was the first one who had to sit through an excited rendition of how cool this series was going to be when I finally got around to writing it. He has been very patient. My other agent, Eddie Schneider, handled the negotiations on these books and has represented them valiantly. Also at the agency deserving of thanks are Sam Morgan, Krystyna Lopez, and Tae Keller.

I'd also like to give a shout-out to my UK agent, John Berlyne of the Zeno Agency. My UK editor on the book was Simon Spanton, an excellent individual and the first person in UK publishing to give me a chance.

My own team includes the ininsouciant Peter Ahlstrom, company VP and editorial director, who handled a lot of the continuity and proofreading on this book, as well as doing a lot of in-house editorial. As always, Isaac $tewart was here to help with art, and my executive assistant was Adam Horne. Kara Stewart deserves thanks for handling our website store (which, by the way, has lots of cool swag for sale).

My writing group on the project included Emily Sanderson, Karen & Peter Ahlstrom, Darci & Eric James Stone, Alan Layton, Kathleen Dorsey Sanderson, Kaylynn ZoBell, Ethan & Isaac Skarstedt, Kara & Isaac Stewart, and Ben Olsen, destroyer of worlds.

Special thanks go out to our on-location team in Atlanta, Jennifer & Jimmy Liang, who scoped out spots for us like superspies, and offered commentary on anything having to do with the city. Beta readers on the project were Nikki

Ramsay, Mark Lindberg, Alyx Hoge, Corby Campbell, Sam Sullivan, Ted Herman, Steve Stay, Marnie Peterson, Michael Headley, Dan Swint, Aaron Ford, Aaron Biggs, Kyle Mills, Cade Shiozaki, Kyle Baugh, Justin Lemon, Amber Christenson, Karen Ahlstrom, Zoe Hatch, and Spencer White.

Our community proofreaders included many of the above, plus Bob Kluttz, Jory Phillips, Alice Arneson, Brian T. Hill, Gary Singer, Ian McNatt, Matt Hatch, and Bao Pham.

And, of course, moral support was provided by Emily, Dallin, Joel, and Oliver Sanderson. The three little boys especially provided me with plenty of commentary on superheroes and how to treat them.

It has been a wild, incredible journey. Thank you again for joining me for it.

Brandon Sanderson